CITY OF WISHES

THE COMPLETE CINDERELLA STORY

CITY OF WISHES

THE COMPLETE CINDERELLA STORY

RACHEL MORGAN

1
THE MEMORY THIEF

ONE

Elle Winter's evening was going exactly according to plan until the moment she smacked face-first into a broad chest and landed on her bejeweled backside on the sidewalk outside Club Onyx. Rough concrete stung her palms, and pain shot up her left wrist. She sucked in a hiss of breath as heat rushed immediately to her face. Lifting her head, she squinted into the flashing neon purple light from the sign above the club's doorway.

"I am so, so sorry," said the owner of the broad chest, blocking the purple glare as he stepped closer and extended a hand toward her. "Are you okay? Can I help you up?"

"I'm fine," Elle answered automatically, darting a quick look over her shoulder. Every eyeball in the queue waiting to get inside the fae-exclusive nightclub was now on her. *Brilliant.* She turned swiftly away from the crowd, blond hair falling across her vision as her heart hammered against her ribcage. This was exactly the kind of attention she tried to avoid.

Peeking up, she found a hand still stretched toward her. Since it was the quickest way out of this situation, she reached for it. In one smooth motion, Mr. I Don't Look Where I'm Going pulled her up. Momentum kept her going, but she managed to jerk to a halt before crashing into his chest a second time. "Are you sure you're okay?" he asked.

Elle let go of him, twisting her left hand in slow, careful circles as she looked up and met his gaze. His silvery blue eyes were piercing in a way that only fae eyes could be, and his dark hair was just the right kind of messy. *Makes sense*, she thought. Of course the guy who'd witnessed her land gracelessly on her butt was heart-stoppingly gorgeous. That was the way the world worked, right?

She cleared her throat and took a step back. Her fingers itched to check whether her hair still covered the pointed tips of her ears, but she managed to resist the urge. Better not to draw attention to them. This close up, he might notice they were fake. "Um, yes, I'm fine," she said belatedly. She uncurled her fingers the tiniest bit and examined her palm. Her skin was grazed, but thank the stars she wasn't bleeding. If anyone saw the color of her blood, they'd know in an instant that she was human. Well, either human or a shifter of some sort, but that was even worse. If the fae outside Club Onyx thought she was human, they'd probably just toss her across the street—onto her ass again. If they thought she was a shifter … well, she might not live to see morning.

"Hey, can you get out of the way?" a woman shouted from somewhere behind her. "You're blocking the door and some of us are trying to get inside."

Eager to remove herself from the spotlight, Elle stepped past the man with the silvery blue eyes, but the bouncer—who'd done nothing until this point except watch the unfolding scene in silence—brought one muscled arm down in front of her. "Hang on, miss. You don't look old enough to be here."

Wonderful. He'd been happy to let her walk right past him a minute ago, but now that she'd embarrassed herself in front of a crowd of fae, she didn't look old enough? Instead of arguing, Elle retrieved her ID card from her purse and held it in front of the bouncer's face. He squinted at it for several moments, his eyes darting between her and the card, which told him her name was Trixie Gold and that she was twenty-two years old. It was an excellent fake that had given her access into many clubs in Vale City, most of which wouldn't have allowed her through the door if they knew she was only nineteen.

"Fine," the bouncer grumbled, stepping aside and jerking his head toward the inside of the club.

"Wait," Mr. Blue-Eyed Fae called after her. "Are you sure you don't need someone to take a look at that wrist before your magic sets it wrong or something?"

"I'm sure," she said without looking back. It wasn't as though she'd broken any bones. Now that the shock of the moment had passed, all she felt was a dull ache. Probably nothing to be concerned about.

"I really am sorry," he continued, catching up to her as she entered the dimly lit passageway inside the club's entrance. She stopped and narrowed her eyes at him. Why on earth was he following her? "Can I at least buy you a drink to make up for knocking you over?" he asked. "I'm Dex, by the way."

Instead of answering, Elle stepped aside to make way for the people behind her. Three women sauntered forward on sparkly heels, leaving a cloud of cloying perfume and the faint gold glimmer of faerie dust in their wake. The tallest one tossed a look over her shoulder and lowered one glittery eyelid in a wink, no doubt directed at Dex. Elle almost rolled her eyes in response. Enchanted perfume hardly ever worked on anyone. Even she knew that, and she was human.

She faced Dex, and something stirred in her chest when she found his silver-blue eyes still on her. Vindication, she decided, pushing her shoulders back a little. *Told you so*, she thought in the direction of the woman who'd tried to catch his attention with her magic perfume. "Weren't you on your way out when you walked into me?" she asked.

His smile stretched a little wider. "Yes, but I can easily change my plans."

She worked hard to maintain his gaze and keep her shoulders pushed back. Saying no to someone without fear of consequences or punishment was always a strange experience. "Well, Dex," she said, "I'm afraid *my* plans can't be changed. I'm meeting someone else here."

"Ah. How unfortunate."

Heat inched its way up Elle's neck. Guys didn't pay her this kind of attention. Or if they did, she'd never had time to notice. She kept her head down, got the job done, and left. There was no other option if she was hoping to stay out of trouble. But if Elle was honest with herself, she longed for just one normal night. The kind of night where she could relax and dance and maybe get to know a cute guy over a vodka unicorn or a piskie sour, neither of which Salvia had ever allowed her to taste. Standing here, staring into Dex's eyes, it was so tempting to say yes.

But that kind of night would be part of Future Elle's life. Present Elle had other priorities. So she wiped away the smile that was trying to find its way onto her lips and said, "Not unfortunate for me." She stepped past Dex and strode forward, trying to convince herself she wasn't disappointed when he didn't follow her a second time.

Swaying bodies, pulsing lights, and the smell of sweat and alcohol greeted Elle as she entered the main part of the club. Drinks hovered around people, and soap-like bubbles floated in the air, rainbow colors visible where the light struck them. Here and there, people jumped to pop a bubble, and faerie dust fell in a rush of gold sparkles, releasing a surprise charm: temporary jewelry, or the ability to breakdance perfectly for two minutes, or a pretty pattern of gold light that erupted into the air before vanishing.

To the right of the club, where a stage floated at eye level, dancers in glowing costumes spun around poles. Elle moved in the opposite direction, away from the deafening speakers and toward the far corner where several booths lined the wall. She was pleased at how well she blended in here. She wore short shorts and a glittery tank top, along with rhinestone-studded combat boots tall enough to hide her ankles. Wearing skimpy clothing was something she still wasn't entirely comfortable with, even after doing so for almost two years. But she'd learned early on that the more skin she exposed, the less likely she was to draw attention. Add some bling, and this strategy became even more effective. Strange, but true.

She sidestepped two girls taking selfies with their phones, and almost bumped into a man with a barcode tattoo on one side of his neck. A little more pushing, shuffling and dodging, and she finally reached the booths. She stopped at the second one from the end and slid onto the cushioned seat on the side that provided the best view of the room. After checking the time on the antique gold pocket watch she wore on a chain around her neck, she leaned back to wait for her client.

It wasn't long before he arrived, dropping into the seat opposite her with a grin and pushing a hand through his shoulder-length hair. "Always on time, Trixie," he shouted above the music.

Elle shrugged and refrained from saying the words that ran through her mind: *I have nowhere better to be.* "Ready?" she asked.

"Definitely," Monty replied, swiping one hand through the air between them. Gold dust glittered at his fingertips as a privacy charm formed over the booth, reducing the club's music to muffled background noise.

"Thanks," Elle said.

"No problemo." Monty lowered his hand and placed it on the table between them. Elle laid her hand over his.

"Is it about—" Her words were cut off as someone crashed into the side of their table, breaking the privacy charm. She jerked back and pressed herself against her seat as a middle-aged man fell halfway across the table. With a groan, he flattened his palms on the table and raised his head. He met Elle's eyes for a second before pushing himself up and straightening. Her stomach lurched as she noticed first the rounded tips of his ears and then the metal collar encircling his neck. A chain joined the collar to the wrist of a fae woman in a black skintight bodysuit.

"What was that for?" the woman shouted. Her anger wasn't directed at the human though. Elle followed her fierce gaze and found the burly bouncer who'd checked her ID.

"I turn my back for one moment and you bring a *slave* in here?" the bouncer demanded. "Don't you know the rules?"

The woman tilted her chin up and looked down her nose at the bouncer. "What rules? My slave goes wherever I want him to go."

"Not in this club, he doesn't. You're leaving. Now."

"Or you could just free the poor man," Monty grumbled, much to Elle's surprise. Her gaze flashed to the woman in the bodysuit, and then to the bouncer, but it appeared no one else had heard Monty over the pounding music.

"Come with me, ma'am," the bouncer said, reaching for the woman's arm.

"Don't touch me," she snapped. "And get out of my way." She tugged the chain, yanking her slave to her side, and sauntered away. The bouncer followed closely behind them.

"Well," Monty said, turning back to Elle. "Now that that little interruption's

out of the way …" He waved a hand and reactivated the privacy charm.

Elle shifted forward in her seat, tucking her hair behind one ear. She didn't generally encourage conversation, but for something like this, she couldn't keep quiet. "You don't agree with the slavery of humans?"

Monty paused before answering, his eyes narrowing slightly. "No, I don't. Is that a problem?"

"Not at all. I completely agree with those who've been campaigning for years to abolish the slave charm."

Monty's eyebrows rose. Elle wondered what surprised him more: that she agreed with him about slavery or that she was talking to him about something other than business. "Cool," he said. "There probably aren't many in this club who feel the same way."

"Probably not. There are plenty of free humans these days, but most fae aren't exactly thrilled about it."

"Yeah, tell me about it. I've had plenty of arguments with people. And don't get me started on the subject of *blood* slaves and vampires. I could go on all night." Monty placed one hand on the table again. "I do kind of understand how it started, though. They're definitely lesser beings, seeing as how they're powerless and all that. But at least employ them as servants or something. And let them donate blood voluntarily instead of forcing them. The whole slavery thing just isn't right."

Elle blinked as the sick feeling returned to her stomach. She made no move to reach for Monty's hand. "Lesser beings?" she repeated.

"Yeah. And don't look at me like that," he added with a roll of his eyes. "You know it's true. I mean, okay. They're technically one of the four High Races, but they're the only ones who can't do anything with magic. Obviously that means they're not on the same level as fae, vamps and shifters."

And if one of these so-called powerless humans could perform some strange, unheard-of magic? she asked silently. *Would that make her an equal to the fae, vamps and shifters?*

"So, are we doing this or what?" Monty asked, rapping his knuckles on the table.

She almost said no. She was so close to standing and walking away. But she needed tonight's payment. Every little bit made a difference. And Monty was a repeat customer. She couldn't afford to burn this bridge. Besides, most of her clients probably felt the same way—or worse—about humans. The only difference was that they'd never had any reason to voice their opinions in her presence.

She exhaled slowly, pushing aside the image of the man confined by a metal collar and chain, then placed her hand carefully over Monty's. "Is it Jilly again?"

"Yes. I saw her this morning. And it was just … it was awful. I want to forget the whole nasty confrontation."

Elle nodded. She didn't ask whether it might confuse things if Monty ran into his ex-girlfriend again—something that seemed to happen fairly often—and had no memory of their most recent verbal clash. She'd asked before, and he'd told her it wasn't a problem. And clearly it wasn't, since he kept seeing this girl, they kept fighting, and he kept asking Elle to make him forget.

"Have you written down anything else you need to remember that happened during the encounter?" she asked. She always checked, even if she'd performed her services for a client multiple times before. "Even if whatever happened had nothing to do with Jilly, you won't remember it. I can only—"

"I know, I know. You can only remove blocks of time, not separate out individual memories within the same time frame, yada, yada." He waved the hand that wasn't currently sitting beneath Elle's. "Nothing else important happened while we were arguing. You can go ahead."

Elle shut her eyes, and within moments, memories that weren't her own began sliding across her vision. She sifted through Monty's surface memories, flicking back through the events of this afternoon and evening, and quickly locating the one he wanted to forget: a heated argument in the middle of a cafe that involved a hot coffee thrown at his chest and bright magic arcing across the cafe to slap his face. All it took was a mental nudge and Elle had removed the entire incident from Monty's memory. Well, except for the very beginning. The moment he'd walked into the cafe and seen Jilly standing in the queue, before any unpleasantness began. Just so Monty would at least know he'd run into her.

Elle opened her eyes and withdrew her hand as Monty let out a contented sigh. "You're amazing. I have no idea what you took away—I know it was something to do with *her*—but I know I'm better off without the memory." He leaned back and rolled his shoulders. "Now I can relax and enjoy the evening."

Elle didn't bother replying as she removed a small glass vial from the front pocket of her shorts. She passed the vial across the table to Monty, and he unscrewed the metal lid. As he held his open palm over the top of the vial, a golden vapor-like substance drifted away from his skin and into the vial. Essence. The name the fae gave to the raw, unformed magic that pulsed through their bodies. When the vial was half full, Monty replaced the lid and passed it back to Elle. "Always a pleasure, Trixie."

"Yeah," she answered, taking the vial and returning it to her pocket.

"Hey, what do you actually do with all the Essence I pay you?" With a smirk, he added, "Planning to go wish shopping?"

"No," she answered, a little too quickly. She could tell from Monty's raised brow that he knew she was lying.

"Well, that's probably a good thing," he said, playing along, "since it would take you years to save for a wish at the rate I'm paying you, even if you're saving up your own Essence as well. But if you *are* in the market, I can hook you up with a great wish dealer I know. Super low prices. Better than what you'd get at the apothecary—"

"No thanks," Elle said quickly. "Not interested." She slid to the edge of her seat. "Anyway, enjoy your evening."

"Hey, come on, why do you always leave so quickly?" He stood and motioned toward the bar with his head. "Grab a drink, come and dance. It'll be fun."

"Um, thanks, but I have somewhere important to be." An attic, to be precise, but that made it no less important.

"Oh, well, maybe next time."

"Maybe," Elle said, though she knew it was a lie.

She made her way back across the crowded dance floor, one hand near her front pocket, just in case someone had seen the Essence in the vial and tried to pickpocket her. Not for the first time, she wondered if it were possible to use her strange power on herself. Wouldn't it be wonderful to wipe away some of her own painful memories? It was so tempting to try, and yet she knew it was a terrible idea. The memory of every horrible moment from the past seven years was exactly what gave her purpose. It was what reminded her why it was so important to collect as much Essence as she could.

She'd just reached the other side of the room when a hand encircled her wrist and tugged her back. Against her will, she was swung around, coming face to face with another chest, this one covered in a tight silver shirt. A tattoo of a barcode disappeared below the collar. It was the man she'd dodged past earlier. "Hey, what are you—"

"Hello there," he shouted over the music. Elle's glare rose to his face—and landed on a pair of blood-red eyes. *Stars above.* What was a *vampire* doing inside Club Onyx? If anyone got close enough to see his eyes … If he pushed aside his straggly hair to reveal ears that *weren't* pointed …

"I've seen you around," he continued.

"I don't think so," she answered, trying to remove her arm from his vise-like grip and failing. Fortunately, he wasn't squeezing the wrist she'd landed on earlier. "You must have me confused with someone else."

He shook his head. "I'm not confused. I've seen you twice in the past two weeks. I know you meet people and do … *something* for them. I have a suspicion about what that something is, but I—"

Elle wrenched her arm free before he could get another word out. She twisted away and tried to run, but a hand grasped for her, scratching down her shoulder before hooking in the back of her shorts and yanking her backward. She lost her balance and tumbled toward the ground for the second time that night—though this fall was at least slowed by the number of bodies around her.

The crowd shifted, dancers shoved against one another, and irritated exclamations mingled with the pounding music as Elle's backside finally hit the floor. A hand grabbed her hair and pulled. She cried out as she tried to get to her back pocket. If she could just reach the small knife she always brought with her—

And then—"Vampire!" someone yelled. The grip vanished from her hair. Several people lunged past her. She put her hand down to push herself up, then snatched it hastily back before a glossy black stiletto heel could pierce a hole through it. She tried to scoot backward, but that left her bumping into knees and swinging purses and several more pairs of shoes.

"Here, let me help you," a voice said just as hands fitted beneath her arms and lifted her swiftly to her feet. "Are you okay?" he asked, turning her around before she could protest. "Oh, hey, it's you." Elle looked up into Dex's silvery blue eyes as he asked, "Did that vamp hurt you?"

"No, no. I'm fine." Though when she stopped to think about it for a moment, her skin burned where the vampire had scratched her. "I, um, I need to go." She was utterly failing in the draw-no-attention-to-yourself department tonight. "Thanks for helping me—" The crowd jostled around them, and she almost lost her balance again. Dex slid his arm across her back and fought against the crowd as he guided her to the edge of the room. The fabric of his shirt stung her skin as it rubbed the scratches on her back, but she was grateful for the assistance. Only once they'd made it safely outside away from the shoving bodies and past the queue of people jostling to get inside did Dex remove his arm from around her.

"Thanks," she said, after taking in a gulp of the cool night air. She almost asked why he was still here, but getting home was her priority now. A glance at the pocket watch around her neck told her it was twenty minutes to midnight. "I really need to go," she said.

"Is it your bedtime soon?" he asked, a teasing edge to his tone.

Without meaning to, she found herself smiling in response. "Something like that." She turned and stepped off the sidewalk.

"Wait, before you go …" Elle stopped and twisted around to look at Dex. His eyes moved back and forth across her face before he asked, "Will you be here tomorrow night?"

Her heart pattered double time at the realization that he wanted to see her again, but there was no way she could agree to that. "I never visit the same place two nights in a row."

One eyebrow inched upward. "How mysterious."

Before he could ask anything else, Elle said, "Goodnight," and hurried away. The scratches running down her back stung like hell, but she waited until she was at the corner of the block and almost out of sight before reaching one hand over her shoulder to gingerly touch her skin. She felt something wet, and her feet stumbled to a halt. Pulling her hand back quickly, she looked down. Her heart lurched. A red smear covered her fingers. She was bleeding. And Dex had wrapped his arm around her.

With a pounding heart, Elle threw a glance over her shoulder toward the club entrance. No one was looking at her. Not even Dex, who was staring down at his hand with a perplexed expression. Then his gaze lifted, landing on hers a moment later, and she could tell in an instant that he knew. *Human*, his eyes seemed to accuse. Without pausing a moment longer, Elle turned and ran.

TWO

DDEX WATCHED THE BLOND GIRL VANISH AROUND THE CORNER BEFORE FROWNING again at the red smear on his palm. He'd assumed she was fae, but her blood clearly told a different story. He wiped his hand on his jeans, then rolled up the sleeve of his shirt to hide the reddish brown marks. He didn't need anyone noticing and getting suspicious. He could prove pretty quickly that he was fae, but there were other reasons he didn't want anyone taking a closer look at him.

"There you are," a familiar voice said behind him, and Dex turned as Oliver ran out of the club.

"Did you get him?" Dex asked.

"No." Olly pushed his hair away from his sweaty forehead and breathed deeply. He nodded to the other side of the street, and Dex took the hint. They crossed quickly before Olly continued. "I couldn't catch him through the crowd, and once he got outside the back and had space to move, he was way too fast. I shot a blood tracker at him, but I must have missed."

"Excuses, excuses," a third voice drawled, and Dex and Olly looked around as Xander crossed the street, hands pushed into his pockets.

"*You* could have caught him if you hadn't been late to your position in the alley," Olly reminded Xander with a punch to his shoulder.

"Hey, this was a spur-of-the-moment operation, remember?" Xander said. "There weren't supposed to be any vamps here tonight. Didn't the message say Tuesday? And didn't they just change the location?"

"Yes," Dex said. He'd been just as surprised as Olly and Xander when he saw the man with the red eyes slip past the bouncer along with a group of giggling women too tipsy to notice the vampire in their midst. It was moments after Dex had spoken to the human girl, and he'd been about to leave. But the sight of a vampire entering Club Onyx changed his plans. "I don't think this vampire has anything to do with the Allegiant, though," he continued. "He wasn't meeting any others. We scoured the place and didn't spot any." A chill crept across Dex's skin as his mind replayed the moment the vampire had lashed out and tugged the human girl back. Was it simply because he had caught the scent of her blood? Or was he after her for another reason? Either way, if he wasn't part of the Allegiant, then he probably had nothing to do with the abductions Dex, Olly and Xander had been investigating. "It looked like he was here for that girl," Dex finished.

"The one you almost flattened on the sidewalk?" Xander asked with a snort. He pushed a hand through his messy bronze hair. "I don't blame her for running from you."

"Yeah, sorry, man." Olly clapped a hand on Dex's shoulder. "I know you saved her from a vampire, but that's not enough to make up for embarrassing a lady in front of a crowd."

"Apparently not," Dex answered, frowning in the direction the girl had run. He contemplated telling his friends the real reason she'd bolted, but decided to keep it to himself.

"Not used to having a girl flee in the opposite direction, are you?" Xander commented.

"Yeah, must be a new experience for you," Olly added. "Don't they normally swoon and fall into your open arms?"

Dex laughed. "Oh, is *that* what I did wrong? You mean I was supposed to use my *arms* to catch her, not the floor?"

"See? You're learning. Soon you'll be—Oof!" Olly's words ended in a grunt as Dex elbowed him in the ribs.

"I don't know why I keep either of you around," Dex said, walking away from the purple glow of Club Onyx and toward the alley behind Jazzers, the all-night pizza joint.

"You'd miss us too much if we were gone," Xander called after him.

Dex shook his head but didn't fight the grin that pulled at his lips. Olly and Xander had annoyed the hell out of him for longer than he could remember, but he couldn't imagine life without them. So different—Olly short and pale and reserved, Xander tall and tanned and confident—yet equally loyal. Which meant that right now, they were just as determined as Dex to find the vampire extremist group known as the Allegiant. "Can we focus on what's important?" he asked as Olly caught up to him. Xander's lazy stride left him several paces behind, but Dex knew he was listening. "You intercepted a message just before that vamp showed up," Dex said to Olly. "Something about the location of Tuesday's meeting being changed?"

"Right, yes. I've got the new coordinates here." Olly produced his phone from a pocket. "You still want to check it out tonight?"

"Yes. So we know what to expect before we get there on Tuesday."

"Okay, let me see …"

Dex glanced away from Olly and turned his gaze upward as a shadow passed over the alley. Dragon shifter? Pegasus? Oversized phoenix? But the shadow was gone before Dex could figure out the shape or scale of whatever creature had flown past.

"It's in Belgravia," Olly announced, drawing Dex's attention back to him. "At the old fairground."

"Abandoned and creepy," Xander said from behind them. "Seems appropriate."

"I don't think they appreciate stereotypes like that," Olly said.

"Which is exactly why he said it," Dex reminded Olly, knowing he would find a smirk on Xander's face if he looked over his shoulder.

"I guess I should be glad he's at least paying attention to what we're saying," Olly said.

"Of course I'm paying attention," Xander answered. "I'm keeping my eyes peeled for more vamps. And pretty girls. You know, in case someone else is about to dazzle Dex so much he can't see where he's going again."

"I was not dazzled," Dex grumbled, hating that there was some truth to

Xander's words. There *had* been something about the girl that made him pause. Something familiar. Something that tugged at the edge of his memory. Probably just the way she smelled, he decided. Like apple blossoms. The scent conjured up fond memories of the hours he used to spend running through orchards as a child. He could probably blame the overwhelming sense of nostalgia for the fact that he'd behaved like an idiot and asked to see her again. Thank goodness she'd said no. *I never visit the same place two nights in a row.* He'd almost laughed at that. It was so similar to the rule he'd been about to break: Never spend more than one evening with a girl.

"You sure she didn't use some kind of charm on you?" Xander asked, startling Dex as he appeared at his side. "'Cause she certainly distracted you enough to keep you from running after the vamp."

"Because I thought you guys had it handled," Dex replied. "Next time, I'll have to catch him myself."

"Next time," Xander said, "there'll be loads of them, and your lazy ass will have no choice but to join the hunt."

"Lazy ass indeed," Dex muttered, reaching out to shove Xander sideways.

With a hoot of laughter, Xander dodged out of the way. "Seriously, how slow are you tonight? I think you've been bewitched."

"Not possible," Dex answered immediately, which only made Xander laugh harder. But it *wasn't* possible. The girl couldn't have bewitched Dex. She was just a human.

THREE

ELLE MADE IT BACK TO HER STREET BREATHLESS AND WITH A STITCH IN HER SIDE. Pressing one hand beneath the right side of her ribcage, she stared up as she caught her breath. Her home was a tall, skinny townhouse wedged between other tall, skinny townhouses on a pretty street in Willowton, a not-too-shabby borough of Vale City. The front door was only a few steps away, but since she hadn't left through it, she certainly couldn't return that way. Her eyes skimmed past the three floors and landed on the attic at the top of the house. Climbing wasn't usually a problem, but her sore wrist might make it more challenging.

She pulled the pocket watch out from beneath her tank top—she'd shoved it down there while running to keep it from bouncing around too much—and her heart squeezed when she saw the position of the minute hand. "Stars," she muttered. She was about to take 'cutting it fine' to a new level.

She hurried toward the ivy-covered trellis that ran from the ground all the way to the roof on the left side of the building. Salvia had got someone to make sure it was firmly secured to the house when they moved in years ago. "If I can't have my gardens and orchards," she'd said, "I'll at least have that damn ivy on the outside of the house."

Elle hooked her fingers into the diamond shapes hidden behind the leaves, raised one boot, and began to climb. She gritted her teeth as the ache in her wrist intensified, but she didn't slow down. Rustling the leaves as little as possible, she ascended the side of her home, quickly reaching the ledge that ran the width of the house beneath the attic window. She pulled herself onto it—sucking in a breath as her wrist screamed at her—and shuffled sideways until she reached the window. Slowly, silently, she slid the window up, sat on the sill, and swung her legs inside. Her boots scuffed the wooden floor, and she cringed at the sound, freezing for a moment. But there was no time to waste. She stood, pulled the window down, and stepped away.

Just in time.

Barely two seconds later, gold lines raced horizontally and vertically across the window, sealing Elle inside. With a quick glance over her shoulder, she saw the same glowing lines barring the door on the other side of the attic. The gold chain-shaped tattoo encircling her right ankle burned briefly in unison with the glowing lines. Then the burn was gone, along with the bright gold light, leaving dull metal bars across the window and door. By morning, when it was time for Elle to go downstairs and begin preparing breakfast, they would be gone.

She crossed the moonlit attic, passing the screen that concealed a basin, toilet, and small shower. An old striped rug covered the center of the room, and on the other side stood her bed. It creaked as she sat on the edge. She reached down and tugged her boots off, then removed her fake ear tips. The ear tips would end up inside the secret compartment at the back of her wardrobe, which was where her sparkly clothing and makeup—the items she'd gathered over the years without Salvia noticing—were hidden.

The only other pieces of furniture in the room were a wooden table and chair, and it was the chair Elle headed for next. After climbing onto it, she reached for the box hidden on top of one of the beams. She pulled it down and placed the vial of Essence inside, then returned the box to its hiding place and climbed off the chair. She removed her watch necklace and pocketknife, and turned her phone off, sliding all three items between the mattress and the bed base a moment later. The pocket watch was the only valuable thing she had left from her father, and if Salvia got hold of it, she'd probably try to sell it.

"Elle?"

As if conjured up by thought alone, Salvia's voice pierced the quiet night and echoed up the stairway outside the attic door. Elle froze. *Don't come upstairs,* she begged silently. But the clack of shoes on the wooden steps announced

Salvia's ascent.

"Stars above," Elle muttered. She had no time to change, no time to remove her makeup. She grabbed the boots and ear tips and hurried on tiptoe to hide them inside her wardrobe. Then she tugged back the patchwork bedspread on her bed and dove beneath it, making sure to pull it right up to her shoulders to cover the glittery strap of her tank top. Turned away from the door, and with her hair partially covering her face, she hoped her makeup wouldn't be noticeable.

The sizzle of magic indicated the confinement charm lifting from the door, and a moment later, the hinges squeaked as the door swung open. A moment of silence passed before Salvia's voice, brittle and cold as ice, reached Elle's ears. "What have you been doing up here, Elle?"

Elle didn't respond. With her eyes sealed shut, she did her best to keep her breathing slow and even.

"Elle," Salvia repeated, her voice drifting through the air like a chill breeze. "You wouldn't lie to me, would you?" She took a step closer. Then another.

Breathe, Elle told herself. *Just. Breathe.*

Salvia muttered something Elle couldn't make out. A curse of frustration, perhaps? Elle didn't care, as long as it wasn't magic. Salvia's shoe scraped the floor and moved again. Toward the door or toward the bed? Elle couldn't be sure. "Nothing's going on up here, my love," Salvia said.

"But I heard something," Meredith's whining voice echoed up the staircase.

"Yes, so you've repeatedly told me. But I've checked your window and Sienna's window, and now I've checked up here, and there's nothing. It must have been a bird or a pixie or some other nasty little critter." The door banged shut, which would have woken Elle if she'd genuinely been asleep. "Go back to bed, Meredith dear," Salvia continued, her voice muffled by the door and another sizzle of magic. "Tomorrow is a big day for you." Her shoes clacked down the stairs, growing a little quieter with each step.

Elle let out a shaky breath. It had been months since she'd come so close to being caught. Salvia allowed her to go out at night sometimes with Sienna, but the rule was that she had to be back home and in the attic by midnight. That was why the confinement charm barred the door and window so late. Salvia liked to remind Elle that this made her one of the luckiest slaves in the city. "Other slaves don't get to stay out until midnight, do they?" she would say. "In fact, other slaves don't get to go out at all."

Other slaves probably aren't *family members*, Elle always wanted to snap back. But there would be consequences for saying something like that. Just like there would be consequences if Salvia ever discovered that Elle left the house two or three nights every week without permission.

She lay motionless beneath the blanket for another few minutes until no other sound reached her from downstairs. Then she tiptoed to her basin and washed her makeup off as quietly as possible before undressing. Back in bed, she stared through the dusty window as her eyelids grew heavier. But even after they slid closed, it took her some time to fall asleep, her thoughts oscillating between the vampire who may have discovered her unique power and the faerie who knew exactly what she was.

Those piercing silver-blue eyes filled her mind. Had Dex told anyone? Had he yelled out "Human!" as she ran away? She would never know, but just to be safe, she could never meet another client at Club Onyx.

FOUR

"This one," Salvia said the following evening, laying a green silk blouse on Elle's bed beside a pair of designer jeans. The items were part of a small collection of clothing Salvia kept aside for Elle to wear on nights like tonight. Nights when Elle was allowed to eat dinner with her stepmother and stepsisters and pretend she was part of the family instead of hiding in the kitchen to clean up and eat on her own. "You can get dressed now. Martin and Meredith should be back here in about half an hour."

"Yes, Salvia," Elle answered quietly without looking up. She expected her stepmother to leave then, but a moment later, Salvia's hand gripped Elle's chin and forced her gaze upward.

"What's wrong with you? You're looking particularly washed out this evening. Don't you dare tell me you're sick. That won't get you out of this."

Elle blinked at her stepmother's steel gray eyes and glossy red hair. She suspected her 'washed out' appearance was from several late nights over the past week. Getting up early every morning so she could begin her household chores the moment the confinement charm lifted didn't help either. But all she said was, "I'm not sick."

Salvia's eyes narrowed as they scanned Elle's face. Her nails bit into Elle's skin. Finally, she let go. "I'll send Sienna up in a minute with her makeup." Then she leaned closer, her cheek almost brushing Elle's. "And remember to smile tonight," she whispered into Elle's ear. "I dislike it when you don't smile."

Salvia marched out of the room, leaving the door open. Elle relaxed her shoulders and dropped onto the edge of her bed. "I dislike it when you don't smile," she mimicked in a whisper. "If only you knew all the things I dislike about *you*," she added softly. She longed to tell Salvia exactly what she thought of her. She came close on a daily basis, but Salvia's particularly wicked form of punishment meant it wasn't worth fighting back. Elle had learned instead to bite her tongue and shove her anger down. Probably not healthy having to do that every day, she reflected, but far better than the alternative.

Elle removed her threadbare jeans and T-shirt—purple with an unraveling hem and a logo for the band Gunmetal Moon on the back—and changed quickly into the blouse and ridiculously tight designer jeans. She wiggled her hips and tried to pull them a little higher, wondering who decided it was fashionable to wear pants so tight they left no room for anyone to have a decent meal. Not that Elle was planning to eat much tonight. She was already feeling ill at the thought of what was to come.

As light footsteps hurried up the staircase, she gave up on the jeans and swiveled her left wrist in slow circles. It still hurt from the night before, and household chores today hadn't helped. "Hey!" Sienna said breathlessly as she reached the doorway, her makeup bag clutched in one hand. She crossed the room and hugged Elle tightly. "I'm so glad you're okay." Her hand pressed against the scratches from the vampire's nails, and Elle winced. Sienna stepped back hurriedly. "What's wrong? Did Mom—"

"No, it's nothing. Just a scratch on my back."

"Were you out last night?" Sienna whispered. "Was that the sound Meredith heard?"

Elle nodded. "I got more Essence."

Sienna scooped her flyaway hair behind one ear. While Meredith had inherited her mother's lustrous red locks, Sienna's hair was a wispy orange that could only be smoothed with a combination of charms and hair products. "It's so dangerous, Elle," she said as she gripped Elle's hand. "I panicked when I heard Meredith complaining she'd heard something up here. I told Mom it was something outside *my* window and not up here. A pixie sneaking around and playing in the ivy. But you know she doesn't listen to me. She insisted on coming up here anyway."

"It's risky, I know," Elle said, "but one of my clients sent a message saying he wanted to meet last night. You know I can't turn down any opportunity to get more Essence."

"I know, I know, it's just …" Sienna set her makeup bag down on Elle's bed and unzipped it. "I'm always scared for you. And with the human abductions going on for over a month now, it's even—"

"It's fine, Sienna. No one knows I'm human when I'm out there at night. I have my pretty pointed ears on, and vampires aren't interested in abducting a faerie girl. It's not like they can drink fae blood." Elle's tone was light, but unease whispered at the back of her mind as she thought of the vampire from last night. What was he doing at Club Onyx? Had he somehow heard about the service she offered? Or had he mistaken her for someone else? Either way, it had nothing to do with the fact that she was human. She looked like every other faerie girl in that club.

"You know they're saying those abductions aren't about blood, right?" Sienna said quietly. She perched on the edge of the bed and began removing makeup items, lining them up neatly on the bedspread.

Elle nodded. "I know." It had been going on for months now, the disappearance of humans. Of course, there were always cases of missing humans, but usually a body would turn up somewhere—in an alley, or floating down a river, or behind an abandoned building—most likely with puncture marks. A victim of a vampire who had grown bored of blood bags and blood slaves.

But what Sienna was referring to now was different. Dozens of humans vanishing every week. Only a few bodies recovered here and there. And nobody knew why.

"What's wrong with your hand?" Sienna asked, and Elle realized she'd been slowly rotating it again.

"Oh, uh … I tripped last night and landed a little hard on it. Probably nothing serious."

"I can get you some of that healing balm, if you want?" Sienna offered. "The one that works on humans too. It's in Mom's bathroom, but if I can sneak in while she's busy, I'll just squeeze a little out of the tube."

Elle hesitated before answering. "Okay, but only if you're sure she won't catch you."

"Definitely. Getting caught isn't an option. I wouldn't do that to you." She tossed a hairband at Elle and added, "Okay, tie your hair up. Let's get this makeup thing done."

Elle twisted her hair into a quick bun and sat on the bed beside Sienna. She was perfectly capable of doing her own makeup, but Salvia didn't know that, and this gave Sienna an excuse to be up here. Besides, Elle's makeup always looked better when Sienna did it, seeing as she could blend and color with magic, not just sponges and products.

"Oh, I got you something when I was out with Nikki yesterday," Sienna said as she began applying foundation with a brush. "A cute little mini skirt on sale. Super bling, so it'll fit right in with the rest of your nighttime wardrobe. I'll bring it up here next time Mom's out."

"Thanks." Elle closed her eyes as the delicate bristles of the brush moved over her skin.

"I don't know how you keep doing it. I'd be terrified walking into clubs and bars and things, all on my own, knowing I'm not old enough. I'd probably freeze up completely and not have any clue what to say."

"It's not exactly my comfort zone either," Elle reminded her, "but you do what you have to do when you're desperate."

"I know. I'm sorry you ended up so desperate though. I'm sorry my mother's such a—"

"Hey, you don't have to apologize for her." Elle opened her eyes and focused on Sienna's face. Freckles sprinkled her nose, and her eyes were a softer shade of green than Meredith's. "And remember that this won't last forever. We'll both get away from her one day."

"I just wish I could help more."

"You *do* help. You bring me new clothes and makeup, and you beg Salvia to let me go out with you sometimes so I can do more jobs while you're hanging out with friends or ... what's his name? That exchange student in your class who likes you so much?"

"Elon," Sienna said, her cheeks flushing faintly. She dropped the foundation brush back into the makeup bag.

"Yeah, him." Elle closed her eyes again as Sienna raised her hand, gold dust glittering at her fingertips. "*And* you're always giving me little bits of your own Essence," she added as Sienna's magic rubbed gently over her face. "So don't tell me you're not helping."

"But it's hardly anything. If it didn't make me so tired, I could give you—"

"It's fine, Sienna. Seriously. You need your energy. If you start falling asleep in class and your teachers tell Salvia, you'll be in huge trouble." Sienna was two years younger than Elle, and still at school. Elle would have graduated last year, but she'd stopped going to school after Salvia put the slave charm on her. When she wasn't cleaning the house or cooking, she read Meredith's old textbooks or listened as Sienna explained whatever homework she was doing.

"Okay, that's done," Sienna said after using a few more makeup products and a bit of magic here and there. "I'll just do a quick charm on your hair." Elle remained still as gold dust drifted around her, and her hair twisted itself into voluminous glossy waves. "There," Sienna said a minute or two later. "Not too fancy, not too casual." She zipped up her makeup bag. "Now I just need to tame my own hair—*again*—so I can look as glamorous as my two sisters, and then we can get this thing done."

Elle let out a grim sigh. "Is Salvia sure it's happening tonight?"

"Yes. Martin spoke to her about it last week. He asked for her blessing, and obviously she said yes."

"Obviously," Elle murmured. "That was the aim of the game with this one."

Sienna nodded, her hands fidgeting with the zip of the makeup bag as she looked away. "Anyway, there's nothing we can do to change it. Not without … you know …"

"Consequences," Elle filled in, a shiver running down her spine. She hated that word.

"Yes." Sienna swallowed, her lips turning downward. She reached out and delicately traced one of the star patterns on the quilted bedspread. Her fingers moved to the tiny words embroidered alongside one edge: *It's written in the stars.* Words from an old song Elle's mother had loved. A few stars to the left were the words *Look to the stars.* Elsewhere on the quilt, alongside a big purple and yellow patchwork star, were the words *Starry night.* Though the quilt was worn with age and the fabric colors had faded, it was Elle's most treasured possession, along with the pocket watch necklace. Her mother had made it years ago, before Elle was even born. It used to cover her parents' bed. Until Salvia came along.

"Anyway." Sienna withdrew her hand and stood. "I'll see you down—"

"Sienna," Elle said, unable to stand the misery on the younger girl's face. She stood and took Sienna's hand. "It won't be for much longer. I think I'll be able to get us out of here soon."

Sienna's eyes rose. "Really? You've saved that much? For a third-tier wish?"

Elle nodded. She hadn't planned on saying anything until she was sure, but Sienna needed hope as much as Elle did. "I think I have almost enough."

Sienna gripped Elle's hand, her eyes brightening as she smiled. "That's amazing. We'll have to start planning our escape soon."

"Yes. Once I'm sure I have enough."

Sienna skipped away and disappeared down the stairs, leaving Elle to wait until Salvia summoned her. She pulled her wardrobe door open and checked her appearance in the mirror. Glamorous, but not overdone. It was exactly the look Salvia always told them to aim for. Elle would fit right in with the modern elegance of the rest of the house. The thought made her ill.

She banged the door shut and turned swiftly away. Cool evening light filtered in through the window, and with a sigh, Elle wandered across the room and peered out. If she squinted hard into the distance, she could just make out Belmont Palace sitting atop Sovereign Hill at the edge of the city. Mountains rose beyond it, while on the left, the land sloped down toward the beach. Not that Elle could see the ocean from here. There were far too many buildings between this house and the coastline, and she wasn't nearly high enough to see over them.

She returned her gaze to the hill that had belonged to the royal family for centuries, ever since the Blood War between fae, vampires and shifters. They'd torn the world apart, fighting over every piece of land, until it became clear the fae would wipe out the other High Races if the war didn't end. The fae claimed most countries—including this one—while vampires and shifters ended up with smaller territories around the world. Humans, of course, ruled nothing. Over time, border restrictions were relaxed, and different races were allowed to travel between territories. Then they were allowed to settle in areas originally claimed by a different race. Eventually, most parts of the world were once again mixed. But the fae never let anyone forget they were truly the ones in power, and Vale City, like many other cities around the word, would always be unofficial fae territory.

"Elle!" Salvia's shout startled Elle from her thoughts. She sucked in a breath and straightened her blouse. Then she turned away from the window and headed downstairs.

FIVE

"ARE YOU BOTH READY?" SALVIA ASKED WHEN ELLE AND SIENNA HAD ASSEMBLED IN the lounge. Salvia reclined in a modern wingback chair upholstered in white linen. The top curved elegantly around her like a pair of sleek angel wings. Elle almost laughed at the ludicrous thought. "Meredith texted to say they're on their way back," Salvia continued, "so I expect they'll be here in a few minutes."

"Yes, we're ready," Sienna said, her tone resigned. Elle didn't need to answer, so she merely nodded.

"You don't look ready," Salvia said to Sienna. She uncrossed her legs, stood, and walked toward her daughter. She raised her hand, causing Sienna to flinch, but all Salvia did was run her fingers from the top of Sienna's head down to the tips of her hair. Magic glittered for a moment as Salvia applied a quick charm to smooth out the remaining frizzy strands Sienna had missed. "There," Salvia said, lowering her hand. "Perfect. Remember, Martin hasn't just chosen Meredith, he's chosen this family. We all need to look the part."

Martin has chosen a lie, Elle almost said out loud. He'd fallen for a story that didn't exist. He believed he'd soon be visiting Meredith's family's real home on a large estate in the foothills of the mountains, not too far from Belmont Palace. This townhouse, while placed in one of the nicer neighborhoods of Vale City, was only their home for a few nights a month, when they needed the convenience of something within the city. This story Meredith had woven for Martin was based on a nugget of truth. Once upon a time, Salvia *had* owned a sprawling estate near the royals, and a holiday villa in the wine lands, and a yacht named Serenity. But not anymore. She'd lost all those assets after Elle's father died.

But the truth wasn't something Martin would want to hear. He came from a family that had been wealthy for generations, and Elle knew that people like that only married into other wealthy families. Fortunately for Meredith and Salvia, Martin wasn't from around here. He didn't know Meredith's real story. He might have discovered it by asking around, digging a little deeper. But it seemed he believed every word she'd told him.

Muffled laughter reached Elle's ears, and she turned to look over her shoulder at the front door. "Ah, it seems they've returned even quicker than I expected," Salvia said. She spun on her heel and returned to her chair. "Sit down and look natural, and I hope the two of you are ready to smile. If you're not convincing, there will be consequences."

Elle and Sienna hurried to the couch, Sienna meeting Elle's gaze for a moment as they sat. Fear flashed through her eyes before she pulled a neutral expression into place. Then she lifted her phone from a side table, while Elle grabbed a magazine from the designer wood and leather rack on her side of the couch. She opened it to a random page and stared unseeingly at the words.

A key turned in the lock of the front door, and Meredith's voice grew louder as the door opened. "I know, right?" she said with a laugh. "It'll be awesome." Elle lowered the magazine—only noticing now that it was upside down—and looked up as footsteps crossed the entrance hall. "Ohmygosh, guess what!" Meredith squealed, stopping just inside the lounge with Martin beside her. She thrust her left hand forward, flashing the largest diamond Elle had ever seen. "We're engaged!" She flung her arms around Martin, and he lifted her from the ground as he swung her around. "I can't believe it. We're getting married. We're getting *married!*"

Martin set her down as Salvia rose and rushed forward to congratulate them. "My darling, that's *wonderful!* I'm so excited for you!" She hugged Meredith, then Martin, as Elle stood and moved forward with Sienna. They joined in the squealing, both threw their arms around Meredith, and then gasped appropriately as they admired the ring.

"I know it seems quick," Martin said, his brown eyes shining as his grin stretched wide. "We've only known each other a few months, and twenty-one is quite young to get married. But when you know you've met the right one …" He gazed adoringly into Meredith's eyes, then kissed her. "I just didn't want to wait any longer."

"Oh, it's so exciting," Sienna exclaimed. "A *wedding*! It's going to be so much fun to plan. And I always wanted a big brother."

"Me too," Elle added hastily as Salvia stared pointedly at her.

Martin beamed at them. "Thank you, Sienna. And … Estelle? Is that right?"

"Yes, but you can call me Elle," she reminded him. They'd only met twice before, so she couldn't blame him for forgetting.

"Right, of course." He gave her a goofy grin. "We'll be family soon. No need to be formal."

Elle nodded, but didn't trust herself to speak. If she opened her mouth again, she might accidentally tell Martin to rip that ring off Meredith's finger and run as if an entire wolf shifter pack was after him.

"Well, this definitely calls for some champagne," Salvia said, her glossy lips fixed in her best fake smile. "Elle, darling, would you grab a bottle please? Choose the very best from our collection here."

"Yes, of course," Elle answered, managing to resist the urge to roll her eyes. Darling? Please? Choose the very best? She knew as well as Salvia that there was only one bottle of champagne in the fridge, and that Salvia had complained repeatedly about how expensive it was.

"Shall we sit?" Salvia said as Elle turned and made for the opposite doorway. "I want to hear *all* about the proposal."

"Yes!" Sienna said. "How did you propose?"

Elle crossed the dining room and entered the kitchen, but Martin spoke loud enough for her to hear the details of the hot air balloon ride he and Meredith had taken from Bremmersford Park at sunset. What a waste. Meredith would have said yes if he'd taken her to a drive-through and presented the ring with a bag of fries.

Elle returned to the lounge with a chilled champagne bottle in one hand

and a tray of five champagne flutes balanced on the other. The glasses were identical except for the one that held a few drops of something extra special. A potion Salvia had mixed up earlier today. "It all sounds so romantic," Sienna sighed, swooning back against the cushions of the wingback chair beside Salvia's. "Don't you think so, Elle?"

"Yes," Elle answered automatically, forcing her own smile back into place. She handed the bottle to Salvia and placed the tray on the coffee table before lowering herself to the couch on Martin's other side—a seat that everyone except Martin had intentionally left open for her. "I can't imagine a better setting for a proposal."

"It was the absolute best," Meredith gushed. "I can't wait to call all my friends and tell them."

Salvia held the champagne bottle up, and with a flourish of one hand and a sprinkle of magic, the cork popped free and hit the ceiling. Bubbly liquid fizzed from the top and spilled onto the carpet. Meredith and Sienna squealed and giggled some more, while Elle groaned inwardly. She'd be cleaning that up later.

Salvia poured champagne into the five glasses and passed one to each of them. They toasted one another, and Elle watched Martin over the top of her glass as she took a sip. Would he notice the odd flavor of the potion mingling with the sweet, fizzy liquid? She almost hoped he would, though it would make no difference to the way this evening ultimately ended.

"I can't wait to start planning the wedding," Meredith said, twirling a strand of glossy red hair around one finger.

"I'm looking forward to it too," Martin said. It appeared he hadn't noticed anything strange about his drink.

"There's the engagement party to plan first," Salvia reminded them.

"Oh yes, of course. We can have it at Fernvale," Meredith said, referencing their old home. "I can't *wait* for you to see it," she told Martin. "The grounds are endless, and it has the most *stunning* views of the Elyn River and the mountains."

"It sounds amazing," Martin said. "A little bit like my family's place back home."

"Oh yes, you showed me pictures." Meredith rested her hand on his arm and added, "I hope you and I can have a beautiful home just like it one day. Somewhere we can live happily ever after."

"Well," Martin said, leaning forward to set his glass down on the table. "If you want to wish for happiness, I think this might help." He slipped a hand into his pocket and produced a bundle of black silk. He placed it on his palm, and the fabric fell away to reveal a glowing green gem the size of a walnut.

A collective intake of breath sounded from around the room. "Stars above," Meredith whispered. "Is that ..."

"A wish," Martin said.

Elle couldn't help leaning a little closer as she stared at it. Magic swirled within the hollow center of the gem, which was what gave it that telltale glow of a wish.

"My goodness," Salvia murmured.

"It's only a first-tier wish," Martin continued, "but—"

"But still so valuable," Meredith breathed as she slowly reached out to take it.

"Yes. It was a gift from my grandmother. The ring was hers as well. I've never been able to decide on what to wish for, so I've been saving it. But now that we're going to be married, I have everything I could possibly want. I don't need to wish for anything else." He squeezed Meredith's knee and reached for his champagne. "It's yours, my love. Wish for happiness or perfect weather on our wedding day or shooting stars on our wedding night. Something money can't buy."

"I wonder if a first-tier wish can buy those things," Sienna said softly. Elle had been wondering the same thing. A lifetime of happiness seemed like a lot to ask for. Perhaps a week or two might be possible for the amount of magic contained in a first-tier wish.

"Well, if it doesn't work," Martin said with a laugh, "just try a different wish."

"This is incredible," Meredith said. "Thank you so much. I'll have to keep it somewhere safe until I decide what to wish for." She placed it carefully on the coffee table as Martin tipped his glass back and finished off the remainder of his champagne.

Meredith, Salvia and Sienna continued discussing party plans and wish ideas, while Martin grew quieter and sleepier. Elle would have to act before he passed out completely. Her strange ability wouldn't work if he was asleep. He needed to be completely relaxed and unaware that there was another presence inside his mind.

"Elle, dear," Salvia finally said. "It looks like you can't stop yawning. Why don't you head up to bed?"

That was the signal. It was time. Elle met her stepmother's gaze, and Salvia gave her a pointed look. Elle knew what she was supposed to say now, but the words were stuck somewhere behind her lips. What if she refused this time? What if she didn't play along? What if she let Meredith and Salvia squirm their own way out of this one without the assistance of Elle's skills?

"Elle," Salvia repeated through gritted teeth, her fake smile stretching a little wider. "You've had a busy day." Which was code for something along the lines of *Don't you dare disobey me now, or someone will pay the price.* Elle's eyes flicked to Sienna, and her resolve wilted at the sight of the fear in the other girl's eyes. An echo of Sienna's bone-chilling screams whispered through her mind. She couldn't do that to her sister.

"Yes, it has been a long day," she said woodenly, glancing again at Salvia before turning to Martin. "I didn't realize I was so tired."

"Me too," he answered, his eyes half closed. "I'm also ... very sleepy."

"Must be all the champagne," Meredith said, her tinkling laugh grating at Elle's nerves.

"I'm so sorry, but I need to get to bed." Elle placed her hand over Martin's. "Congratulations again. I'm so happy for the two of you." The lie tasted bitter on her tongue.

Martin turned a sleepy smile toward her. "Thank you."

She slipped effortlessly into his mind, detecting the memories at the surface with ease. There was a lot she had to remove—the past three months—and she couldn't help wondering what other memories she'd be erasing along with the memory of Meredith Leroux and her family. What other important moments in Martin's life would be gone from his mind forever?

She was vaguely aware of Meredith speaking to him in a soothing voice, keeping him distracted for the few remaining moments it would take Elle to race back through his mind to that moment, just over three months ago, when he'd first met Meredith. She tumbled through his thoughts—and there it was, a brighter memory than the others around it. Meredith in a polka-dot dress, bumping into his table at Cafe Rouge and spilling her latte across his chest. How beautiful her wide green eyes were as she'd apologized repeatedly and grabbed every napkin she could find to try to blot up the mess. And then the two hours they'd spent chatting and getting to know each other while Martin's work went untouched and he missed his morning meeting. With one mental swipe, Elle erased everything from the start of that morning up until the present moment. In an instant, the memories were gone from both Martin's mind and her own.

She opened her eyes, removed her hand from Martin's, and breathed through the nausea that rose into her throat.

"Aaaaand he's asleep," Meredith said, leaning away with a satisfied sigh. "Another one done."

SIX

In a quiet part of Willowton, a man stood in the shadows with his eyes fixed on one of the townhouses across the street. Last night, he'd watched a girl climb into the highest window of that house. He'd been waiting ever since for her to leave. Well, he hadn't waited during the day. He'd paid someone else to keep an eye on the house then. But after sunset, he'd returned to his post.

A repeated chirp in his pocket alerted him to an incoming call. He removed his phone, touched the screen, and held it to his ear. "Azriel?" asked the man on the other end of the call.

"Yes."

"Have you caught her yet?"

"No."

A pause. "Are you sure you're in the right place?"

Azriel's hand clenched around the phone. "Of course. I followed her here last night."

"If you were close enough to see which house she entered, why didn't you catch her before she got inside? You're a vampire. You're supposed to be *fast*."

"I didn't catch her because she didn't enter through her front door. I reached the street just in time to see her climbing through the attic window."

"Are you sure she's the right girl?"

Azriel shut his eyes for a moment, resisting the urge to break the phone. All these questions. Couldn't he be trusted to take care of this on his own? "I'm not yet certain," he bit out, "but I have compelling evidence to believe it's her."

"Well, she'll have to come out at some point. Catch her when she does."

"That's why I'm here," Azriel growled.

"And if she doesn't come out again, then make a plan to get yourself invited inside. We need her before Tuesday."

"How about you do your job, and I'll do mine," Azriel suggested. "I'll figure something out." He ended the call and shoved the phone back into his pocket. Whatever plan he came up with, it wouldn't involve him wasting time trying to get himself invited inside. Sure, he could go to the effort of getting contacts to hide his red eyes and fake ear tips to pretend he was fae, but even then, it was unlikely anyone would invite a stranger inside, no matter what story he gave. People weren't stupid.

For now, he would wait and watch a little longer. Perhaps the girl would climb out of her window. Perhaps she would leave for another meeting at a club. But as more time passed and he watched shadows moving behind the curtains, a new idea began to take shape in his mind. Perhaps it would be better if he stopped wasting his time waiting and hoping and instead made sure the girl had a reason to leave the house again soon.

Azriel reached for his phone and checked the time as his thoughts turned back to Club Onyx. It was a little early, perhaps, but he wanted to be there when it opened so he could watch the people who entered. He would recognize the man this girl had sat with last night, if he was there again tonight. Azriel could force some information out of him.

He was about to leave when a car stopped in front of the house he'd been watching. A stocky man stepped out, ran up the stairs, and knocked on the door. Azriel watched in curious silence as the man disappeared inside, then reappeared less than a minute later with a large shape—a *body*—draped over one shoulder. Azriel's eyebrows shot up. He watched as the man carefully descended the stairs, then lowered the body into the trunk of the car.

"How strange," Azriel murmured as the car drove away. But as long as that body wasn't the girl he was waiting for—and it had looked too big to be her—he wasn't particularly interested. He had a new plan now. He stepped out of the shadows and sped away.

SEVEN

"BEAUTY," MEREDITH STATED THE FOLLOWING MORNING AT BREAKFAST. "THAT'S what I should wish for. I can be the fairest in the land."

Elle, walking into the dining room with a platter of croissants, cheese and fruit in her hands, caught Sienna's eye before quickly looking away and smothering her smile. If she were able to speak her mind without fear of consequences, she would tell Meredith there probably wasn't enough magic in even a *third*-tier wish to make her the fairest in the land.

"Meredith, love," Salvia said as Elle placed the platter in the center of the table, "that's completely nonsensical. The wish is worth more to us if we sell it."

Elle stepped back to stand beside the sideboard, watching Meredith pout. "But I could be the most beautiful girl in the city. In the world!"

"You're beautiful enough already, darling. Increasing your beauty won't buy us food, and clothes, and the latest home decor, and tickets to art galleries."

"It might," Meredith grumbled. "If I'm so beautiful that no one can say no to me, then I can just take whatever I want."

Elle turned her eyes toward the ceiling as she let out a quiet sigh. She'd been forced to listen to Meredith and Salvia arguing for hours last night while she tidied everything up, and now they were at it again.

"Elle!" Salvia said with a snap of her fingers, causing Elle to flinch. "You haven't poured the coffee yet."

"Sorry," Elle murmured, quickly lifting the antique silver coffee pot from the sideboard. She was grateful Sienna had snuck her some healing balm last night while Meredith and Salvia were arguing. Preparing and serving breakfast were much easier when she didn't have an aching wrist or scratches on her back that pulled her skin when she bent over.

"Fine, sell the wish," Meredith said as Elle stood beside Salvia's chair and poured ready-made coffee into her mug. Someone had enchanted the pot years ago so that it poured a perfect latte every time, including latte art swirling across the surface of the magically steamed milk. This morning's pattern looked like a mermaid. "In the meantime," Meredith continued. "I shall continue to admire the ring." She displayed her hand and waggled her fingers. Morning light shining in through the dining room window glinted off the oversized diamond.

Salvia exhaled sharply through her nose. "Meredith, darling, what are you still doing with that? You were supposed to leave it in my room last night."

"I know, but I wanted to pretend it's mine for just a few hours."

"Fine," Salvia muttered.

Conversation ceased as Elle finished pouring coffee for Meredith and Sienna. "Thanks," Sienna murmured. Elle nodded before returning to stand by the sideboard. "Martin should be waking up right about now," Sienna added, reaching for a slice of pineapple. Gut-wrenching guilt tortured Elle's insides at the mention of Martin's name. She'd been trying her best not to think of him since his unconscious form had been removed from the house last night.

"Yes, he should," Salvia said. "With absolutely no memory of any of us."

"Where did you ask Branson to leave him?" Sienna asked.

"Behind that bar that overlooks the Radley Canal."

"He'll be so confused," Sienna murmured.

"That's the point," Meredith said with an eye roll.

Elle clasped her hands tightly together as she stared at the floor, imagining Martin waking up alone and confused, a gaping hole in his memory. She hoped every con might be the last, but deep down, she knew Salvia would never stop. She *couldn't* stop. Cons paid for Sienna's schooling and the upkeep of the house, and filled their pantry with food. Salvia didn't work. Her first husband earned himself a fortune before he died and left it all to Salvia, and the money was more than enough to keep them going after Salvia married Elle's father. But when he died, most assets were seized to cover his debts, and Salvia was left with only the Willowton house in Vale City. Salvia and Meredith began their first con the day they moved in here. Salvia knew she couldn't pull it off without Elle's help, and by the end of the first week, Salvia had burned the slave charm into Elle's skin to make sure she would never run away.

"Anyway, we should get a lot for this ring," Meredith continued. "This might be our most profitable con yet, don't you think? The diamond is enormous. Whatever we get should keep us going for a while."

"Definitely," Salvia said. "And Elle came close to ruining it." Her quiet tone was more threatening than if she'd shouted. Elle knew she probably would have dealt out her favorite punishment last night if she hadn't been so busy arguing with Meredith. Now, she leaned back and draped one leg over the other as her eyes settled on Elle.

Elle's hands clenched together behind her back. They shook with both fear—at the thought that punishment might still be on its way—and anger. She longed to launch herself across the table and tear her nails across Salvia's glacial expression. But one glance at Sienna reminded Elle why she would never do that. "I'm sorry for hesitating last night," she said. "I didn't mean to. I was tired."

"I'm sure," Salvia answered, her tone suggesting she didn't believe Elle for a second. "Anyway, Meredith, dear." She refocused on her favorite daughter, leaving Elle to exhale slowly as her shoulders relaxed. "You'll have to give me the ring after breakfast. Lucius needs to examine it for a serial number. But it sounds like it's probably old enough that we don't need to worry about—"

Elle startled at the sound of a metallic clang. Along with the other three women in the room, she looked toward the entrance hall. "Was that ... the mail slot?" Sienna asked.

"I think so," Meredith said. "How weird. I can't remember the last time we received paper mail." A moment of silence followed as they all continued to stare through the doorway into the entrance hall. "Well?" Meredith demanded sharply, and Elle realized her stepsister's eyes were boring into her. "Are you going to fetch it, or are you planning to simply stand there gaping at nothing like an idiot?"

Elle hurried from the room. They both knew Meredith could easily have summoned the mail with magic, but that wasn't the way things were done in this house. As Salvia continually liked to remind Elle, the point of a slave was to perform all those mundane tasks one didn't want to waste an ounce of Essence or time on.

Elle bent and lifted the cream-colored envelope from the floor. It was heavy, and the address and name on the front—The Leroux Household—were written in elegant, looping calligraphy. She ran her thumb over the gold-embossed words, then turned the envelope over. On the back was the crest of the fae royal family.

"Well, what is it?" Meredith called.

Elle straightened and returned to the dining room. "I don't know, but it looks like it might come from the palace." She placed the envelope into Salvia's outstretched hand before resuming her position near the sideboard.

"Ooh, how exciting," Meredith said, leaning forward over her plate.

Salvia sliced through the top of the envelope with a quick spark of magic, then slid a thick card from within. She cleared her throat. "Prince Chevalier of House Belmont cordially invites you to the Moonlight Masquerade Ball."

Silence greeted her words. Then Sienna said, "*We're* invited? Like, us regular people?"

Salvia leaned back, a slow smile curving her lips. "Well, well. The rumors must be true."

"What rumors?" Meredith asked.

"Haven't you been paying attention to the gossip every Saturday at high tea?"

"No, I've been busy with Martin, remember?" Meredith reached across the table and snatched the invitation from Salvia. "What rumors, Mom?"

"The king wants his son to marry and is tired of waiting for him to find someone."

"Well how's he ever supposed to find someone if he never leaves his stuffy palace?" Sienna muttered.

"Because people can *visit* the palace, you moron," Meredith snapped. "And don't say it like it's his fault he can't leave," she added. "You know he isn't well enough. He has some … I don't know. Immune deficiency or something." She downed the remainder of her coffee and held the mug out toward Elle, shaking it to let her know she wanted a refill.

"I thought that was also a rumor," Elle said as she picked up the coffee pot. She moved forward and filled Meredith's mug. "The part about him being unwell."

"As if you'd know anything about it," Meredith replied, not even bothering to look at Elle. She lowered the invitation to the table and sipped her coffee.

"Anyway, back to the point of this ball," Salvia said, delicately tearing off a piece of her croissant. She spread strawberry jam over it. "Since the prince seems uninterested in choosing a wife from among the fae nobility, I've heard the king is becoming desperate. He's decided he doesn't mind his son choosing from among the common class."

"Common class," Meredith muttered. "Such an archaic term. And it in *no* way describes us. We're certainly not common. Well, not all of us," she added with a sneer in Elle's direction.

"Exactly," Salvia said. "Which is why you, my love, stand just as much chance as any other girl."

"Just as much chance of …" Meredith trailed off, and Elle watched as realization dawned on the girl's face. Stars above, she was slow sometimes. Elle often wondered how she managed to successfully con anyone. "Just as much chance of being *chosen*," Meredith said, her tone heavy with meaning. "By Prince Chevalier. As his bride."

"Yes," Salvia said with a smile.

"Holy stars, that would be amazing."

"Really?" Sienna asked. "Why would you want to be married to some sickly, pale-faced prince who's never well enough to leave home?"

"Because he's a *prince*, Sienna," Meredith said, giving her sister a withering glare. "I would be queen one day."

Like he'd really choose you, Elle thought.

"It doesn't matter how sickly or pale he is," Meredith continued. "I don't care if he's butt ugly. Can you imagine being *queen*? Besides, with a name like Chevalier, he can't be that bad. *Prince Chevalier.*" She swirled her coffee as a dreamy expression came over her face. "I can imagine him in old-fashioned shining armor, riding a white horse, ready to rescue me."

Elle exchanged a glance with Sienna, then looked away as she suppressed a snort. Sienna didn't bother hiding hers. "Sounds like a pompous snob to me," she said. "A pompous snob in a limo, not on a horse, because he's probably allergic to animals or dirt or something."

Salvia smacked her palm down on the table, causing all three girls to jump. For several heart-pounding moments, no one said a word. Then, in a voice that was deadly quiet, Salvia said, "Sienna, you're going to be late for school. Can't be late on a Monday morning. It sets a bad tone for the whole week. And Elle." Her gaze swung across the room. "I'm not sure why you're still in this room. You should be in the kitchen, waiting to be summoned when I need you."

Elle nodded and strode swiftly from the room, listening to the scrape of chair legs against the floor as Sienna stood. "I'll just finish this in my room while I'm—"

"You will not take that food to your room," Salvia said. "I don't need rats running around in there nibbling on crumbs."

"But I won't make a mess—"

"Sienna, if you're hungry, then you should have eaten *now* instead of talking nonsense about Prince Chevalier. Now go and get ready."

"Beastly woman," Elle muttered. She crossed the kitchen, grabbed one of the leftover croissants from the baking pan on top of the stove, placed it inside a container, and added it to Sienna's lunch bag. She was about to start clearing away the dishes she'd used while preparing breakfast when a repeated squeaking reached her ears. She looked around at the pantry. "Not again," she muttered, hurrying toward the open door. Inside the tiny room, her eyes scanned the shelves until she spotted a pixie tugging at the lid of a glass jar containing chocolate chip cookies. It was tough to tell pixies apart, but Elle recognized this one from the pistachio shell she always wore as a hat.

After a quick glance over her shoulder to make sure Salvia wasn't on her way into the kitchen, Elle hurried forward. She reached for the jar, but the pixie smacked her thumb and screeched something unintelligible in high-pitched tones. "Hey, I'm trying to help you!" Elle protested in a whisper. "And if you don't stop making so much noise, Salvia will hear you."

The pixie let go and dropped onto the shelf. Her gossamer-thin wings quivered as she stared with tiny, bright eyes at Elle. Elle picked up the jar and unscrewed the lid. She was about to stick her hand inside and remove a cookie when the pixie swooped toward her and began pulling at the edge of the lid again. No, not the lid, Elle realized. The gold ribbon that was tied around the lid. "Should have known," she muttered. Pixies had a fondness for shiny things. Elle pulled the ribbon free and handed it to the tiny creature. She struggled a bit, managed to wrap it around her arm a few times, and then flew away, the ends of the ribbon trailing behind her. Elle followed and watched as the pixie disappeared through an open window.

"But seriously, Mom, this could be it," Meredith said, her voice reaching Elle through the doorway between the kitchen and dining room. "The answer to all our problems. We would never need to do another con. We'd be set for life."

"I know," Salvia answered as Elle reached for the board she'd chopped all the fruit on earlier. "I was thinking the same thing. We must begin preparing immediately. You need to stand out. Make sure he notices *you* above all the other girls."

Elle paused near the sink. Salvia couldn't possibly be serious, could she? With every girl in the city vying for Prince Chevalier's attention, did she really think he'd choose *Meredith*? Shallow, vain, self-centered Meredith? And yet, Elle reminded herself with a shiver of unease, Meredith had managed to make men fall for her before. She could do it again.

The sick feeling she'd been trying to push aside since Martin had been carried away last night hit her once again. Meredith marrying into the royal family would be bad news for Elle. If the rumors were true, the king was in favor of human enslavement. She'd heard he wanted to put the slave charm on all free humans. If Meredith and her family ended up living at Belmont Palace,

Elle would end up there too. It would be even harder to gain her freedom from within those walls.

She slowly lowered the chopping board with all its peeled fruit skins onto the counter beside the sink, her mind spinning. She had to talk to Sienna about this. Make sure the ball ended up being a complete disaster for Meredith. She would leave an impression, all right, but it would be for the wrong—

"Elle!" Salvia's sharp voice rang through the open doorway. Elle turned away from the sink and walked quickly to the dining room. "I have an errand for you," Salvia said, scrolling through something on her phone. "I've just been notified that my dress for the Fords' cocktail party on Friday is ready for collection."

"From Harrington's?" Elle asked. The dressmaker's boutique was on the other side of the city, situated on the upmarket Cavalli Avenue.

"Yes, and I won't—"

"Is it safe?" Sienna asked, poking her head back into the dining room. "I just saw an alert on my phone about another abduction yesterday—"

"Don't be such an idiot, Sienna," Meredith interrupted. "Of course it's safe. It's *daytime*. No vampire's going to whisk Elle off the streets while the sun is up."

"Exactly," Salvia said smoothly. She turned in her seat to face the doorway. In a tone low and threatening, she said, "I believe I told you to get ready for school."

"I'm ready," Sienna said. She pointed to the bag hanging from her shoulder. "I just had to get my bag, that's all."

"You're not ready. Your hair looks atrocious. Go and deal with it." Sienna's face fell, her eyes meeting Elle's for an instant before she spun around and marched away. "As I was saying," Salvia continued as she turned back to Elle. "You will go to Harrington's and collect my dress, and I will not be giving you a transportation charm. I might have considered it if you hadn't been hanging around during breakfast, listening in on our private conversations and quietly giggling along with Sienna. But now you'll have to walk."

Elle nodded and simply said, "I understand," as she tried to keep her expression neutral instead of letting her delight show through. She didn't care that she would have to spend hours treading the sidewalks today. All she cared about was that Harrington's was very close to Apollo's Apothecary—a high-end supplier of charms and potions, and the only legitimate seller of wishes in Vale City. It was closed after hours, which meant Elle could never visit when she snuck out at night. And most of the errands Salvia sent her on during the day were close to home, and Salvia strictly monitored the amount of time Elle was out of the house.

"You'll leave as soon as you've cleared up all the breakfast dishes," Salvia continued, pushing her chair back and standing. "You can collect your phone from me on your way out, in case I need to contact you. And don't forget that I'll be checking it when you return."

"Yes, Salvia," Elle said, wondering how stupid her stepmother thought she was. No way would she ever use that phone to contact anyone except Salvia. Sienna's old phone, currently sitting beneath Elle's mattress upstairs, was the phone her clients contacted her on.

"Quickly now." Salvia clapped her hands, and Elle hurried forward to begin gathering dishes from the table. The routine was a mind-numbingly familiar one: collect dishes, stack them in the kitchen, scrape peels and remnants of food into the trash, load the dishwasher, wipe all the counters. It was such mundane work, but today, Elle found she didn't mind it. In a few hours, she would find out exactly how much Essence she needed for a wish. She would find out how close she was to buying her freedom.

EIGHT

A happy melody of tinkling bells sounded somewhere in the depths of Apollo's Apothecary as Elle pushed the door open and stepped inside. A potent combination of scents greeted her, along with a warm glow from the dozens of candles floating near the ceiling. The shelves were packed with jars of potion ingredients and bottles of different sizes, shapes and colors. She walked around the center display table, where ice-blue smoke rose from a bowl, and stopped in front of the counter. Beneath its reinforced glass top lay rows and rows of colorful, glowing gems. *Wishes*, Elle thought with a shiver of awe.

She looked up at the woman behind the counter and met a flawlessly made-up face framed by sleek purple hair. Tiny sparkling stones ran all the way to the tips of her pointed ears, and gold bangles flashed on her arms, creating a striking contrast to her dark skin. The rectangular gold badge pinned to her chest announced her name was Cress.

"Can someone help me over here?" a man called from behind Elle.

"Just give me a minute, honey," Cress said to Elle before bustling away. Elle crossed her arms and looked around, trying to push away the flutter of nervous anticipation that rose in her chest. *Don't be silly*, she told herself. *You're just making an enquiry. Nothing to get excited about.* But the possibility of her freedom being so near—that it might be just a few jobs away—was enough to send her heart racing.

Bells tinkled again, and Elle peered over her shoulder to see another man enter the apothecary. His eyes brushed over her, and his frown turned to a sneer of disgust. He'd probably noticed her ears—perfectly round and perfectly human. Elle lifted her chin a little higher and made a point of not looking away. She may be human and she may be dressed in clothes so old they resembled cleaning rags, but she had just as much right to be in here as anyone else. Certain parts of Vale City were off limits to everyone except the fae, but this wasn't one of those places.

The man finally broke eye contact and stalked toward the shelf of chocolate bonbon charms. "Will that be all?" Cress asked, sashaying back toward the counter, and Elle realized she was talking to the customer she'd been assisting. Elle moved over to make space for him to finish his transaction.

"And a first-tier wish," he added. "In a red gem. It'll go well with the red glass." He placed a red bottle on the counter and slid it toward Cress before Elle could read the label. "The perfect gift, I'd say."

"Lovely," Cress said, ringing up the purchase. From the corner of her eye, Elle watched the man pay with a combination of Essence—collected in multiple vials inside a clear box—and credit card. She tried to ignore the resentment that burned briefly through her veins. The fae's magic gave them everything—longer life, good health, the ability to perform thousands of simple tasks with the snap of their fingers—and on top of that, they were the only ones who could afford wishes. *As if they don't have enough already*, Elle thought bitterly.

"Now, what can I help you with, honey?" Cress asked as the man picked up the gift bag and turned away.

Elle waited a moment, making sure no one else was within earshot, before she said, "Wishes."

Cress quirked an eyebrow. "Interesting. I don't often get humans in here enquiring about wishes."

"Makes sense," Elle said quietly. The only acceptable form of payment for a wish was Essence, and it wasn't as though humans had readily available supplies of it. They had to acquire it the way Elle did—payment or gifts from fae. Or by taking it illegally by force, through methods Elle had no desire to learn. "Um, so, I need to know how much Essence a wish costs."

"You'll need to be more specific, honey. There are different tiers of wishes."

"I know." Elle shifted her weight to one side and tapped her fingers on the counter top. "I'm not sure exactly which one I need. It could be third, but I'm hoping it may have changed. It's for—" She leaned a little further forward and lowered her voice. "My freedom."

Cress pursed her glossy purple lips. Her gaze dropped, but even if the counter hadn't been in the way, Elle's jeans concealed her ankles. "So you want to break a slave charm, is that it?"

"Yes."

With a sigh, Cress turned to her computer screen. "Okay, let me check the catalog. It's not exactly a common request, but it's not unheard of, so it must be in here somewhere. If not, I'll need to send a request to—Ah, there it is. Freedom from Enslavement Charm." She looked at Elle. "It requires a third-tier wish. The most expensive kind, I'm afraid."

Elle nodded. That's what she'd been told when she first came in here, a little over two years ago. "That's what I expected," she said quietly, "though I hoped it might have changed. So what's the price of a third-tier wish?"

"Twelve elixion ounces of Essence."

Elle's stomach dropped. She'd measured her Essence collection last week while she was alone at home, sneaking into Salvia's bedroom to use her special Essence calibrator wand. The glittery gold number that drifted into the air told her she had just over eight elixion ounces. It had taken two years to save that much. "Are you serious?" she asked. "Last time I enquired, it was six. I expected it would be more now, but—"

"Six?" Cress let out a rich, husky laugh. "When was that? A decade ago?"

"Two years."

Cress dabbed her finger delicately beneath each eye as she sighed. "You're aware that prices go up over time, aren't you?"

"I know, but by that much?"

"Yes, by that much. I'm sorry, sweetie, but that's the going price of a third-tier wish these days."

Elle set her jaw and pushed her shoulders back. "I bet a dealer could sell it to me for less."

Cress's expression darkened. "A dealer? You want to buy dodgy, illegal wishes on the black market? Even if that wasn't a recipe for disaster, you still won't get one for the price you're hoping for."

Elle exhaled slowly. "Okay, I'm sorry. Is there anything else you'd accept as payment?"

"Now you're being silly. Who do you think I am? The Godmother?"

"No, I just mean that maybe you could consider taking *money* instead of—"

"Oh, honey, don't be ridiculous. Essence is the only accepted form of payment for a wish. You know that. Everyone knows that. I don't have time for people coming in here expecting special treatment. Now off you go." She made a shooing motion with her hands, her bangles jangling loudly. "I want to help you, I really do. But you need to come back when you're ready to take this seriously."

NINE

A few hours later, Elle sank onto her bed in the attic. She had less than ten minutes until she was expected to be downstairs in the kitchen, preparing dinner. She pressed both hands over her face and willed herself not to break down. She would not give in to despair. She would find a way to make this work. To save enough for a wish. It was the only option. Nothing else—aside from Salvia's own words—could break the slave charm. The alternative was to remain a slave forever, and Elle refused to accept that.

I'll just have to do more jobs, she decided. *And I'll have to charge more.* She climbed off the bed, stuck her hand beneath the mattress, and removed her phone, planning to search through her list of clients for someone who hadn't contacted her in a while. But there was already a message on the screen. An enquiry from someone new. A flash of hope warmed Elle's insides. This was exactly what she needed. She lay down again and read the message.

Unknown: My friend Monty gave me your number. Said you're really good at what you do. I'd like to meet you tonight if possible? Sanguinious Maximus

Elle rolled her eyes at the obviously fake name. She dropped her head back onto the pillow, the phone clutched loosely in her hand as she considered how to reply. Salvia was entertaining tonight, which meant it would be a busy evening for Elle. It would be late by the time Salvia's friends left, and even later when Elle finished cleaning everything up. Tomorrow night would be better.

First, though, she needed to make sure this person's story checked out. That—along with the fact that she only ever met with people in busy, public places—was the only security measure she could take. She typed a quick message to Monty.

> **Trixie:** Did you give my number to a friend of yours? Someone who might be using the very strange alias Sanguinious Maximus?

She waited another minute or two, then sat up to put the phone away. But it buzzed in her hand before she could stand.

> **Monty:** Sounds like my friend. Hope it was ok to pass on your number? You said I could refer people to you if they sound serious about needing your services.

> **Trixie:** Yes that's fine. Thanks.

She tapped her way back to the message from Mr. Maximus and typed a reply.

> **Trixie:** Thanks for your query. I can't meet tonight. Tomorrow night?

At that moment, footsteps sounded on the stairs. Elle shoved the phone beneath her pillow and shot up off the bed, but then she recognized the footsteps as Sienna's. She crossed the room and met Sienna in the doorway. "Did Salvia send you? Am I supposed to be downstairs already?"

"No, don't worry, she hasn't said anything. And she won't notice I'm up here." Sienna moved past Elle into the attic. "She's been busy on her computer for hours, totally absorbed in her current research."

Elle turned around. "Current research?"

"Dress designers." Sienna rolled her eyes. "According to her, Meredith will be wearing the most jaw-droppingly stunning creation of all time to the

Moonlight Masquerade Ball. Apparently that's supposed to make the prince fall for her."

Elle groaned. "It would be better if he fell *over* her. Like if he tripped on her silly dress or something. Then he'd never choose her."

Sienna laughed. "There's no way he'll ever choose her."

"You don't think?" Elle crossed her arms and leaned against the doorframe. "She knows how to get what she wants."

"Sure, but she has way too much competition this time."

"That might not be enough to stop her. Seriously, Sienna, we can't let him choose her. You know what the royal family is like. I've heard how the king treats slaves."

A frown creased Sienna's brow. "But even if Meredith does end up marrying into the royal family—which is *highly* unlikely—you'll be free by then, won't you? That's what I came up here to ask you about. I figured you'd probably go to the apothecary today. I know it's close to Harrington's." Her eyes shone as her smile reappeared. "How close are you to being able to afford that wish?"

Elle let her eyes slide shut as disappointment caved in on her again. "I'm sorry. It's bad news." She opened her eyes. "I shouldn't have said anything to you last night about having almost saved enough. If I'd known I was getting your hopes up for nothing, I would have kept quiet."

Sienna's face fell. "Has the price gone up way more than you thought?"

Elle nodded. "Like, a *lot* more."

"Man, that *sucks*." Sienna stared at the floor, her brow furrowing. "What if … I mean … I'm scared to even say it, but what if …" Her eyes rose to meet Elle's. "What if you didn't *buy* a wish." Her gaze was heavy with meaning, and Elle knew at once what she was suggesting.

"I'm not summoning the Godmother," she said immediately.

"Look, I know it's dangerous to bargain with her, but it might be the only way to get your freedom."

"It isn't the only way," Elle said firmly. "I just have to keep saving."

"But, Elle, if the rate at which the price goes up is faster than the rate at which you can save Essence, then how is this ever going to work?"

"I'll just have to save Essence faster. I'll start charging more. After all, there isn't anyone else who can do what I do, so I can afford to charge more, don't you think?"

"Yes, I suppose …" Sienna's tone was still full of doubt. "But what if you still can't save enough? What if a bargain is the only way to get your hands on a pure, high-quality, third-tier wish?"

Elle tightened her arms over her chest and stared at the floor. She couldn't possibly consider this as an option, could she? But what if Sienna was right? Pure wish magic was rare, produced only by highly skilled fae who'd trained for years at the Mages' Guild. Wish production was closely regulated, and the wishes produced were supplied only to registered sellers. Dealers like the one Monty had mentioned sold wishes produced by fae who hadn't been properly trained. The wishes they produced weren't the best quality, and sometimes they went horribly wrong. Which left the Godmother as the only other option for anyone seeking a genuine, high-quality wish.

Elle had no idea what her real name was, but rumor had it that decades ago, she was the very best mage at the Mages' Guild, producing magic that could grant the most incredible wishes. Then, for some reason, she wanted to leave. She was supposed to have the knowledge of wish magic removed from her mind before cutting ties with the Guild—that had always been the rule—but instead, she managed to escape. She hid her identity and had been supplying wishes illegally ever since. Anyone could summon her, or so the rumors said, and apparently she could grant almost any wish your heart might desire. The only catch, however, was the price.

It wasn't Essence or money that the Godmother wanted. She dealt only in *bargains*, and what she asked for in exchange for a wish was always different. Something specific to each wisher, in proportion to the magnitude of the wish. Someone's eyesight, or the first three years of their child's life, or the one possession that brought them the most joy. Elle had never heard of anyone who'd been happy with the price they'd had to pay. Which was why she would never do it.

"I won't bargain with the Godmother, Sienna," she said, looking up. "You know it's a terrible idea. It might be the easiest short-term solution, but I don't want to spend the rest of my life regretting it."

Sienna covered her face and groaned. "Ugh, I know. I shouldn't have even brought it up. It just feels like we're never going to get away from Mom."

"I know, but we will. It's just going to take longer than I thought."

"You're right." She lowered her arms to her sides. "It's okay. We can handle this. And if you still haven't saved enough by the time I'm a legal adult and supporting myself, then *I'll* find a way to free you from Mom. At least then you won't have to worry about getting *me* away from her as well."

Elle's heart sank a little deeper. Could she really wait for however long it took Sienna to finish school, study further, find a job, and earn enough to support herself? Even then, how long would it take her to save enough of her own Essence for a third-tier wish?

"It sucks that Meredith's wish from Martin is only a first-tier one," Sienna added. "I got so excited when I first saw it last night. If it was third-tier, we could have stolen it, and you might have your freedom already."

"I know," Elle said quietly. "But it isn't, so there's no point in even thinking about it." She sighed and pushed away from the doorframe. "I guess I'd better go downstairs before Salvia notices I haven't started prepping dinner yet." She was about to turn back toward the stairs when a muffled buzz issued from the vicinity of her bed. She hurried across the room and pulled her phone out from beneath the pillow.

Unknown: Tomorrow night works. Meet at The Topaz Lounge at ten? I'll be on the right-hand side of the bar, wearing an old-fashioned hat.

The Topaz Lounge. Elle hadn't heard of that one before, but she could easily look it up. She smiled at Sienna. "I have another job. And I'm going to start charging more. I'm going to make this work, okay? Somehow, I'm going to save enough."

TEN

ELLE STEPPED OUT OF THE GLASS ELEVATOR THAT HAD JUST SHOT UP THE SIDE OF one of Vale City's tallest buildings and walked into The Topaz Lounge. It was a good thing she'd read a little about this place instead of merely looking up its location. She would have been underdressed in her usual attire. Fortunately, her secret wardrobe included a glitzy silver dress that was mid-thigh length and high-heeled black boots that reached to her knees. She would far rather have worn her combat boots, but she didn't want to stand out by pushing any fashion boundaries.

She looked around, noting the bar on one side of the room and stylish couches on the other, where floor-to-ceiling glass provided an extensive view of Vale City. This was by far the most upper class club she'd ever been inside. With its slow, seductive music, sleek black and white finishings, and well-dressed patrons sipping cocktails or swaying in time to the irresistible beat of the music, it oozed class and elegance.

She walked slowly past the couches, trying to act as if she belonged here. At one of the low tables between two couches, a woman and two men played poker. Towers of chips and several jewels, gleaming with the wish magic within them, sat at the center of the table. As Elle passed, the woman placed her cards on the table with a flourish. Over the sultry music, Elle heard her shout out, "Yes!" Both men slumped back against the cushions. The woman leaned forward and scooped her winnings to her side of the table. She lifted one of the wishes, encased within a green gemstone. Elle slowed, watching the way the light refracted off the faceted stone. The woman wrapped both hands around it, and Elle found herself coming to a stop as she watched. Was the woman going to use the wish right now? Elle shouldn't stare. She knew it was rude, and it might bring her unwanted attention. But she couldn't help it. The woman's hands tightened around the gem as she used a charm to break it. A gold substance, heavier than Essence but lighter than water, poured out over her arms and lap. For a moment, her whole body seemed to glow. Her lips moved, but Elle couldn't figure out what she was saying. Within a few seconds, the wish magic had vanished, leaving the woman looking exactly as before. Well, except for the satisfied smirk that curved her lips. Curiosity burned within Elle. What had the woman wished for?

One of the men looked up then, catching Elle's gaze before she could look away. She smiled politely before pointing her eyes forward and resuming her journey toward the bar. In the time that she'd stopped to watch the woman with the wish, her new client had appeared at the right-hand end. Hunched over, with an old-fashioned hat atop his head, he took the glass the bartender held out toward him and swirled it. He turned his head slowly to look over his shoulder, then paused. Elle guessed he'd seen her, though she couldn't tell because of the shadow cast by the hat.

She approached him warily. It was always risky meeting a new client. That was one of the reasons she brought her pocketknife with, just in case she needed to fend someone off and get away. Tonight, she had no pocket in which to keep the knife, and it wouldn't be easily accessible inside her purse. Slipping it into her boot meant it slid all the way down to her ankle, which wasn't helpful either. So she'd ended up wearing socks almost as high as the boots so she had something to secure the knife to the side of her leg. People in movies—the few she'd watched at home with Sienna on occasions when Salvia and Meredith were out—made it look so easy. Hopefully, she would have no need for the knife tonight.

She took a seat on the stool next to him and swiveled to face him. "Sanguinious Maximus?" she asked, a wry smile on her lips.

"Yes," he answered. He turned toward her, not bothering to remove his hat.

Elle tried to peer beneath the brim, but he tilted his head further downward in response. Perhaps he was a regular here and didn't want anyone recognizing him while he met with a strange girl. "You take memories," he said quietly.

"Yes."

"What do you do with them?"

"Sorry, I should have been more specific." Elle shifted closer to the bar and leaned her arms on it. "I don't *take* them. I *erase* them. They're gone forever."

"Is that so?"

She frowned. "Yes, that's so. I give people freedom from the memories they don't want to live with. You tell me what you want to forget, and those will be the only memories I take."

"I see." He fell silent. Then his hand stretched past the side of Elle's face, as if to tuck her hair behind her ear.

She jerked back. "Don't touch me."

"I'll do as I please," he said. Then his hand flashed forward, almost faster than she could see. He gripped her ear and ripped the fake ear tip right off.

"Hey!" she gasped, trying to shove him away as ice-cold fear shot down her spine. But his hand was around the back of her neck now, his fingers digging into her skin as he forced her closer. And finally, she saw him properly. His red eyes. A barcode tattoo barely visible above the collar of his shirt. A face she recognized from Club Onyx.

"I know who you are," the vampire hissed. "Human freak. You're coming with me." Something sharp and stinging pierced the inside of her arm. She wrenched it back before diving down toward her boot, but he grabbed her wrist before she could get to the knife. Then his hand was over her mouth. Surely someone would see. Someone would come and help her. Someone would …

She blinked as her thoughts began to bump into one another. She was suddenly sleepy, and everything was blurring together, and the world was tilting to the side. "Had a little too much to drink, have you, darling?" the vampire said, his voice bleeding into the music and the chatter and the clink of ice cubes in glasses. "Let me just cover your ear there for you. Wouldn't want anyone else to see."

She was vaguely aware of his arm around her as the scenery and people of The Topaz Lounge swam past her. Then everything became darker, and lights blinked past her vision in a repetitive pattern. Was she in the glass elevator? The one with the view of the city? She managed to unstick her tongue from the roof of her mouth and said, "You're not … a friend of Monty's."

"Monty has no friends," the vampire said. "Not anymore. A dead man can't have friends, can he?"

Fear encompassed her, temporarily blacking everything out. But she heard the ding of the elevator and the whoosh as the doors opened. "Where are you … taking me …"

He answered, but she couldn't make sense of his words as the world faded in and out. Then his face was suddenly right in front of hers. "She tried to keep you from us. She thought we'd never find you. But she failed."

"Who?" Elle mumbled.

"Your mother."

"My … what?"

But before she could catch his reply, everything vanished into complete darkness.

ELEVEN

neck. He was hiding with Olly and Xander between the plastic unicorns of a merry-go-round at the old fairground in Belgravia, not too far inland from the beach. The place had closed down about five years ago when a large amusement park opened next to the pier. Apparently no one had decided what to do with this land yet, and most of the old rides and equipment were still here.

"They're late," Olly whispered.

"Maybe we're in the wrong spot," Xander replied.

"We're not. We double-checked the other night. The coordinates point to that exact empty patch of ground over there."

"I don't know if I trust the map on your phone," Xander said. "Remember when it took you to that pole dancing studio instead of a gin bar?"

"They had the same name!"

"Hey, I see someone coming," Dex whispered as he squinted into the distance. Two figures walked slowly past a Ferris wheel. They paused, then sped up, moving supernaturally fast before coming to an abrupt stop a few seconds later in the area Olly's phone had brought them to the other night.

"Told you," Olly whispered, almost too quiet for Dex to hear.

Over the next few minutes, another six people arrived. From this distance, they could have been vampire, human or shifter. Their ears were round, and it was impossible to see the color of their eyes. But their speed gave them away.

Dex remained as still as possible behind the purple and gold unicorn that was mostly shielding him from view. The vampires were probably far enough away that their ears wouldn't pick up whispers, but their sharp eyes would notice movement.

"Not many of them," Olly murmured. "The Allegiant has far more members than this."

"But we knew they weren't *all* meeting tonight," Xander reminded him. "It's better this way. Easier to catch them."

"Yeah. Ready when you are, Dex," Olly said.

"Give them another few minutes," Dex replied. "In case more are joining them."

They waited. Crouched in an awkward position, Dex slowly began to lose feeling in his toes. The swings continued squeaking nearby, and the vampires' voices reached his ears as indistinguishable murmurs. He was about to tell Xander and Olly it was time to move when he noticed someone else approaching the gathering. Another vampire, though he didn't move quite as quickly as the others had. Probably because he was carrying a body in his arms. A woman, her blond hair trailing over the vampire's arm. Her silver dress sparkled in the moonlight, and a purse hung from her shoulder, swaying as the vampire walked.

"Another abduction?" Olly whispered.

Dex cursed beneath his breath. This complicated things. They desperately needed to catch these vampires, and now they would have to do it without hurting the human.

"Is that her?" one of the women called out as the newcomer reached the group.

"Yes. Finally found her."

The woman let out an excited whoop, while several of the others clapped.

"Hey," Xander whispered. "I think … Dex, isn't that the fae girl from Club Onyx? The one you walked into?"

Dex squinted harder. Something tightened in his chest when he recognized her face. "Yes, I think it is. And that's the same vampire," he added as the man turned enough for moonlight to illuminate his face. "Which means he *is* part of the Allegiant."

"And this isn't like the other abductions," Olly added, "since those were all humans, and this girl's fae."

"Actually," Dex admitted, "she was pretending to be fae. I realized after she ran that she's—" He cut himself off as one of the vampires whipped his head toward him. In an instant, the group became silent, all of them turning to look the same way. "We've been spotted," Dex whispered. "Time to move. And be careful of the girl."

They launched out from behind the plastic unicorns. Dex's hands and lower arms glittered with magic, and as he raced forward, he brought his arms up and around in a throwing motion. Streams of light arced away from him. Olly did the same, while Xander's magic shot forward in the form of golden bullet-like shapes. One vampire fell—hopefully injured, not dead—and the others scattered. Dex hurled magic at the one carrying the girl. It caught him on the shoulder and knocked him forward. He stumbled but didn't let go of her. Dex lunged after him and caught the vampire's arm. Golden dust turned to flames, igniting the vampire's shirt and licking its way up and down his arm. With a cry, he finally dropped the girl. Dex ran after him, but he was already speeding away, a blazing figure disappearing into the night.

He turned back toward the girl. She was awake now, pushing her hair out of her face and trying to scramble away. Dex dropped down beside her. "Are you o—"

"*You?*" Her brows pinched together. A second later, her boot landed square in his stomach.

"Hey!" he wheezed. *I'm trying to save you,* he would have added, if only his lungs could find the required amount of air.

Another figure appeared abruptly at her side and grabbed her arms. Dex pushed himself up and launched across the girl, slamming into the woman vampire and rolling several times. Faerie dust raced across her skin, transforming into tiny needle-like shapes. She howled in agony, but even after tearing herself free from Dex's grip, she didn't run. She went straight for the human girl again.

A brilliant flash of magic sped toward her from the other side of the girl. It struck her in the chest and punched her backward. Time seemed to slow as Dex watched. The vampire was weightless, soaring past him through the air while all around him, offensive magic lit up the fairground like a fireworks display. For a single moment, he was reminded of what this place looked like in its heyday, with all the rides lit up and the grounds filled with people. Then the vampire hit the ground. Magic crackled across her body and vanished. She didn't move.

"Dex!" Xander shouted. Dex looked up and saw his friend with one arm still stretched forward from throwing magic. A split second later, he saw the figure rushing toward him. Dex rolled, jumped up, and sliced his hand through the air. Golden flames shot away from him and leapt up his attacker's body. The vampire writhed and slapped at the enchanted flames. With a cry, he raced away, still burning.

Dex spun around, his hands raised and curled into fists, ready to fight off anyone else who got too close to the human girl—who appeared to be lying motionless on the ground again. "They're all gone!" Olly shouted.

"I'm heading that way!" Xander yelled, already taking off in the direction of the Ferris Wheel.

"'Kay, I'm after the others!" Olly shouted back, launching himself in the opposite direction.

Dex almost lurched forward, torn between hunting down the vampires and staying beside the girl. On any other night, he would have followed Xander or Olly without hesitation. But it was clear this human girl was somehow important to the vampires, and he couldn't run off and leave her here. That consideration aside, chasing vampires once they were on the move was almost always futile. He probably wouldn't have much success even if he did run after them now.

He looked down at the girl, passed out on her side with one leg drawn up and her hand slung over her knee. Blood trickled from a cut at the top of her left arm. The surrounding skin was an angry red. Magic must have got a little too close to her. Maybe it knocked her down and she'd hit her head. The thought filled him with guilt, even though he had no idea if it was his magic that had caused the injury. He couldn't heal the wound—in its raw form, healing magic was too much for a human—but he could at least clean it. Not right here in the middle of the fairground, though. Who knew if there might be more vampires on their way. Without further delay, Dex knelt down, scooped the girl into his arms, and lifted her from the ground.

TWELVE

Elle blinked slowly, becoming aware of a stinging ache near the top of her left arm. Memories of the moments before she lost consciousness—for the second time that night—flashed across her mind. A Ferris wheel. Vampires and fae crowding around her. Magic arcing through the air. The faerie guy who'd walked into her at Club Onyx.

She blinked again, moved her arms, and felt her purse beneath one palm and a hard, dusty surface beneath the other. She pushed herself up, looking down at her arm. A cut marred her skin, but it didn't look too bad. A faint smear below it suggested someone had wiped blood away. She shivered at the thought. Lifting her eyes, she looked around at a room furnished with two desks, a few chairs, and some filing cabinets. Dull moonlight filtered through a dusty window. Was this an office? She'd recognized part of the old fairground when she woke earlier, but she could be miles from there by now. Her vampire captor had obviously moved her. The vampire who'd said something about her mother …

Movement caught her attention. She whipped her head toward it and found a dark-haired faerie with silvery blue eyes. "Are you okay?" Dex asked.

She scrambled away from him, her heart racing as she fumbled for the pocketknife she hadn't managed to reach earlier. Finally, she got her hand into the top of her boot and grabbed the darn thing. A second later, she'd flipped it open. "Stay away from me," she hissed, brandishing the tiny knife as she climbed to her feet.

"Hey, it's okay. You're not a prisoner." He held both hands up, then motioned to the open door with his head. "You can leave, if you want. I'd prefer to talk to you a bit before you run, but if you don't want to hang around, I understand."

Keeping her back against the wall and her eyes trained on him, Elle edged toward the door. A desk blocked her way. She wondered how quickly she could get around it.

"Seriously, I'm not going to stop you." Dex backed up against the wall opposite her and took a few steps away from the door. "I'm not with the vampires. I was trying to *catch* them. You're free to go."

Elle thought back to the few conscious moments she'd had in the middle of the fairground. It *had* seemed there was a lot of fighting going on. And she'd never heard of vampires and fae working together. So Dex's story was probably the truth. Still, he was a stranger and she had no idea if she could trust him. She took another step, glancing at the door before focusing on him again. Then her eyes slid up to the clock on the wall above his head. The motionless second hand indicated the clock no longer worked, but the position of the minute and hour hands—both pointing almost exactly at twelve—was enough to send Elle into a panic. "Oh, shoot. Do you know what the time is?"

"Uh …" Dex's brow creased. That was probably the last thing he thought she'd ask about. Why worry about something as trivial as the time after being kidnapped by vampires? But he slid his phone from his pocket anyway. "It's eleven twenty-five."

"And where are we right now?"

"At the old fairground. Inside an office above the entrance."

A chill of fear raced over Elle's skin. She would never make it home in time. It would take over an hour by foot, and she didn't have enough cash to pay for a cab ride that far. She had Sienna's old phone with her, but she couldn't make payments with it the way other people did with their phones. Without a bank account of her own, the only option was cash, and Sienna never had much to share with her.

"Are you late for something?" Dex asked.

"Yes. Very late. Um …" She tried to clear the panic from her mind so she

could think properly. "I need to be somewhere by midnight. It's urgent."

"Urgent?" His lips twitched into a half-smile. "You were just kidnapped by a vampire. I'm sure whoever you're supposed to meet at midnight will understand if you're late."

"No." Elle shook her head. "She won't. I *have* to be there by midnight."

"Okay, okay. Well, I have a car. I can drive you wherever you need to go."

She hesitated. Swallowed. When was it ever a good idea to get into a car with a stranger?

"I swear I won't take you anywhere else," Dex said. "Or I could call you a cab, but this side of town isn't exactly the center of Vale City's nightlife. You'd have to wait a while for one to get here."

"Okay. You promise you'll take me straight to where I need to go?"

"Yes, of course."

Elle breathed deeply in and out. He sounded truthful, but one could never be too careful. "Make a blood oath."

He raised his eyebrows. "Seriously?"

"If you're not lying, then you shouldn't have a problem making an oath."

"True." Dex pushed back one sleeve of his shirt, then the other. "It's just that you said you're in a rush, so—"

"So you'd better make the oath quickly," she said, gripping the knife a little harder as she kept it pointed at him. "I know it takes less than a minute."

Dex's fingers glowed as faerie dust formed on his skin. A moment later, it coalesced into a laser-straight, glittering line, which he swiped briefly across his palm. A thin cut appeared as he looked up. "What exactly do you want me to—"

"Promise you won't lie to me," Elle said. Dex frowned, his eyes slipping away from hers. "Is that a problem?" she asked. "Because if it is, then ..." She trailed off. Then what? Then she wouldn't get into a car with him. She would run as if wildfire nipped at her ankles, and she would be late, and there would be *consequences* of the most severe kind.

"It's not a problem," Dex said, turning his attention back to his palm. The cut glowed as he spoke a few quiet words. Then he raised his voice a little and added, "I need to approach you in order to finish this. Can I do that? Or are you going to use that pocketknife on me?"

Elle narrowed her eyes, getting the feeling he was making fun of her. "You can come closer. But if you do *anything* except finish the oath, I won't hesitate to use this on you."

A small smile lifted his lips. "I wouldn't dare." He walked closer, his arm stretched out in front of him, his palm facing the ceiling. When he was almost close enough to touch her, he stopped.

Keeping the knife raised in one hand, Elle lifted her other arm. Though no one had ever made a blood oath with her before, she'd seen others perform them. She knew she needed to extend her hand toward Dex's, as if they were about to shake hands. She lifted her gaze to his, and he didn't break eye contact as he said, "I swear I won't lie to you." The moment felt strangely intimate, and it seemed to Elle that an almost magnetic force kept her from looking away. Her heart pattered a little faster before she finally managed to tear her gaze away and look down.

The blood vanished from Dex's palm. Magic wound itself like a rope around his hand, then extended through the air to wrap itself around Elle's hand and wrist. She flinched at the tingling heat, but it wasn't painful. Nothing like the slave charm that burned her ankle for a few seconds every night when she was confined in her attic. The golden rope of magic glowed even brighter, then vanished.

"Done," Dex said, lowering his hand.

"Great." Elle took a step away from him. "So, will you take me exactly where I ask you and nowhere else? And you won't hurt me?"

"I'll take you wherever you want, and I most certainly will not hurt you."

Elle lowered the knife and folded the blade away. "Thank you. Okay, we need to go quickly."

"Yes." Dex was already taking his phone from his pocket as he moved toward the door. Elle grabbed her purse before following him.

"Wait, who are you calling?" she asked as he lifted the phone to his ear.

"Friends. They were with me on the fairground, fighting the vamps. They ran after them, but—Hi, Xander?" Dex didn't break his stride as he crossed a landing toward a staircase. "Yeah, I figured. They're way too fast. But you had to try. Listen, how quickly can you bring the car around to the fairground entrance? We need to take the girl—" He paused and looked at her. "Sorry, what's your name?"

"Elle," she said, then mentally kicked herself for letting her real name slip out. She was supposed to be Trixie when she was with strangers.

"We need to take Elle somewhere. It's urgent." He descended the stairs two at a time, and while Elle appreciated his haste, she struggled to keep up with him in her silly heels. She should have just gone with her normal combat boots, fashion be damned. "Oh, no, she's fine," Dex continued, "but she needs to be somewhere quite urgently. Okay, great. Thanks." He ended the call and looked at Elle. "They're almost at the car. We parked it round the other side of the fairground so it was nowhere near the vamps' meeting spot. They'll drive straight to the entrance and pick us up."

"They?" Elle asked.

"Xander and Olly. Friends of mine."

"So now I'm getting into a car with not one strange man, but three?"

"We're not strange. Well, maybe *they* are," he added with a laugh, "but not in the way you mean. And I *swear* to you—" he looked pointedly at her as they reached the bottom of the stairs "—that none of us mean you any harm." He crossed a room that looked like it was once a reception area and pushed open a door. "This way." He stepped back while holding it open for Elle. She hurried past him into the night. They moved quickly between run-down buildings, through a ticket booth, and toward the tall arched entrance where two halves of a rusty metal gate were locked together by an equally rusty chain. The chain was so loose, though, that it was easy to slip between the two sides of the gate.

"They should be here soon," Dex said. Elle nodded in response. Her eyes scanned the road and the overgrown bushes on the other side, just in case another vampire was about to leap from the shadows. But her mind was racing backward, trying to remember exactly what the one who'd caught her had said about her mother. Something about … keeping Elle from him? "Can I ask you something?" she said to Dex, at the exact moment he asked, "How did you end up—"

He cut himself off, smiled, then said, "Sorry, you first. What did you want to ask?"

"The vampires … did they say anything about my mother?"

Dex frowned. "If they did, I didn't hear it. Is that why they abducted you? Something to do with your mother?"

Elle looked away. "I don't know. I thought I heard him say something after he drugged me, but …" She shook her head. "Maybe I was confused or dreaming or … something."

The revving of an engine greeted her ears, and a moment later, a black car sped around the corner. She took an involuntary step back as it screeched to a halt in front of her. Tinted windows hid the occupants from view. Dex moved forward and opened the back door. "Come on," he said to Elle. After one more beat of hesitation—during which she reminded herself that he *did* make a blood oath—she hurried forward and slid inside. Dex shut the door, and Elle looked forward at a pale blond guy in the front passenger seat, and a head of unruly bronze hair sticking above the driver's seat in front of her.

"Um, hi?" she said as they both turned to look at her.

"Elle?" the blond guy asked. "I'm Olly. This is Xander."

On the other side of the car, the door opened and Dex climbed in. "Okay, where do you need to go?" he asked as he pulled the door shut.

Elle almost gave her real address before reminding herself that she didn't need these people watching her climb into an attic window. And even if she were able to use the front door, it was probably best if they didn't know where she lived. So she gave them an address two roads away from hers.

"Okay then," Xander muttered. He tapped the address into the car's navigation system before pulling away with a smooth rush of power that forced Elle back against her seat.

Olly, still facing the back seat, said, "So, Elle. How'd you end up knocked out and abducted by a vampire? I would assume it's because you're human, but when you arrived, someone asked, 'Is that her?' and they all seemed really excited when the dude carrying you said yes."

Elle blinked. "Um, okay."

"Do you know why they might be so interested in you?" Dex asked.

"No." She looked away as she shook her head so neither of them would see the lie in her eyes. She was fairly certain it had to do with her strange ability to remove memories, but that wasn't something she told most people about.

"The vamp who caught you is the same one who was at Club Onyx," Dex said. "He must have been tracking you for some time."

"Yes, I recognized him." She was beginning to wonder just how long he'd been looking for her. If she hadn't imagined what he said about her mother, then it could have been years. "So, I assume they all got away?" she asked.

"Yes," Xander grumbled. Elle looked forward in time to see his grip tighten on the steering wheel. "Well, except for the two who ended up dead during that whole mess on the fairground. We could have caught them all if we hadn't had to be so careful."

"Careful?" Elle asked. Blurred memories shifted across her mind—flashes of magic and someone yelling about being careful—and she realized what he meant. "Because of me. You had to be careful with magic because you didn't want to hit me, and that's why they got away." She tried to catch Dex's gaze, but his frown was pointed forward.

"Correct," Xander muttered.

"We don't know that," Dex said quietly. "It could have gone badly whether Elle was there or not. Hopefully we'll get another chance to track them down."

"Not like this," Xander replied. "It took us weeks of following one tiny snippet of information after the next—plus a good dose of luck—to get this information. We may never get another chance like the one we had tonight."

"I'm sorry, but I didn't exactly ask to be drugged and abducted and wind up in your way," Elle said. "And who are you guys anyway, following vampires and trying to catch them?" A whisper of fear nudged her mind. "Are you with the police?"

"No," Dex said. "This is more of an unofficial, off-the-records kind of operation. We believe they're part of the group responsible for all the human abductions that have happened recently. We're trying to find out what that's all about so we can stop it."

Well, it was a relief they weren't involved with the police. She *really* didn't need anyone in authority knowing that she, a human, liked to masquerade as a faerie. She would wind up in a prison cell somewhere, and once Salvia got her out, her fury would know no bounds. "Why are you doing your own investigation?" she asked. "I heard the police had a lead on who was behind all of that. Don't you trust them to get to the bottom of it?"

Dex gave her a pointed look. "Do you?"

She almost laughed. "I'm human. I have a hard time trusting anyone who's fae, whether they're in law enforcement or not."

"Clearly," Dex said, rubbing his thumb across the cut on his palm that was now little more than a faint scar. "Anyway, I don't trust them either. Humans aren't exactly high on their priority list. They make announcements every now and then to keep the public happy—at least, that small part of the public who actually care about humans—but we all know there isn't much behind their words."

"And *you* guys care about humans?" Elle asked, unable to keep the skepticism from her voice.

"Would we be fighting vampires if we didn't care?" Xander asked. He swung the steering wheel hard to the right as he turned a corner, and Elle gripped the seat with one hand and the door handle with the other.

"I suppose not," she muttered. "Sorry, it's just unusual to come across fae who care *that* much. Most fae are probably glad someone's ridding the world of humans."

"One of many things that's wrong with the world," Olly muttered.

Elle loosened her grip on the seat and looked at Dex. "So, I've been wondering …"

"Yes?"

"The other night at Club Onyx, you saw the color of my blood and realized I'm human. But did you say anything? Did you tell the bouncer or anyone?"

"No. I didn't even tell Olly and Xander, actually. I figured it wasn't my secret to tell."

"I'm so hurt right now," Xander deadpanned, his head still pointed forward.

"Thank you," Elle said quietly.

"Why were you there?" Dex asked. "I assume you're aware of how dangerous it is. Not just because of all the fae who could have discovered you were pretending to be one of them, but because there are vampires out at night. Those abductions have been going on for weeks. And I know you were disguised, but if they get close enough, they can smell—"

"There was no way that vampire could distinguish the smell of my blood among all the other odors in that club," Elle pointed out.

"Okay, maybe not. But out on the street?"

"Look, I don't have a choice, okay? I need to go out at night sometimes. It's a risk I have to take to get Essence." Which, she realized now that a look of horror was growing on Dex's face, she probably should have kept to herself.

"To get Essence?" he repeated. "You mean … fae are *paying* you for something?"

"Whatever you're thinking," Elle said quickly, "I can guarantee you're wrong."

"Okaaaaay."

"I need Essence for … something. I offer a service—nothing dodgy—and people pay."

"Now I'm definitely intrigued," Dex said.

"Is this where you need to be?" Xander asked, turning hard yet again. Elle grabbed hold of the door to keep herself from being flung into Dex's lap.

"Uh, yes," she said, peering between the two front seats and recognizing the road she'd told Xander to go to. "Wow, that was fast."

"Dex said it was urgent."

"Yes, it was." Elle's eyes landed on the time displayed on the car dashboard. "Thankfully, it isn't quite so urgent anymore." She pulled the door handle and opened the door, then turned back to face Dex. "Thank you for getting me away from the vampires. And for not saying anything at Club Onyx about me being human. Maybe I don't seem like I'm grateful, since I made you do that blood oath back there, but I was just being careful."

Dex nodded, a small smile lighting up his silver-blue eyes. "I understand."

"Wait," Xander said as Elle moved toward the door. "What do you think about helping us catch those vampires?"

A beat of silence passed in which Elle replayed the words in her head, wondering if she'd misheard him. "Me? Are you serious? How would I do that?"

"They want you. You could be bait."

Elle's eyebrows jumped up. "Um, what?"

"That sounds like a dangerous idea," Dex said.

Xander looked at him. "You've never been opposed to dangerous ideas."

"*I'm* opposed to dangerous ideas," Elle said. "I mean, sure, my nighttime escapades aren't exactly safe, but this would be far worse. Intentionally putting myself in the path of a bunch of vampires? No thanks."

"What if we pay you?" Xander suggested. "In Essence. That's what you want, right?"

Elle narrowed her eyes. "How much?"

"You can't possibly be considering this," Dex said.

"What do your other clients pay you for your time?" Xander asked.

Elle's gaze shifted between Dex and Xander. She didn't like this idea, but Essence was hard to turn down. "Half an elixion vial per job. And a job only takes a few minutes."

"But how many jobs do you do in a night?"

"Usually only one," Elle admitted.

"I am *so* curious about whatever these jobs are," Olly said.

"I can probably part with a full vial without suffering any adverse effects," Xander said. "And so can you guys," he added, looking first at Dex and then Olly. "So how about that? Three full vials per night until we catch at least one vamp who can give us useful info."

"This is a bad idea," Dex said, a deep furrow forming across his brow.

"Obviously we won't let anything happen to her," Xander said. "You know that. But we need to catch them, Dex. This could be our best chance."

Dex groaned. "I don't know. Maybe." He looked at Elle. "I know you're in a rush though, so why don't you take my number." He raised his hand and wrote quickly in the air, leaving glittering gold digits hanging in front of Elle. "We can meet and discuss this further. If we can make sure it's a plan that guarantees your safety, then—"

"No," Elle interrupted as she slid away from him to the edge of the seat. It was tempting—*so* tempting—but even if she didn't mind risking her life, it wouldn't be possible to leave the house whenever Dex might need her. "I'm sorry. I don't want to get involved. I *can't* get involved. It's … it's complicated. Thank you again for your help tonight. I really appreciate it." She pushed the door further open and climbed out of the car.

"Wait!" Dex called. "Just take my number. In case you change your mind."

She almost didn't, but something—probably the promise of all that Essence—made her duck back inside the car and swipe her hand through the numbers still floating in the air. They transferred themselves to her arm. Then she leaned back, slammed the door shut, and hurried toward the nearest townhouse. She climbed the stairs, stopped on the porch right in front of the door, and pretended to fish inside her purse for a key. Then she looked back over her shoulder and waved at the waiting car. "You can go now," she muttered beneath her breath, forcing a quick smile onto her lips. "I'm fine. You don't have to watch me go inside."

Fortunately, Xander took the hint, and as Elle turned back toward the door, she heard the car pull away from the sidewalk. The moment it was around the corner, she hurried down the stairs and back onto the street. She walked as briskly as possible in her high-heeled boots, aware of the fact that her fake ear tips were gone. But she was so close to home, she reminded herself as she moved her hair to cover her ears. It was unlikely anything would go wrong now.

She glanced repeatedly at the numbers glowing faintly on her arm. They would wash off easily. She knew the spell Dex had used. It transformed his magic into something like paint once it came into contact with skin or paper or some other hard surface. It was silly, but she couldn't help admiring his elegant script. The slant of the numbers and the way he drew his twos with a loop at the bottom.

Don't be an idiot, she told herself, forcing her gaze upward as her cheeks burned. *It's just handwriting.*

She turned into her street, expecting to be greeted by the usual quiet stillness of near-midnight. Instead she saw two police vehicles parked directly outside her house. The door to her home was wide open, spilling yellow light onto the road. A police officer jogged up the stairs, while another two hurried down, and behind the curtains, shadows paced. Loud voices and the crackle and beep of radio communicators met her ears. Then one of the police officers turned her way. He called out and hastened across the road toward her.

"Crap," Elle whispered as dread sank into the pit of her stomach.

THIRTEEN

"You made a blood oath with her?" Xander demanded the moment the car started moving.

"Dex, what the hell?" Olly said. "What did you swear to her?"

Dex stared through the windshield as Xander turned out of Elle's road. He wanted to smile at the memory of her standing in that dusty office with her feisty expression and her tiny knife pointed at him. He was fae and infinitely more powerful, but that clearly hadn't daunted her. "Look, we needed to get her to safety," he said. "She's important to the vampires, which means they could have been circling back toward the fairground while you guys were chasing after them. I couldn't just leave her—"

"Dude, just tell us what you swore to her," Xander said.

Dex sighed. "She didn't want to accept a ride from me. She didn't trust me. She told me to swear I wouldn't lie to her, that's all. No big deal."

Olly turned in his seat to face Dex. "No big deal? Really? You lie to *everyone* you meet."

"I don't." Dex looked away, his expression darkening. "I omit the truth. There's a difference. The blood oath knows that, and so do you. This won't be a problem."

FOURTEEN

Elle's heart pounded so hard she thought it might break free from her chest. The police officer hadn't explained anything. He'd merely ushered her across the road after she gave him her name, saying something about getting her inside the house where she'd be safe. *It's all relative*, she thought bitterly. Dangers might lurk in the shadows outside, but she knew what awaited her inside the house. There was no way she would classify it as 'safe.'

The officer steered her into the lounge, where she found Sienna standing with her arms crossed tightly over her chest, and Salvia sitting beside Meredith on the couch. Meredith's eyes were red. She held a healing aid patch over her cheek. All three were in their pajamas.

Salvia looked up, and her expression hardened as her eyes landed on Elle. She stood slowly, saying nothing, but her eyes seemed to burn with hatred, and Elle imagined she could feel the fury rippling off her in hot waves. Her gaze moved past Elle to the uniformed man beside her. She pulled her signature smile into place and asked, "Are you done here?"

"Yes, I think we've taken—"

"Thank you very much then, officer. I appreciate your speedy response. More than you can possibly know."

"I—of course. Officers Cole and Rushmore will be posted outside tonight—and for the next few nights—keeping watch in case the vamp returns."

"Thank you, we're all *incredibly* grateful to you for helping us feel safe. I assume you can show yourself out?"

"Yes, of course. Uh, goodnight then." He turned away. Moments later, the front door clicked shut.

Salvia's smile vanished. She tilted her head. Her eyes traveled down Elle's silver dress, which sparkled beneath the warm lamplight. "Where have you been?" she asked, her voice deadly quiet.

Elle had been trying to come up with an explanation since the moment she turned onto her street and saw all the police activity. It didn't matter what she said though. She'd left without Salvia's permission, and there was nothing that could make up for that. "I was meeting someone," she said, since Salvia had probably figured that out already, given Elle's outfit.

"A vampire?"

Elle's pounding heart tripped over itself for a beat or two. "Why would you think—"

"Because he showed up here. At our front door." Salvia took a step closer. "Meredith was up, watching TV, so when he knocked, she answered. She accidentally stepped beyond the doorway boundary, and he grabbed hold of her." Salvia moved forward another step. "He said he was looking for you. That he wouldn't let Meredith go until she invited him into the house. She fought him, and he tore his dirty nails down her face. Fortunately, I had reached the door by then. I struck his face with magic and pulled Meredith inside. We called the police immediately, but the vampire, of course, was long gone."

"When—when did this happen?" Elle asked.

"Not long ago," Sienna whispered, hugging her arms a little tighter around her middle. "Twenty minutes, maybe a bit more."

Elle swallowed. The vampire must have come straight here after Dex and his friends chased him away, probably hoping to get inside the house and wait until she returned home.

"Imagine if a vampire scratch was like a bite," Salvia hissed. "Meredith could be *turning* right now! You would have essentially *murdered* your own sister!"

Stepsister, Elle corrected silently. She liked to pretend Sienna was her real sister, but Meredith had always remained firmly in *step* territory. "I'm so sorry," she said, "but I had nothing to do with—"

"What have you brought upon us?" Salvia demanded.

"I don't know, I swear. I have no idea why a vampire would be looking for me, and I have no idea how he knows where I live."

"Liar," Salvia spat. "You have broken every rule I set for you. You left this house without permission." She spun around and slapped Sienna.

"No!" Elle gasped, then pressed a hand over her mouth. She knew protesting would only make things worse.

"You got involved with a vampire." She raised both hands and shoved Sienna so hard she fell with a cry. "And then you led him right to our front door." Faerie dust flashed on her fingers. She threw her hand out, and her magic coalesced into a glowing whip that lashed across Sienna's arm.

"Stop, stop, stop," Elle pleaded behind her hand.

"You were disobedient," Salvia said. "And now Sienna has to pay." She struck Sienna again, causing her to cry out as she tried to scramble away across the carpet.

"You know how this usually works, my dear Elle. Whoever disobeys causes the other one to be punished. But you hurt Meredith. You hurt my sweet, darling favorite. Which means this time, the usual rules don't apply. This time, you have to pay too." She raised her hand and pointed one glossy fingernail toward the kitchen. "The cellar. Now."

"No, wait," Sienna whimpered from the floor. "Please don't take her down—"

"Shut it," Salvia snapped, stepping over her daughter. She grabbed Elle's arm and shoved her toward the doorway. Elle tripped and dropped her purse, but managed to catch herself against the doorframe. "What is *that*?" Salvia demanded. Elle looked around and realized her stepmother's eyes were on the phone number written in magic gold on her arm. "Whoever he is," Salvia said, "you won't ever be contacting him." Her hand swiped through the air. Magic flashed down, zapping across Elle's skin. A hiss of pain escaped her as the numbers vanished and a long red welt took their place. "Now *move*!" Salvia said.

Elle stood her ground, giving herself just a few seconds of defiance. She sought out Sienna's eyes but instead caught Meredith's. Meredith The Favorite.

Sitting there with a triumphant smirk, despite her red-rimmed eyes and the healing aid patch stuck to her cheek.

Elle whipped her head back around, pushed away from the doorframe, and walked out of the room. Meredith had been Salvia's favorite ever since the day Sienna had stamped her tiny foot as tears streamed down her face and yelled, "I wish *you* were dead and he was still alive!" It would have been bad enough if it had been her own father she'd been shouting about, but it wasn't. It was Elle's dad, and that made it even worse. Sienna loved him more than she loved her own mother, and she wasn't afraid to scream it at Salvia. Until later. Later, after Salvia's heart had hardened and she'd come up with the most effective way to punish her disobedient daughter and stepdaughter, then Sienna's fear became real.

"You're despicable," Elle said as she marched into the kitchen with Salvia right behind her. She was about to be punished anyway. May as well say what she wanted to say.

"You made me this way," Salvia replied bitterly. "You and your father. Vile humans."

"You loved him," Elle said, whirling around to face Salvia. "And he loved you. He did *not* make you into this—"

Salvia's hand cracked across Elle's face. Hot, stinging pain flared in her cheek. "Yes, I loved him. And it was the biggest mistake of my life." She stepped past Elle. "Now follow me. And if you dare disobey, it'll be Sienna who ends up in the cellar." She headed for the door in the opposite corner of the kitchen and opened it.

Elle followed, taking a deep, steadying breath. But her hands were already beginning to shake at the thought of what was coming. She tried to focus on other things. The uneven stone steps, smooth with age. The chilly, stale air. The dark cellar lit only by a bare bulb hanging from the ceiling. The shadows cast by the boxes and old possessions stored down there.

The wall was cold beneath her palms as she bent forward and pressed her hands against it. There was that familiar crack between two bricks. The crack she stared at every time. Salvia had never bothered to ask anyone to fill it—

Burning, white-hot pain slashed across her back, tearing her focus from the wall. She sucked in a breath through her clenched teeth. Magic flashed a second time, striking her back and eliciting a whimper despite how hard she tried to clamp her lips together. She squeezed her eyes shut and silently repeated the same words she always focused on when Salvia punished her.

It'll be over soon.

It'll be over soon.

It'll be over soon.

FIFTEEN

Later that night, Elle lay on her stomach on top of her quilted bedspread, her head twisted to the side and one hand clamped around the gold pocket watch. She still wore her sparkly dress, which had been torn to shreds across the back by Salvia's magic. It would be too painful to try to remove. She would suffer in agony through the night, and early in the morning, Salvia would send Sienna up with some human-safe healing balm. Sienna would help Elle remove the dress, use the limited magic that was allowed on humans, and by the time Elle had to begin her chores for the day, the pain would be bearable. It would remain her companion throughout the day and night tomorrow, but by the next day, her back would be free of pain and scars. Until next time.

Elle squeezed the pocket watch tighter and stared at the sliver of the moon and a few tiny twinkling stars through her dusty window. *Look to the stars*, her mother had embroidered on the quilt, but both the moon and the stars faded out of focus as tears glazed Elle's eyes. She always tried to be strong, to never despair, to live in hope. Her parents wouldn't have wanted her to give up. But on nights like tonight, alone in the darkness with the searing pain almost too much to bear, she couldn't help but break down. Tears trickled down her cheeks and wet the pillow.

Elle didn't know how long they continued to fall, but eventually they slowed. Then they dried up. The outline of the window and the moon—in a different part of the sky now—came back into focus. She breathed in a shuddery breath and sought out the determination that lived deep inside her. The resolve that

Salvia could never truly destroy, no matter what she did to Elle. "Freedom," Elle whispered through shaky lips. She held onto that word like a promise. One day, it would be hers.

Carefully, she pushed herself up and turned around. Her purse sat on the end of the bed. Sienna must have brought it up here while Elle was in the cellar. Thank goodness. At least Salvia hadn't got hold of it. In her fury, she seemed to have forgotten that Elle returned home with a purse in her hands.

She leaned forward, trying not to pull the skin on her back too much, and tugged the purse closer. She opened it and pulled her phone out. Salvia had wiped the numbers from her arm, but Elle's gaze had traced them so many times while walking home that she could see them clearly in her mind's eye. She lifted the phone, opened a new message, and entered the numbers. Then, after taking another deep breath, she started typing.

Elle: Three vials a day. If the offer still stands, I'm in.

2

THE VAMPIRE TRAP

ONE

In the back aisle of Lunar Cherry, Vale City's best baking supplies store, Elle Winter tapped her left combat boot against the floor as she scanned the shelves of unicorn-related items. "There you are," she muttered, her eyes landing on the tiny glass bottles of Lawson's Unicorn Tears on the top shelf. She stood on tiptoe and reached for a bottle, wincing as the partially healed cuts on her back pulled tight. The healing balm Sienna applied this morning had helped a lot, speeding up Elle's recovery with its magical properties, but the wounds wouldn't be completely gone until tomorrow or the next day.

Elle lowered the unicorn tears into the basket floating beside her, then checked the note in her hand to make sure she had everything. "Check, check, and … check." She crumpled the paper and pushed it into her shorts pocket. But instead of moving to the checkout queue at the front of the shop, she hung out in the back aisle, pretending to examine the vast array of cookie cutters and piping nozzles as her basket followed dutifully alongside her. Dex should be here soon. She'd told him she only had a few minutes to talk. If she took any longer than that, Salvia would get suspicious—especially after last night.

After breakfast this morning, Salvia had put a confinement charm around the entire house, telling Elle she was never allowed to leave again. But then tea time arrived, and Elle hadn't been able to bake any more of Salvia's favorite pearl crunch cookies because some of the ingredients were finished, and at that point Salvia decided she was too tired to go shopping herself. So she temporarily lifted the confinement charm and shoved Elle out the front door with the threat of *consequences*—her favorite word—if she didn't return within an hour.

A squeak reached Elle's ears, and she squinted at the collection of edible glitter spray in front of her. There certainly shouldn't be anything *alive* among the bottles. She moved one aside to see if a mouse or some other tiny creature might be hiding back there, but all she saw were more bottles of glitter spray. She pulled the straps of her canvas bag further up her shoulder and walked forward. Another squeak greeted her, sounding suspiciously as if it came from beneath her arm. She peered into the bag and pushed aside the purse of cash Salvia had given her. Right there, between the two bottles of vitamins she'd picked up from the pharmacy next door, was the pixie she'd caught in the pantry the other day. Her pistachio shell hat sat cocked to one side on her tiny head. She gave Elle a mischievous grin and hugged one of the vitamin bottles.

"What are you doing in there?" Elle hissed. "Don't you dare open that bottle. Salvia will—"

"Elle?"

Elle's head shot up and she found Dex in front of her. "Oh. Hi. Hello." *Typical*, she thought. The first time they met, she was on her butt on a sidewalk. The second time, she was unconscious. Now, she was talking to her bag. She would hate to know what he really thought of her.

"Everything okay?" he asked, his eyebrows rising slightly above his too-gorgeous blue eyes.

"Um, yes. Sorry, there's a—never mind." She tugged at the end of her blond ponytail as she decided not to mention the pixie. For some reason, she felt stupidly self-conscious about her appearance. Old shorts, a faded T-shirt, and her favorite scuffed black combat boots with cheap rhinestones sprinkled across the front. Meredith had bought them several years ago and worn them once before deciding they were too chunky for her delicate feminine tastes.

Elle noticed Dex's gaze focused somewhere near said chunky boots, and for one heart-pounding moment she feared he could see the gold chain-shaped tattoo encircling her right ankle. Her head snapped down, despite the fact that she knew—she *knew*—her boots and socks were high enough to conceal the tattoo. She let out a quiet breath of relief as she confirmed that the symbol of the slave charm placed upon her was still hidden.

She looked up and found Dex's eyes on her face again. "I know you said you don't have long to talk," he said, "but I figured we should make some plans in person instead of arranging everything by text. You never know who might intercept that kind of information."

Elle lowered her hand as she looked around to see if anyone might be close enough to overhear them. "I understand."

"So are you sure you want to get involved in this? It's going to be dangerous. Possibly even deadly."

She met Dex's eyes so he would know how serious she was. "I'm sure. I *need* to do this."

"If it's just about the Essence—"

"It isn't." Elle let out a long breath and decided to tell Dex what had happened. "A vampire attacked my stepsister."

"What? When?"

"Last night. One of them must have run from the fairground straight to my house. My stepsister Meredith answered the door, and I guess she was stupid enough to step beyond the doorway. The vampire grabbed her. Said he wouldn't let go until she invited him inside, but then my stepmother managed to pull her back, and the vampire disappeared."

Dex cursed beneath his breath. "Is she okay?"

"She's fine. But I can't have vampires appearing at my front door again. My stepmother—well … I just need to make sure it doesn't happen again." If it did, Salvia would punish Elle by hurting Sienna. That was Salvia's twisted way of keeping her disobedient stepdaughter and daughter in line.

Dex shook his head. "It's bad news that they know where you live. Is that where that vampire caught you last night? Outside your home, as you were leaving?"

"No. I, um, used the back entrance of my house," Elle said vaguely. She didn't need Dex asking why she had to sneak out of the kitchen door, tiptoe past garbage bins, and slip through a hole in the wall into the next street over. "Maybe he was waiting for me, but he wouldn't have seen me if he was out the front."

"So then … maybe the attack on your stepsister was a coincidence," Dex suggested. "Maybe it was an attempt at another random human abduction."

Elle shook her head. "My stepsister is fae. Besides, the vampire apparently said he was looking for me."

Dex let out a heavy sigh. Then he frowned. "Perhaps this makes things easier. We don't have to orchestrate anything elaborate in order for them to come and get you. If they know where you live, they'll probably be waiting for you the next time you leave at night."

Ignoring the fact that simply leaving the house was going to be a problem, given Salvia's new restrictions, Elle said, "Maybe, but there'll be two police officers stationed outside my home for the next few nights, so a vampire might not dare to come close enough."

"If they're desperate enough to get their hands on you, a whole group of them might show up. They could probably take down two officers."

"Probably." Elle crossed her arms. "But I want to keep this away from my home, if possible. If I can get out safely, then maybe—"

"Oh, dammit." Dex's eyes focused on something behind Elle. "Okay, we need to go. Right now."

"What?" Elle whirled around, her mind turning immediately to the vampire who'd abducted her. But of course it couldn't be him; it was still daytime. The only person Elle could see was a fae woman reaching for a container of cookie cutters.

"I can't let her see me," Dex said. Elle turned back as he raised a hand and partially covered his face. He turned, hurried to the other end of the aisle, and peered around the shelf.

"I guess I can understand that," Elle muttered. She would have had the same response if Salvia had caught her somewhere she wasn't supposed to be. "You should be able to leave without her seeing you," she whispered as she caught up to Dex. Shooting a look over her shoulder, she added, "She seems completely focused on those cookie cutters."

"Yes, I think—No, wait. Her husband's here too. Heading this way. Wonderful." Dex spun around, his eyes searching behind Elle as he kept one hand up near his face.

Elle looked about, hoping to see another way out of the store, but there was none. Then her eyes fell on a staircase with a Staff Only sign hovering above the first step. "Over here." She reached for Dex's arm and pulled him toward the stairs. They ducked beneath the floating sign, Elle glancing behind her to make sure her basket was still following, and hurried up the stairs. At the top was a room piled haphazardly with boxes and wooden crates, and at the far end—in danger of being buried beneath reams of paper, stacks of files, and numerous cables sticking out of an old computer—was a desk.

"We should move out of sight of the door," Dex said, placing one arm loosely around Elle's back. It was a casual movement he probably hadn't even thought about, but Elle flinched at the sudden pressure against her wounds. Dex snatched his arm back as if he'd been burned. "What's wrong?"

"Nothing. Um, do you think that woman saw us?" she asked quickly.

"Uh …" He frowned for a moment before turning away and crouching down at the top of the stairs. "I don't see anyone coming, and I don't hear anyone shouting at us to get out of the Staff Only area, so I think we're all good."

"Great." Elle sat on the edge of a crate and pulled her basket closer. She was curious to know why Dex wanted to hide from a woman shopping for cookie cutters, but she had more urgent matters to discuss with him. "I don't have much more time, so …"

"Right, yes." Dex shifted another crate closer to Elle and sat on it. His knee was almost touching hers, which was a silly thing to notice, and yet she could barely drag her attention away from that tiny gap of space between his leg and hers. "You were saying you want to keep the vamps away from your home," Dex said, "which I totally understand."

"Yes." Elle cleared her throat and looked up. "My stepmother—she just wouldn't react well. What were you going to suggest before you realized they know where I live?"

"Oh, well, there's this event the night after tomorrow. One of Gizella Munroe's parties. You know, where she invites her friends of all races and tries to show the rest of the world that we can all be friends."

Elle nodded slowly. "I've heard of them." Gizella Munroe was a popular fae actress who firmly believed in the equality of all races. She held extravagant parties in her numerous homes around the world. Meredith had managed to score an invitation once or twice. Elle had obviously never been.

"They're usually well-attended," Dex continued. "Anyone who's anyone likes to be seen there. Not because they *agree* with Gizella, necessarily, but because—"

"They want to be popular by association," Elle guessed. Meredith had spoken endlessly about how unsettling it was to attend parties with vampires and shape-shifters—"And *humans*, can you believe it?"—and yet she bent over backwards to get herself invited.

"Yeah, pretty much," Dex said.

"And you think one of those vampires who tried to kidnap me will be at this party? Doesn't sound like the right kind of scene."

Dex's lips curved up on one side. "I know. Gizella Munroe's vamp friends have never tasted a drop of human blood, right? Her shifter friends have never attacked anyone while in beast form. Her fae and human friends all respect and admire each other. They're all upstanding citizens of the law, aren't they?" He laughed. "I've been to a few of these parties, and I can tell you that's not the case. Gizella likes to be inclusive, which means she doesn't exactly supervise who her friends invite. It was actually at one of those parties that I first overheard a whispered discussion about the Allegiant, though I was never able to actually *see* the man and woman who were talking."

"The Allegiant?" Elle asked as her brow drew lower.

"Sorry, I forget sometimes that the name hasn't been publicized anywhere. I don't know if the police even know that's what this group calls themselves. They're the ones responsible for all the recent human abductions. The abductions where no bodies have been found."

Elle clasped her hands together in her lap. "Okay, so we go to this party on Friday night, and hopefully the right vampire sees me and tries to abduct me, and you and your friends get hold of him instead?"

"Yes. And then we'll find out what's really going on and who else is involved.

We'll make sure the police know everything, and soon—hopefully—you and your family will be safe again."

"Sounds so straightforward," Elle said, unable to keep the doubt from her voice.

"We'll make sure nothing happens to you, but if you're not comfortable with this idea, then you don't have to—"

"Dex, I already said I need to do this," Elle reminded him as she stood. "For my family and for the Essence." And for the chance to ask that vampire exactly what he knew about her mother. Her mind kept taunting her with the vague memory of those few words he'd spoken—*She tried to keep you from us*—and she couldn't bring herself to believe she'd imagined that moment.

"Oh yes, the Essence." Dex stood and slid one hand inside his jacket. "Three vials a day until we catch a vamp who knows something. That's what we agreed, right?" He withdrew his hand and held three vials glowing gold from the vapor-like substance within.

"Um, thank you." She wasn't about to turn down the Essence, but she still felt awkward taking it. She hadn't done anything to earn it yet. "Let me know where to meet you on Friday," she added as she slipped the vials into the canvas bag still hanging from her shoulder. "I'll figure out how to leave my house safely."

"You don't want me to pick you up? That way I can make sure no vampire grabs you off the street and—"

"No, it's fine," she rushed to say. "That, um, won't work. I'll ask one of the cops for a lift. He can escort me straight from the front door into his car."

"Okay," Dex said slowly, his brow furrowed once again. "I guess that should keep you safe."

"Yes." Elle nodded, though she hadn't been thinking of lurking vampires when she'd mentioned leaving her house safely. Salvia and her rules and confinement charms were the bigger problem. But Elle had already begun to formulate a plan to deal with Salvia. She just had to be brave enough to execute it. "Anyway, I really have to go," she said, nudging her basket back into the air as she stepped past Dex. "See you on Friday."

TWO

That night, Elle ate her dinner alone at the kitchen table, listening to her stepmother and stepsisters in the dining room. The first time Salvia banished her from the dinner table—"It isn't proper for our *slave* to eat with us," she'd stated—Elle had cried hot, angry tears while eating alone. These days, she was grateful for any time away from Salvia and Meredith. If she could just block out their conversation, her mealtimes would be almost perfect. Unfortunately, the door had to be left open in case Elle was needed for something. Stars forbid Meredith might have to refill her own glass, or dish her own second helping from the hot plate on the sideboard, or wipe her own darn face when she spilled gravy on her chin.

Elle snickered at that last thought. If Meredith ever reached the point where she asked Elle to wipe her face, she would end up with a lot more than gravy on it. Then, of course, there would be consequences. Sienna would have to pay for Elle's disobedience. Elle sighed as she chewed slowly on a mouthful of peas. It wouldn't be worth it.

The annoying pop song Meredith used as her phone's ringtone interrupted Elle's thoughts, followed by someone coughing and then a repeated smacking sound. Elle paused with her fork halfway to her mouth but didn't move from her seat. She'd made the mistake of returning to the dining room unbidden before. If someone needed her help, they would call for her.

The coughing and smacking ended. "It's Quentin," Meredith spluttered over the sound of her phone ringing. "One of Martin's friends."

Goosebumps rose across Elle's arms at the mention of Martin's name. He was the target of Salvia and Meredith's most recent con. The young man Elle had been forced to use her memory-wiping ability on.

"So don't answer it," Sienna said.

"I have to answer it!" Meredith hissed. "It'll be suspicious if I just ignore him from now on." She cleared her throat. The ringing stopped, and her voice dripped syrup as she said, "Hello?"

Elle stood quietly, picked up her plate, and moved closer to the door. After angling herself so she could see Meredith through the doorway, she pierced a roast potato with her fork and nibbled on it as she watched.

"Oh, yes, Quentin. Hi. How are you?" Meredith smiled her flirty smile and dragged her hand through her shiny red hair, as if Quentin were in the room and could be seduced by her charms. "Oh my goodness, *really*? And he doesn't know how he ended up there?" Meredith lowered her hand, an expression of fake horror encompassing her features. "He doesn't remember *me* either? Well, I mean, we weren't together for very long, so it's not as though—Wait, he was *what*?" Her tone climbed a few notches. "*Propose*? Are you sure?" Another moment passed as she listened. Salvia and Sienna watched her in silence. "I think you've got that wrong. I mean, we really weren't—My idea? He said *I* wanted to get married?" Meredith laughed. "No way, I am *not* ready for that. If Martin told you anything about marriage, it was totally his idea. And he—Oh, wow, his grandmother's ring?" She gasped, placing a hand over her mouth. "Oh no, he must have been robbed." Elle almost rolled her eyes. Of course poor Martin had been robbed. Meredith was the one who'd done it. "Well, yes, I could come to the hospital and see if it sparks his memory. But, I mean, the last time I saw him, we actually ended things, so even if he does remember me, I'm not sure he'd be happy to see—" She played with her fork, listening for another few moments. "Yes, certainly, I can come through tomorrow morning. I'll see you then." She ended the call and let out a groan.

"I assume someone found Martin behind that bar," Salvia said.

"Yes, and now he's in hospital with no memory of the past three months. His stupid friends think maybe it'll help if he sees me." Meredith dropped her phone on the table and let out a dramatic sigh. "This is why we don't do this sort of con very often. We have to get too involved in a person's life. Too many other people to deal with afterwards."

"It'll be fine," Salvia assured her. "Elle!" she shouted, and Elle took a hasty step backward before anyone noticed her watching through the doorway. "More roast beef and gravy," Salvia called. Elle lowered her plate to the kitchen table before hurrying into the dining room. With the aid of an oven mitt, she lifted the platter of roast beef from the hot tray and brought it to Salvia's side.

"I know it'll be fine," Meredith said as Salvia used her magic to transfer a few pieces of meat onto her plate. "Martin won't remember me, and I can explain the rest away. I'll tell his friends that he became obsessive after I tried to break up with him. He insisted we were meant to be together, and that's why he was telling people stories about proposing to me."

"Sounds good," Salvia said. "And the gravy, Elle," she added with a snap of her fingers. "How many times do I have to ask?"

"My *point*, Mom," Meredith continued as Elle returned the platter to the hot tray and grabbed the small gravy jug, "is that we need to let enough time pass before we do this particular con again. People will grow suspicious if too many young men end up losing their memories after telling their friends and families they're about to propose to Meredith Leroux."

"Of course, and that's why we have a different one lined up for—That's *enough*, Elle! My goodness, do you want to drown my plate?"

"I'm sorry," Elle muttered, stepping away quickly as she imagined drowning Salvia instead.

"Ugh, another con already?" Meredith complained. "But we just finished one. Can't I have a break?"

"Actually, I was thinking Sienna could do this one."

Sienna's hand jerked, knocking her knife to the floor. She bent hastily to retrieve it. "Um, what was that?" she asked as she straightened.

"It's about time you started adding to the income of this household."

"But—I—uh—"

"There's that nice exchange student who's taken a liking to you. Elon, is it?

He's related to the royal family on that tiny little island he comes from, correct?"

"By, um, by marriage, I think," Sienna said faintly.

"Same thing," Salvia said. "My research tells me he comes from a very wealthy family. I'm sure you can steal something of value from him."

Sienna's grip tightened on her knife. Elle shook her head, hoping Sienna would notice. *Don't argue now*, she wanted to tell her. *Salvia won't listen. We can come up with a way to avoid this later.* Sienna's eyes flicked toward Elle before returning to her plate. She cleared her throat. "Um, of course. Just—just let me know what I need to do."

"Ha, what a joke," Meredith retorted. "I'm sure he'll see right through you."

"Meredith, that isn't very supportive of you," Salvia said, but her lips were turned up in an amused smile.

Sienna opened her mouth, clamped it shut, then opened it again. "Elle, can you please get me some, uh, some more juice. And I think I need more gravy. And another roast potato. They're so delicious." Elle nodded and returned to the sideboard, recognizing Sienna's numerous requests for what they were: a plea to not be left alone right now with her horrid mother and sister.

"Oh my stars, I know what I can wish for!" Meredith exclaimed, slapping her hand down on the table. "You know, with the wish Martin gave me." With the pitcher of juice in her hand, Elle turned in time to see Meredith leaning forward with a crazed gleam in her eyes. "It's so simple, I don't know why I didn't think of it before. I'll wish—wait for it—*for the prince to marry me.*"

"Don't be silly," Sienna said immediately. "You can't wish for *love*. It's one of the impossible wishes. Everyone knows that."

"I'm not wishing for love, idiot. I'm wishing for marriage. There's a difference."

"It's only a first-tier wish," Sienna reminded her as Elle topped her glass up. "I doubt it can grant you a marriage."

"I may as well try, right? Right, Mom?"

"Actually," Salvia said, "I took the wish to Apollo's Apothecary yesterday."

Meredith's jaw almost hit her plate. *"What?"*

"Calm down, darling. I haven't actually sold it yet. We don't have an authentication certificate for it, so someone needs to examine it and make sure it's legitimate, not some low-grade, black market wish. I'll hear from them once the authentication is complete and they offer me a price. I can still back out if I change my mind."

"Thank goodness for that." Meredith pressed a hand dramatically to her chest as she sighed. Elle made a superb effort at keeping her eyeballs pointed forward instead of rolling them toward the ceiling. She moved to the sideboard and swapped the juice pitcher for the gravy jug and the dish of potatoes.

"But remember, Meredith," Salvia added, "that we decided the wish would be worth more to us if we sell it."

"Not if I wish for the prince to marry me and it actually works," Meredith retorted.

"Yes, well … Hmm. Yes." Salvia trailed off while Sienna took her time choosing a single roast potato from the dish. Elle watched Salvia carefully, wondering if she might actually be considering Meredith's preposterous idea.

"What?" Meredith demanded.

"I'm thinking," Salvia said. Elle remained motionless, dread settling in the pit of her stomach. Sienna took the gravy jug from her and poured it ever so slowly over the potato sitting at the center of her plate. Across the table, Salvia rubbed her chin. "We just … yes, we need a plan." She refocused on Meredith. "Some of those dressmakers I contacted will be here over the next few days to measure you and show us samples and give us quotes. And you've been reading every article I sent you about the prince, I hope?"

"Of course."

"We need to—Elle, why are you standing there gawking? You're not needed right now. Put those things down and return to the kitchen." Elle replaced the dish and jug on the hot plate without a word. "We need to put all the pieces together and devise a solid plan," Salvia continued. "Something that has a real chance of working. Then, if we can word it properly, it might be worth wishing for something like the prince asking you to marry him."

Sienna's knife clattered to the floor a second time. "Ohforgoodnesssake," Salvia snapped. "Do you have to be so clumsy?"

"Sorry," Sienna muttered, reaching down at the same moment Elle crouched to retrieve the knife. "We can't let her make that wish," Sienna whispered. "Neither of us will ever be free if this family ends up stuck behind palace walls."

"I know," Elle whispered back. Then she raised her voice and added, "Wow, that knife really fell far." Though the offending piece of cutlery was already in her hand, she crawled a little further under the table. "Okay, got it. Here you go." She reversed and handed it to Sienna.

"Thanks so much, Elle," Sienna said, straightening and brushing her wispy hair out of her face.

"Any time," Elle answered, climbing to her feet. She returned to the kitchen—to her plate of food that was now cold—while behind her, Salvia muttered something about being surrounded by circus folk.

THREE

Later that night, after Elle had finished cleaning the kitchen, she hovered outside the lounge where Salvia was reclining with her laptop. Probably searching for more dress ideas for Meredith, or reading the latest gossip about Prince Chevalier. Bothering her stepmother after dinner was a risky move, but Elle had to do this before she chickened out.

She took a deep breath and knocked on the lounge door. Salvia's head appeared around the side of her favorite white linen wingback chair. "What?" she snapped.

Elle placed her shaking hands behind her back and walked into the room. She stopped in front of Salvia's chair, her eyes landing on the little side table. On it sat a plate with a pearl crunch cookie and the shimmering crumbs that remained from the one Salvia must have already eaten. Elle had baked a batch this afternoon before starting dinner. White chocolate chips and chopped nuts gave the cookies their crunch, while the unicorn tears gave them their pearlescent sheen. They were delicious, and if Elle ever wanted one, she had to sneak it off the baking tray soon after the batch came out the oven. Once the cookies were packed away in a jar, Salvia kept count of how many were left.

"I'm sorry for disturbing you," Elle said, looking up from the plate, "but there's something I want to talk to you about."

"You're supposed to be in your room now," Salvia said. "It's almost half past nine. You know the kind of pain you'll have to suffer if you're not inside that room at the right time."

"I know," Elle said, her mind going to the slave charm tattoo on her right ankle. Salvia had adjusted the confinement charm on Elle's attic so it would seal her inside at nine thirty instead of midnight. That was long enough, she'd told Elle, for her to finish cleaning the kitchen and dining room after dinner. If she was a moment too late, however … Well, she'd felt the searing agony once before when she accidentally fell asleep in Sienna's bedroom and didn't make it into the attic in time. She had no desire to experience that pain again. "But this is important," she said. "And it won't take long. I'll be back in the attic before it's too late."

"Important?" Salvia asked. "Really?" She placed her laptop on a side table, tucked a strand of glossy red hair behind one ear, and interlaced her hands in her lap. "It had better be very important indeed. If you end up boring me with something insignificant, Sienna might have to suffer the consequences."

Elle's jaw tensed. Sometimes she hated her stepmother so much she could taste it. But losing her temper now would only cause pain for Sienna. "There's something you and I both want," she said carefully.

Salvia raised an eyebrow. "Is there now?"

"We don't want any vampires to show up at this house ever again."

"I told you—"

"It's my fault, I know, so I need to make sure it doesn't happen again. If you let me out at night, I can deal with the problem. It shouldn't take more than about a week, and then we never—"

"No," Salvia said immediately.

"Just listen—"

"Absolutely not. You want me to let you out at night to go and meet vampires who'll probably end up killing you? Who will help me cover up the evidence of our cons if you're dead?"

Elle exhaled slowly. She'd prepared for this argument. "You don't actually need me for your cons. I know I make it easier, but you and Meredith are good enough to con people without me taking their memories." It was dangerous to play the flattery card, but she spoke her words with an edge of bitterness, as if she were grudgingly admitting the truth rather than buttering up her stepmother.

"Well, I suppose that's true, but that doesn't mean I have to let you go anywhere. The police will catch the vampire who was here last night. They can make the problem go away."

"Can they really?" Elle asked. "There are many problems in this city that the police haven't managed to get rid of. And in a few days, they won't be patrolling our street anymore. They'll have new problems to deal with. What if vampires come back then and force their way into this house?"

"Not possible without an invitation."

"But you can't hide inside forever. What if they catch you or Meredith while you're leaving or returning home at night? What if they threaten to kill you if you don't invite them in? And what if you *do* let them in and they kill you anyway once they've got me? I know I'm not worth that much to you. I know you wouldn't risk Meredith's life just to keep me."

Salvia's eyebrows lowered. "You're playing a dangerous game, Estelle."

"I promise I'm not. I don't know what these vampires hope to get from me, but I want to be rid of them as much as you do. All I'm asking for is a chance to go out—somewhere far from this house—and deal with them."

"Deal with them," Salvia repeated with a snort. "You're hilarious. How could you possibly *deal* with them?"

"Maybe … maybe I can take their memories. It doesn't matter how I deal with them, as long as they don't return. And if something happens to me, well …" She lifted her shoulders. "You'll have lost me, but at least you'll be free of the threat of vampires. You and Meredith and Sienna will be safe."

Salvia cocked her head to the side. "Tell me what you've really been up to all the times you've snuck out of this house, and perhaps I'll consider granting your request."

Elle took a deep breath and decided to go with a version of the truth. "I met someone."

"A human?"

"A faerie."

Salvia laughed. "What terrible taste he has."

Elle lifted her chin. "He doesn't care that I'm human."

"Is that so?" Salvia arched an eyebrow. "And does he care that you're a slave?"

At that, Elle remained quiet. She could have lied, but Salvia probably would have seen right through her.

Salvia shook her head slowly and made a *tsk, tsk* sound. "Keeping secrets from him already. What an unhealthy start to your first relationship." Again, Elle remained silent. "Fine," Salvia said. "I'll let you go out and 'deal' with this. You have one week in which to make it happen, and you still have a curfew. I'll adjust the confinement charm so it's back to midnight, as before. You don't need to be out any later than that. *Don't* argue with me," she added, raising her index finger as Elle opened her mouth. "This is the most freedom I've ever given you. You'd damn well better use it to get rid of that vampire—or *vampires*, plural—instead of hanging out with your faerie *boyfriend*." She spat out the last word as if it tasted bad.

"Don't worry," Elle said quietly. "I won't be seeing him again once this is done."

"You most certainly will not. You won't leave the house at night ever again once this is done."

Elle nodded and, without another word, stepped away. But Salvia stuck her arm out to stop her. "Remember the consequences if this doesn't work."

"I'm fully aware of the consequences," Elle said bitterly. "You'll hurt your own daughter if I fail."

Salvia pulled her hand back and laid it in her lap. "You see my actions only as a punishment. Don't you realize I'm doing her a favor as well?"

"A *favor*?"

"The world is a cruel place. If I don't teach her that at home, she might not learn this important lesson until it's too late."

"Do you really have to *beat* her in order to get the message across?" Elle demanded. A second later, she wished she'd held her tongue. That was exactly the sort of comment that would end with Sienna getting hurt. But instead of retaliating, Salvia simply let out a weary sigh.

"You don't have to be so dramatic about everything. Sienna will be fine. My father beat me when I was young, and it only made me stronger. I'm doing the same for her. Now go. You're wearing down my patience."

Elle almost asked why Salvia wasn't teaching Meredith the same lesson, but she'd pushed her luck far enough tonight. Best to keep her mouth shut and return to her attic before she found herself locked out by the confinement charm.

FOUR

On Friday night, Officer Cole brought his car to a stop outside the restaurant Elle had asked him to drive her to. She leaned forward in the passenger seat and checked the restaurant name before her eyes slid down and landed on Dex's car parked just ahead of them. "Is this the right place?" Officer Cole asked.

"Yes, thank you so much." Elle reached for the passenger door handle. "I really appreciate the lift."

"Well, your mom asked so nicely," Officer Cole said with a goofy grin. "I couldn't exactly say no."

Elle forced a smile onto her lips and decided not to correct him on the mom part. "Yes, she can be very persuasive."

"Right, so, she said I should pick you up at eleven thirty?" he said.

"That's right. Thank you. She had to go somewhere tonight, so she isn't able to pick me up herself." Not that Salvia would ever have gone out of her way to fetch Elle from anywhere, even if she wasn't busy.

"All righty. See you then."

Elle climbed out of the car and crossed the road. She opened the front passenger door to find Dex talking to someone on speaker phone. "… worry every time that someone will recognize us," a voice said as Elle bent and slid onto the seat. It sounded like Dex's friend Olly.

"You worry too much," came a second voice through the phone. Probably Xander. "It's not healthy."

"My worry is completely founded. What if—"

"Okay, I need to go," Dex said. "Elle's here. Make sure you keep your eyes peeled for any of our unpleasant friends. We'll be there soon." He ended the call and looked up. "Hi."

"Hi," Elle answered, unable to look away from his gaze. It was ridiculous the way his eyes took her breath away. She really had to get that under control. She forced herself to turn and pull the car door shut. "Um, do I look okay for tonight? I mean, will I fit in? I'm not exactly familiar with celebrity parties."

"Yeah, you look good."

"Okay. Thanks." Elle rubbed her hands self-consciously over her legs. She was wearing one of the outfits Salvia kept aside for the occasions Elle had to pretend she was a normal part of the family while helping out with a con. A flared, high-waisted skirt that ended just above her knees, and a cute polka-dot blouse. Plus her combat boots. Meredith had remarked loudly about how the boots completely ruined the outfit, but there was something about them that Elle found comforting. Besides, she thought they added a bit of attitude to the whole look. Far more interesting than if she'd gone with stockings and flats. But she'd kept that thought to herself as she walked out of the house with Salvia and Meredith's eyeballs burning holes into her back. Leaving with permission wasn't nearly as pleasant as sneaking out.

Elle reached for the chain at her neck and pulled her pocket watch necklace out from beneath the blouse. It was safe to show it off now that Salvia wasn't around. It probably didn't go with the outfit either, but Elle drew as much comfort from it as she drew from her familiar boots. "I like that," Dex said as the car rumbled to life. "The necklace, I mean. I don't think I told you that the other night."

"Oh, thank you. It belonged to my father." Why had she said that? She'd never felt the need to tell anyone that before.

"Cool." Dex pulled into the street and drove away from the restaurant. "And you mentioned a stepsister?"

"Yes."

"So one of your parents remarried? Or both?"

"My father." Elle twisted her hands in her lap. This was new territory for her, talking about her family with a client. Then again, Dex wasn't like her other clients. He'd saved her from a vampire abduction, and now he was hunting them with her help. He might be paying her Essence the way her clients did, but he was more of an accomplice than anything else. Besides, part of her *wanted* to share more of her story with him. She never got to share anything with anyone else. "He remarried when I was seven. But then, um, he died when I was twelve."

"Oh, wow, I'm so sorry." Dex shot a look at her before returning his gaze to the road. He raised one hand and rubbed the back of his neck. "So … now you live with your stepmother and stepsister?"

"Two stepsisters. Meredith is horrible—she was the one silly enough to step outside the house and let a vampire grab hold of her—but Sienna's amazing. She feels more like a real sister." Elle shifted slightly to face Dex. "Do you have siblings?"

"Oh, uh, no. Unfortunately not. It's just me. So does your mother live far away?" he asked before Elle could comment on him being an only child. "Is that why you live with your step-family?"

Elle turned her eyes toward the windshield. Street lights and flashing billboards zipped by. "My mom isn't alive either."

"Oh, jeez, I—I'm an idiot. I'm so sorry. I shouldn't be asking you all this personal stuff. Do you want to talk about the weather? That's probably a lot safer."

Elle laughed. "And a lot more boring too." She shook her head. "It's okay. I mean, it's not *okay*. I still miss my parents every single day. What I mean is … I don't mind you asking."

"Okay. Well … I'm really sorry you lost both of them. I can't imagine what that's like. And … uh …" He tapped his fingers on the steering wheel. "So, it's a great evening for a party, right?"

Elle chuckled. "Yes, such lovely weather."

"Amazing weather."

Elle pressed her lips together, trying to keep her smile from growing. "This conversation is deteriorating quickly."

"I know, I'm sorry," Dex said with a groan.

"So where's this party happening?" Elle asked. That seemed like a topic that was both safe and relevant.

"Gizella Munroe's home. In the Arabesque Hills."

"Okay. I wonder if it has a good view of the palace." The Arabesque Hills, home to some of the most lavish estates on the outskirts of Vale City, weren't too far from Sovereign Hill, where Belmont Palace sat in all its glittering glory. Elle's old home had been situated somewhere amid those rolling hills. One of the smallest properties in the area—but still sprawling compared to the townhouse she lived in now—it had belonged to Salvia's first husband before Salvia inherited it.

"Yeah, maybe, I'm not sure," Dex said. "Anyway, we need to stop somewhere first so I can pick up something. Sorry about that. I forgot I needed this—thing. But it'll be quick. Do you know Apollo's Apothecary?"

"Yes. But it's closed at night, isn't it?"

"It is, but we'll be going onto the roof."

"Oh." Elle tried to picture the roof of Apollo's Apothecary, but all she saw in her mind's eye was the domed glass top. "Do you mean the greenhouse?" she asked. "Isn't that part of the apothecary?"

"Yes, but we'll be able to get in." Dex offered no other explanation. The car moved speedily toward the upmarket part of town, and Dex made idle conversation about the landmarks they passed. Clearly he was too scared to venture anywhere near personal territory again. "Okay, we're here," he said, bringing the car to a stop and cutting the ignition. He looked around, and Elle noted that the street was empty. "I don't want to leave you alone in the car," Dex said. "It might not be safe."

"I'll be fine," Elle told him. "I mean, I think I'll be fine," she added as the thought of a bunch of vampires all trying to break into the car at once came to mind. "How strong are vampires again?"

"Just come with me. It won't take long. We'll go up to the roof, get the parcel that's waiting for me, and come straight back down."

Elle raised an eyebrow. "A parcel. How mysterious."

"It's just a medicinal thing I forgot to pick up earlier." He climbed out of the car and hurried around to her side, opening the passenger door before she'd finished unbuckling her seat belt. She noticed the gold dust glimmering at his fingertips.

"Ready to throw some magic at someone?" she joked.

"Gotta be prepared when there might be vamps hanging around. I assured you I wouldn't let anything happen to you, didn't I?"

Elle nodded. "True. Can't go back on your word now."

"I don't intend to."

FIVE

Dex's heart thumped a little too fast as he and Elle climbed the spiral staircase attached to the outside of Apollo's Apothecary. What the hell was wrong with him? He was normally so composed, so confident, and here he was making a complete idiot of himself in front of her. Chatting with strangers usually came easily to him. Perhaps because he knew it was unlikely he'd see any of them a second time. There was no pressure to impress anyone. Not that there was any pressure to impress Elle. Was there? There shouldn't be, he reminded himself.

And what was he doing asking about her *family*? What a stupid move. Aside from hurting her by bringing up painful memories, asking about her family left the door open for her to ask about *his* family, and he certainly couldn't go down that road. He should have kept things strictly non-personal. "You can't get too close to her," Xander had reminded him earlier this evening. Dex was aware of that, and he'd said as much, but Xander still gave him that look that said, *I know you. Don't be an idiot.* Dex had to admit that Xander was probably right. He'd already crossed a line with Elle. He'd made a blood oath with her, for goodness sake. How many other strangers had he done that with? Precisely zero.

"I think it's locked," Elle said, and Dex realized she was trying the door at the top of the stairs.

"Let me," he said, reaching around her. He placed his hand over the lock and uttered the charm Cress had given him. Something clicked, and when Elle turned the handle again, the door opened. They stepped inside, and he heard

Elle's quiet intake of breath as she looked around. Plants and flowers of all sizes, shapes and colors filled the circular space, separated by a few winding paved paths. White stone statues were visible here and there, and a fountain with water spilling over the edges of its three tiers sat at the center of the greenhouse. The domed glass roof let in some light from the moon and streetlights, but most of the illumination came from the numerous small lights placed among the plants at floor level.

Dex left Elle to admire the magnificent purple blossoms of a clem-fever bush while he headed for the pegasus statue between the phoenix leaf trees on the right. He bent down and reached behind the statue, expecting to feel a small paper-wrapped parcel. When his hand found nothing, he leaned further to the side and looked behind the statue. There was nothing there. "Dammit," he muttered. Straightening, he brushed the sand from his hands and looked around.

"Is something wrong?" Elle asked.

"It's supposed to be behind this statue here, but I can't find it."

"Can I help you look? How big is this parcel?"

"It should fit in your hand. Wrapped in brown paper."

"Okay, I'll—Holy stars!" Elle breathed. Dex looked up in time to see a large winged shape swooping overhead. "Am I imagining things," she asked, "or was that a dragon?"

Dex swallowed. "That was a dragon." He took a deep breath and resisted the urge to grab Elle's hand and run back down the stairs. He couldn't leave here without the astaleaf potion. Besides, maybe the dragon that had flown past wasn't the dragon he was thinking of. *Unlikely*, his brain reminded him. There weren't exactly loads of dragon shifters around.

Elle rushed to the edge of the greenhouse and pushed a fern aside as she looked down. "It landed in the street in front of the apothecary, but I can't see it anymore. This is so crazy. I've never seen one so close before."

"They're just people, you know," Dex reminded her, smiling a little at her awe.

"I know, I know, I'm sorry. I'm sure they don't want to be gawked at by other races. I just think they're so cool." She turned away from the glass, scooping her hair behind one ear. "Sorry, we're supposed to be looking for your parcel. Um, we can check behind all the other statues? Maybe you just got the wrong—"

"Dex, you're here," a female voice said. Elle whipped around just as Dex turned to face the door and the woman with sleek purple hair. "And you brought a friend," she added, her eyes moving to Elle.

"A new friend," Dex said, hoping Cress would catch his meaning. *A new friend who doesn't know anything about me*, he would have said if Elle wasn't within earshot. "This is Elle," he added, moving closer to her. "Elle, this is Cressida."

"Call me Cress," Cress said, crossing the greenhouse and holding her hand out toward Elle. Gold bangles jangled on her arms.

"Um, hi," Elle said, grasping Cress's hand and shaking it. "Wait, was that— was that you? The dragon. I saw it fly overhead, and then it landed in the street in front of the apothecary."

Cress seemed to examine Elle for several moments before answering. "Yes, that was me." She smiled. "You look shocked, honey. Are you okay?"

"I've just never met a dragon shifter before. And I thought you were fae. Your ears ..." She trailed off.

"I was born fae," Cress explained. "Bitten when I was young. There aren't many of us dragon shifters in Vale City—born or bitten—so I'm not surprised you haven't met any." Her eyes turned to Dex. "You look a little uncomfortable too, Dex," she added with a knowing smile.

He let out a sharp breath. "I just didn't expect you to be here, that's all."

"Right. I'm sure that's it." Cress's eyes moved to Elle, then back to him. She smiled. "Don't worry, I'm not in the business of sharing other people's secrets."

Dex's brows pulled lower over his eyes. *Was it really necessary to say that?* he would have demanded if he'd been alone here with Cress. Then he noticed the way Elle's eyes widened, and suddenly he wondered if Cress might have meant her instead of him. Or had she been referring to both of them? "Have the two of you met before?" he asked.

"She's come into the apothecary," Cress said, at which point Elle's lips pressed together and her cheeks turned pink. "Anyway, I need to speak with you, Dex. That's why I'm here."

Right. The astaleaf potion. He'd been so scared Cress might say something she shouldn't that he'd almost forgotten about it. "I looked behind the pegasus statue, but—"

"It's not there. I know. Come, let's talk." She ushered him to the far side of the greenhouse, and Elle, clearly polite enough to understand that Cress wanted to talk in private, didn't follow. She might still be able to overhear them, but hopefully Cress wouldn't give away anything too important. "I'm afraid I couldn't get any shadowbane to finish the potion," Cress explained. "I went looking again now, which is why I didn't call you, but the plants are all bare. It's the wrong time of month for the flowers to bloom."

"Shadowbane. Is that an important ingredient?"

"It's vital. Astaleaf is the major component, hence the potion's name, but it's ineffective without shadowbane."

Dex felt invisible ropes tighten around his chest. "But this is urgent. I don't have any potion left."

"I'm sorry, Dex, but you didn't give me much notice."

"I know, I'm sorry. I've been distracted with all this vampire business. I didn't realize I was almost out. How long do you think it'll be before you can get this shadowbane?"

"I'll look again tomorrow, just in case some of the plants bloom early, but it could be another four or five days. I'll let you know as soon I've got some."

Dex let out a long sigh. "Okay. Thanks. I guess I can't ask for more than that."

"Will you be okay? Perhaps you should stay home until I can get more for you."

Dex looked across the greenhouse at Elle. If something went wrong tonight at the party ... He shook his head, banishing the thought. "I'll be fine. I had the last few drops this morning. That should keep me going."

"For how long?"

"I don't know. Tonight at the very least. Hopefully longer. But I'll be fine. Xander and Olly are always nearby."

After a pause, Cress nodded. Her bangles clinked as she patted his arm.

Dex looked past a giant-leafed pixie catcher to where Elle was standing, her arms crossed over her chest as she faced away from him and Cress. "I guess we should get to that party then," he called out to her.

She looked over her shoulder with the kind of innocent expression that probably meant she'd heard every word he and Cress had spoken. "Ready when you are."

They returned to the car, and Dex spent the entire ride to the Arabesque Hills waiting for Elle to ask what Cress had meant by keeping other people's secrets. But she didn't bring it up once. Which, he supposed, made sense if she had her own secret to hide. He certainly wasn't about to ask though. He had too many of his own to worry about.

SIX

By the time Dex's car drove below an impressive arched entrance, past a security check, and up a long driveway lined with tall trees, Elle had recovered from her shock at seeing Cress on the roof of Apollo's Apothecary. She'd been terrified Cress would say something about her being a slave. Though it was rude to eavesdrop, she'd held her breath and tried to listen in on as much of their conversation as she could. She didn't hear everything, but Dex hadn't looked at her with horror or revulsion at any point, so that was a good sign. If Cress had told him the truth, he probably would have run a mile by now, abandoning her and his car and their vampire hunting plans. It was one thing to hang out with a human, but to spend time with a slave? People didn't do that. The only reason Sienna's friends occasionally put up with Elle's company—when Elle actually spent an evening with them instead of sneaking off to meet clients— was because Sienna always reminded them that Elle was, first and foremost, family. They'd probably be relieved when they found out she was never allowed to leave the house again with Sienna.

Dex followed the driveway around a huge fountain and parked alongside a row of flashy vehicles. All Elle could do once she was out of the car was stare. The magnificent mansion rose up before her, all clean white angles and huge glass windows and cleverly placed exterior lighting. It put Fernvale, her old home in this area, to shame.

"Ready?" Dex asked.

Elle pulled her gaze from the palatial home. "For an attempted abduction?

Sure. Any time."

"Emphasis on 'attempted'" Dex said. "We won't let anything happen to you."

"I know."

They walked toward the entrance together, and Elle wondered if this was what life was like for normal girls. Not the celebrity mansion part, but the part where it was Friday night and she was walking into a party with a handsome date beside her. *This is not a date*, she reminded herself. Dex wasn't here to hang out with her. He was here to catch vampires. But for someone who spent most of her time either locked in an attic or doing her stepmother's bidding, this was probably as close to a date as she was likely to get. May as well pretend for a few moments before she had to start worrying about vampires pouncing on her.

"Message from Xander," Dex said, looking at his phone. "He's seen someone he might recognize from the fairground the other night, but Olly isn't sure he agrees."

"Well, I guess I just need to hang out near this person and see what happens."

"He says the vamp is currently on the deck overlooking the pool, chatting with a …" Dex frowned at his phone. "Pretty sure that's meant to be 'fae woman,' not 'fell woman.' Anyway." He returned his phone to his pocket. "We can head that way."

Inside the grand entrance hall of Gizella's home, people mingled around a marble sculpture of a naked woman reaching up to touch the two-story high ceiling. Among the many unfamiliar faces were plenty Elle recognized: models, actors, singers, social media personalities. She almost pinched herself to check she wasn't dreaming.

A little further inside, where the lights were dimmer and the music was louder, people hung out in groups or pairs. They stuck their straws into the different colored bubbles of drinks that floated around, or grabbed snacks from the branches of the silver trees that sprouted up here and there, or danced in time to the beat of the music.

If this were a normal date, Elle thought, she and Dex might dance together. What would it feel like to have his hands slide around her waist and pull her closer? Her face warmed, and she gave herself a mental smack over the head for allowing such a silly thought to cross her mind. She hardly knew Dex and here she was daydreaming about him because he was the first guy she happened to spend any amount of time with. She had far more important things to focus on. Like vampires. And getting answers about her mom. And not dying tonight.

She and Dex pushed their way through the crowd and onto a wooden deck that spanned the length of the house. The party continued out here, with people laughing and chatting or reclining on loungers. Below the deck was a rectangular swimming pool with a cascading water feature at one end, and beyond that, a gloriously untamed garden of tangled bushes and glowing neon flowers and meandering streams. Elle leaned against the railing and stared into the twisted mass. "I didn't expect that," she said to Dex with a smile. "The house is so … clean. Straight lines and hard angles and square spaces. And then you get that beautiful overgrown forest down there."

"Yeah. I've never actually met her in person, but from everything I've heard, that's the real Gizella down there. Wild and vibrant. I'm pretty sure someone else picked the house for her."

Elle nodded slowly. "I suppose when you have so many houses, it doesn't really matter if they don't all reflect your personal style."

"I suppose not." Dex turned and leaned his back against the railing. "Okay, that must be him on one of the loungers," he said quietly. "He's the only vampire I can see sitting with a fae woman."

"Yes," Elle answered, not looking around. "I noticed him when we walked out here. He looked up at me briefly, and I *think* his expression changed a little, but it was hard to tell."

"Yeah, I can't say for certain if he was one of the vamps at the fairground the other night. There was too much going on. I didn't get a close look at all of them."

"Me neither," Elle said. "For obvious reasons."

"Okay, I'm going to get us some drinks." Dex pushed away from the railing. "Or pretend to, at least," he added in a lower voice. "If he comes over here and speaks to you, just go along with it. He might want you to follow him somewhere more secluded."

"Which I should also go along with, right? So we can get him somewhere quieter before you guys try to catch him?"

"Yes. Xander, Olly and I will be paying close attention to you, so don't worry. We'll all be close behind, ready to act."

Elle glanced over to her left and spotted Xander laughing with a woman who could have been human or shifter. It was impossible to tell without getting closer and shining a light in her eyes, which was considered rude. "Paying close attention, huh?" Elle asked. "Looks like Xander's paying much closer attention to that woman over there than he is to us."

Dex chuckled. "Don't worry. He's not nearly as distracted as he seems. I trust him with my life."

Elle caught his arm before he could walk away. "What if you don't get the answers you're looking for?" she asked quietly. "He might refuse to tell you anything."

"There are charms the police use to get the truth out of people."

"And you know these charms?"

Dex grinned. "I know a lot of things I probably shouldn't know." He walked away, leaving Elle to lean idly against the railing and try her best to look lonely and in need of a companion. Since she generally tried to do the complete opposite, this wasn't an act she had much experience with. Either she was doing a terrible job, or the vampire genuinely wasn't interested in her—or he'd decided it wasn't the right time for him to act. He didn't move an inch from his comfortable spot on the lounger with the fae woman nestled against him.

Eventually, Dex returned and handed Elle a glass of champagne. "So you weren't just pretending," she said as she took the drink.

"Well, I watched for a while, but our vamp friend showed no sign of moving. I figured I may as well grab some drinks from the waiter I almost bumped into on my way back to you."

"Thanks." Elle took a sip and savored the sweet bubbles dancing across her tongue. She never got the chance to properly enjoy champagne while at home. Salvia only ever gave her a glass during pretend family dinners while entertaining a mark, which usually meant Elle was about to steal someone's memories. Nothing tasted good when she knew that was coming.

"We'll just have to be patient," Dex said. "And maybe walk around a little more. If this vamp here isn't the right one, then somebody else at this party probably is."

Elle turned her head to look at Dex. "Why do you care so much about all of this? The whole human abduction thing. I mean, we're not your own race. Why get so involved?"

He frowned. "It's the right thing to do. Isn't that enough?"

"So you don't have any other agenda?"

He opened his mouth, appeared to choke on something, then thumped his fist against his chest as he recovered.

Elle straightened, unsure if she should do something to help him. "Are you okay?"

"Yes, I just …" He cleared his throat. "That was weird. Um … I forgot I made an oath not to lie to you."

"Oh." The implication of his words settled over her. "I see."

"Look, I don't *want* to lie," he added quickly. "I don't mind admitting I have another agenda. It's just that it's kind of … personal. It seemed easier to say no."

"Oh, okay." Elle nodded. "That's fine, don't worry. You don't have to explain anything. It really doesn't matter to me what your motives are. You're trying to help humans, and that's great. And, I mean, there are things in my life I'd prefer not to talk about, so I completely—"

"No, it's okay," Dex said. "I don't mind—"

"It's fine, really," she insisted. "We don't have to get personal."

He hesitated, his mouth half open. Something shifted in his expression. Something … was he *hurt* by what she'd said? "Right. Of course." He looked away, leaving Elle with the distinct impression she'd just done something wrong. But if she'd let him talk about whatever this personal issue was, then he might have expected her to reciprocate, and she couldn't do that. She'd told him about her parents, but that was enough. He didn't need to know what a messed-up home situation she had now.

"Um, you suggested we walk around a bit more," she said.

"Oh, yes." He smiled at her, and it seemed the awkward moment may have passed. "If there are other vampires around, it'll give them a chance to see you, and hopefully some of them are Allegiant vampires."

"Good idea." Elle took another sip of her champagne before moving away from the deck railing. She and Dex returned to the inside of the home and made their way slowly through the crowd. "Do you mind if I look for a bathroom quickly?" she asked after another few minutes, her voice raised over the music.

"Sure. Want me to hold that?" He nodded toward her drink.

"Thanks."

"And don't worry about anyone following you," he added. "I'll keep an eye on things."

Elle made her way between the partygoers and around the silver trees with endlessly replenishing snacks until she noticed a passageway leading off the entrance hall. Moving closer, she spotted a closed door a few feet into the passageway and three women—all fae—waiting outside. "Is this queue for the bathroom?" she asked as she reached the women.

One looked over her shoulder at Elle. "Ugh, yes. I feel like I've been waiting forever." She turned away and slumped against the wall, her shoulder rubbing the edge of a canvas painting that was probably worth millions.

Footsteps stopped behind Elle. Someone sighed and said, "And the bathroom on the other side of the hallway is busy too. I'm going to find one upstairs. Want to come?"

"Yeah, okay," Elle answered, realizing only as she turned that the woman behind her was a vampire. Fear shot through her, and she almost declined the woman's offer, but she was *supposed* to let someone attempt to catch her, not try to avoid it. Hoping she hadn't paused long enough for it to be noticeable, she followed the woman, her eyes scanning the crowd for Dex. She found his gaze, inclined her head in the smallest of nods toward the woman, and looked away. She knew he would follow.

She increased her pace and reached the woman's side as the two of them made their way through the crowd toward the stairs. Elle snuck a sideways glance at the woman—smooth milky skin, hair so dark it was almost black, a serene expression on her face—but it was impossible to tell whether she meant Elle any harm. She was about to look away when she noticed a gold letter A hanging from a chain around the woman's neck. "What does the A stand for?" she asked. The thought that it might stand for Allegiant flashed through her mind, but that was far too obvious.

"Alissa," the woman said as they reached the stairs. She didn't ask for Elle's name, which Elle figured was probably because she already knew it.

"Are these parties always so crowded?" Elle asked.

"Oh, I haven't been before. I came with someone. Well, followed someone, if we're going to get technical," she added.

Followed someone, huh? Elle thought. She almost asked if that someone was her. "How'd you get past security if you weren't with someone on the list?"

"Slipped in as part of a larger crowd. It wasn't that hard. Oh, wow, that is the most hideous piece of art I've ever seen." As they reached the top of the stairs, Alissa stopped in front of a sculpture of a giant, wrinkled thumb with an amateurish smiley face drawn onto the cracked, ridged nail. "I sure hope Gizella Munroe didn't choose this herself."

"Probably not," Elle said, thinking of the bright splashes of color in the tangled garden below. "Don't people in positions like hers pay someone else to fill their homes with expensive and completely unnecessary stuff?"

Alissa gave Elle the kind of genuine smile that made her think the two of them could have been friends if Alissa wasn't about to abduct her. "You're right. That is how it works."

Elle looked past the giant thumb and noticed a few other people milling around. If Alissa was going to attempt something without an audience, she would have to lead Elle somewhere else in order to do it. "That looks like a bathroom through there," Elle said, pointing to an open door. "Do you want to go first?"

"That's okay. You go."

Elle took a hesitant step forward, still watching Alissa. Was it possible she'd got this all wrong and Alissa had nothing to do with the Allegiant?

"Everything okay?" Alissa asked, a small frown creasing her brow.

"Yes, sorry, I just … thought I saw someone I recognized."

"Oh, okay." Alissa flashed a wide smile—which froze a moment later as her gaze flicked past Elle, then bounced back to her. The smile vanished. "You need to get out of here. Immediately."

Elle's heart skipped a beat. "Why?"

"Because someone's here for you."

Elle paused. Was this part of the vampires' plan to get hold of her, or was Alissa genuinely trying to help?

"Seriously, you need to leave!" Alissa grabbed Elle's arm and pulled her in the opposite direction. Elle's instinct was to fight her off, but she managed to remain compliant. She knew Dex or one of the others would be watching, ready to pull her out of harm's way when the moment was right.

"You're one of them," she said as Alissa dragged her into a bedroom.

"I don't know what you're talking about," Alissa answered. She slammed the door shut, locked it, and pushed a dresser in front of the door as if it weighed no more than a flimsy chair. Then she tugged Elle toward the window.

"Do you know about my mother?"

"What?" Alissa flashed a confused look in Elle's direction.

"The last vampire who dragged me out of a bar said something about my mother. I want to know—Whoa, hang on. You're pushing me out of a window?"

"We're jumping," Alissa said. A second later, Elle found herself draped over Alissa's shoulder, and as something crashed against the door behind them, Alissa jumped. Elle screeched as the wall flashed past her. She squeezed her eyes shut, bracing for the impact of hitting the ground, but the jolt as Alissa landed wasn't nearly as bad as Elle expected.

"Show-off," she gasped, struggling for breath.

"I'm going to run now," Alissa said. "Please don't throw up on me."

"Tell me about my mother."

"I don't know—Hey!"

Someone landed behind Alissa, and Elle looked up in time to see the face of a vampire she recognized. His hands flashed forward, and then Alissa was falling, taking Elle down with her. "Don't do this, Azriel!" Alissa shouted.

Azriel. So that was his name. The vampire with the barcode tattoo and the answers about Elle's mother. Something gripped her waist. She was tugged upward, and the night whirled around her. *Don't fight*, she reminded herself, but her self-preservation instinct was too deeply ingrained, and before she knew it she'd shoved her elbow in his face and kicked backward as hard as she could. *And* that's *why I'm wearing chunky boots.* The random thought flashed through her mind as Azriel grunted in her ear. But his grip on her remained just as tight. With a burst of speed, he began running. The garden blurred past.

Then, with a flash of golden sparks and dust, everything slowed. The next thing Elle knew, she was tumbling across the grass. She came to a halt on her back, but the stars seemed to bounce around in the sky far above her. "Are you okay?" Dex asked, his face in front of hers. The world spun around as he lifted her to her feet.

"Yeah … just … everything's spinning." She stumbled sideways and blinked repeatedly.

"A little help over here!" Olly shouted.

Dex raced away as Elle caught herself against a tree. *Don't throw up and don't fall over*, she told herself as she blinked rapidly and breathed deeply. As the world slowly settled, she squinted at the golden glow not too far away and tried to figure out what was going on. A loop of magic was wrapped tightly around Azriel, and three golden glowing ropes were attached to the loop. Dex, Xander and Olly each hung onto the end of one of these ropes, and all seemed to be struggling to keep Azriel from writhing wildly about.

"Just hit him with enough to make him pass out!" Xander shouted.

"I'm trying!" Dex yelled back, throwing one hand out and releasing a flash of magic. "If you could get him to stop moving, that would be great." With a fierce cry and a powerful tug on the rope, Dex heaved Azriel toward him and slammed his outspread hand into the vampire's chest. Gold dust radiated away from the point of contact. Azriel staggered backward before falling to his knees.

In a flash of motion too fast for Elle to shout a warning, someone raced up behind Dex and leaped onto his back. It was Alissa, Elle realized. Just minutes ago, she'd helped Elle, and now she was attacking Dex. And if she bit him …

"No," Elle said out loud. She ran forward. Olly and Xander were trying to restrain Azriel—who *still* hadn't passed out—and no one was helping Dex. So Elle did the only thing she could think of—which turned out to be the exact same thing Alissa had done. Elle jumped onto the vampire woman's back and tried to wrench her away from Dex.

"What the hell?" Alissa shouted. She thrust backward with one elbow, but her angle was wrong, and Elle only wrapped her arms tighter around Alissa's neck. "Get *off!*" Alissa hissed. Her grip loosened on Dex. She turned a little, exposing her chest, and a flash of magic—from Xander or Olly, Elle wasn't sure—sizzled by, catching Alissa's shoulder. She let go of Dex with a cry and finally managed to dislodge Elle, who landed on her backside on the grass.

With a roar, Azriel jerked one shoulder forward, and then the other, yanking the two remaining ropes away from Xander and Olly. Alissa was by his side in a second, helping him to his feet. He stumbled forward a step or two, then seemed to recover enough to start running. A moment later, he'd taken off with Alissa, while Dex and the others hurled magic uselessly after the two vampires.

"What the hell?" Dex gasped. "How strong was that vamp?"

"Are you okay?" Xander asked.

Elle climbed to her feet. "Did she bite you?" she asked as she ran toward Dex.

"I don't think so." Dex clutched his neck. "I don't feel anything. Do you see any blood?"

Elle pulled his hands away from his neck. "No."

"Hey!" a new voice shouted.

"What now?" Xander grumbled, looking around.

"Security guards," Olly answered. "Lots of them."

"Definitely time to leave," Dex said.

They ran through the tangled garden, dodging bushes and trees and couples making out, and eventually curved around the side of the house and came out near the parked vehicles. "Hurry up!" Xander shouted, opening one of the back doors of Dex's car before climbing into the front passenger seat. As Dex reached the driver's side, Elle tumbled through the open back door. Olly threw himself in after her. "Drive!" Xander yelled, but the car was already moving. Olly yanked the back door shut as Dex pulled away with a screech of tires.

"Everyone okay?" he asked. "Elle?"

"Yeah. Yes." She pushed her hair out of her eyes as she sat up. "I'm fine."

"Do you think anyone got a good look at us?" Olly asked.

"Worried you won't be able to show your pretty face at one of these parties again?" Xander asked, turning in his seat to face Olly with a grin.

"You know why I'm worried," Olly said.

"I doubt most of the people at that party are even aware something just happened," Dex said. "And the security guys didn't get close enough to see us. We're fine." He sped past the security check and turned sharply at the bottom of the driveway. Elle slid across the seat and crashed into Olly.

"I'm sorry, I'm sorry," she said, then started laughing.

"What?" Dex asked.

She scrambled back to the other side of the car and pulled the seatbelt across her body, still chuckling. "Nothing."

"You sure you're okay?" Olly asked.

"Yes." Well, that wasn't strictly true. She'd missed out on her chance to pee and her bladder was starting to complain, but that wasn't the kind of thing she needed to share with three guys. "It's just … I don't know. Is it crazy that part of me thinks that was kind of fun?"

Dex caught her eye in the rearview mirror. He grinned. "Only the good kind of crazy."

SEVEN

SOMEWHERE NEAR THE TOP OF A HIGH-RISE APARTMENT BUILDING IN VALE CITY, Azriel sat at a polished oak table contemplating his most recent failure. The aches and pains from his earlier encounter with the three fae had just about faded, but his wounded pride remained.

On the other side of the table, a blond man poured himself a drink. He could have been about thirty years old, or he could have been three hundred. He could have been older or younger than Azriel. It was impossible to tell with vampires, and it didn't matter. Age was simply a number.

Without offering Azriel a drink, the man dragged a chair out from beneath the table, letting it scrape slowly across the floor. He sat. He swirled the amber liquid in his glass before placing it on the table. "I'm disappointed, Azriel. You came highly recommended, but I'm starting to doubt your abilities. After Leroy spotted her at that party and called you, I figured it was a done deal. What happened?"

Azriel folded his arms and took a calming breath as he stared out of the apartment's floor-to-ceiling windows at the glimmering city lights. He didn't appreciate being told off like a child, but it wouldn't do to lose his temper. "It was a setup, Lev. Somebody wanted to catch me."

"I see. Well, aren't you special."

Azriel's hands clenched into fists beneath his arms. "Not particularly. I assume somebody wants answers, and they'll take them from whoever they can get hold of."

"Well, if it really was a setup—and who knows whether you're simply being paranoid—then I can't send you out again. This girl and her friends will recognize you. The only way we'll make this work is if I send someone they haven't seen before."

"Like me?" The voice came from the shadowed doorway leading to the bedrooms. Azriel knew without having to look that it was Nik, Lev's son. He'd met Nik several times when he first joined the Allegiant.

"Perhaps," Lev said as Nik walked forward. With their matching white-blond hair, red eyes and unlined faces, they could have been brothers instead of father and son.

"Nik," Azriel said, inclining his head in a brief nod of greeting. "How's it going being experimented on?"

Nik rolled his shoulders. "To be honest, I've never felt better. Younger. More powerful. I wonder if this is what those insufferable fae feel like all the time."

Azriel hated to show an interest, but he couldn't hide his curiosity. "So it's working?"

"Feels like it."

Azriel looked at Lev. "If you've figured out how to do it, then why are we hunting down this girl?"

"I don't know the complete method," Lev said. "It's possible I'm leaving something out. Something important. That's why I need her. And I'd have her by now if you hadn't failed three times."

"I did find her," Azriel reminded him quietly.

"True. That is something. But not enough. She's currently still out there."

Azriel decided not to argue. He was certain he could catch the girl if given another chance, but if Lev had other plans, that was fine. "Well, if you have no further use for me—" Azriel placed his palms on the table and pushed himself up "—then my work here is done." He stepped around the chair and pushed it back into place beneath the table. He would have preferred to slam it, perhaps cracking both the table and the chair, but he didn't need these people knowing they could so easily get under his skin.

"Don't think you're off the hook," Lev said. He raised his glass to his lips and tipped the contents down his throat. Ice blocks clinked as he lowered the glass to the table. "You'll be required here tomorrow night for another meeting."

"Regarding what?"

"Azriel, don't tell me you've forgotten the meaning of the word allegiant."

Azriel narrowed his eyes. "Of course I haven't forgotten. My *allegiance*—" he bit the word out angrily—"is to the true king."

"Then it doesn't matter what tomorrow's meeting is about. If it's to serve your true king, you'll do whatever's required of you."

Azriel let out a long breath. "Of course."

Lev cocked his head, his gaze sliding down and settling somewhere near the collar of Azriel's shirt. "You never did tell me about that tattoo of yours."

"And I don't intend to." With that, Azriel strode to the door, yanked it open, and left the apartment. He allowed himself the duration of the elevator ride to wallow in the dark memories that had surfaced at Lev's mention of the tattoo, but when the doors slid open, he banished them.

Out on the street, he was about to run when a familiar voice called his name. He turned back to face Alissa, his hands fisting at his sides. "How dare you get between me and that girl? Don't you know who she is? I was *so* close. I almost—"

"Of course I know who she is," Alissa answered. "That's why I had to stop you."

"You don't know what you've cost us."

Alissa's red eyes glinted in the light cast by the street lamps. "Az, why are you still involved with these people? Their agenda is … it's insane."

"You know why. And as my sister, you're supposed to be on my side."

"I don't have to be on your side when you're doing the wrong thing."

"Maybe you're the one who's wrong." It was a stupid, petty thing to say, and it reminded him of a time many years ago when the two of them were children.

"I'm not," she said, and as Azriel turned to race away, part of him feared she might be right.

EIGHT

"**T**HEY MUST SUSPECT BY NOW THAT IT WAS A SETUP," Elle WHISPERED INTO HER phone. "I mean, you and the others were right there at the correct moment, ready to catch him. They can't possibly think that was a coincidence." It was Saturday morning, and after gathering all the breakfast dishes and cleaning the kitchen, she'd hurried up to the attic to answer a call she was expecting from Dex. They tried not to speak in specifics. No names or places. It wasn't something Elle would have considered, but Dex was worried someone might be listening.

"Yes," he said. "I'm sure they must—Wait, why are you whispering?"

"I'm not whispering," she whispered. "Just … talking quietly. I don't want to disturb my family."

"Oh. Okay. Anyway, yes," he continued. "They probably suspect something. But if they want you badly enough, that won't stop them from trying again. There'll probably just be more of them next time."

"Which means you need more people on your side as well."

Dex sighed. "That isn't possible. It's just the three of us. Nobody else knows about this."

"What if you tell—" She stopped, reminding herself about the 'no specifics' rule. "We need to talk in person again," she said.

"Elle!" Meredith's screech reached all the way up the stairs and through the closed attic door.

"I'm sorry, I have to go," Elle said.

"Okay, I'll text you about meeting up somewhere."

Elle switched her phone off and shoved it beneath her mattress before hurrying downstairs. She rushed into Meredith's bedroom, where Meredith was standing in front of her mirror in a plain, cream-colored dress. Sienna sat on the bed with a tablet in her hands. "Is everything okay?" Elle asked.

Without looking around at her, Meredith waved toward a wet patch on the carpet. "There's a mess over there."

"Oh. I see."

Meredith met Elle's gaze in the mirror and narrowed her eyes. "So you need to clean it up."

"Yes, of course. What is it?"

"Jeez, it's just water. The wind blew the curtain and knocked my glass over or something. Why does it matter what it is?"

"I'll help you," Sienna said before Elle could get herself into trouble by explaining that it was useful to know whether soap was needed or not. Sienna scooted to the edge of the bed. "It'll be quick. I've perfected the sponge charm with—"

"Don't," Meredith snapped, spinning around and glaring at Sienna. "It's Elle's job to clean. Don't waste your magic."

"It's fine," Elle said to Sienna. She hurried to the kitchen and returned with a small towel. "Where's the dressmaker?" she asked as she crouched down and pressed the towel against the carpet. "I thought I heard someone arrive a few minutes ago."

"Ohmygosh, you are so behind the times," Meredith said. "They don't send actual people anymore to do measurements and quotes and things."

"Well, some of them do," Sienna corrected. "The ones who cost a lot. The ones who work for recognizable designer names. But we can barely afford the fee to get a quote from people like that, let alone an actual custom-made dress."

"Yes, okay, but the people who send the magic sample dresses are just as good," Meredith said. "And besides, all you're getting is a ready-made, store-bought dress, so you don't get to judge my dressmakers and their process."

"Whatever," Sienna said with a shrug.

"Is that a magic sample dress?" Elle asked, nodding at the dress Meredith was wearing. She refolded the towel and pressed it into the carpet again.

"Yes. And there's this book that comes with it ..." Meredith moved to her desk and lifted a large hardcover book into her arms. "You can select different styles." She turned several pages before touching something, and her dress changed instantly from a simple sleeveless shift dress to a ballgown with a tight bodice and a huge poufy skirt. "Ooh! Cool, right? And then the second half of the book has all these fabric samples." She flipped to where the paper pages became fabric pages of different colors. She touched one, and the stiff cream fabric became a softer glittery purple.

"That's actually really pretty," Sienna said begrudgingly.

"Yeah. So then I send my style choice and fabric choice back to the dressmaker—and the dress itself records all my measurements—and then the dressmaker sends a quote for how much the dress will cost. Easy peasy."

"That is quite cool," Elle admitted. The wet section of the carpet was now a barely visible damp patch, so she stood and balled the towel in her hands.

"It is. I guess you can stay if you want," Meredith added imperiously. "I doubt you'll ever get to experience something like this yourself. You may as well watch me."

How generous of you, Elle thought. She looked at Sienna, who didn't bother hiding her rolling eyes. Suppressing a smile, Elle asked, "Where's your Mom? I thought she'd want to be here for this."

"She was supposed to be back by now," Meredith said, "but I guess her coffee date went on too long or something. She was meeting Mrs. What's-Her-Face with the giant mole. You know how she can talk forever."

"Yes," Elle said with a nod, though she had no idea who Meredith was talking about.

"Is this everything?" Sienna asked, looking up from Meredith's tablet. "All the articles you have about the prince? 'Cause this is a lot. I don't know when you're going to have time to read it all before the ball."

"No, that's just one of three folders. And what do you mean I won't have time? I've read most of it already."

"Oh. But … don't you have college courses you're supposed to be doing tons of reading for?"

"Yes, but obviously this is more important. What do you think of this style and color?" Meredith turned to the right and then the left, admiring her form-fitting ruby dress from all angles. Aside from a few small pieces of opaque fabric that covered the important bits, it was made mainly from sheer lace.

"Too sexy," Sienna said immediately.

"No such thing," Meredith answered.

"Yes there is. You don't want to look like you're wearing lingerie."

"Don't I?"

"No," Sienna and Elle said at the same time.

"But I want to grab his attention. This might be the best way."

Elle bit her lip. She and Sienna needed to *prevent* Meredith from grabbing the prince's attention, but it was going to be difficult if she insisted on walking into the palace wearing little more than underwear.

"Why don't you ask Mom when she gets home?" Sienna suggested.

"Obviously I'm going to ask Mom as well. Her opinion is way more important than yours."

Sienna sighed and returned her attention to the tablet. Elle crossed the room and sat beside her on the bed. "So you've memorized all this random stuff?" Sienna asked. "His favorite color and hobbies and …" She brought the tablet closer to her face. "Is there seriously an article about how he likes his *eggs* cooked?"

"Yes. Medium poached. There are articles about *everything*, Sienna. Mostly from the past two years, ever since Prince Remy died and everyone started talking about Prince Chevalier instead. But one of my other folders has all the articles I could find from when he was younger."

Elle leaned back on her hands and watched Sienna swiping through articles and photos. She remembered when the older prince had died. There'd been a huge show of mourning, but it wasn't long before all the gossip turned to Prince Chevalier, the new heir to the throne.

"He's only twenty-three," Sienna said, zooming in on some smaller text.

"Why is his father so desperate for him to marry? Surely he's still got time."

"No idea." Meredith tapped her book and changed her dress style yet again. "It's probably some royal thing we don't know about. Thou shalt be married by age twenty-four or something."

"Seriously? That's one of the stupidest things I've ever heard come out of your mouth, and you say a *lot* of stupid—"

"Sienna! If you're going to be mean, then get out of my room."

"Sorry, sorry, sorry." Sienna swiped the screen again. "Why aren't there any recent photos of him? I can't find anything where he's more than like … ten years old."

"Quite a cute ten year old, though," Elle added, leaning forward to get a look at the fair-haired boy.

"Oh my gosh, don't you *ever* pay attention to any of the gossip?" Meredith asked.

"No," Sienna said.

"It's because of his illness. It's bad luck to photograph fae who are seriously ill. It, like, condemns them to eternal sickness."

Elle met Sienna's gaze. Sienna rolled her eyes again, and Elle bit her lip to keep from laughing. Did Meredith honestly believe all the stupid things she said?

"That's the main reason all my friends are so excited to go to this ball," Meredith continued, swaying her hips and swishing her many-layered tulle skirt from side to side. "None of them think they'll actually be chosen. They just want to see what Prince Chevalier looks like. I, however, don't actually care. I just want to be a princess and live in a palace."

Sienna opened her mouth, but the sound of the front door banging shut interrupted whatever she was going to say. "Must be your mom," Elle said, standing up. Salvia wouldn't be happy if she caught Elle 'lazing about' on Meredith's bed. It would be better if she thought Elle was patiently waiting to serve one or both of her stepsisters.

"We're in here!" Meredith shouted. "Come and see the magic sample dress they sent over from Darcy's Delightful Dresses."

"In a minute," Salvia called back. Her footsteps moved past Meredith's bedroom to her own. Several moments of quiet followed before those footsteps rushed back out. Salvia raced into Meredith's room and stopped at the sight of Elle. Fury burned in her eyes. "Did you take it?"

Instinctively, Elle raised her hands. "No. What? I didn't take anything."

"Mom, what are you talking about?" Sienna asked.

"The wish is gone."

"*What?*"

"The wish. I picked it up from Apollo's yesterday afternoon, along with the authentication certificate. They offered me a price, and I told them I'd need to think about it. Sometime between last night and right now, the wish has gone missing from my bedroom." Her eyes returned to Elle. "And since there's no sign of a break-in—"

"I wouldn't dare," Elle said, her hands still raised in surrender. She almost added that Salvia could search the attic if she wanted to, but that would be a bad idea. She might find Elle's hidden collection of Essence.

"It was me," Meredith said quietly.

"What?" Salvia's gaze snapped toward her favorite daughter.

With her eyes fixed on the floor, Meredith said, "You told me last night that the wish was real and they offered a decent amount of money for it. I knew you'd probably want to sell it instead of letting me use it, so I—I took it and made a wish."

"You *used it?*" Salvia demanded.

Meredith finally raised her eyes and met her mother's gaze. She set her jaw. "I did."

Salvia took in a deep, shuddering breath. "What exactly did you wish for?"

"When the prince sees me, he'll want to marry me."

"That's what you said? Those are the exact words you used?"

"Pretty much. I said, 'I wish that when Prince Chevalier sees me, he'll want to marry me.'"

Salvia sighed.

"What?" Meredith asked. "Don't you think that's good enough?"

"I suppose it might work," Salvia said, "if a first-tier wish is strong enough to grant something like that."

Meredith folded her arms. "What were you going to suggest then?"

"I was thinking that perhaps we scour the entire catalog of wishes and find something we *know* would work for a first-tier wish, and somehow use it to our advantage."

"That's ridiculous, Mom. The catalog is ginormous. There aren't enough hours between now and the ball to read every entry in the first-tier wish section."

"That's probably true," Sienna murmured.

"I didn't ask you," Salvia snapped. "And what are *you* doing in here?" she asked Elle.

"I—I was cleaning." Elle pointed at the faint patch on the carpet. "Meredith asked me to."

"Well, you can both leave now. Meredith and I have important work to do. Give me that," she added, snatching the book from Meredith's hands. "Let's see if we can make this work."

Elle left the room without having to be told twice. Sienna's quiet footsteps followed closely behind her. "This is a disaster," Sienna whispered as they reached the kitchen. "The wish thing. What if it *works*? I don't want to be stuck in a palace for the rest of my life with a mother who abuses me. And I know she'll have plenty of other things to keep her busy while living in a palace, but she'll still be able to hurt us. I know she will."

"I know." Elle pushed her hand through her hair. "I mean, you'll probably still have enough freedom that you could run away at some point, but loads of people will recognize you by then. It'll be so much harder."

"And you ..." Sienna shook her head. "I don't think the king treats slaves very well."

"I'll probably be chained up like an animal. It'll be impossible to earn more Essence and buy a wish."

Sienna pressed her hands over her face. When she lowered them, her eyes were red and rimmed with tears. "Okay, so what do we do? Meredith's made this stupid wish now. We can't undo that."

"You just have to make sure the prince doesn't see her. If he does, the wish might work."

"It's going to be almost impossible to keep her away from him."

"I know. But you'll have to do whatever it takes. Even if she hates you for it. Even if Salvia sees you and ends up punishing me because of your actions."

"Elle …"

Elle gripped Sienna's shoulders and stared determinedly into her eyes. "You can do this."

NINE

That evening, Elle descended the stairs leading from the side of Penryn Pier down to the beach and stepped onto the sand. The outdoor bar Dex had asked her to meet at was a little further along the beach, its tables and chairs arranged on the sand beneath a rickety structure fashioned from bamboo poles and palm fronds. Despite its rundown appearance, it was clearly popular, as were the other establishments lined up along this part of the beach. It was comforting to know there were so many people around, but Elle still found herself walking faster than necessary, aware of the possibility of lurking vampires.

"Hey." Dex waved her over as she neared the bar. He sat at a small table, and she slipped into the chair opposite his. "I was hoping you'd be able to meet earlier in the day," he added.

"I'm sorry, I had—family obligations." She removed her canvas bag from her shoulder and dumped it on her lap. "Why, do you have other plans tonight?"

"No, it's just that it's safer to meet during the day. There could be vampires out here tonight. Allegiant vampires." He shifted forward in his seat and leaned his elbows on the table. His arresting silver-blue eyes didn't move from her face, but she was definitely getting better at pretending they had no effect on her breath or her pulse.

"There could be," she said as she tucked her hair behind one ear. "And that would be a *good* thing, remember? Then we wouldn't need to make another plan to try and lure them in."

He paused, then nodded. "Right, yes, of course."

"But we don't know if that will happen, so we should make a new plan just in case."

"Do you have a suggestion?" he asked. "There was something you wanted to say on the phone."

"Well, I think we might need to be more direct about this. Rather than going out at night and hoping the right vampires show up, I could contact them and ask to meet. I still have the number for the vampire who first abducted me. The one who tried again last night. So what if I just send him a message and say I want to meet at a certain time and place? Obviously he'll be suspicious, but I can say that I realize he wants me for some reason, and that I'll agree to help him if he gives me answers about my mother."

"Your mother?"

"Yes, remember I told you I thought he said something about her?"

"Yes." Dex frowned. "But even if you say you want answers, he'll still suspect it's a trap. So why would he agree to meet?"

"You said it yourself when we spoke on the phone: If these vampires want me badly enough, then they'll come even if they know it's a trap. Azriel will probably bring a whole load of other vampires with him, which is why you need more backup."

"Azriel?"

"Yes, I heard Alissa—the other vampire—say his name last night."

"Okay, but I don't have more backup."

"But the police do. That's the part I was going to say on the phone." Elle shifted forward slightly. "You should tell them what we're planning. You said you're going to tell them whatever you manage to find out once you catch a vampire, so why not tell them now? Surely that's the more legal route anyway? I mean, you're not actually authorized to hold people in custody and question them, are you?"

Dex opened his mouth and choked on whatever he'd been about to say. He cleared his throat and said, "That blood oath we made is getting annoying."

Elle raised her eyebrows. "You were about to lie to me?"

"No. I was going to use the words 'not exactly' instead of the word 'no,' which I guess isn't the complete truth, so the blood oath's magic decided to choke me."

Elle blinked. "Now I've forgotten what my question was."

"You asked if I'm authorized to hold people in custody and question them. The completely truthful answer is *no*."

"Right, I didn't think so. Which means you should tell the police *before* this happens. You can call them with an anonymous tip or something. Tell them an attempted abduction is going to take place and there's a chance to catch lots of vampires and finally get to the bottom of this abduction thing. Then they can lie in wait and catch all these vampires instead of you and your friends trying to do it and probably getting yourselves arrested in the process."

Dex watched her for several moments. Then the corner of his mouth lifted in a half smile. "Okay. I guess we can do that."

"Really?"

"Yes."

"Okay, then I'm going to send Azriel a message now." She reached into her bag. It didn't contain much. Just her a phone—which Salvia still didn't know about—and a sweater in case the night grew colder. "Should I ask him to meet tomorrow night?"

"Yes. And it doesn't matter what location you suggest, since he'll probably insist on a different one."

"Okay." Elle quickly typed a message before lifting the edge of her bag and dropping her phone inside. A barely audible squeak ensued, followed by a rush of motion as a small creature zoomed past her hand and landed on the table. The pixie's delicate wings quivered as she righted her pistachio shell hat. Then she dove off the table and flew away.

"Scared of pixies, huh?" Dex asked with a grin.

Elle laughed. "Completely terrified, clearly. What's your biggest fear?"

"My father," Dex said without missing a beat. Then his grin vanished. His eyes widened.

"Crap," Elle whispered. "The blood oath. I'm so sorry, I didn't mean for you to—"

"It's … it's okay." Dex's face was turning red. "I didn't even think, or I would have tried to make something up, and then the oath would have … Anyway. Moving on."

"Yes, definitely. Um, so, the pixie. I think she lives somewhere in my house because I keep finding her in random places—the pantry, inside a flower pot, under a bed—and every time I shoo her away she disappears out of a window, but then I end up finding her somewhere else in the house or in my bag."

Dex's lips pulled into an almost-natural smile. "So you are afraid of pixies?"

"What? No, not at all."

"But you said you shoo her away."

"Oh, yes. That's because my stepmother kills pixies when she finds them in the house."

Dex raised his eyebrows. "That's quite extreme."

"Yes, my stepmother is … extreme." At a loss for what to say next, Elle lapsed into silence. Dex didn't say anything either. It seemed the awkward moment hadn't entirely passed yet. Elle looked around. "Allegiant vampires could be here right now," she said in a low voice.

"Yeah. They could be."

"So …" She looked at him. "Should we hang out here for a while? Are Olly and Xander nearby, in case you need backup?"

"Yes. Are you able to stay out for a while longer? I mean, you don't have to get back home yet?"

"Not just yet. My lift—the police officer—isn't coming back here until eleven."

"So they're still patrolling your street?"

"Yes, though I think they might finish up tonight or tomorrow. They certainly seem to be tired of hanging out there. And what about you? You definitely don't have anywhere else you need to be tonight?"

"Nope. Not yet. I'm all yours. I mean, you know—"

"I know," she said with a smile. *This is not a date*, she reminded herself firmly. *This is not. A. Date.* But her grin refused to disappear.

Until her phone buzzed in her bag. Her heart climbed into her throat as she reached for the phone and turned it over. Her pulse raced faster as she read the message on the screen.

"What did he say?" Dex asked.

Elle looked up. "He said okay. He'll meet me tomorrow night."

TEN

A chill breeze lifted Elle's hair as she waited alone at one end of a bridge in Belgravia. Interestingly, this spot wasn't far from the abandoned fairground where she'd woken up surrounded by vampires. Clearly they liked to hang out in this area. She wrapped her arms around herself as a winged creature—too big to be a bat, but nowhere near the size of a dragon shifter—swooped overhead and disappeared. Silence descended again. It was easy to believe she was truly alone out here. But Dex, Xander and Olly were hiding nearby, and hopefully the police had taken Dex's anonymous tip seriously and weren't too far away either.

A blur of movement on the other side of the bridge caught Elle's attention, but when she looked more closely, it was gone. She squinted into the night, her eyes scanning the outline of trees, lamp posts, a warehouse in the distance, a manhole cover in the road. Then her breath caught and her heart stumbled over itself at the sight of the shape leaning against the railing at the other end of the bridge: a man. A man who hadn't been there seconds before.

He peeled himself away from the shadows and began walking slowly toward Elle. She took a deep breath, clenched her shaking hands into fists, and moved forward. *I'll be fine*, she told herself with each step. Dex was beneath the bridge, Xander was on the road somewhere ahead of her, and Olly was behind her. If Azriel grabbed Elle and ran, someone would stop him with magic, no matter which way he chose to go.

They were several paces away from one another when she realized the vampire coming toward her wasn't Azriel. The lamplight behind him caught on the edges of his white-blond hair, forming a halo-like glow around his head.

Elle stopped. "You're not Azriel."

"No. My name is Nik." He took another step toward her, and then another. By the time he stopped, he was close enough that Elle could make out his red eyes through the darkness. "You're Estelle Winter, correct?"

"Correct. What do you know about my mother?"

"It doesn't matter what I know. We want to know what *you* know."

"Well I want to know what Azriel meant when he said my mother tried to hide me from you. Why did she do that? How was she involved with vampires?"

Nik looked around. "Where are your friends hiding?"

"What do you mean?"

"I know they're here."

"Where are *your* friends hiding?" Elle countered.

"I don't need friends. I can handle this on my own."

"I don't believe you."

He laughed. "Would you like to see what I can do?"

Elle shivered. She wanted to say no, but it wouldn't make a difference, so she kept her mouth shut. Nik slowly raised his hands, palms facing upward. Elle took an instinctive step back. Another few seconds passed before she made sense of what she was seeing: gold dust—*faerie* dust—falling from his fingers. *Not possible*, her brain said, pushing back against what her eyes were telling her.

Gold light flashed away from him, shoving Elle backward and almost knocking her to the ground. But after several stumbling steps, she caught her balance. Magic rippled off Nik in gold waves, then zapped forward and wrapped around Elle. It tugged her right up against him, and for a moment all she could see was his manic grin. "I bet you taste delicious," he whispered.

Then something flashed between them, and a strong wind shoved her to the side. "Run!" came Dex's shout. Elle didn't need to be told twice. A vampire in possession of magic? She was totally out of her league. As she ran away, Xander tore past her in the opposite direction. Thank goodness. Dex might be strong and powerful, but could he take down a vampire who might be even more powerful?

She raced off the end of the bridge and onto the road, heading for the empty car that was waiting a little further around the bend for her. She couldn't drive it, but Dex had given her a transportation charm. The car would take her to whatever destination she thought of.

But why was it still so quiet out here? Where were all the cops who supposedly wanted to get to the bottom of the abductions? And where were the rest of the vampires she'd been expecting? Was Nik so arrogant that he honestly didn't think he needed—

Her thoughts scattered as something slammed into her, knocking her into the bushes alongside the road. "Got you!" someone hissed in her ear as pain shot up and down her right side. She saw red eyes, dark hair, but it wasn't Azriel. She kicked with as much strength as she could muster. Her combat boots would have done more damage, but she had jeans and sneakers on tonight, knowing she might have to run and that sneakers would be best.

The vampire swore at her and yanked on her hair. "You're dead once we've picked everything out of your brain." He tried to tug her out of the bushes—and then everything became a confusing blur. Shouts, lights flashing beyond the twigs and branches, a magically magnified voice telling someone to surrender, the crack of a gunshot. Elle shrieked and instinctively ducked further down into the bushes. On the other side of her closed eyelids, another light blazed—gold this time—and she feared this vampire was about to use magic on her as well. But the grip on her hair was gone, and when she opened her eyes, she saw the vampire lying motionless a few feet away on the road, and Dex was leaning into the bushes, reaching for her. She grabbed his hand and let him pull her up.

They ran in the direction of the car, but a crackling sound and a flicker of light told Elle something was wrong before they'd even rounded the curve in the road. "Wonderful," Dex said, slowing to a halt. "Somebody set fire to my car."

"The warehouse," Elle said, pointing across the road. "We can hide there. Figure out what to do."

"Yeah, okay." They took off in that direction, and Dex used magic to aid them both in climbing up and over the fence. The main entrance into the warehouse had a protective charm on it, but after running around the side of the building, they found a smaller door that Dex was able to unlock with magic. They shut the door, ran up a ramp and into an office, and only then did Elle allow herself to sag against a wall and catch her breath.

"Holy stars," she gasped. "He used magic. *Magic*, Dex! But he was definitely a vampire, right? I mean, he can't be some sort of … hybrid?"

Dex shook his head. "Not possible for a vamp."

"I know, I know, it's just … *how*? How could he use magic like the fae do?"

"I have no idea."

"Maybe it's the result of a wish? There are no rules when it comes to wishes. At least, not the kind the Godmother grants."

"I don't know." Dex began pacing. "Yes, maybe that's it. I can't think of how else a vampire would have Essence in his system."

"Right, because even if they drink fae blood—"

"—they don't get Essence," Dex finished. "But the Godmother doesn't deal with vamps. Would she really grant one of them a wish that would make him more powerful than he already is?"

"I don't know. If the benefit was great enough to her, then maybe."

"But if it's something else … if there's some other way this vampire got his magic …" Dex stopped pacing, leaned on the edge of a desk, and faced Elle. "He might not be the only one."

"There could be more just like him," Elle whispered.

"Fae have always been the most powerful. Vampires have speed and strength, but magic has always given us the edge. But *vampires with magic* … This would put them at the top. If there are enough of them, Elle, this could change everything."

"I know," she said faintly.

He rubbed one hand over his face, then exhaled a long, slow breath. His eyes moved over her as he frowned. "I'm sorry, I didn't even ask if you're okay." He pushed away from the desk and came toward her. "There's blood on your hand—"

"Oh." Elle looked down. "It's just a scratch. I landed in the bushes. I've probably got scratches everywhere." She raised her eyes to his again. "What was happening out there? Did the cops come?"

"Yes. Xander and I got out of the way as quickly as possible. I ran after you, but Xander went looking for Olly. I should probably—"

The squeak of door hinges interrupted Dex. He and Elle both looked in the direction of the door they'd entered through. Dex raised a finger to his lips, then moved to the other side of the office where a second door stood ajar. He pulled it open and motioned for Elle to follow him. They hurried along a passageway and into a large room with hundreds of boxes lined up on shelves that reached all the way to the ceiling. High windows allowed moonlight to filter in. On one side of the room, a metal staircase led up to a gangway and another door. Dex ascended, his shoes making barely any noise on the stairs, and Elle followed.

At the top, they slipped through the door into the next room. Even larger than the one they'd just left, this one was piled high with wooden crates. Elle looked back and saw Dex peeking through the crack of the almost-closed door. "It's him. The vampire from the bridge."

"What? I thought the cops would have him by now."

Dex turned away from the door. "We need to get out of here. If a bunch of fae cops can't restrain him, I'm pretty sure I can't fight him on my own."

"I'm happy to get as far away as possible." Elle turned and faced the room. "We just need to find a way out past all these crates." She assumed there must be another door somewhere, but after a hurried examination of the room—darting in and out of all the gaps and makeshift passageways between the towering piles of crates—it turned out they couldn't access any section of the wall.

"There's no other way out," Dex said.

"Can't you use magic?"

"I could make a hole in the wall if we move all these crates, which I could also do with magic, but he would definitely hear us."

Elle swung back toward the door as she heard a noise. "I think he's on the stairs. What do we—"

"We have to hide. Just be quiet, and we'll be fine. Maybe he won't even come into this room."

They moved as far away from the door as they could get and squeezed into an impossibly skinny gap between two rows of crates. Elle strained her ears for any hint of Nik, but all she could hear was her thundering heart and her shuddering breath.

"You okay?" Dex whispered.

"Yes. Sure." She wasn't, though. Half of her was terrified Nik would find them, and the other half was hyper-aware of every point of contact her body was currently making with Dex's. Shoulder, arm, hand, thigh. She swore she could feel his body heat emanating from him. Then his hand moved a little, his pinkie finger wrapped around hers, and if anything could have made her pass out right now, it was this. "So ridiculous," she muttered, squeezing her eyes shut.

"What?"

"It's like a scene from a movie," she blurted out in a whisper. "The hot guy and the awkward girl end up in a confined space. You can feel the tension between them. Next thing they're kissing, and that's supposed to make total sense. No! Kissing should be the furthest thing from their minds! They're about to be caught by a crazy magical vampire! Why aren't they devising a plan to get out of there alive?"

Dex let out a sound that was somewhere between a choke and a snort. "There are so many things I want to say right now, I don't even know where to start."

"Unless one of them is a brilliant plan for how we get out of here alive, I'm not interested."

A beat of silence passed before he said, "You think I'm hot?"

"Oh come on, you *know* you're hot."

"And you know you're not awkward."

"That's definitely debatable."

"You're very ... *open* all of a sudden."

"Yes, well, maybe it's the idea of impending death."

"We're not about to die."

"You're right. We're probably about to be tortured. Apparently they want to pick my brain apart and *then* they're going to kill me. Do you have anything else super helpful you'd like to add?"

"Yes. What terrible movies have you been watching?"

Elle sighed. "Not many, I'll admit. But Sienna always seems to choose—" Dex silenced her with a squeeze of his finger around hers.

"He's here," he whispered into her ear, so quiet she could barely hear him over the pounding of her heart. She sucked in a breath and held it for as long as possible, listening for the sound of footsteps. Eventually, as she was breathing out as slowly and quietly as possible, she heard something. Though she couldn't see anything beyond the crate in front of her face, she could track the quiet sounds as they moved around the room. Nik was searching, looking around every pile of crates, and eventually he would—

An irritatingly upbeat melody filled the air, startling Elle so much she was in danger of squeezing Dex's finger right off. The noise stopped, and Nik said, "Yeah? No, but I'm pretty sure she ran in here." He paused, and when he spoke again, he was closer to Elle and Dex than before. "Are you certain about that? Which side of the warehouse?" He paused again. "Was she with someone? Okay, that could have been her. I'll head out that way."

A sizzling sound and a flickering of gold light suggested Nik was using magic. Then came the sound of crates bumping together. Then there was silence. Elle and Dex waited until at least a minute had passed, and then Dex whispered, "I'm going to look." He shuffled sideways to the end of the gap and peered out past the crates. "Wait here," he whispered. He disappeared, and Elle spent the next few moments wondering what she would do if he never came back.

"All clear," he said, startling her as he peered back around the crates.

"Are you sure?"

"Yes. He made a hole right through several crates and then the wall. He must have crawled through and jumped down."

Elle squeezed her way out before slumping against a pile of crates. "Okay, we're not dead."

"Nope. See, I told you." Dex smiled.

"Remember the other night, at the party, when I said this was kind of fun? I was wrong. This is definitely *not* fun."

"Yeah, I think I can agree with you on that."

"Okay, so now what?" Elle asked.

"Now we …" Dex trailed off as a shadow flitted across his face. Elle looked up and around at the windows in between the crate piles, but whatever had cast the shadow was gone. When she looked at Dex again, he was leaning over, his hands pressed against his knees.

"Dex?"

"Damn," he muttered, and then he collapsed onto the floor.

"Dex!" She rushed to his side and knelt down. As she rolled him over onto his back, a gasp escaped her lips. Dark shadow-like streaks rippled continuously across his skin. "Holy stars," she murmured. "Dex, can you hear me?" She shook him, but he didn't respond. She leaned closer and lifted one of his eyelids, then lurched back in fear when she saw his eye was solid black. "What on earth?"

She reached into her back pocket and pulled out her phone—but it was cracked down the middle and wouldn't turn on. When had that happened? Did she land too hard on something when she was thrown into the bushes? It was all too much of a blur to remember.

She searched Dex's pockets and found his phone. After pressing his thumb against the screen to unlock it, she searched for his recent contacts. "Xander or Olly," she muttered. One of them would know what to do. Xander's name was at the top of the call history, and she was about to tap it when she saw Cress's name further down the screen.

Suddenly, she realized what must be wrong with Dex. This *thing* that was happening to him was probably the reason he needed a potion from Cress. Elle hadn't overheard everything they'd said in the greenhouse, but she knew Dex needed that potion badly, and that Cress was worried he wouldn't be okay without it. And Cress was a dragon shifter, which meant she could travel fast. Maybe she could get here faster than Olly or Xander, since they may have run off after vampires.

Without another thought, Elle tapped Cress's name and brought the phone to her ear. With every ring, her chest grew tighter. "Please answer, please answer," she muttered. Finally, the ringing stopped.

"Dex," Cress said. "I was going to call. I just found some—"

"Dex needs help," Elle blurted out. "Urgently."

ELEVEN

Elle had never dreamed she would fly one day. She'd imagined what it might be like, shifting into a dragon and taking to the skies, but at no point had she ever considered she might one day know firsthand what it felt like.

Now, as she sat in a small lounge at the back of Apollo's Apothecary while Cress tended to Dex in the adjoining room, she closed her eyes and allowed herself to relive the thrill of swooping through the air. She imagined the chilly night air whipping past her, and the feel of Cress's dragon hide—knobbly, but also smooth and slippery—beneath her fingers, and the glittering city rushing beneath her.

"Elle?" Elle's eyes jerked open as Cress said her name. Anxiety returned instantly, blotting out the delight that had lifted her spirits at the memory of her first—and probably only—flight.

"Is he okay?" she asked, standing as Cress entered the lounge.

"He will be." Cress slid her fingers through her purple hair before folding her arms. "Right now, he's still asleep. Though I suspect it won't be long before he wakes. He's still much stronger than the darkness trying to eat away at him. And, fortunately, I had just finished gathering the final ingredient necessary for his potion when you called."

"So ... wait, what did you say about darkness eating away at him?" Elle asked. "What's wrong with him?"

Cress hesitated, looking over her shoulder into a second lounge where Dex lay on a futon amid a mound of colorful cushions. "It isn't my place to say. He can tell you, if he chooses to."

Elle nodded slowly. "Okay. Can I sit with him until he wakes?"

"Certainly. I'm going to tidy up my workshop. I tend to leave quite a mess when making potions in a hurry." She turned away, then looked back. "Had any luck collecting more Essence for that third-tier wish you so desperately want?"

Heat gathered in Elle's cheeks at the reminder of her ugly secret, but she was fairly certain by now that Cress wouldn't tell anyone. "I'm working on it."

"Good. I hope you're successful." With that, Cress left the room.

Elle padded across richly colored rugs toward Dex. Scarves were draped across the windows of the second lounge, while numerous leafy plants placed on shelves and tables around the room provided some relief from the riot of color. Elle perched on the edge of the futon and watched the last of the faint, rippling shadows disappear from Dex's skin. Her eyes traveled down to his hand, and she wondered if she should hold it. She wanted to, but that would be weird, wouldn't it? Holding hands with someone she barely knew. They'd held pinkie fingers earlier, but that was only because he'd been trying to comfort her as a vampire who thought she would 'taste delicious' came closer and closer to finding her.

Before she could decide whether touching Dex was appropriate or not, he sucked in a deep breath and shifted. His fingers clenched briefly, and then his eyelids squeezed tighter before opening. He blinked a few times, a deep frown forming across his brow.

"Oh. Hi," Elle said, surprised he'd woken so quickly. Feeling suddenly as if she were sitting way too close to him, she slid backward a little on the futon. "Are you feeling okay?"

Instead of answering, Dex looked around. Recognition settled in his gaze. "Apollo's," he murmured.

"Yes. Cress brought us here. She made more of your potion, which I'm guessing is what she gave you now."

Dex pushed himself up so he was sitting instead of lying down. "You didn't run," he said quietly.

"What? No, of course I didn't run. Why would I leave you in a state like that?"

"Because … I don't know." He ran a hand through his hair. His gaze moved around the room, never landing on Elle. "I thought you'd be scared. All those dark shadows on my skin, and my black eyes. I thought you'd want to get far away from me."

"Of course I was scared. But I wasn't about to leave you on your own like that. I thought—I thought some evil magic entity was attacking you or something. And then I figured out Cress might be able to help. I thought it might be something to do with that potion you were supposed to get from her the other night. So I used your phone to call her. I'm sorry, that was probably a violation of privacy, but I was kind of desperate in the moment. I figured you wouldn't mind."

"I—no, I don't mind. I'm grateful. Thank you."

"Is … is it a curse?"

Dex shook his head, still not looking at her. "No." He reached for the glass of water on the low table beside the futon and took several long gulps. He set the glass down. When he made no move to explain further, Elle decided not to ask. He would be forced to tell the truth, and he clearly didn't want to share any more about this mysterious malady.

"Okay. But you're feeling all right now?"

He nodded. "I think so. Pretty much back to normal."

"What's wrong then? Why won't you look at me?"

He covered his face with his hands and groaned. "I'm sorry. This just isn't right."

"What isn't?"

"You shouldn't have had to see me that way." He dropped his hands into his lap and looked toward the ceiling. "I'm supposed to be … not helpless."

Elle finally realized what the problem might be, and her lips curved into a wry smile. "So it's fine if you save my life, but it's not fine if I save yours?"

He sighed, his eyes finally settling on her. "Something like that."

She couldn't help laughing. "You need to let go of gender stereotypes like that."

He gave her a rueful smile. "I know, I'm sorry. And it's not even that. Not really. I don't have a problem with strong women. This is more about … me. I just hate how out of control I end up when this … *thing* happens. I didn't want you to see that."

Elle leaned back on one hand. "You should try being human sometime. It's good practice for that whole out-of-control thing. When every other race is more powerful than yours, it's a feeling you just have to get used to."

His smile stretched a little wider. "You may be human, Elle, but you don't seem like someone who's out of control much."

She groaned. "If only you knew."

He raised an eyebrow and shrugged. "You could tell me."

"Maybe another time," she said, knowing it was a lie. "We've had quite a night already."

"True. Apparently it's possible for vampires to acquire magic, but that wasn't shocking enough to keep you from daydreaming about kissing me while we were hiding from said vampire."

Elle's mouth fell open. "That is *not* what happened. I was merely commenting on the difference between the reality of our situation versus the exact same situation if it were in one of those silly movies Sienna likes to watch."

"Oh, I see." Dex nodded. "So you don't want to kiss me?"

"I—I didn't say that either." Imaginary flames engulfed her face, and she decided it should be criminal to have eyes as captivating as his. They held onto her, refusing to let her look away. "What?" she asked, her voice coming out embarrassingly breathless. "Stop looking at me like that."

"Like what?" he asked with a grin.

"Just … like that."

His eyes dipped down toward her lips. He leaned forward, and his hand gently grazed her chin.

"Wait, um—"

"Oh, I'm sorry." He leaned back. "I shouldn't have assumed—"

"No, no! It's fine! It's just … what if I'm terrible at it?"

Confusion crossed his face. "Terrible at what?"

"I mean … ugh." Elle buried her burning face in her hands. She couldn't believe she was about to admit this to him. "Iveneverkissedanyone," she mumbled.

"What was that?" He gently removed her hands from her face, interlacing his fingers with hers.

"I, um ..." She took a deep breath and stared at the ceiling. "I've never kissed anyone."

A beat of silence passed. Then: "How?"

She looked at him. "What do you mean *how*?"

"Well you're ... you're beautiful and funny and interesting, and I can't imagine how no one's—"

"I've just—been busy."

"Too busy to kiss anyone?"

"Yes. Busy with more important things. I haven't had time for boys. I mean men. I mean—" She rolled her eyes. "Whatever. You know what I mean."

His fingers tightened a little around hers, and his smile melted something inside her. "Do you have time right now?"

"I ... I do," she said faintly.

With his eyes on her lips again, Dex moved closer.

"But what if I'm really bad at it?" she whispered, and he paused a few inches from her mouth.

"If that happens to be the case, I don't mind practicing until you get it right."

Elle smiled and let out a quiet laugh. "I guess that wouldn't be so—"

Bright, hot pain bloomed out of nowhere, searing her right ankle. She jerked back, sucking in a breath against the pain. "Stars!" she hissed between clenched teeth. "No, no, no." She reached for her ankle, slipped off the edge of the futon, and landed on the floor.

"Elle!" Dex pushed himself forward and crouched on the floor beside her.

She gripped her leg just above the pain. "Crap, no," she gasped. "What's the time?"

"What? It's—I don't know." He looked around the room, and his eyes landed on something behind her. "It's midnight. Elle, what's wrong?" She let out a wordless moan as the burning intensified. "What's happening? Tell me what to do." She shook her head, her hand squeezing tighter around her calf. Dex looked down. He reached for the lower edge of her jeans.

"No, no. It's fine. Don't—" But she couldn't pull her leg back in time, and before she knew it, he'd pulled her jeans up a few inches.

"You're a slave," he whispered at the sight of the gold chain-shaped tattoo glowing on her skin. "But … how … who did this to you?"

She couldn't answer. She couldn't explain. The pain was too intense for her to do anything except try to breathe her way through it. But Dex was looking at her in horror, and *she had to get home*. That was the only way the agony would end. Somehow, she found the strength to push herself up. She launched toward the door.

"Wait, where are you—"

"Leave me alone," she gasped. He knew the ugly truth now, and there was no going back. No chance at a kiss. No chance at anything more. Not that that was ever a real possibility.

She hurried out of the apothecary as fast as possible, half running, half limping. Movement didn't make the pain any worse than it already was, but it was blinding, sickening, and as she lurched her way around corners and through alleys, steering away from any main streets, she struggled to keep her balance.

She couldn't tell if Dex had tried to follow her. Probably not, because surely he would have caught up to her by now. She'd told him to leave her alone, and he'd listened. For some reason, that hurt almost as much as the pain of the slave charm.

The night seemed to press in on her. The moon grew dimmer. She staggered onward for another minute or two before the agony finally consumed her and the cobblestones of whatever street she was in rose to meet her face.

TWELVE

Dex cursed the lightheadedness that had sent him reeling when he jumped up and tried to follow Elle. Everything had gone white and then dark. By the time he regained consciousness and found himself staring at the ceiling, he had no idea how many minutes had passed. He should have remembered it always took him a bit of time to recover from an episode.

He rushed through the back rooms of Apollo's Apothecary. The door Elle must have left through was still open. He ran outside, looked both ways, then chose left. But when he reached an intersection, he saw no sign of her in any direction. He ran back, past the open door, and stopped at the intersection on the other side of Apollo's. But again, there was no indication of which way Elle had gone.

"Dammit." Dex patted his pockets for his phone, but found nothing. His thoughts tumbled over one another as he ran back inside Apollo's. How could Elle be a slave, and yet she roamed the city freely whenever she wanted? And yet … that wasn't exactly true, he reminded himself. She was always checking the time, and he'd never seen her stay out beyond midnight. And she hadn't wanted him coming to her home to pick her up. In fact, that spot he'd once dropped her off at probably wasn't even her home. He hadn't actually seen her go inside, had he?

Back inside the colorful lounge, he found his phone on the table beside the glass of water. He picked it up and immediately saw several missed calls from Xander. He clenched his hand around the device. Phone Elle, or phone Xander? Which was more important right now?

Leave me alone. That was the last thing Elle said to him. And Xander and Olly had repeatedly told him not to get too close to her. They would be even more insistent if they knew about her slave status. Then Dex's eyes landed on something on the floor that answered his question for him: Elle's phone, with a single crack running from top to bottom.

A light inside him went out as he realized he would never find her, and that that was the way it was always going to end. He'd known he shouldn't feel anything for her. He'd known he shouldn't kiss her. But he was stupid and reckless, and fate had been forced to step in and remind him of his place in the world—and hers, it would seem.

He swallowed, turned back to his own phone, and tapped the screen to call Xander. *Time to move on*, he told himself as the dial tone sounded in his ear. Less than a full ring later, Xander answered. "Hey, where are you? I've been trying—"

"I know, I saw. Are you guys okay?"

"Yeah, you?"

"I'm … fine." He didn't need to go into detail right now about passing out because of the Darkness. He would only end up with an earful from Xander about how irresponsible he was to have let that happen. "What happened to you two?" he asked.

"Just so happens," Xander said, "that we found someone useful lurking near the bridge."

Dex's heart rate quickened. "Who?"

"The vamp who first abducted Elle."

"And you caught him?"

"We did."

Dex's lips pulled into a grin. "Well done. Were there others around?"

"Yeah. Cops caught a bunch. We got this one. But the magic vamp got away." He cursed beneath his breath. "I can't believe I just used the words 'magic vamp.'"

"I know. We have to figure out what's going on here. Where'd you take the vamp?"

"My place."

"Good. I'll get there as soon as I can."

THIRTEEN

Elle woke up to find the ground sliding by beneath her. Not the ground, exactly, but a carpet. The carpet in the entrance hall at home. Another moment passed before she realized she was hanging in the air. She gasped in fright and threw her hands out, expecting to fall, but the floor of her home remained the same distance away from her as it moved by. Or rather, as she moved over it.

"Wonderful," came Salvia's voice from behind her. "You're awake. Now you can tell me why you dared to stay out beyond your curfew, and why you made me come all the way to the other side of the city to find you."

The stairs to the attic came into view beneath Elle as she remembered exactly how the slave charm worked. If she wasn't in her room at the required time and the mark of the charm began to burn her skin, Salvia would know. It wouldn't hurt *her*, of course. Not the way it hurt Elle. But it would alert her to the fact that Elle wasn't where she was supposed to be, and Salvia could then use the charm to locate Elle. Salvia must have found her passed out and brought her home, and was now using a levitating charm to get her upstairs.

"I was trying to get to the bottom of our vampire problem," Elle explained, "just like we agreed. But I lost track of time."

"Not acceptable. And you're pretty useless at dealing with your *vampire problem*, since all the vampire activity was happening in a completely different part of the city tonight, near the beach in that crummy old area. Belgravia."

"Yes, that's where I was before I ended up—"

"Stop lying to me." Magic sizzled around Elle, and she found herself tossed forward onto the wooden floorboards of her attic.

"I'm not lying," she said as she scrambled up to her feet. Her body ached everywhere, from earlier when a vampire had crashed into her, and then from hitting the road as she'd passed out, and now from landing on the hard floor. But it was nothing compared to the pain Sienna would have to endure if Salvia decided Elle's disobedience tonight was worth a punishment. "I promise I'm not lying. I lured a vampire onto the bridge there, and it turned out he—"

"Perhaps you should be asking her to explain *this*."

The person who interrupted her was Meredith, and Elle looked around to see that she was sitting on the edge of the bed. And beside her—

No.

Nononono.

The bottom dropped out of everything and Elle sank to her knees. It was her box of Essence. Her future. Her hope.

"What is that?" Salvia demanded, stalking past Elle and taking the box from Meredith. She yanked the lid off, and Elle heard a quiet intake of breath. For a moment, no one moved. No one said a word. Then Salvia faced Elle. Elle expected to see anger or outrage in her stepmother's eyes, but all she saw was shock. "Where did you get this?" Salvia whispered.

Elle didn't answer. What would be the point? Nothing she said now would make a difference. Salvia would take the Essence from her, like she'd taken everything else, and that would be the end for Elle.

"Did you *steal* all these vials of Essence? Is that what you've been doing every time you sneak out of this house? What were you planning to do? Buy a wish? Blindside me by wishing for your freedom and simply *disappearing*?"

Again, Elle said nothing.

"I've tried to be lenient with you. I gave you freedom with barely any restrictions because you were once *family* to me. You've had more freedom than any other slave in this city. And this is how you thank me? You and Sienna will both be punished for this."

"No, wait," Elle said, pushing herself onto her feet. "Sienna doesn't know anything about this."

"Meredith, leave," Salvia said, ignoring Elle's protests. "And thank you, my love, for searching this attic and revealing the true extent of Elle's betrayal."

"Only a pleasure," Meredith said with a gloating smile. She rose from the bed and sauntered past Elle. For one wild moment, Elle considered tackling her to the floor and striking that smile from her face. But then Meredith was at the door, and the moment had passed, and Elle was as weak as she'd always been in her stepmother's presence.

Salvia strode past her with the box of Essence vials tucked beneath her arm. "Please don't hurt Sienna," Elle said as self-loathing almost choked her. She could barely stand to beg, but she was willing to do anything to keep Sienna from suffering.

"Sienna is not your problem," Salvia snapped, turning in the doorway to face Elle.

"Please," Elle said, rushing forward.

"Get back in there!" Salvia shouted, throwing her hand out. Gold dust flashed, and magic stung Elle's cheek. She gasped in surprise and pain, raising her hand automatically to her cheek. "You will *never* be free!" Salvia hissed. "The confinement charm will be on here permanently. The only time you'll leave this room is when I require your skill at memory removal. You won't clean the house. You won't go out on errands. We earned enough from the last con to hire a new maid. Congratulations, my dear *Estelle*. You've graduated from slave to prisoner." She slammed the door and disappeared along with every last shred of Elle's hope.

FOURTEEN

With shaking fingers, Elle traced the various star shapes on the quilted bedspread her mother had made. She didn't know what to do, what to feel. She had always had a plan. She had always had hope, no matter how slim. And now she had … nothing. There was a gaping hole in her chest, and she didn't know what to fill it with.

She looked up as Salvia's shouts reached her ears from downstairs. Then Sienna's cry. Salvia was probably interrogating Sienna, trying to figure out if she knew anything about Elle's Essence collection. Would Sienna give in and tell the truth? Salvia would only hurt her more if she did.

As Sienna's cries intensified, Elle squeezed her eyes shut and let her tears tumble over her cheeks. She drew her knees up to her chest and wrapped her arms around them, rocking herself back and forth. But she didn't try to block her ears. It was her fault Sienna was being punished, and it didn't seem right to try and escape the terrible sounds.

When the shouting, crying and stomping footsteps eventually faded to silence, Elle unwrapped her arms. She climbed off her bed and went to the window. "Look to the stars," she whispered. It was a line embroidered somewhere on her quilt. But the stars had no answers. They held no hope. "I can't do this anymore," she whispered into the night.

She raised her finger to the dusty window. In a way, she had known since the moment she saw her Essence box sitting out in the open on her bed that it would come to this. But she'd resisted it for so long that she needed just a little more time to accept that this was now the only way out.

She traced a symbol in the dust of her window. A symbol she shouldn't know. Good, law-abiding citizens were supposed to avert their eyes from things like this. But Elle had seen it around the city, spray-painted onto walls in alleys, or scratched onto tree trunks. A curve, almost like an S, with three lines and a loop. The symbol of the Godmother.

Elle took a step back and stared at the shape. Her voice shook as she whispered, "I need your help, Godmother."

Then she waited, her heart pounding, unsure of how long this was supposed to take. When a voice spoke behind her, she almost fell to her knees in fright. She spun around, and there, perched on the edge of her bed, was a woman. Her short, elegantly styled hair was completely white, while her eyes were a deep, rich brown. Her skin—like that of most fae—was flawless, exquisite.

"Y—you're the Godmother?" Elle asked, though the question was entirely unnecessary.

"Yes. And you're … Elle. Estelle Winter."

Elle blinked. "You know me?"

"We've met before. I never forget an essence."

"I'm human," Elle said faintly. "I don't have Essence."

"Not that kind of essence." She crossed one leg over the other. "I mean that inexplicable quality that makes you you. Faces change with time. Names can change too. But no one's essence ever changes. It's the sense I get from your spirit, your soul, whatever you want to call it. The part of you that is not physical."

"So—wait." Elle shook her head. "When did we meet?"

The Godmother's lips curved into a smile. "That is someone else's story, not yours."

"But … what? That doesn't make sense. If I was there, then it's part of—"

"I decide what makes sense, Elle. Don't forget that. Now, let's get down to business. I assume you summoned me because you'd like to wish for something."

"I—yes." Elle took a steadying breath. "I would like to wish for my freedom."

"I see. Well, that's fairly straightforward."

"Um, okay. That's good."

"The price, however, is never straightforward."

Elle sighed. "I didn't think so."

"Come closer," the Godmother commanded, and after a moment's pause, Elle stepped forward. "Give me your hand."

"Why?" Elle asked, at which the Godmother merely raised a single, perfectly arched eyebrow. "Right, of course," Elle muttered, reaching her hand out.

The Godmother took it. Her skin was smooth and cool, but not icy. She closed her eyes, and Elle felt something like a tiny zap of electricity dance along her skin. She waited, holding her breath, until finally the Godmother opened her eyes and let go of Elle's hand.

"Interesting," she said. "Very interesting indeed."

"I would ask what it is you find so interesting, but I know you won't tell me."

"No, I won't." She smiled. "But it seems I do have a use for you after all."

"Okay. Great. What do I need to do?"

The Godmother tipped her head to the side. "How badly do you want your freedom?"

Elle's eyebrows jumped. "Do you have to ask? I mean, I summoned you, didn't I? So I must be pretty desperate."

"Well," the Godmother said, looking somewhat taken aback. "I would pretend to be offended, but I have to admit I'm impressed you would dare to say such a thing out loud."

"Look, I know the price is going to be something I don't want to pay," Elle said, "but I'm out of options, and this isn't just about me. My stepsister needs to get away from this abusive household too, but she's too young to be out there on her own. I need my freedom so I can run away and take her with me. *That's* how badly I want this wish."

"Your stepsister is more important to you than anyone else?"

"Yes. She's the only true family I have left."

"Good," the Godmother said. "Let's talk specifics then, shall we?"

"Yes," Elle answered, steeling herself for whatever was to come.

"There's a masquerade ball happening soon at the palace."

"I know." Elle frowned as she wondered what this had to do with anything.

"If you want your freedom," the Godmother said, "you will go to this ball."

"Okaaaaay."

"And you will kill the fae prince."

3
THE MOONLIGHT MASQUERADE

ONE

On a quiet street in Vale City's Willowton borough, moonlight shone through a dusty attic window where Elle Winter stood blinking at the glamorous, white-haired fae woman perched on the end of her bed. It was surreal enough that the Godmother herself was sitting in Elle's bedroom. Perhaps their entire conversation—and the Godmother's presence—was actually a dream. Elle pressed her nails into her palms, and the pain felt very real. So, not a dream?

"I'm sorry," she said to the Godmother. "I know it's really late, so maybe I zoned out for a second and misheard you. But it sounded like you said you want me to *kill* the prince?"

"Yes. Prince Chevalier of House Belmont."

Elle let out a choke of a laugh. "Is—is that a joke?"

The smallest of frowns marred the Godmother's perfect features. "I don't ever joke about the price of a wish."

"N-no!" Elle blurted out. "I won't *kill* someone. You can't ask me to do that."

"Elle, you just told me how important it is that you wish for your freedom. That it's the only way you and your stepsister can run away together, and that she means more to you than anyone else. Has that changed within the last few seconds?"

"No, of course not. But … I mean … you're asking me to commit murder."

"I am," the Godmother said, as simply as if she were asking Elle to pick up something she'd just dropped on the floor.

"But … this … this doesn't even make sense," Elle said, hoping to bring some rationality to the conversation. "Why me? I'm not even allowed to go to the ball. Surely it's far less complicated if you ask someone who's actually going? There must be people summoning you for wishes all the time. I'm sure you'll find someone else in the next few days."

"I'm not asking someone else, Elle. I'm asking you. You can get close to him."

"And someone else can't? *You* can't? You're the Godmother. You can do anything."

"Well, I'm flattered you think so." The Godmother smoothed one hand over her perfectly styled hair. "But there's a limit to the extent of my reach. Prince Chevalier has certain magical wards placed around him. Wards that specifically target me. I can't get close enough to him. It has to be you."

Elle shook her head. "I'm … I'm really not the right person for this job," she insisted, her voice trembling slightly as despair began to inch its way up her chest and into her throat. "Even if I was happy to end someone's life, I would have no idea what to do. I'd mess up the whole thing."

"You are exactly the right person for this job. Your talents make you uniquely equipped."

"My talents?"

"I know you're not entirely human, Estelle Winter."

"Excuse me? I'm definitely human. My blood is as red as any other human's."

The Godmother leaned back on one hand. "Forgive me. That isn't quite what I meant. I know you're human, but I also know what you can *do*, and it isn't something any other human can do."

For several moments, Elle was silent. She longed to ask when exactly she and the Godmother had met and how the Godmother knew these things about her, but the mysterious woman had already made it clear she wouldn't answer questions about the past. About 'someone else's story,' as she'd put it. "Yes, okay," Elle said eventually. "I can remove people's memories. I have no idea how I possess this strange magical ability while also being human, but that's the way it is. What does that have to do with killing the prince?"

"Your power doesn't simply remove memories," the Godmother said patiently. "If you take it further—if you remove *all* memories, if you remove the mind itself—the body cannot survive on its own."

Elle felt a sickening jolt in her stomach. "What? How do you know that?"

"You've done it before."

"I most certainly have not."

"You don't remember. You took the memory from yourself."

Elle could only stare, her heart pounding, dread building inside her. "That … can't be true. I've—I've never used my ability on myself." She realized the absurdity of what she was saying as the words left her mouth. If she had taken a memory from herself, then of course she wouldn't remember doing it. Her clients had their memories of meeting with her; they knew she'd taken *something*, even if they didn't know what it was. But if she had done something terrible and then immediately removed that space of time from her own mind, she would have no way of knowing it ever happened if she didn't write herself a note or leave some other clue.

The Godmother let out a sigh. "It honestly doesn't matter what you believe. What you've done in the past isn't relevant right now. My point is that you need no weapon. You need no killing expertise. You will simply do what you've been doing for years. You'll convince the prince to accompany you to a quiet spot away from all the activity of the ball, and then you'll take his memories and his mind, to the point where he slips away from this world."

Elle swallowed past the rising nausea in her throat. "And what if he doesn't want to follow me anywhere? What if I don't even have the chance to get near him? There'll be hundreds of women vying for his attention."

"And you will be the one to capture it. I'll make sure of that. And your hairstyle will hide the tips of your ears so he won't know you're human. Trust me, Elle. Prince Chevalier will follow you anywhere."

"But … I …" Elle trailed off. She'd run out of things to say, used every argument she could think of, but it seemed the Godmother wasn't open to negotiating. She'd decided on her price, and now Elle had to say yes or no.

A noise reached her ears from downstairs. Elle looked over her shoulder, terror wrapping its fingers around her heart and squeezing tight. What would Salvia do if she walked in here and found the *Godmother*?

"Don't worry," the Godmother said. "No one can hear us while I'm in this room. Now, I need your answer, Elle. Do you accept this price or not?"

"Oh, I, uh …" Elle's scrambled thoughts tumbled over one another. "Can I have a day or two to think about it?"

"Don't you know the rules?"

The hand of fear squeezed a little tighter. "What rules?"

"If you summon me and refuse to pay the price I set, you don't get to summon me again. That will be it. The end of all our dealings."

"But—then—"

"It's a simple decision, Elle. This is what it comes down to: who would you rather save? Your stepsister who means the world to you, or a fae prince who is exactly like his father. You know how the royal family feels about humans. If it were solely up to them, no human would ever be free. I'm sure you're aware of how hard King Belaric has been working to get the National Council to vote in favor of making the slave charm mandatory for all humans once more. If he succeeds, all humans will be returned to slavery. His son has been working just as hard to get this proposed change voted in. What's wrong with removing a person like that from the world?"

"I … I don't …"

"Fine." The Godmother rose from the bed. "This meeting is over then. I don't have time for—"

"Wait, okay!"

She paused. Raised an eyebrow. "Okay?"

"I'll do it," Elle said, her heart thumping so hard it hurt.

"Good. I'll see you on Saturday evening then." She snapped her fingers, and an instant later, she vanished.

Elle turned on the spot, just to make sure the Godmother was really gone. Then she sank down and sat right there on the floor, allowing herself to breathe freely for the first time in minutes. Was this real? Had she really just done that?

Yes. She had.

She'd *lied* to the Godmother. And now she had to figure out how to pretend to kill Prince Chevalier.

TWO

Though she wasn't required to do household chores, Elle raised her weary, aching body from bed at the usual time the following morning. She may not have physical tasks, but her brain had work to do. It was Monday, and the ball was on Saturday. She had six days to figure out how to pretend-kill a prince who would have hundreds of women—and probably at least a dozen guards—following him around.

She also had no idea how she was going to get past the confinement charm on the attic, or what she would wear, or how she would actually *get to* Belmont Palace. But she assumed the Godmother would take care of all the details. This whole go-to-the-ball-and-kill-the-prince thing was her idea, and she was well aware of Elle's situation.

It was still early when footsteps sounded on the stairs leading up to the attic. *Sienna*, Elle thought instantly. Years of practice had made Elle an expert at identifying exactly which of her three family members was climbing the stairs.

The footsteps stopped outside her door, and she listened for the sizzle of magic as the confinement charm was temporarily lifted. The handle twisted, and the door swung open. Sienna stood on the other side, a plate of toast in one hand. At the sight of the yellowish-brown patches on her face, Elle inhaled a quiet gasp of air. How badly must Salvia have beaten her if she still had visible bruises after a night of her fae magic working its healing power?

"Stars above," Elle whispered. "Are you okay? What did she—"

Sienna thrust the plate at Elle, her eyes downcast. "I'm fine. I can't talk.

Mom is—"

"What did I tell you, Sienna?" Salvia shouted up the stairway. "You are *not* to speak to her. You've taken too long already."

"I'm fine, I promise," Sienna whispered before pulling the door shut with a bang and reactivating the confinement charm.

Elle stared at the door, her hand gripping the plate tightly as Sienna descended the stairs. If Salvia truly didn't want the two of them conversing, she wouldn't have allowed Sienna to come up here. She would have come herself, or sent Meredith. Or, more likely, she would have let Elle go hungry for a day or two. No, there was a reason for this. Salvia *wanted* Elle to see Sienna's bruises. She wanted Elle to see what her disobedience had resulted in.

Any remaining doubts Elle had about bargaining with the Godmother fled her mind. Whatever she had to do to convince everyone the prince was dead— for a few hours, at least—would be worth it. She needed to get Sienna away from this house before Salvia took things too far. Before she hurt her own daughter so badly she might not recover.

Elle carried the plate to her bed, sat down, and eyed the two pieces of toast covered in honey. Anger had robbed her of her appetite, but she wouldn't be helping anyone by not eating. Her brain needed food if it was going to function. So she nibbled on the toast as she tried to figure out how she would trick the Godmother.

She spent most of the morning pacing the attic, ridiculous half-ideas flitting through her mind. If the Godmother couldn't get close to the prince, how would she know if he was really dead? What if Elle gave him something to knock him out, hid him somewhere, and then started a rumor about him being killed? It would spread lightning fast among the ball's guests. By the time Elle got away from the palace, the rumor would probably have reached the Godmother. But she would want to know for sure. She'd probably wait for an official statement from the royal family before granting Elle her wish. So that wouldn't work.

Elle passed her wardrobe for the hundredth time, then stopped. She stared at the closed doors, then pulled them open and dug out an old photo album from beneath her socks and underwear. Sitting on the edge of her bed, she flipped through the cardboard pages, yellow around the edges with age. She didn't often look at this album—wandering through memories of the good old days was always bittersweet—but she felt she needed the encouragement of seeing her parents' faces. It was hard, but it would give her strength.

The album began with pictures from the time her parents had only just met, mostly taken while they were hanging out together with friends and family. There was one of Dad with his brother—before his brother was killed in a car accident—and one of Mom with her best friend Liana, a woman who was fae. Then a group photo with friends: a mixture of fae, humans and shifters. Elle wondered what had happened to them all. She had vague memories of Liana, and of the shifter with the beard. Eric? Merrick? Merrick, that was it. He was a wolf shifter. But Elle couldn't remember seeing much of Liana, Merrick or the others after her mom died when she was six. Then Dad remarried soon after Elle turned seven, and she definitely didn't remember seeing any of his friends once Salvia was in the picture.

Elle turned the page, shoving aside all thoughts of Salvia. They didn't belong in the same brain space that was dedicated to reliving happy memories of her parents. The following pages were filled with photos of holidays and fun dates and more hanging out with friends. Finally, she turned a page and landed on a photo from her parents' wedding day. Just one. There had been another album dedicated entirely to their wedding, and Salvia had made sure it disappeared soon after she married Elle's father. Elle lingered for a while on the wedding photo, smiling at her parents' faces filled with joy, Dad's hand around Mom, confetti raining down around them, and Mom's free hand raised as if she were about to catch some of the falling petals.

Elle moved on and found a few photos of herself as a baby with her grandparents—none of whom were still around by the time Dad died, or they would surely have put a stop to Salvia's slave charm—and finally, a photo of baby Elle with both her parents. Elle traced her forefinger over her mother's blond hair, wondering what secrets those smiling eyes hid. *She tried to keep you from us.* That was what Azriel had said. But *why*? It still made no sense to Elle that her mother was somehow involved with vampires. If anything, she would have guessed it was her father who had something to do with them, given the way he'd died …

She tightened her hand into a fist and looked away, trying to focus on something else—the wardrobe, the window, the carpet—to blot out the heart-shattering memory of her father turning. She squeezed her eyes shut until all she could see was blackness. Then she opened them and looked down at the image of her smiling parents. That was the way she wanted to remember them. Not the pale skin and straggly hair of a woman struck by an incurable illness. Not the dull, unseeing eyes of a man who'd ended his life before the vampire transformation was complete. Elle placed her fingers over the photo once more. "I'll figure this out," she promised them. Then she stood and returned the album to her wardrobe.

Time passed achingly slowly as she paced the attic and tried to think her way out of this kill-the-prince mess she'd landed in. Occasionally, thoughts of Dex slipped in to distract her, which were far more pleasant than thoughts of murder. The memory of sitting in a lounge at the back of Apollo's Apothecary surrounded by colorful cushions and wild plants in mismatched pots was so vivid. If she'd had just a few more minutes with Dex, what might have happened? He'd wanted to kiss her. She had wanted to kiss him too, and if she hadn't been so scared and silly, she would have had the chance before the stupid slave charm started burning her leg. Dex was probably immensely relieved the kiss hadn't happened though, now that he knew the truth about her.

She stopped at her window and pressed her forehead against the cool glass. There was a dull ache in her chest at the thought of never seeing him again, but at least she knew he was okay. Thank goodness for Cress and her dragon shifter speed and her skill at potions. Elle had never heard of anything like the strange shadowy blackness that had darkened Dex's eyes and skittered across his skin and made him pass out. But Cress had come up with something to combat this strange affliction.

And yet … there was something about the way Cress had spoken about Dex that left concern gnawing at the back of Elle's mind. Cress had said he was stronger than the darkness trying to eat away at him. *Trying.* Present tense. As if it was still happening. But hopefully, if he kept taking this potion Cress made for him, he'd be fine. Or maybe Cress could come up with something else to—

Elle's thoughts crashed into one another and her heart jumped an extra beat or two as an idea popped into her head. Cress knew all about potions. She managed an apothecary brimming with elixirs and concoctions. The shelves in the back rooms had potion manuals and ingredient textbooks squeezed into the gaps between all the plants. Maybe, just *maybe*, she knew of a potion that could simulate death.

Elle began pacing again, her bare feet crossing the attic faster now, and her breaths coming quicker. If she could slip a potion into the prince's drink that would make him *appear* to be dead for several hours—no, it would need to be longer than that; at least a day?—then that would give her enough time to get away from the ball and for the Godmother to confirm the prince's death and grant Elle's wish. Then Elle and Sienna could run, and they'd finally be free of Salvia, and by the time the Godmother discovered Elle's deception, they'd be free of her too. It seemed like a good plan. The best she'd come up with so far. The only problem was that she had no way of leaving the house and no way of contacting Cress.

A familiar squeak caught her attention as she turned near her window. She looked back over her shoulder and saw a pixie—the one with that silly pistachio shell she wore as a hat—standing on the windowsill. She must have crawled through the open gap at the bottom of the window. The confinement charm, of course, had no effect on her.

"Oh, hey." Elle knelt by the window and placed her hands on the ledge beside the pixie. "You're probably wondering why you haven't seen me in the kitchen or the pantry today. Sadly, I'm no longer allowed to leave this attic." The pixie stared with bright eyes the size of pinheads. One wing quivered. Elle sighed. "You shouldn't hang around here. Seriously, you should find another home to live in. One where they don't kill pixies. I won't be the one working in the kitchen downstairs anymore, and if the new maid sees you and tells Salvia, you won't last long. She'll probably try to lure you into a pixie trap with a shiny button or something."

The pixie took a step closer and placed her tiny hand on top of Elle's pinkie knuckle. Then she patted it. Her hand was so small and light that Elle barely felt a thing. It was silly, but emotion welled up in her chest and all of a sudden she felt like crying. Had her life really come to this? Were things so terrible that the only one left to provide her with any comfort was a pixie? She sniffed and blinked her tears away. "Thanks," she whispered. "I hope you find a better home than this one." She stood and turned away.

And then an idea clicked into place in her brain.

"Oh, wait." She swung back around. "Wait, wait! You can understand me, right?" She knelt down again and faced the pixie. Research suggested pixies understood the languages of the High Races. It was the High Races who struggled to understand pixies. Apparently pixies could respond in the same language, but they spoke so fast and their voices were so high-pitched that it was impossible to make out much more than a squeak. Sienna had read up about it for one of her school subjects, and then told Elle about all the research she'd found. But if the research was correct, this pixie wasn't doing much to confirm it. She simply stared at Elle.

"Okay, I'm going to take that as a yes," Elle said, mainly because she didn't have any other options. "Can you do something for me? Please, this is important, and I can't leave this house." The pixie continued to stare, which, again, Elle decided was a good sign. "I need you to go to Apollo's Apothecary. I'll write a note for you to take, and you must give it to Cress. *Only* Cress. Do you understand?" The pixie patted Elle's hand a second time. "Okay, great. You just wait there, and I'll quickly write a note."

She hurried to her wardrobe and dug inside a box for a notebook and pen. Then she moved to the wooden table that stood near her bed and began scribbling down a message to Cress.

Cress, I need your help. I need a potion that will simulate death. The drinker needs to appear to be dead for at least a day, longer if possible, but he needs to return to normal health when he wakes. If such a potion exists, I need it by Saturday afternoon. I have no money to pay you. I don't even have Essence. It's all gone. But I'm desperate. More desperate than I can put into words. After the ball, I'll be free, and I'll do anything I can to pay you back. Work in the apothecary. Collect ingredients. Make potions. Whatever. PLEASE.

She signed the note simply with an E. Then, after a moment's pause, she added 'Dex's friend' in brackets. She didn't add that she would also need Cress to hide her and Sienna for a while. *Cross that bridge when you reach it*, she told herself. She tore the page from her notebook and folded it as small as she could.

"Are you able to carry this?" she asked as she hurried back to the window. Crouching down, she held the folded note out to the pixie. The tiny creature reached for it with both hands before clutching it to her chest. Then she turned back to the window. Elle hastily lifted it so the pixie wouldn't have to squeeze through such a narrow gap at the bottom. The pixie raced forward and leaped into the air. Elle placed her hands against the invisible barrier of the confinement charm and watched her miniature ally zoom away, hoping this plan would work.

THREE

Nik folded his arms tightly across his chest as he surveyed Vale City from one of the vast windows of his father's apartment. The last rays of the setting sun slid across the city, but this building was already in shadow.

"Honestly, you're as useless as Azriel," his father said from behind him. A chair scraped the floor, and Nik guessed his father had just sat. "You now have *magic* coursing through your vampire body, and you still couldn't catch a simple human girl last night."

"A human girl aided by fae," Nik reminded his father. "One helped her run. The others tricked us." He turned toward the table, his arms still tight against his body. "They tricked *you*. Made you think you saw a man and woman fleeing from the warehouse."

"They didn't *make* me see anything. I definitely saw a man and woman hurrying away from that warehouse."

"Well then they were a decoy. Fae who disappeared before I could find them."

"Or they were the girl and her fae friend, and they managed to elude you."

Nik turned back to the window and stared beyond the many buildings. Though it was small and distant, he had a good view from up here of Sovereign Hill and the palace that sat atop it, gleaming in the setting sun. The Allegiant would soon tear Belmont Palace to the ground. Every last stone would tumble into the sea, and a new age would begin. The age of vampires. He'd believed that 'soon' might be only a matter of days away. Now, he wasn't so sure.

"It doesn't matter what went wrong last night," he said quietly. "We don't have the girl, which means we don't know what she knows. If we can't find her before Saturday—"

"Oh, we're still going ahead with plans for Saturday," his father informed him. "I received word this morning."

Nik lowered his arms and faced the table. He moved closer, gripped the back of a chair, and leaned forward. "Is that wise? We don't know how to finish the—"

"You don't get to question your king," his father snapped. "*You* screwed up, which means our plan isn't as perfect as it could be, but it can still work. We won't get another opportunity like this ball in a long time, which means we need to take advantage of it. And if there are negative side effects because we couldn't complete the spell, it's on you. Literally."

"And on everyone else who's gone through the process I went through," Nik muttered. "We might all be too weak for this plan to succeed."

"The others will be fine. They began the process after you. If anyone's going to weaken before the ball, it's you. And if that happens, you're out. You won't be going."

Nik worked hard to keep his hands from fisting. He'd worked so hard for this. Practiced endless hours with his newly acquired magic. He wouldn't miss out on the biggest move vampires would make against the fae in centuries. "I'll be fine on Saturday night," he assured his father.

"I certainly hope so. When the true king rules this country, I plan for us to be handsomely rewarded. That's only going to happen if you don't let me down again."

Nik pinned his gaze once more on Sovereign Hill. "Trust me, I won't."

FOUR

To Elle, the days passed by achingly slowly until finally, Saturday arrived. Unfortunately, her pixie friend did not. Perhaps she hadn't understood a word Elle said. Perhaps all the research Sienna told Elle about was pure nonsense. Whatever the reason, Elle was left with no potion that could simulate death and no reasonable backup plan—and a great deal of panic threatening to overwhelm her.

She had to keep closing her eyes, sitting on the edge of her bed, and taking deep, slow breaths. *What's the worst that could happen?* she kept asking herself. She would fail at paying the price, and the Godmother wouldn't grant her a wish. That was all.

Except that *wasn't* all. Her freedom was on the line, as was Sienna's. And possibly Sienna's safety. Sure, Sienna would be a legal adult in less than a year, free to leave home if she was brave enough to go against Salvia's wishes, but what if she didn't survive that long? What if Salvia's irrational anger caused her to do something before then that even magic couldn't heal?

Footsteps echoed in the narrow staircase beyond the attic door. Elle turned toward the sound. Sienna? It didn't sound like Salvia or Meredith, but it didn't sound entirely like Sienna either. Elle moved from the bed and hovered near the door, waiting. Salvia's new maid had been delivering meals to the attic, and Elle hadn't seen Sienna since Monday morning when they'd barely had two seconds to talk. She still wasn't sure if she should tell Sienna about the wish and the Godmother's price. What if something went wrong and Elle's last remaining

"

hope at freedom slipped through her fingers?

The door opened, and for a moment or two, Elle didn't recognize the girl who stood on the other side. "Hey," Sienna said quietly. "Mom doesn't know I'm up here. She's busy with Meredith." She half turned and glanced down the staircase before facing Elle again. "They're both taking far too long to get ready, and I doubt either of them would notice if a fire started or the house fell down or something exploded."

"Sienna," Elle said, the name leaving her lips on an exhale of breath. Her eyes traveled over Sienna's dress, which was a shimmering gray-green that perfectly complimented her auburn hair. The style was simple—a fitted bodice with a skirt that flared out slightly—but the lace detail Elle had seen across the back when Sienna turned was beautiful. With her usually wispy, out-of-control hair styled into a perfectly chic updo, she looked glamorous and elegant. "That's … just … you look incredible."

"Do you think so?" Sienna laughed. "For the first time in my life, I actually feel … I don't know. Pretty? Sophisticated? It's so weird. I'll have to try and not trip over something or spill anything on my dress."

"It looks amazing on you. Absolutely perfect."

"Yeah, Meredith keeps pointing out how simple my dress is in comparison to hers, but I actually prefer mine, even if it wasn't custom-made for me. And even if—as Meredith keeps saying—someone else is wearing the same dress, who cares?" She shrugged. "I'll just walk in the opposite direction if I see someone else wearing it."

Elle smiled. "I hope you manage to enjoy some of tonight, even though you'll be trying to keep Meredith away from the prince the whole time."

"I know. That would be nice, even though it's not a priority. Anyway, I just wanted to come up here and tell you that I'm determined not to fail." She pushed her shoulders back and gave Elle a firm nod. "I'll do whatever I have to. Even if it means causing an embarrassing scene so Meredith and I are asked to leave. It's just … you know. Mom will probably punish one or both of us severely for something like that, so I thought I should warn you."

Guilt struck Elle square in the chest. "It's not as though you had any warning after she found my Essence collection and punished you for it," she said quietly. "Are you okay now? You still had bruises on Monday morning. She must have hurt you badly."

"I'm—yes, I'm fine," Sienna said, but her smile was strained, and a shadow crossed her features. "I'm so, so sorry about the Essence, Elle. I can't imagine how—I mean, you worked so hard for it, and now it's all gone, and that must have been utterly heartbreaking."

Elle nodded, still unsure whether she should mention the bargain she'd made with the Godmother. "It was a pretty low point for me, but listening to you being punished because of it was worse."

"No, that's not the worst of it," Sienna said with a shake of her head. "Mom told me the next day that I couldn't go to the ball. That she was going to lock me in my room tonight while she and Meredith go out. I thought for sure Meredith's plan was going to work and the prince would end up proposing to her. But then Elon was here for dinner on Wednesday—Mom made me invite him because she's determined I'm going to con something valuable out of him—and he said he was looking forward to seeing me at the ball, and Mom couldn't very well tell him I wasn't allowed to go. He might have asked why, and she would have had to come up with a very good story. Besides, now she thinks tonight is an excellent chance for me to get closer to Elon." Sienna rolled her eyes. "Which I'd love to do if I knew I wasn't going to have to *steal* from him at some point. Now I just want to stay away from the poor guy so he doesn't get caught up in one of Mom's plots."

Elle sighed. "I'm sorry. But maybe … maybe you won't have to go through with the con."

Sienna wrinkled her brow. "Why? What do you—" She looked over her shoulder as Salvia shouted her name. "Oh, stars, I should go. Mom probably needs help squeezing into her dress—or magically adjusting the size, more likely. She was way too optimistic about the amount of weight she thought she could lose since we received that invitation."

"Sienna," Elle said, gripping her stepsister's shoulders and making a quick decision to tell her at least part of the truth. "Something's going to happen tonight. At the ball. Something terrible."

"What—what do you mean?"

"I can't be more specific."

"Elle, you're scaring me. Is it going to be dangerous for us to be there? Should I try to convince Mom we shouldn't go?"

"No, no. You'll be fine. Besides, there's nothing on earth that could convince your mother to stay at home tonight. What I'm trying to say is … if this thing does happen, you need to get out of there as quickly as you can. Come back home and come up to the attic. Wait for me here."

"*Wait* for you? But—where are you going? You can't get out."

"I can't explain. Just promise you'll do that, okay?"

"Okay. Yes, of course."

"Siennaaaaa!"

"Right, gotta go. Love you." Sienna pulled the door shut before Elle could reply. She stared at it for a second or two before her shoulders drooped. She stepped forward, shut her eyes, and pressed her forehead against the door. Perhaps she shouldn't have said anything to Sienna, not when the chances were slim that tonight would actually end with the Godmother granting Elle's wish. But part of her believed this could still work. There was still time. She could still come up with a brilliant plan that hadn't yet occurred to her. Like … like abandoning the ball, breaking into Apollo's Apothecary, and stealing a wish. Then she wouldn't need the Godmother.

"Ugh, that's a *terrible* idea," she moaned out loud.

In response, someone squeaked at her.

Elle whirled around, and there on her bed, as if her desperate thoughts had summoned the tiny creature, was her pixie ally. "You came back!" Elle said. She rushed across the room and knelt beside the bed so she was almost eye level with the pixie. The miniature winged woman handed her a tiny glass bottle with a small, folded note tied to the side. Elle opened the note with shaking fingers.

This potion isn't exactly legal. I almost ignored your request. But I like you, E, and I'm choosing to believe that your desperation is genuine. Since you're not killing anyone for real, I'm happy to help you. I hope this moves you forward in the journey toward your freedom.

Add just a few drops of this potion to your target's food or drink, and he or she will pass out within minutes. Your target will appear to be dead and will remain that way for at least a day. Longer, if you use more of the potion.

Good luck, and be careful.

Elle wrapped her hand around the note and clutched it against her chest, her relief almost overwhelming her. "Thank you so much!" she said to the pixie. "I wish you were big enough for me to hug you. Thank you, thank you, thank you. You may have just saved my life, and I don't even know your name."

The pixie squeaked. She swept one tiny hand through her short blond locks before bobbing in a way that might have been considered a curtsy.

"I wish I could understand you. I'm sorry. It must seem to you that I'm speaking frustratingly slowly."

In response, all she received was a shrug.

"I would call you Pistachio," Elle continued, "but that's kind of a mouthful. How about Stash? Oh, or Tash. That's better. What do you think?"

The pixie patted her hand.

"Okay, we'll go with Tash. Then I can stop thinking of you as The Pixie with the Pistachio Shell Hat."

Tash bent over and plucked a loose silver thread from one of the stars on Elle's bedspread. Then she flew up to the top of Elle's wardrobe and disappeared from view. "Payment?" Elle wondered out loud. If so, she didn't mind. Tash could have all the silver threads she wanted.

Elle opened one of the wardrobe doors and hid the potion among her socks. Then she wandered over to the window and peered out. She watched the sun set. She watched Salvia, Meredith and Sienna climb into a chauffeur-driven limousine. Meredith could barely fit through the limo door in her gigantic, puffy skirt, and Salvia's frilly, mermaid-style dress was so tight she had to shuffle rather than walk. The limo disappeared down the road, and Elle continued watching. Then she watched the moon rise higher and higher, until eventually the panic of the last few days began to grip hold of her again. Where was the Godmother? What if she'd forgotten all about her deal with Elle?

"Estelle."

Elle jumped at the sound of the familiar voice, almost knocking her head against the window. How did the darn woman appear so silently? Not a footstep nor a sizzle of magic nor even a breath.

"Ready for a party?" the Godmother asked as Elle turned to face her. She was leaning against the wardrobe, her arms folded and one high-heeled ankle boot crossed in front of the other.

Elle couldn't help frowning. "I thought you'd be here sooner. I'm already late for the start of the ball."

"Exactly, my dear. There's no other way to make an entrance."

FIVE

"RIGHT THEN," THE GODMOTHER SAID, PUSHING AWAY FROM THE WARDROBE AND walking toward Elle. "This shouldn't take long." She snapped her fingers near Elle's hair, then again in front of Elle's face. Elle blinked and coughed as the smell of powder filled her nose. And her hair was … no longer hanging lifelessly down her back?

"What did you just—"

The Godmother snapped her fingers a third time, and a mirror with a pretty silver frame appeared on her open palm. She held it up with both hands in front of Elle's face. Elle blinked at her reflection. Her makeup was flawless— eyes startlingly blue amid shimmering, dark eyeshadow, cheekbones perfectly accentuated, full lips painted dark red—and her hair appeared to have been partially French-braided before being expertly gathered up at the nape of her neck. All within the space of about two seconds.

"Stars above," she whispered. "That was fast."

"I'm the Godmother, darling. Did you expect anything less?"

"It's just … most fae have to speak spells out loud or wait for magic to appear in their hands," Elle said, "but you didn't say a word, and I didn't see any faerie dust either."

"I've had plenty of time to perfect all the magic any faerie could ever dream of using, including the visualization of spells as opposed to utterances. And faerie dust itself isn't actually necessary."

Plenty of time, Elle repeated silently. As the Godmother tapped her chin with one shiny black fingernail and scrutinized Elle from the neck downward, Elle wondered if the rumors were true. The rumors that said the Godmother had used wish magic to extend her life beyond that which was normal for the fae. And fae had long lives to begin with. "Exactly how old are you?" she asked.

"Elle!" The Godmother clenched her hand, an affronted look on her face. "You never ask a woman her age."

"Right, sorry."

With another finger snap, Elle's jeans and T-shirt vanished, leaving her standing in only her underwear. Underwear, she noted with surprise, that was brand new and far prettier than anything she owned. "Is, um, is the finger snap necessary?" she asked, mostly to divert attention from her near nakedness.

"Not at all." The Godmother snapped her fingers once more, and layers of soft blue fabric sprouted out of nowhere and wrapped themselves around Elle's form. "But that doesn't mean it isn't fun." The fabric tightened itself around Elle's chest and waist, while growing more voluminous around her legs. More layers than Sienna's dress, but nothing near the size of Meredith's monstrous gown. "Oh, and shoes," the Godmother added with an effortless twirl of her fingers. Elle felt her heels rise as something rigid formed around her feet. "Take a look," the Godmother said. Elle realized the hand mirror was now floating in the air, and within seconds, it had expanded to the size of a door.

Elle gaped at her reflection. From its sweetheart neckline and off-the-shoulder sleeves to its cinched waist, the dress fit her perfectly. Perhaps it was the way the moonlight shone in through the window, but the dress seemed almost to glow, and tiny pinpricks of light glistened within the fabric like stars in an early evening sky. A string of diamonds sparkled around her neck, and in her right hand was a mask of delicate silver filigree.

"It's absolutely magnificent," she breathed. "Is it my imagination, or are the stars in the fabric actually twinkling?"

"It's not your imagination. And neither is the subtle glow of moonlight emanating from the dress. Of course, there will be other girls wearing dresses with magic woven into them, but I like to think you'll stand out in a creation that's not only stunning but perfectly fits the theme."

"Moonlight Masquerade," Elle whispered.

"Exactly."

"The only thing …" she added, trying to wiggle her toes. She lifted the skirt and looked down to see glittering crystal heels encasing her feet. She raised her eyes and met the Godmother's gaze in the mirror. The woman pinned her with a glare.

"The only thing is *what*?" she demanded.

"Well … the shoes are quite uncomfortable. I'm not sure I'll be able to walk in them."

"Well then." The Godmother clapped her hands, and the discomfort vanished. "You can go barefoot."

"Oh. I didn't mean—"

"Those are the shoes, Elle. Take them or leave them. I've used enough magic on you already."

"Well … can't I just wear some of my own shoes?"

The Godmother tipped her head back and laughed. "You think you have something appropriate?"

"No, but it's not like anyone's going to see them." Elle placed the mask on her bed before swishing her way to her wardrobe. She pulled the doors open, and her eyes fell on her rhinestone-studded combat boots. *Perfect*, she thought as she reached for them. They were, after all, her favorite shoes. More importantly, they would give her somewhere to hide the potion.

"Stars help me," the Godmother muttered as Elle grabbed a pair of socks—and the tiny potion bottle. "This girl has *zero* fashion sense."

"It's fine," Elle assured her as she sat on the edge of her bed. "Like I said, no one will see them." She pulled the skirt up, put her socks on, and surreptitiously slipped the potion bottle into the top of the right sock. Then she pulled the boots on.

"Those might be the most hideous shoes I've ever seen," the Godmother commented.

"I love them," Elle replied. She stood and let the skirt fall down to cover her feet. "See? All gone. No one will ever know. And if someone does see them and comments on how *hideous* they are, I promise I won't tell them it was the Godmother who dressed me." She looked up with an innocent smile. The Godmother narrowed her eyes.

"As long as you can kill the prince while wearing them, I don't particularly care what you choose to put on your feet."

Elle's smile vanished as quickly as if someone had dumped ice water over her head. "Of—of course. I can do that."

"Good."

"Why do you want him dead?" she blurted out.

The Godmother merely stared.

"Right," Elle muttered. "None of my business."

"Exactly. Now, I think it's time to get you to the ball."

Elle nodded. "I assume you can take care of the confinement charm on the attic?"

"Taken care of already," the Godmother said. "And as long as you're back in here by midnight, there won't be a problem."

"But … if it's gone, then why—"

"Because that is the time limit I've set for you, Elle. I can't have you taking all night trying to decide if you can really do this or not. At midnight, if you're not already back in this attic, magic will bring you back. I'll meet you here. If you've paid your price, I will then grant you your wish."

"But what if something goes wrong and it takes me longer to complete the task than expected?"

"Well, then you'll wind up back in this attic without having completed your side of our bargain. I won't grant you a wish, you'll still be a slave, and the confinement charm will reappear."

"But—"

"Please stop arguing with me. Your task is not that complicated, and you'll have more than enough time. Just get it done, and everything will be fine. Can you handle that?"

Just get it done. It should be easy. The potion should work. But what if it didn't? What if Elle put it in his drink and nothing happened? What if she was left with no other option but to do as the Godmother asked and actually kill the prince? As she stared at the woman, Elle wondered if she could actually go through with that. To be honest, she didn't know. She wouldn't know until she was faced with the certainty that there was no other way out. "Will it hurt him?" she asked quietly. "Will he feel pain? When I take all his memories, I mean. When I take … his whole mind."

"No," the Godmother said, and Elle wasn't brave enough to ask if she was lying. "Now." She clasped her hands together. "Time to go. And don't forget your mask." She moved toward the bed, and the mask floated up to meet her hand. She half turned toward Elle, then paused. She stared at the bed with a frown.

"What?" Elle asked.

The Godmother looked up and flicked her hand. The mask spun lazily through the air toward Elle. "Nothing. I like the quilt. That's all."

"Oh. Okay." *That was weird.* She caught the mask as the Godmother raised her hand, smiled a glossy-lipped smile, and snapped her fingers. The room vanished. Something jolted Elle's body, and when her surroundings reappeared, she was standing on the sidewalk in front of her house. She took in a gulp of air and pressed her free hand to her chest. "That, um, didn't feel so good."

"My apologies. I always forget that humans don't respond well to being hurtled through space by magic."

As Elle took another few breaths and felt her body return to normal, she glanced both ways along the road. The police were no longer patrolling this street, and though it had been almost a week since she was locked in her attic, there was always the possibility of a hopeful vampire or two hanging around, waiting for her to leave her house.

"Looking for something?" the Godmother asked.

"Just … checking things out."

"Vampires can no longer see this street, in case that's the thing you were checking for."

"They … what? What do you mean?"

"They simply walk right past it from the street on one side to the street on the other. As simple as that.”

Elle blinked as her eyebrows pulled into a frown. “But …”

“I heard you had some vampire problems on this street. I thought I should take care of that for you.”

Elle was about to ask how the Godmother had heard of the vampire attack—and why she even cared—but she knew without opening her mouth that she wouldn’t get answers. So all she said was, “Thanks?”

“Good, that’s what I was hoping you would say. And now for some transportation.” She rubbed her hands together, then spun her arm in circles before sweeping it out to the side. The distant roar of a revving engine reached Elle’s ears. “Before you ask,” the Godmother said, “the answer is no. The hand gesture wasn’t necessary. But I enjoy a good flourish.” The engine roar grew louder, and seconds later, a streamlined, low-slung vehicle zoomed into Elle’s street and came to an abrupt halt in front of her house.

“A sports car?” Elle asked, unable to keep the doubt from her voice.

“Yes. Isn’t it fabulous? I haven’t conjured up one of these in ages.”

“It’s pumpkin orange,” Elle pointed out.

“It is.”

“It’s probably visible from the moon.”

“Would you prefer to walk?” the Godmother asked, her tone icy.

“No, no. Not at all. I’m happy with the flashy orange car. It’s just … you know. Not exactly subtle.”

“No, it is not.” The Godmother waved her hand, and the passenger door opened. “I never intended for your arrival at the ball to be subtle. Now, climb in. You’ll find it a little more spacious than most sports vehicles. I had to make room for your lovely dress.”

Having never been inside a sports car of any kind, Elle had nothing to compare the interior space to. But the seat was comfortable—perfectly molded to her body, in fact—and there was plenty of room for her dress. There was also a noticeable lack of anyone resembling a driver. “Um—”

“Don’t worry. The car knows where to go. I hope you have fun tonight, Elle,” she added, placing one hand on top of the car and leaning down to peer at Elle. "Other than the murder part, of course. Though that can be fun too, if you let it."

"Uh …" Elle couldn't think of a single thing to say to that.

"Anyway, I have other wishes to attend to." The Godmother tilted her arm and narrowed her eyes at the gold watch on her wrist. *Not a watch*, Elle corrected herself as she caught a glimpse of the circular face that had tiny images flashing across its surface instead of a clock face. "Yes, things are looking busy tonight."

"What do you do if multiple people summon you at the same time?" Elle asked, the thought only occurring to her now. "And what if people summon you while you're asleep?"

"Elle, my dear. You can't possibly think this is a one-woman show. You're aware that I run an entire *empire* based on the trade of wishes? I have many people who work for me. They answer the summons if I'm busy. They liaise with me, communicate prices, follow up on whether the other party has completed their side of the deal. Then I grant the wishes. Not everyone is lucky enough to spend so much time with me. You should be honored that I've taken such a personal interest in your situation."

Honored—or scared, Elle thought. "And you've never been worried that you'll be caught? That someone's wish is actually a trap for you? That your whole … empire, as you call it, will come crashing down around you?"

"Is that a threat?"

"No, not at all," Elle hastened to say. "I need a wish, and you're the one giving it to me. I'm not about to mess that up." *At least, I hope I'm not*, she added silently.

"Some have tried to betray me over the years," the Godmother said. "It's never worked out well for any of them."

A shiver zipped its way along Elle's arms. Would the Godmother see it as a *betrayal* if Elle managed to successfully trick her tonight? Hopefully not. Elle wasn't threatening the Godmother's empire in any way. And she kind of technically was following through on her side of the bargain. She *would* kill the prince. If only for a few hours.

"One last thing," the Godmother said. "I've added a little something to the magic I've placed on you to help you locate the prince."

"Oh. But I doubt I'll have any trouble locating him. I'm sure it'll be obvious who he is."

"I'm sure it will be, but the ballroom will be crowded, and everyone will be vying for his attention. He'll be moving around, dancing with numerous women. And everyone will be wearing masks. You may find it hard to get to him without a little magical assistance."

"Okay," Elle said with a shrug. "Whatever you think is best."

"And don't do that, dear," she added, placing a hand lightly on Elle's shoulder. "Princesses don't shrug."

"But I'm not a—"

"Doesn't matter. Prince Chevalier needs to think you could be." She stepped back, waved, and the car door swung shut. The engine revved. Then, in a rush of speed, the pumpkin orange sports car shot forward, carrying Elle toward the ball and her last hope at freedom.

SIX

Belmont Palace sat in all its glittering glory beneath twinkling stars and a crescent moon, making Elle feel as small as Tash the pixie as she stood in front of it. Her mouth fell open while her eyes traced over towers, domes, pillars, statues, and a vast, sweeping staircase. She definitely didn't belong in a place like this.

And yet, she'd had no trouble getting through the massive gate about halfway up Sovereign Hill. Several guards and a glowing barrier of magic had stopped her car, and Elle had just about had heart failure when the driver's window slid down and a guard peered inside, saying, "Invitation, please."

She'd held her breath, barely moved, and stared at the empty driver's seat, hoping something magical would happen. And something magical *must* have happened because several moments later, the guard said, "Perfect, thanks. Go ahead." Then he stepped away from the car, the magic barrier disappeared, and Elle continued her journey up a magnificent, rose bush-lined driveway.

The car dropped her off at the foot of the staircase leading up to the grand entrance, which was where she currently stood, gawking at the magnificent palace and seriously rethinking her level of bravery. Could she really do this?

Yes, you can, she told herself firmly. *It's just a party. He's just a guy. And it's just a few drops of a potion.* She raised the delicate silver mask to cover the upper part of her face and tied the ribbons behind her head. Then she ascended the stairs.

Inside, she passed between two lines of uniformed fae, a mixture of men and women, all standing perfectly upright with their hands clasped together in front of them. Feeling about a thousand percent awkward, Elle kept her gaze pointed forward. Unless someone stepped in front of her, she wasn't about to stop moving. *Pretend you belong here*, she reminded herself as she swallowed. *You do this all the time. You have confidence. And you most certainly are* not *wearing cheap, chunky combat boots beneath this gorgeous ball gown.*

The last man in the right-hand line of fae extended one arm toward another staircase on the other side of the vast hallway. "That way, my lady." Elle glanced at him and inclined her head in a small nod. Perhaps this was the way it worked for every guest, or perhaps it was a product of the Godmother's magic. Elle didn't care. She continued forward at the same pace, though it took all her willpower not to break into a run to get away from the fae she knew were watching her. She could have managed it pretty easily in her combat boots. She was grateful she'd chosen them, despite the fact that they were completely out of place. She never would have made it up all those stairs outside—and now another staircase inside—in those crystal heels the Godmother had conjured up.

At the top of the stairs, she was directed by another two fae toward a pair of closed doors, large and intricately inlaid with patterns of gold. As she approached, the two men standing in front of the doors straightened a little. They pushed their shoulders back and lifted their chins, and Elle remembered that she was late. These men probably didn't think they'd be opening the doors again until guests started to leave later tonight. After a curious glance in her direction, they each reached for a door handle. The doors swung open, and Elle was finally at the Moonlight Masquerade Ball.

She stepped through the doorway and looked around. A staircase—yes, more stairs—led down to the main part of the ballroom, which was filled with beautiful people in extravagant clothes. But it was the ceiling of the ballroom that caught Elle's attention. Or rather, what the ceiling was enchanted to be. It appeared that the ballroom was open to the sky, and an enormous moon—far bigger and fuller than the real moon outside—illuminated the room in silvery light. Tiny stars glittered all around the moon, as well as within the walls and the glossy marble floor, which Elle caught glimpses of as the guests mingled and danced. Floating globes of golden light added to the moon's glow, ensuring the ballroom was well lit.

Elle moved forward. She wasn't royalty or nobility, so nobody announced her arrival in the ballroom—she'd heard that was a thing the fae liked to do—but she noticed dozens of heads turning toward her as she descended the stairs. She was grateful for the mask that partially concealed her face. Her family had never seen her dressed in such finery, and with her face half covered, there was no way on earth they'd recognize her.

The crowd made way for her as she reached the ballroom floor. The Godmother would be pleased if she were here. She'd hoped Elle would stand out enough to grab the prince's attention. Elle hadn't thought about the fact that this meant grabbing everyone else's attention too. How was she supposed to put a potion into the prince's drink if half the people here were watching her? But as she swished her way through the crowd, the heads slowly turned away from hers and back toward whatever they'd been focused on before she arrived. Conversation or dancing or prince-watching.

They were mostly fae, Elle noted, but she spotted a few vampires and shifters. At least, she assumed they were shifters and not humans. Based on all the gossip she'd overheard while out running errands for Salvia last week—before she was permanently confined to her attic—the royal family was making a show of being inclusive by inviting certain vampires and shifters. But they hadn't stooped so low as to include any humans on the guest list.

Oh, and there was Sienna! Elle almost called out to the girl in the gray-green dress and butterfly-shaped mask before reminding herself it was better if Sienna didn't know she was here. There would be far too much explaining to do otherwise. Besides, she was currently dancing with someone, and it looked as though she was actually having a good time. Though this someone was not Elon, Elle realized as she noticed the young man's very tanned skin. Elon was as pale as Sienna, and only a little taller than her. This guy was ... *Hang on.* Was it Dex's friend Xander? Elle took a closer look at Sienna's dance partner. He wasn't wearing a mask, and when he turned again, it was easy to see that it was him.

Elle frowned with disapproval. Xander seemed like a nice enough guy, but he also liked to hunt vampires and operate outside the law. He would only be trouble for Sienna. Besides, wasn't he too old for her? Elle guessed he was in his early twenties, while Sienna was only seventeen. She shouldn't be getting involved with—

Elle caught herself mid-thought and almost laughed at her overprotective instincts. She had nothing to worry about. It was just a dance. Besides, she and Sienna would be on the run later tonight—tomorrow morning at the latest—and neither of them would have time for trouble-making boys while trying to hide from Salvia and the Godmother. The more important question was this: Why wasn't Sienna working to keep Meredith away from the prince?

Elle continued in the direction most of the crowd seemed to slowly be moving—that was surely the direction in which she would find Prince Chevalier—and only then did her thoughts take the logical next step they should have immediately taken the moment she saw Xander: If he was here, maybe Dex was too.

No, you have to focus, she told herself firmly. She was here to pretend-kill a prince—hopefully *before* he got a chance to lay eyes on Meredith—not to find the guy she'd almost kissed and then run away from.

"Have you had a chance to dance with him yet?" The question wasn't louder than any of the other voices nearby, but it was the chilling familiarity of it that grabbed Elle's attention. She inhaled sharply and turned away from the source of the voice.

Salvia.

How, in an entire ballroom crowded with people, had she managed to almost bump into her horrid stepmother so quickly?

"No!" a second familiar voice exclaimed. That was Meredith. Elle kept her face turned away and her ears tuned to their voices. "I only just got out of the bathroom," Meredith added. "That custard was super sticky and the cleaning spell took forever. I swear Sienna did it on purpose."

"She'll be punished, don't worry," Salvia said. "When I find her later."

"Ugh, I haven't even *seen* the prince yet," Meredith complained. "I can't get close enough."

"He's the one in the gold mask. It's covering most of his face."

"I *know*. I heard something about a gold mask. I just haven't seen anyone wearing it yet."

Gold mask, Elle thought. *Good to know. And well done, Sienna, for spilling food on Meredith's dress.*

She moved away from Salvia and Meredith as quickly as she could, heading for the center of the room where the dance floor was located. Whenever groups of people stood on tiptoe and stared in a certain direction, she altered her course slightly. If she followed the crowd's attention, she would find him eventually. Or—Hang on. Why was the crowd parting again? Nobody was turned toward her this time, so—

Holy stars, he was coming toward her. A man in a gold mask. Prince Chevalier of House Belmont himself. Was it really going to be this easy? *He* was coming to *her*? Suddenly, she wanted to flee in the opposite direction. She couldn't do this. How exactly had the Godmother expected her to lead the prince away to a quiet corner and use her special ability on him? There were no quiet corners in a ballroom of a thousand gossiping voices and two thousand gawking eyeballs!

"Hi," the prince said, stopping in front of her. His mouth was visible, but the mask—which was solid, unlike the intricate wire work of her own—covered most of the rest of his face.

"Hi," she answered, but her voice was so quiet even she couldn't hear it. She cleared her throat and tried again. "Hello."

"I saw you come in," he said. "On the stairs. It's daring of you to arrive so late to a royal function."

"Oh, right. I'm so sorry about that. Car trouble. It … arrived late to pick me up. Your highness—er, royal highness," she added hastily at the end. That was something she should have gone over with the Godmother. How to properly address a prince so she didn't offend him within seconds of meeting him.

"It's fine, you don't have to worry about being so formal," he said with a laugh. "And I admire the fact that you were still brave enough to come inside, even though you were so late. Do you want to dance?"

Oh crap. Oh stars. Why hadn't it crossed her mind that she might actually have to *dance* tonight? Like, formal dancing with formal steps. Why hadn't she discussed this part with the Godmother? It probably would have been a simple spell—just another snap of the Godmother's fingers—if only she'd thought to mention it. "I can't dance," she blurted out. "Maybe we can—talk?"

"Talking's good too. I'm quite tired of all the dancing, actually. Should we move out of the way?"

"Sure," she said, though it was hardly necessary. He could have planted himself in the center of the dance floor and everyone would still have parted around him.

They walked together toward the edge of the ballroom, and something niggled at the back of Elle's mind as she snuck sideways glances at the prince. There was something familiar about him. The way he held himself, the shape of his face, the color of his hair. He looked almost like …

But it couldn't be …

They stopped moving, and in a rush of bravery and shock, Elle reached up and tugged the prince's mask away.

SEVEN

"You're—"

But it wasn't him. She'd been so sure for a moment. So sure that the fae prince she was standing in front of was actually Dex. But of course it wasn't him. What a crazy notion. It didn't even *sound* like him, though with all the noise in the ballroom, it had been difficult to tell.

"Excuse me," Prince Chevalier said, stepping hastily away from her. She caught a glimpse of his disapproval before he slid his mask back into place. "I'm afraid this conversation is over." He turned and strode away, and Elle felt her hope slipping through her fingers like fine sand.

No, this is NOT over yet. She could still make this work. She crouched down and pulled the tiny potion bottle from her right sock. Clutching it against her palm, she hurried after the prince. She probably looked ridiculously desperate, but she'd already made a fool of herself in front of him; how much worse could things get?

"I'm so, so sorry," she gasped, pushing past several women and placing herself in the prince's path. "You said you admire my bravery, so I thought … I mean … well, we all know why we're here. We know you're supposed to be choosing someone to marry. But if you and I can't even see each other, then how can we really know each other? And how can you choose someone from this room if you don't actually know any of us?"

To Elle's great surprise, the prince paused instead of running in the opposite direction. She wished she could see his expression. "That's probably the most honest thing anyone's said to me tonight," he told her. "But why does it matter what we *look* like? I think it's far more important to get to know one another without our outward appearances getting in the way."

"True," Elle admitted. Darn, that was actually a good point. Why did she have to blurt out something that made her sound so shallow? "The masks just feel like additional barriers between us, that's all. As if they're helping us pretend to be someone we're not. But when the masks are removed, we have to be ourselves." That sounded good, didn't it? Hopefully it was a believable enough excuse for why she'd so abruptly pulled his mask off. "At least have a drink with me," she said as a waiter approached the prince with a tray of champagne flutes. "One glass of champagne. They don't even have that much in them," she added, eyeing the bubbly liquid in the glasses. "It's not like you'll be stuck with me for long."

The prince actually smiled. "I suppose one drink wouldn't hurt." He looked at the waiter and asked, "They've been checked?" He gestured to the glasses.

"Yes, your highness," the waiter responded. "You can confirm with Lord Hinton." He looked over his shoulder, and the prince followed his gaze. Elle tried to see over the tops of people's heads, but before she could locate whoever the prince was looking at, he stepped forward and lifted two glasses from the tray. He handed one to her, and she took it, sensing her fingers shaking. Hopefully he didn't notice.

Now or never, she told herself. *Just get this thing done.* She took a step to the side and pretended to stumble over something. "Oh, oops!" She made a show of looking down near her feet for this imaginary something, and the prince followed her gaze. With her eyes still peering down and her hands holding the glass close to her chest, she flicked the tiny cork out of the top of the potion bottle and quickly tipped the contents into her own champagne. "I don't see anything," she said, frowning at the floor. Then she laughed, hoping it didn't sound as fake to him as it did to her. "Probably just my own clumsiness. Here, would you hold this for me?" She handed her glass back to him. "I just want to straighten the bottom of my dress."

"Oh, okay."

There was nothing to straighten, but Elle spent a few moments crouching down anyway, fiddling with the layers of fabric while stealthily wiping the potion bottle free of her fingerprints. She dropped it on the floor somewhere near her feet. "All good," she said as she straightened. "Thank you." She reached out and took the glass without the potion. She saw the prince start to protest, to tell her the other glass was hers, but he stopped. Probably for the same reason she would have chosen to say nothing: Neither of them had actually drunk anything yet. It didn't matter whose glass was whose. They were exactly the same, as far as he knew.

"Cheers!" Elle said, raising her glass quickly and taking a sip before the prince could say anything. "Oh, this is delicious," she rambled, and drank again. The prince's eyebrows rose the tiniest bit, but he lifted his glass, and Elle watched as a decent amount of potion-laced champagne slid past his lips.

Yes! She almost shouted out loud with glee but somehow managed to keep her mouth shut. It was a little harder, though, to keep her triumphant smile to herself. She sipped her champagne again to try to cover the smile and ended up choking a little. The prince's eyebrows climbed a fraction higher. Wonderful. She was digging herself a deeper and deeper hole here. Not that it mattered. She'd done what she came here to do. Now she just had to wait a few minutes to make sure it worked.

"You okay there?" Prince Chevalier asked.

"Yep, all good. I'm just enjoying the champagne so much." *Oh, dear stars. Stop. Talking. Now.*

The prince's mouth quirked up on one side. "What's your name?"

"I'm—uh—Trixie Gold." She'd come scarily close to using her real name. She needed to stop sipping the champagne.

"Gold? Interesting. Is that a fae name?"

Crap. She let out a giggly, high-pitched laugh. "Last time I checked."

"Well, Trixie Gold. I'd love to spend a little more time with you, I really would, but I can see some of the other ladies around us getting impatient."

"Oh, yes, of course. I wouldn't want to hog your attention for too long." And she definitely didn't want to be the one standing in front of him when the potion started working.

"I hope you enjoy the rest of the evening," the prince said, and after a final nod, he walked away and greeted another woman.

Elle let out a long breath, placed her glass on a passing tray, and began to inch her way toward the edge of the ballroom while still keeping the prince in her line of sight. What exactly had Cress's note said? The potion should start working within minutes, right? But roughly how many minutes? She wished Cress had been more specific. The prince hadn't finished all the champagne in his glass, but that shouldn't be a problem. She'd tossed more than just a few drops in there. But what if the darn thing didn't actually work? How long did she need to wait before confirming this?

But then the prince staggered forward. He caught himself against the woman he was currently talking to, who didn't seem to mind in the least that Prince Chevalier of House Belmont was currently using her to prop himself up. Then he lurched to the side and landed on his knees. Gasps filled the air, accompanied by a few laughs from people who obviously thought he'd tripped.

A shout reached Elle's ears. She assumed it was something to do with the prince—someone calling for help or shouting to ask if he was okay—but when more shouts joined the first and the undulating motion of a flag—a flag?—caught her eye, she realized the shouts had nothing to do with Prince Chevalier.

In the center of the dance floor, a small group of people were raising colorful flags and banners with words written in bold, block letters across them: END THE SLAVE CHARM, and HUMANS ARE OUR EQUALS, and FREEDOM: EVERYONE'S RIGHT. People jumped and waved their flags, tugging fake ear tips off to reveal that they were human. Though it appeared there were fae among their number as well. And even … a vampire or two?

"Oh, stars," Elle muttered. She was fully in support of their cause, but this was not the time to start a protest. It would only anger the king, and he was already opposed to the idea of free humans. Not to mention someone was probably about to discover that Prince Chevalier was 'dead.' That would not look good for the anti-slavery campaign.

It was *definitely* time to get out of here. She shuffled back a little more. She was on the side of the ballroom opposite the staircase, where arched doorways led into the garden. Uniformed fae stood beside each arch, but they didn't appear to be stopping anyone from walking outside. It was probably easier to leave that way than to try to get past the protesters and across the crowded room to the stairs.

She was about to turn toward the garden when someone caught her eye. Someone with red eyes and blond hair and a dark blue mask that covered only part of his face. It had been dark on the bridge that night in Belgravia, but she'd seen his face in the glow of unnatural magic that rippled off his body and she recognized it instantly now. Fear froze her to the spot.

Nik.

Elle's eyes slid down, and as Nik pushed his way between the ball's guests, she made out the faint glimmer of faerie dust somewhere near his hands. Then another gold flicker grabbed her attention: Another vampire, unsmiling, inching through the crowd without speaking to anyone. And there was a third, she noticed suddenly. And with everyone's attention focused on the protest, it seemed no one noticed these strange vampires in their midst, slowly making their way toward … the fallen prince?

"Oh no," Elle whispered. "No, no, no." There were Allegiant vampires *right here in this ballroom*. Things were going to go south very quickly. She had to get away. And she had to get Sienna out of here too. She spun around. "Where are you, where are you?" she muttered. As soon as she found her and they got to the edge of the ballroom, she could yell out a warning about the—

What was that? There, on the far side of the ballroom, was the shimmer of a gray-green dress. The one Elle had been looking out for. Sienna was running up the stairs and away from all the commotion. Of course, Elle realized. Because that's what she had told her to do when something went wrong tonight. Sienna must think she'd been referring to the protest.

Well, Sienna was safe then. Now Elle only had to worry about herself. And a ballroom full of innocent people. She turned toward the garden and pushed against the crowd to get to the closest archway. "Excuse me, sir," she said to the faerie who stood guard there. "Do you see that vampire there?" she pointed behind her. "And those two there. Oh, stars, and there's another one. They have magic. And they're heading for the prince. They're—"

She was interrupted by a blood-chilling scream. The fae guard launched away from her, magic glowing all around him. Elle didn't wait to find out what would happen next. She grabbed handfuls of her skirt and raced into the garden. At the sound of footsteps and screams behind her, she threw a glance over her shoulder and saw she wasn't the only one fleeing this way. She hesitated and slowed, watching as most people ran left around the outside of the building. Was that the quickest way to get back to the front of the palace? These people would surely know better than her.

But seconds later, a gold mesh-like barrier appeared in the air, blocking the path of everyone running around that side of the palace. Probably all part of tonight's security, Elle thought. Maybe there were private buildings that way. She took off in the opposite direction, skirting around a fountain and keeping her eyes peeled for an open door or window. It might be that the only way back to the front of the palace was to go through it. In fact, now that she thought about it, that made sense. The royal family wouldn't want people wandering around the entirety of the palace grounds. They'd probably enclosed a small section of the garden for guests to enjoy, while making sure to keep the rest private. She wouldn't be surprised if that magic barrier she'd seen arced through the garden and came back around to meet the other end of the palace. In which case, she would run into it sooner or later.

Something made her slow near a trellis covered in climbing roses. Had she seen something move there? She couldn't be sure, but some instinct made her want to take a closer look. She hurried to the trellis and carefully pushed aside several white roses, careful to avoid the thorns. She expected to see bricks there—after all, the trellis was secured directly to the palace wall—but instead, she found a door. "Yes," she whispered. She hooked her fingers into the diamond shapes of the trellis and tugged on it. It swung away from the wall easily, and she realized it had hinges on one side. It was meant to open and close.

She reached for the handle and turned it, whispering, "Please, please, please—" And the door opened. She rushed inside, leaving the door open for anyone else who might want to escape this way. Except, she now realized as she ran along the dark passageway, the moonlight from behind her just barely lighting the way, this might not be an escape. She might end up lost inside this enormous palace, unable to find her way back to the garden or back to the front. But when she came to a simple staircase, she ran up it anyway.

She reached the top, stepped quietly around a screen, and found herself in a small sitting room. Moonlight filtered through the large windows, illuminating antique furniture, thick rugs, and old portraits of people Elle didn't recognize. The only sound was her breathing. She made for the door toward her right, then stopped when she realized there was another on the left side of the room. Crap, how was she supposed to know which way to go? Left? Right? Back down to the garden? But she felt an odd pull toward the door on the right. Hopefully that was her directional instinct kicking in—if such a thing existed.

She tiptoed to the door, opened it a sliver, and peeked out. The corridor beyond, embellished with wooden paneling and lamps sitting on decorative sconces, was empty. She closed the door quietly behind her and hurried along the corridor, trusting her instincts again and heading in the direction that *felt* right, rather than deliberating over which way was most likely to lead her to the front of the palace.

She passed through another sitting room, then another corridor, and then a small dining room. More stairs, more turns, more portraits and tapestries and flower arrangements tall enough to reach the ceiling. She was aware with every passing second that she was probably about to land herself in enormous trouble, rather than escape it. But she couldn't stop. Something urged her forward. And so she hurried on.

When she finally approached a set of wooden double doors with a pattern of leafy vines etched around the edge, it felt as if something that had been tightly coiled within her began to relax. This was the way out. She was sure of it.

She put her ear against the door, but all she heard was silence. A smothering, all-encompassing kind of silence. For several moments, she couldn't even hear her quick breaths or her racing heart. She pulled back quickly, away from the strange vacuum of sound. But silence was *good*, she reminded herself. It meant no one was on the other side of these doors. And this was definitely the right direction to head. So she gripped the knob of the right-hand door, twisted, and pushed the door open just enough to look beyond it.

Warm light fell through the opening, and voices greeted her ears as abruptly as if a TV had just been switched on. She should turn and run, but she was too surprised to move. In the space of about three seconds, she took in the strange scene: A mixture of fae and vampires, all standing around a giant antique desk in the middle of a large study, discussing something while moving papers and diagrams around. Not fighting or arguing, as fae and vampires were prone to do. Looking for all the world as if they were working together.

But that wasn't the strangest thing of all.

No. The part that hit Elle in the gut and made her simultaneously burning hot and icy cold was the sight of the man standing behind the desk, pointing at a page and saying, "… probably try to come from this side."

It was definitely him this time. There was no mistake.

"Dex?" Elle said.

Silence. Every eye in the room swung toward her. In a flash of motion, two vampires were beside her. One grabbed her right arm and whipped her mask off, while the other took her left arm. The doors clanged shut behind her with a sizzle of magic. "Your highness," one of the vampires said, and Elle realized his words were directed at Dex. "What do you want us to do with her?"

EIGHT

Five Days Before The Moonlight Masquerade Ball

DEX PACED THE STONE FLOOR OF THE DUNGEON BENEATH XANDER'S FAMILY'S HOME. The dungeon hadn't been used in decades. At least, not that Xander's family knew of. Take right now, for example. They had no idea a vampire sat bound in chains of magic beneath the polished floors of their stately home.

The vampire, Azriel, had been here since the night before, when Xander and Olly had spotted him in the vicinity of the bridge where that magic-wielding vampire had revealed himself. They'd knocked Azriel out with magic—a feat that was probably only possible because he didn't know it was coming—and brought him straight back here, far from the prying eyes of Dex's parents and everyone else at Belmont Palace.

They'd given Azriel the night to sleep off the effects of the magic, but now that he was awake, it was time to get some useful information out of him. "Has it been long enough?" Dex asked.

"Still another minute," Olly said, taking a look at his cell phone screen and continuing to tap one foot quietly against the floor.

"You're very impatient," Azriel commented, his eyes pinned on Dex. "You should try some relaxation techniques. Meditation, perhaps."

Xander took a step closer to Azriel, muttering something about meditation and sticking things where the sun didn't shine. If Dex wasn't concerned with sparing his energy, he might have responded. But the truth spell he'd performed was a complicated one, and once it began working, it would tire both him and Azriel. Azriel more so, since he would be the one struggling to hide the truth as the magic of the spell pulled it out of him. But Dex would suffer too.

"I know who you are," Azriel said to Dex, and that was enough to stop Dex mid-stride.

Don't let him get to you, he reminded himself. He was supposed to be the one in control here, not this vampire. "I doubt it," he replied.

"You may have gone to a great deal of trouble to hide your face from the public," Azriel said, "but I do my research. I know what everyone in your family looks like, *Prince* Dex."

Dex forced himself not to show his alarm. So what if this vampire knew who he was? It made sense, given the main goal of the Allegiant vampires. He should have expected it.

The alarm on Olly's phone beeped shrilly, breaking the tense moment. A second later, Dex felt a tingle across his skin. Olly quickly turned the alarm off. "Okay, it should be working now."

"Yes, I felt it activate," Dex said. He stood in front of the chair Azriel was bound to and folded his arms. "What are the Allegiant vampires planning?"

Azriel pressed his lips together for a long moment before giving in to the spell. "They plan to kill the fae royal family and place Vincenzo Savoy, last remaining heir of House Savoy, original rulers of this country, on the throne."

Dex sighed. "I know that already. I need to know specifics of when and how they're planning to move against my family."

"Well, then you'll have to be more specific with your questions."

Dex narrowed his eyes. "Let's start a little further back. I want to know how reliable your information is. How long have you been with the Allegiant?"

"A little under two months."

Dex frowned. Behind him, Olly stopped tapping his foot. "That isn't very long."

"And that isn't a question," Azriel replied.

"Were you working for Savoy in other ways before joining the Allegiant?"

"No."

"Did you only recently decide to pledge your allegiance to Savoy?"

Azriel breathed out heavily before answering, "No."

Xander stepped in front of Dex and leaned closer to the vampire. "Do you actually believe Vincenzo Savoy should be king?"

Azriel lifted his gaze and simply glared at him.

"Ask him the damn question," Xander muttered, straightening and turning away.

With increasing curiosity, Dex repeated the question. Azriel seemed to struggle, but the word that finally escaped his lips was, "No."

"No? Then why are you working with the Allegiant vampires?"

"Because they have … they have …" Azriel shook his head and clenched his jaw, but he couldn't hold back the truth. "They have Mariel," he finished in a rush of breath.

"Who's Mariel?"

"The woman I love."

Dex felt his brow furrow. That was the last thing he expected to hear. For a moment, his thoughts turned to Elle. Which was crazy, because he didn't love her. He was attracted to her, without a doubt, and if he was free to follow his heart wherever it wanted to go, then he might have come to love her. But as it stood, he barely knew her. Well, he knew her laugh, and the exact blue of her eyes, and that she was one of only a handful of people who hadn't fled when she'd seen the Darkness. Okay, so it was definitely more than just *attraction*, but—

Focus, dammit, he instructed himself.

"Wow, so you actually have feelings," Xander said to Azriel. "Sucks for you, doesn't it. Ow!"

Dex glanced over his shoulder to see Olly's elbow extended and Xander clutching his side. "It probably does suck for him," Olly pointed out.

"I know. I was being serious."

"Oh. Sorry, sometimes I can't tell with you."

Dex looked away from them with a sigh. "Okay, so just to clarify," he said to Azriel. "Do you believe vampires should rule this country?"

Azriel rolled his shoulders and tilted his head from side to side before answering. "No."

"So you don't agree with anything the Allegiant are doing?"

"No."

"And you wouldn't have tried to abduct Elle on numerous occasions if you hadn't been told to?"

"No."

Well, that was good. Dex suddenly felt considerably less hostile toward this vamp. "Which means you should be working for us instead."

"Dex," Xander said, and there was a warning in his tone.

"What?" Dex looked over his shoulder. "It's true. The vamps who are helping us already aren't on the inside like Azriel is. He could be extremely valuable."

"I can't work with you," Azriel said. "I told you why I'm with the Allegiant. I need to get Mariel back. That isn't going to happen if I flip sides."

"Well obviously they don't have to *know* that you've flipped sides," Dex said. "Look, we have vampires who are working with us already. They've been trying to help us discover exactly what the Allegiant are planning. Please. You can help us too. You can make a difference."

"You have vampires on your side? That doesn't sound like your father. He may be hosting a ball in your honor and inviting a few token vampires and shifters, but we all know that's just for show. He's made it clear in the past that he only trusts fae, and it'll be a fae woman he chooses as your bride."

Dex let out a sound that was half grumble, half sigh. He'd always hated how the public seemed to know just as much about his life as he did, even when they weren't supposed to. Nowhere had it been mentioned that the point of the Moonlight Masquerade Ball was for him to find someone to marry because his father was tired of waiting for him to choose a bride, and yet somehow, everyone knew. "When I said *our* side," Dex said, ignoring Azriel's comment about the ball, "I didn't mean my father."

With a laugh that sounded like it cost him a great deal of effort, Azriel said, "Treasonous thoughts from the king's son himself?"

"Not at all. I don't plan to take anything from my father. On the contrary, I'm trying to help him keep his throne by figuring out what the Allegiant are up to. And, unlike him, I *do* think other races can be trusted, so if they're able to help me, then I'm happy to work with them."

"Well, that still doesn't give me much incentive to help you," Azriel said. "I may be opposed to Allegiant vampires ruling this part of the world, but that doesn't mean I think your father should remain on the throne."

Dex pressed his lips together. He happened to agree with Azriel, but that wasn't something he was supposed to even think, let alone speak out loud. "One day there will be a new king," he said quietly. "Don't you think it would be better if the kingdom that exists at that point in the future is a happy, united one instead of a war-torn mess?"

"Yes," Azriel said. He sighed and closed his eyes. "But it doesn't matter what I think. I can't help you even if I wanted to."

"Fine. Then you can help by answering a whole lot more questions. When are the Allegiant planning to make their move against the fae royal family?"

"I don't know."

"But you must have heard something," Dex pressed. "Rumors or whispers."

Azriel remained silent with his eyes closed. "That wasn't actually a question," Olly pointed out.

"Yes, fine, okay," Dex muttered. "Have you heard any rumors of when the Allegiant will make a move against the royal family?"

Azriel sucked in a breath and tried to hold it. "Yes," he said finally.

"What is this rumor?"

"They will attack at … at …" The vampire clenched his teeth together, but he was weakening now, and he couldn't hold the words back for more than a moment. "The ball."

A shiver raced down Dex's spine. He exchanged a glance with Xander and then Olly. "That would be a stupid move," Xander muttered, but Dex was thinking back to the bridge, and the vampire with magic, and the conversation he'd had with Elle where he wondered out loud if there might be more of them.

"Are the Allegiant vampires aware there will be plenty of security?" he asked.

"Yes."

"Plenty of fae guards and magical security?"

"Yes."

The shadow of apprehension grew in Dex's mind. "Is the vampire with magic going to be part of this rumored attack at the Moonlight Masquerade Ball?"

A pause. Another deep breath. But Azriel was struggling now. "Y … yes."

Though Dex feared he knew the answer already, he asked, "Will there be *more* vampires with magic at this rumored attack at the ball?"

Azriel stamped his foot and bit his lip, but the answer was unmistakable when it escaped him: "Yes."

"How?" Dex demanded. "How have vampires acquired magic?"

But Azriel's eyelids slid closed, and his shoulders slumped as his head fell forward.

"Great," Xander muttered. "We'll have to carry on later."

"At least we know they're planning to hit the ball," Olly said.

"Well, we don't know that for sure," Dex reminded him. "Apparently that's only a rumor."

"Better to be careful though. You should speak to your father about this. See if you can get him to cancel the event."

Dex shook his head. "You know he won't. I mean, I can speak to him, so at least he's aware of the possibility, but he won't cancel the ball just because of a rumor. He's probably received a dozen threats already. That always happens, and they're almost always hoaxes."

"Except for when they're not," Xander said grimly. "This is different. If an army of magical vampires gets onto the palace grounds, the guards may not be enough to stop them, even though they're fae."

"I'm aware of that," Dex said, "and I'll tell my father what I know. But I'll be surprised if he takes this threat seriously. You know he doesn't believe anything will ever threaten his reign."

"Yes, we know that very well," Olly muttered.

"So the best we can do is plan for an attack and hope it doesn't happen," Dex said. He pinched the bridge of his nose and took a deep breath. "I need some fresh air or I'm going to fall asleep."

"Sorry, man, that spell's a rough one," Olly said. "Should we go get some breakfast?"

"Yeah, it's probably ready by now," Xander said, sliding his phone from his pocket and looking at the screen. "Not quite the spread we'd get at Dex's place, but my parents' chef isn't too bad."

"Your parents' chef is amazing," Olly said as he and Xander walked out of the dungeon ahead of Dex. "Didn't he win all those awards last year?"

"No, that was the last chef. He threatened to leave and go get a job at the palace, so my mom fired him. This guy was on one of those TV shows."

Dex looked back at Azriel, letting Xander and Olly's conversation become background noise. There were still so many questions to ask. How did these vampires get their magic? Why did they want Elle? And what were all the human abductions about?

They slipped out of the dungeon and around the back of the house so no one would see where they'd come from. When they reached the pool, Dex said, "You guys go ahead. I'll see you inside. I just need some sunlight and fresh air."

Xander nodded, but Olly paused. "Is everything okay? You've been kind of weird since last night."

"Yes, sorry, I'm fine." Dex attempted a smile. "It's just … a whole new threat we didn't realize we had to fight. Vampires with magic. I'm just wrapping my head around it, that's all." And wrapping his head around the fact that Elle was a slave. To be honest, it was Elle who'd filled his mind every time he woke last night, not the threat of a magic-wielding vampire. How could she be a *slave*? And how was he supposed to move on without ever seeing her again? He had so many questions. He wanted to *help*. Surely he could do something to free her?

He sat down on the warm paving stones beside the pool. What he actually needed to do was focus on more urgent matters, like vampires possibly showing up at the ball on Saturday. He would have to—

A shadow fell across him, and he jumped immediately to his feet. "Oh, sorry," he said when he saw it was a fae woman with a black umbrella and not a vampire about to launch a magical attack on him. Which he should have realized was unlikely, given the bright morning sun. "You startled me, that's all," he said with an awkward laugh. The woman looked vaguely familiar. One of Xander's sister's friends, perhaps.

"I don't want to hurt you," she said.

A chill raised the hairs on the back of Dex's neck. "Excuse me?" And then he recognized her. If he took away the pointed ears and imagined her with red eyes instead of blue, she was the vampire who'd led Elle upstairs at Gizella Munroe's party. The vampire who'd then attacked him while he was trying to get hold of Azriel.

He raised his hands, gold dust already flashing at his fingertips, but pain cracked through his skull. He sensed himself falling as darkness gathered in his vision, and the last thing he saw was the vampire frowning down at him.

NINE

About half an hour later, Dex sat with Xander and Olly in Xander's father's home office, checking the security footage. "Yep, there they are," Xander said, nodding at the computer screen. "Two vamps. Each with a blackout umbrella."

"Brave," Olly murmured. "Those things don't always work well."

"Aaaaand there they are again, less than two minutes later, leaving with a third vampire and a third umbrella." Xander swiveled in the desk chair to face Dex. "So they found the dungeon, broke through the dungeon gate, and through Azriel's chains—probably with magic they're not supposed to have— and got him off the property in under two minutes."

"How did they know we were holding a vampire here?" Dex demanded. "You said you weren't followed last night."

"Yeah, well, maybe I was wrong. I didn't think anyone saw us, but vampires are fast and stealthy."

"Man, this sucks," Olly mumbled. "It took us so long to get our hands on one of them, and we didn't even get to ask half our questions."

Dex pushed away from the desk and stood. He walked to the window and ruffled his hair as he stared out. He could see the tall towers and glittering domes of Belmont Palace not too far away. His home. His prison. He would have to get back soon. He'd promised his mother he would join her for tea. Well, she'd insisted and he'd given up on trying to find excuses. Telling her he had far more important things to do—which was the truth—never worked out well.

"Hey, Xander?" Dex looked toward the door as Xander's younger brother walked into the room. "Some shifter chick is here to see you," he said.

"Oh." Xander sat a little straighter. "Did you tell security to let her in?"

"No. I told them to keep her outside and watch her every move."

"Becket …" Xander sighed. "She's not going to bite you, little bro."

"I don't care. She's your problem, not mine. You go deal with her. Just make sure she's gone before the parentals see her."

"You don't get to tell me what to do!" Xander shouted after him.

Olly raised his eyebrows. "So mature."

"What? I'm older than he is. I should be the one bossing him around."

"Not when it comes to shifters, it would seem," Olly said.

"Yeah, well, you know how my family feels about shifters," Xander said, swinging his chair back to face the computer. "Apparently they're as bad as vamps." He clicked through the various security camera feeds until landing on the one from the front gate. "Oh, looks like it's Astrid."

Dex leaned over the desk for a closer look. The girl's honey-colored hair was piled on top of her head in a messy bun, and she was staring up at the camera with her arms crossed over her chest. "Yeah, that's Astrid. Must be something important if she's come all the way here."

Xander picked up the phone beside the computer and called the front gate to let her in.

The three of them headed outside to meet her in the garden, and her grumpy expression disappeared when she saw Dex. "Oh, hey, I'm actually looking for you."

Xander let out a sigh. "Most women generally are."

Astrid rolled her eyes and punched his shoulder. "Not like that, you moron." She turned to Dex. "Anyway, I've been trying to reach you. Rothman said you weren't at home, so I figured you might be here."

"Sorry, I haven't looked at my phone for a while."

"He got hit on the head by a vampire," Xander supplied.

Dex glared at him. "Thank you for sharing that."

"Any time," Xander answered, flashing his favorite I-know-I'm-pissing-you-off-right-now grin.

Dex turned his attention back to Astrid. "Everything okay? Is it something about the Allegiant?"

"No, it's about the Godmother, actually. I saw her at The Red Layne Cafe when I was grabbing a coffee this morning. She was meeting this older guy—fae—and they spoke for quite a while."

"You're sure it was her?"

"Yes. I mean, she's probably long gone now, since I couldn't reach you sooner, but you said you wanted to hear about any sightings, anywhere, any time of day, so …"

"Yeah, this is good," Dex said with a nod. "Thanks. I'll go check it out, even though she's probably gone."

Astrid twirled a stray piece of hair around one finger. "You ready to tell any of us yet why you're after her? You said you don't want a wish from her, which makes me even more curious."

Dex glanced at Olly and Xander. They were the only ones who knew, and they would take the secret to their graves unless Dex told them otherwise. "Nope, sorry," he said to Astrid. "Still keeping that one to myself." And that's the way it would stay. Taking on the Godmother was personal. No one else needed to get involved.

TEN

Four Days Before The Moonlight Masquerade Ball

AZRIEL DIDN'T OFTEN FIND HIMSELF FACE TO FACE WITH THE VAMPIRE KING HIMSELF, and when he did, it was never a pleasant experience. Today was no different.

Lev had informed him early that morning that their lord king—who was not yet a king, Azriel always wanted to point out—required an audience with him. And so he'd dutifully traveled to the closest Eternal Night, which was where Vincenzo Savoy currently resided, and crossed into a land of darkness.

The Eternal Nights—pockets of land scattered here and there around the world—had existed for many centuries. Long enough that no one remembered exactly how they'd come into being. Magic, most likely, which meant the fae had possibly been involved. And yet the fae, who had longer lives than vampires, knew of the existence of only a few of the Eternal Nights. The location of the others was a closely guarded secret among vampires. The Fae King Belaric had no idea that one of the Eternal Nights existed within his own country.

"You let me down," Vincenzo Savoy said to Azriel that afternoon. He sat on his 'throne'—an imposing chair made of black glass—while Azriel was required to kneel before him. The room was devoid of all other furnishings, but large windows provided dramatic views of the rocky landscape and the starless, moonless night sky. Azriel had heard that the rest of the palatial home was tastefully decorated in shades of red and turquoise, but perhaps Savoy didn't want anything to divert his followers' attention from himself while in this 'throne room.'

"I can still prove myself to you, my lord king," Azriel said. That was how

Savoy liked to be addressed, and though it made Azriel want to throw up, he would say whatever he had to in order to free Mariel from this place.

"I wanted you for your superior strength, speed and tracking skills, but you failed to get me the girl."

Azriel focused on the polished gray floor at his feet. "I can still get Elle Winter for you."

"You're too late, Azriel. We'll have to make do without her now, which means I have no further use for you."

"There must be something else I can do for you, my lord king."

"There isn't. Which, to be honest, is a relief. I've been waiting months to see your face when Mariel tells you the truth."

Azriel raised his gaze a few inches, just enough to focus on Savoy's shoes. "What truth?"

"This conversation is over." A moment of silence passed before footsteps entered the room. Azriel looked behind him as two men and two women filed into the room. He recognized three of them. They were enhanced, like he was. He wondered if they'd chosen to be here, or if they were also being coerced in some way. "Get rid of him," Savoy said.

"Wait, please." Azriel stood quickly. "I can give you information. I know who it is that's been protecting the girl. Prince Chevalier."

"And how does that help me?" Savoy asked. "It only makes it less likely that I'll ever get my hands on her."

"He's been acting without his father's permission. There are vampires working with him."

At that, Savoy finally appeared to pay attention. "Give me names, and I might reconsider your worth to me."

"I don't have names. I didn't have long enough to speak with the prince, but if you give me more time—"

"And here we go again. It's always 'more time' with you, Azriel."

"That's because it takes time to do a job properly."

"Oh, just give up already, would you? This is over. You can't save Mariel. She never needed saving. You fell for her tricks, like so many lovestruck men before you."

Azriel let his eyes fall shut as he tried to gather his patience. "I know you're lying," he said.

"Am I?"

"Yes. Mariel wouldn't have helped me and all the others escape if she was only ever out to trick me."

Savoy laughed. "She didn't help any of you escape. She brought you all to me. She wanted full payment, you see. She didn't want to share with dear daddy."

"What a convenient story," Azriel said, opening his eyes and fixing his glare on the pretend-king he hated. "But that's all it is. I know what you're trying to do, but your lies won't work on me."

Savoy's lips curled into a condescending smile. "Does it even matter? I have no use for you anymore, Azriel. The only way you could change that is if you bring me Estelle Winter—since I can use her information for our future plans, if not right now—but I'm tired of giving you more chances only to watch you fail."

"Not this time," Azriel murmured as he turned and launched past the guards. He sprinted as if his life depended on it—which it did—but he sensed the guards close behind him. He was usually confident he could outrun any pursuer, but not this time. This time, he had no idea if he was faster. Death might finally catch up to him.

But this was his last chance to get his hands on that damn human girl, and if he got out of here alive, he would tear down her home piece by piece just to get past the vampire protection. None of this waiting around for her to come out, or looking out for her at parties, or agreeing to meet her at random locations. The cops would be gone from her street by now. The security on her home was minimal. This game was over.

ELEVEN

The Present

ELLE'S EYES REMAINED FIXED ON DEX—HIS PARTED LIPS, HIS FURROWED BROW—AS the two vampires dragged her to the center of the study somewhere inside Belmont Palace. "I thought there was a charm on the door," one of them said.

"The sound charm was definitely there," someone else in the room replied. "I did it myself. Who was supposed to do the lock charm?"

"Quiet," Dex said. He straightened and wiped the startled expression from his face. Hurrying around the desk and coming toward Elle, he added, "You can let go of her. She's on our side."

"You're … I don't understand," Elle said. "He called you …"

"Elle—"

"He said, 'Your highness.' To you." Her eyes flicked to the vampire hovering nearby, watching her with a wary expression.

"Yes," Dex said carefully. "He did."

"But—the man in the ballroom. The man in the gold mask. Everyone's following him around and—"

"And he's not actually a prince," Dex filled in quietly.

"So … *you're* him. The prince? Prince Chevalier?"

Dex grimaced as he nodded, as if admitting to something embarrassing.

"But you're Dex."

He made another face. "Chevalier Adex Norville Belmont. A pompous mouthful, and the only normal bit I've ever been able to extract is Dex, so that's what people call me. Well, if they expect me to answer, that's what they call me."

"And the guy out there in the gold mask is …"

"My body double. I'm not supposed to be using him tonight. My parents don't know. But that ridiculous ball is the last place I want to be, and my father made things a lot easier when he decided this party should include masquerade masks."

Elle blinked a few times. Dex gave her a sheepish smile. "So you're really … you're him," she said.

"Yes. I'm him. I mean me. He's me."

"Your highness?" someone asked.

"You know what I'm trying to say," Dex grumbled.

"It makes sense now," Elle murmured. This was why the Godmother said it had to be her. This was why she'd been so sure the prince would follow Elle anywhere. She must have seen something when she took Elle's hand. Seen that Elle and Dex had spent time together, had almost kissed. And that extra magic she'd added—something about making it easier to find the prince—was what had led Elle to this room. She hadn't found it by accident. Every pull around every corner was because of the Godmother's magic.

The Godmother.

Who wanted her to *kill* the guy she'd slowly started falling for.

It struck Elle only now that she had failed to pay the Godmother's price. And there was nothing on earth that could convince her to follow through on her side of the deal now. She would never get that wish. She was still a slave, and she would remain that way.

"What makes sense?" Dex asked.

"Um, nothing."

The sound of shouts and something crashing nearby made everyone turn toward the door.

"What's happening out there?" Dex asked.

"Oh, right, of course. Allegiant vampires," Elle said hastily. "With magic. They were in the ballroom."

"So Azriel was right," Dex said.

"What?" Elle asked.

"They can't possibly know we're in here," a fae woman said. "We can hear them, but they can't hear us."

"Does that matter?" another woman asked. "They're probably breaking down every door they come across." She was human, Elle realized, with honey-colored hair and pretty hazel eyes. She leaned against the desk, and the lamp that was sitting atop a stack of papers shone directly up into her eyes, making her pupils shift shape for a moment. *Shifter, not human,* Elle corrected silently.

"Your highness," someone behind Elle said. "We should—"

A resounding crash interrupted him, and the doors splintered open. "Stars above!" Elle gasped. Magic zapped across the room from multiple sources, creating a shimmering barrier between them and their attackers. Dex grabbed her hand and rushed to the wall, where he pressed his shoulder against one of the wood panels. Then he tugged her into the darkness beyond.

TWELVE

They raced through hidden passageways between the walls, magic lighting their way. Elle had no idea if the footsteps and shouts behind her were friend or foe, and the fear that phantom hands might grab hold of her at any moment chased her around every corner. "Split up!" Dex called back at one point, and Elle saw a moment later that the passage branched three different ways. Dex pulled her to the left, and she followed without question. The noises behind her diminished as the group she was running with grew smaller.

"I hope," she gasped, "all those people … in the ballroom … are okay."

"They should be fine," Dex answered. "I warned my father about this. He didn't believe the threat was real, so he wouldn't cancel the ball. But he did increase security. Extra guards and magic … protective charms in the champagne … to be handed out to all non-vampires."

In the champagne? Elle thought. And the prince—the fake prince—had drunk champagne. Was the protection enough to counter the effects of the potion she'd given him? Hopefully, since he was the wrong guy.

"Okay, slow down," Dex said, and Elle almost bumped into him. "And don't say anything," he added. "We're approaching the ballroom. All the mirrors on this side of the ballroom back onto this passage. We'll be able to see through them into the—"

"No way!" someone hissed behind them. It sounded like one of the vampires who'd first grabbed her. Elle looked back and saw two or three others behind her. "You can't stop there," the vampire said.

"I have to!" Dex replied. "I need to know what's going on. They might need my help in there. If they do, I can throw magic through those air vents along the bottom of the wall, and you guys can take Elle—"

"Don't be stupid," the vampire said. "Your highness," he added quickly. "There might be Allegiant vampires chasing us through these passages still, and if you end up dead along with the rest of your family, then Savoy will have won. None of us want that. We have to keep moving and get to that garden you mentioned."

"I'm not going to end up dead."

"Shh," Elle said, looking ahead and seeing patches of light filtering into the passage. They had just about reached the ballroom. Dex hurried forward, still pulling her along, and stopped at the first mirror. It looked like most of the guests had fled, but fae guards and vampires were still fighting, along with a few people in tuxedos and ball gowns who'd somehow become involved in the fray. Fragments of plates and glasses littered the floor, and flashes of gold illuminated the room like fireworks.

"My parents," Dex whispered, and Elle followed his gaze toward the stairs. They must have been in the ballroom earlier—where else would they have been?—but Elle was so focused then on finding the prince that she hadn't spared them a thought. But there they were now, near the top of the stairs, with a ring of guards in front of them deflecting magic and throwing their own spells.

And then, with a bright flare of sparks, one of the guards fell. A vampire sped forward, throwing both arms out. Was it Nik? Elle was almost sure it was. His magic zigzagged away from him like lightning, through the gap in the line of guards, heading straight for King Belaric.

"No!" Elle gasped. Dex's hand clenched so tightly around hers, she thought her fingers might break. But both of them stood frozen, watching the terrible scene, knowing it was too late to do a thing. The magic struck the king—

—and rebounded instantly. A darkness, like ink or shadows, or some strange combination of both, radiated out from him, mixed with the glittering gold of faerie dust. It arced over the guards and struck every remaining vampire, throwing them clear across the room. Not one of them moved again.

Elle realized she was holding her breath. From the silence around her, it seemed the others were doing the same. Then: "What the hell kind of magic was that?" someone murmured behind her.

"They're okay," Dex whispered. "I think—everyone's okay." And Elle's brain chose that moment to remember Dex telling her his greatest fear was his father, and then a terrible thought crossed her mind: would he have been relieved if his father had died tonight?

"Oh, hell, they're still coming," someone said.

"What?" Dex looked back and finally loosened his grip on Elle's hand.

"Allegiant in the passages. Keep moving! Get to the garden!"

They rushed past the ballroom. Images of destruction flickered in Elle's peripheral vision with every mirror that flashed by. And then they were in the darkened passages again, turning this way and that, almost stumbling over each other around corners and down stairs. Elle would have been utterly lost on her own.

"I think they're gaining on us!"

"We're almost at the gate!" Dex shouted back.

"I can't tell if they're—Argh!"

Elle stumbled into Dex as he slowed and looked back. She twisted around. In the dim light of glowing faerie dust, all she could see was one figure on the floor—the vampire?—struggling to get up, and another two—a man and woman—with magic brightening at their fingertips. A little further back along the passage, dark shapes raced toward them.

Magic flew from the hands of the two faeries, speeding through the air in a rush of sparks and wind that slowed their attackers' advance. "Out the way!" Dex gasped in Elle's ear. Time seemed to slow as his arm came around her and swept her against his right side while he pivoted his left to face the oncoming threat. He thrust his left hand forward, and a pulse of glittering magic shot away from him. Flames rushed past his fae companions and over the vampire busy dragging himself upright. A wall of fire formed across the passage.

"Run!" Dex said, spinning around again and pulling Elle with him. They reached a metal gate, which Dex shoved open. He flattened himself against the wall as the others rushed through. The vampire, despite being injured, seemed to have no problem keeping up with the fae. The gate clanged shut, and Dex said, "Help me reinforce this," as he raised his palm to the metal bars. The other two fae joined him, and bright gold light flashed along the crisscrossing bars.

Then, once again, they were running. Curving to the right, and then racing up more stairs. The skirt of Elle's dress was bunched in one hand, while her other hand held on tightly to Dex. *Crystal heels most definitely would* not *have helped me tonight,* she thought as they reached the top of the stairs. There was a ceiling directly above them, but Dex placed his palm against it, and after a moment of glowing faerie dust, a circular portion of the ceiling disappeared.

Dex climbed through the hole, then reached back to help Elle. The first thing she saw was a bench. But as she stepped hurriedly around it, adrenaline still racing through her body, she took in a garden full of roses, ivy-entwined archways, and trees with slender branches and softly glowing pink and white blossoms.

"Are we supposed to be running still?" she gasped, twisting to face Dex as her lungs continued to struggle for breath. But Dex was crouched on the ground, sealing the hole they'd just climbed through, and one of the faeries was examining the vampire's shoulder as he dropped onto the bench.

"No." Dex stood and reached for Elle's hand. "We'll be safe here."

THIRTEEN

"**A**RE YOU OKAY?" **D**EX ASKED.

It took Elle a moment to process the question. Was she okay? "I—yes. I think so."

"Good." Dex squeezed her hand before looking at his vampire friend. "Are *you* okay?"

"Yeah, of course." A strained smile pulled at his lips. "You fae are frustratingly slow. I could have got to the garden within seconds if you hadn't all been in my way."

One of the faeries rolled her eyes. "He's fine."

"Okay, see if you can contact the others and find out where they ended up," Dex said to the other faerie. "Hopefully everyone reached one of the safe zones—and took out a bunch of Allegiant vampires in the process."

Elle's mind flashed briefly back to the ballroom. Whatever the king had done, it had definitely taken out all the vampires left in that room.

"Elle?" Dex said. She blinked at him and sucked in another deep breath. "Do you want to … talk?"

She nodded, and he led her away from the other three. "We're safe here," he told her again. "This section of the garden has always been well protected by magic—it's my mother's favorite part of the grounds—but I placed extra wards around it over the past few days, as well as in another few spots around the palace. I just thought … well, I didn't know what to expect. You never know if you might need to send people to a safe place to hide."

They stopped beneath one of the blossom-laden trees. "Okay wait," Elle said. "Just wait. I have about a thousand questions, and … I'm still trying to catch my breath." She bent over, pressed her palms against her knees, and took a few slow breaths. She swallowed. Then straightened. "You're freaking Prince Chevalier!"

His lips twitched as though he might be trying to hide a smile. "Yes. We went over that bit already."

"Oh, well, forgive me if my mind is still in the process of being blown by this revelation."

This time, he didn't hide his smile. "Forgive me if *my* mind is blown to see you standing here, in my home, looking …" He shook his head. "Like the most beautiful woman to ever walk through the doors of this palace."

Elle's cheeks burned. "I—no. Don't do that." She took a step back. "I'm trying to put puzzle pieces together in my head, and you're making it difficult."

"Elle, I thought I would never see you again. You were just *gone*, and you left your phone there, and you were in so much pain because of that awful slave charm, and I had so many questions—"

"*I* have so many questions," she said, mentally shoving aside the reminder that she was still a slave. A *slave*, for goodness sake. Standing in front of a prince! "Like … how do you go out into the city all the time without anyone recognizing you?"

"Well, hardly anyone knows what I look like, so it's easy."

"But *how* have you gone this long without people knowing what you look like? Why aren't there any recent photos of you? And you were *blond* when you were a kid, just by the way. And now your hair is dark. So that's just … really confusing. I mean, I would never have guessed that you could be him."

He quirked an eyebrow. "Really? My hair color is the sole reason you would never have guessed I'm actually a prince?"

"Oh come on, just answer my questions!"

"Okay, okay." But that smile of his was still there, and she kind of wanted to smile in return. This was *Dex* standing right in front of her. Like him, she thought they would never see one another again. She thought he might even be repulsed by the fact that he'd almost kissed her. But he was looking at her now as though nothing in the world could draw his attention away from her face.

That is, until his expression clouded and he looked down. "It's because of the Darkness," he said quietly.

"Darkness? Like ... with a capital D?"

"Yes. Well, that's the way I think of it."

"You're talking about the thing that happened the other night in the warehouse?" Elle asked.

"Yes. It started happening years ago, and my parents investigated all sorts of ways to try to cure me of it. One thing my mother came across was the suggestion that curses can be cast over the image of someone. It's an old wives' tale, and that's not even how this whole Darkness thing started, but it freaked her out. She thought someone could make me even sicker if they wanted to. Since then, she hasn't allowed anyone to take photos of me."

Elle couldn't help her quiet chuckle. "So Meredith was actually right about those rumors. Well, partly right."

Dex groaned. "Do I want to know what rumors you're referring to?"

"They're not too bad. She just said that Prince Chevalier never leaves the palace because he has an immune deficiency or something, and she also mentioned that it's bad luck to photograph fae who are seriously ill, which is why there are no recent photos of him."

Dex sighed. "I always wonder how these little bits of the truth get out there and fuel all the rumors about me and my family. Anyway, the no-photo rule is ridiculous and unnecessary, but I've used it to my advantage. Since no one knows what I look like, no one recognizes me when I sneak away from here and go into the city."

"And no one's ever figured out who you are? Like, someone who's visited the palace and then happens to see you at a party like Gizella Munroe's?"

"There isn't really much overlap of the crowd I mix with out there and the people who visit Belmont Palace. Actresses, singers ... they're not really my father's kind of people. Most of them don't have a noble history attached to their family name. And ... well, it helps that I don't form attachments with people out there. I don't share my number with people or make plans to meet up a second time. If I did, it would become harder to keep the truth of who I am a secret."

"So, the other night at the apothecary," Elle said carefully, her heart beating faster as the memory of almost kissing him flashed across her mind. "How does that fit into your philosophy of not forming attachments?"

"It doesn't." Dex moved closer and took both her hands in his. "I've broken quite a few of my rules when it comes to you."

She couldn't look away, and she didn't want to ruin the moment, but she had to *say something*. She had to remind him of the truth. "Dex, I'm … I'm a slave."

"I don't care," he said simply. Then he frowned. "I mean, I do *care*. Nobody should ever have had the right to enslave you, and I want to know who did it so I can personally make sure that you're freed. What I mean is, it doesn't change what I think of you."

"But … even if I'm free …" She wanted to remind him that she would still be human. And he was a fae prince. What more could possibly happen between them other than a kiss?

Dex stepped closer, and his shoe bumped into hers. He looked down and started laughing.

"What?" she asked, looking down. "Oh." The bottom of her dress had been torn at some point since she'd fled the ballroom, and her sparkly combat boots were now sticking out the bottom. "So, uh, I know they don't go with the dress. They were never meant to be visible."

"They're perfect," he said.

She rolled her eyes. "They're definitely not perfect."

"I mean they're perfectly *you*."

"Well, I'm glad you think so, because the woman who dressed me—"

His lips pressed against hers, cutting off her remaining words. She was so startled she couldn't move, couldn't think, couldn't breathe. But then Dex's hands slid up her arms and around her waist, and something inside her melted. Her eyelids fluttered shut as he pulled her against him, and her hands, somehow, were gliding up to his shoulders. His lips moved against hers, and a tiny, panicked voice screamed, *I don't know what I'm doing!* But there were far too many other sensations to lose herself in: his hands pressing into her back, the taste of his tongue, the goosebumps rushing across her skin.

When the warmth of his lips eventually vanished from hers, she was flushed and embarrassingly breathless. "Sorry I interrupted you," Dex murmured before kissing her lightly again. "I didn't want to miss my chance a second time around."

"That's … that's okay." Holy exploding stars, it was *definitely* okay.

He placed his hands gently on either side of her face and kissed her again. When he pulled away, her eyes finally opened, but she was far too shy to meet his gaze. "Was I terrible?"

He let out a quiet laugh. "No. Not at all."

"But, you know …" She dared to look at him. "We should probably practice some more anyway."

His grin told her he fully understood the hint. "Definitely." He kissed her lips again, and then her jaw, and then he was murmuring, "Didn't you say you have about a thousand questions for me?"

"Mm hmm." She found his lips again as her hands slid around his neck. "Just … just give me a minute," she said between kisses, "and I'll … I'll think of them."

He laughed quietly against her mouth. "I think there were some things I wanted to ask you too. Isn't it funny how I can't remember a single one either?"

Elle chuckled—and then her breath caught in her throat as something wrapped around her middle and tugged her away from Dex. "What the—"

"Elle!"

She stumbled backward, but managed to keep herself from tripping. Looking down, she found there was nothing around her waist, but something was definitely *pulling*.

"What was that?" Dex asked, coming closer. "What just happened?"

Somewhere in the distance, a bell chimed. Then it chimed again. Suddenly, Elle knew exactly what was happening. She met Dex's eyes for a moment—just long enough to whisper "Midnight"—and then the Godmother's magic yanked her clear across the garden.

"Hey!" Dex yelled, racing after her. Her feet left the ground and she was swirling through the air, past the trees and archways and the bench where Dex's companions were sitting. She caught a glimpse of them jumping up and joining Dex before the Godmother's spell spun her higher and higher as she flew faster. And then—

A cry escaped Elle as she rammed into something hard and invisible in the air. Magic sparked around her as her body seemed to roll against an invisible barrier. *The wards?* she wondered. Dex said there was lots of magic around this part of the garden, and that he'd placed extra wards here. She almost managed a smile despite the fact that magic was busy tossing her around high above the ground. Surely all the wards here were stronger than whatever simple spell the Godmother had placed on her? They would keep her inside this garden, and Dex would find a way to get her down.

But her momentary relief vanished when something began to tug her higher. Higher and higher, she was gaining speed, and she just had time to wonder if the wards were in the shape of a dome or were more like walls when she felt herself suddenly tossed sideways. She let out an angry cry as her body sped over the palace grounds, heading in the direction of Vale City. She couldn't let this happen. She couldn't go home to Salvia. Dex had promised to free her, and she had to get back to him. To tell him she needed a wish. It was as simple as that. Maybe he could get her one. The royal family probably had dozens of wishes lined up next to their jewelry and crowns and designer watches.

As she swirled low enough to touch the trees, she tried to grab hold of branches and leaves, but they tore through her fingers, leaving scratches on her palms. "Dammit, just *slow down!*" she yelled, but of course the magic didn't listen. Her body somersaulted through the air, and when she was upright again, she discovered her hairstyle had unraveled itself. And then—holy stars—her dress vanished in the blink of an eye. She let out a startled yelp, then breathed again when she realized she was back in her jeans and T-shirt and not naked. She had a feeling that if she could look in a mirror, she'd find all her makeup gone too.

She tried to push her hair out of her eyes and saw that she was finally nearing the palace itself. Zooming toward it faster and faster, and CRAP she was going to slam straight into the wall! But at the last moment—with her eyes closed and a scream tearing itself from her throat—Elle swooped up and up and up, and flew right over the top of Belmont Palace.

She lost height so quickly on the other side that she thought the magic had dropped her. But it caught her just before her feet brushed the polished tiles outside the entrance and sent her soaring forward just above the stairs. She was close to the railing on one side of the staircase, so she reached for it, hoping to grab hold of one of the balusters. Her hand slapped against them as she passed, and then *finally*, she grabbed hold of one.

Her body slammed against the railing, and the force of the magic threatened to pull her arm from its socket, but she held on with all her strength. She wrapped both arms around the baluster, then wedged her boots in between two balusters further down. "Just try to pull me away now," she said through gritted teeth, aware of how extremely odd she would look to anyone who happened to walk up or down these stairs right now.

The magic, as if it could hear her and had decided to respond, suddenly pulled backwards instead of forwards. Then it tried to spin her body. As she jerked to the side, her upper body lost its grip on the baluster. "No!" she gasped, her hands flailing, trying to catch hold again. And though her boots were firmly stuck between the two balusters further down, the magic tugged and tugged until she felt her feet begin to slip free of them. "Nonono!" she gasped. Why hadn't she tied the darn laces tighter? Before another thought could cross her mind, the magic had sucked her clean out of her shoes, and she was flying away again.

Then a hand grabbed hers, jerking her to a halt. "Oh thank goodness," she gasped, looking back and expecting to see Dex's face. But it was someone else whose powerful grip was slowly pulling her back, hand over hand, fighting against the Godmother's magic.

"I don't know what spell's got hold of you," he said, "but I'm willing to bet I'm stronger." He reached the top of her arm and grabbed her shoulders, then pulled her against his chest, wrapping his arms around her to keep her from flying away. Elle, shaking now, looked up into familiar red eyes. "Got you," Azriel said. "And this time, I'm taking you where no one will find you."

4
THE ETERNAL NIGHT

ONE

In a stylishly furnished lounge in one of Vale City's most expensive apartments, the Godmother dropped into an armchair with a huff. She smacked her fist down on the cushioned arm of the chair. "Why can't I *find* her?" she demanded, though there was no one else present to hear her question. Midnight had come and gone hours ago, and the slave girl, Elle Winter, should have returned to her attic. But she wasn't there, and no amount of magic seemed to be able to locate her.

A small creature fluttered in through the open window. "Yes?" the Godmother said. The pixie zoomed closer and alighted on the arm of the chair, just in front of the Godmother's fist. She tilted her hat—or was it half a shell?—and squeaked something. "No sign of her anywhere near the house?" the Godmother asked. After another few squeaks, she sighed. "Well, thank you for looking. I appreciate it. In fact, if you don't mind hanging around, I may have further use for you. What's your name anyway?" She listened as the pixie squeaked something unintelligible. "I'm afraid you'll have to repeat that." The pixie tried again, her words a fraction slower. "Oh, well if you like that nickname," the Godmother said, "we can go with that. Tash. Easy enough to remember."

Her phone rang, and she reached to pick it up from the side table. She tapped the screen, brought the phone to her ear, and said, "Yes?"

"I've confirmed that it's true, Godmother," said the man on the other end of the call. "The vampires who invaded the ball had magic."

"I suspected as much." The Godmother sighed. "Well, I suppose we couldn't expect that spell to stay a secret forever. Not while there was still a record of it out there somewhere, even if that record is incomplete." She crossed one leg over the other. "But as long as the vampires don't perform the ritual in full, their power will never last. But if they *do* complete it ..." She frowned. There was still the problem of the missing girl. If no magic could locate her, there was a strong possibility the vampires had her. Was it too late already?

"This is becoming a mess," she muttered into the phone. "I don't like mess. Not unless I'm the one causing it." As an afterthought, she added, "Did the royal family survive?"

"Yes."

"Including the prince?"

"Yes."

A smile pulled at the Godmother's glossy lips. "So the slave girl failed to pay her price. Well, there's a small bit of good news. Still, this Allegiant mess changes things. What to do, what to do ..." She drummed her fingers across the top of her leg, her mind flicking through all the options and the possible outcomes.

"There's something else," the man on the other end of the phone said. "There was a protest at the ball. Humans campaigning against the slave charm."

The Godmother groaned. "That helps absolutely no one."

"I know. I think the king will use this to strengthen his case. He may finally be able to get the National Council to vote in favor of making the slave charm mandatory for all humans again."

"More mess," the Godmother muttered. "Well, thank you for keeping me updated." She ended the call without saying goodbye. Then she let out a long sigh and returned her attention to the pixie.

"Do you know what it says in our country's constitution, Tash? Well, in every constitution in every country in the world, if we're going to get technical." Tash replied with a disbelieving squeak. "Why, yes. I have memorized the Constitution of Astranerica," the Godmother said. "I've been around for a very long time. Sometimes I get bored. I need to find things for my brain to do.

Anyway, Tash, the part I'd like to bring your attention to is that little bit in the Bill of Rights that mentions freedom. This, my dear young pixie, is what it says." She waved her hand and gold letters appeared in the air as she spoke, matching her word for word. "Every member of a magic-blooded High Race has the right to freedom."

Tash sat on the arm of the chair and leaned back on her tiny hands.

"The key, of course," the Godmother said, "is in the words 'magic-blooded.' We fae have our Essence, which lengthens our lives and allows us to do a great many fantastical things no other race can do. The vampires have a type of magic that gives them long life, speed and superior strength. And shifters have a type of magic that allows them to change their physical shape. But what do humans have?" She nodded slowly as Tash replied, an amused smile curling her lips. "Correct. It does appear to suck a great deal for humans. It makes you wonder why they were ever considered a High Race, doesn't it." She steepled her fingertips and pursed her lips. "Unless, like me, you know the answer."

She sat in silence for another few moments, then lifted her phone again and searched for a name she hadn't contacted in quite some time. Raising the phone to her ear, she murmured, "It's time to move a few pieces around the game board, Tash. Would you like to stick around and observe the fun?"

TWO

The morning after the most disastrous ball Belmont Palace had ever hosted, Dex found himself walking along a nondescript street in a quiet borough of Vale City with a pair of woman's black combat boots sitting on his upturned palms. After spending several hours this morning listening to his furious father rage about vampires and humans, he'd finally managed to get away.

Sneaking out of the palace grounds without his parents' knowledge was a skill he'd mastered years ago. It was his nanny who'd first helped him, when he was very young and had begged to explore the forest on the other side of the palace wall. He'd learned a few tricks from her, like befriending the right people on the palace staff. These days, that included the security team who monitored the back entrance near the garages where all the palace vehicles lived. The guards didn't mind turning a blind eye as long as Dex wasn't alone. Xander or Olly, sons of trusted noble fae families, generally accompanied him, and that always seemed to keep the guards satisfied.

Dex looked down at the shoes again as he reached the intersection of two streets. The rhinestones sparkled in the morning sun. He'd found the shoes wedged between the balusters alongside the palace front steps while searching for Elle the night before and recognized them instantly as hers. He wanted to get started immediately on a tracking spell, but his father's guards had found him at that point, and it had been impossible to get away from them for the remainder of the night. It wasn't until mid-morning that he'd come up with a good enough excuse to escape his father's office.

The shoes shifted ever so slightly on Dex's palms, pointing toward the left now. He turned that way and continued walking, Olly at his side. The two of them had parked a few streets back and left the car behind after blindly following the shoes' directions, accidentally turning up a one-way street, and almost crashing into a taxi. Olly had convinced Dex that walking was safer, though Dex found it frustratingly slow. He'd earned himself a few odd looks, wandering around holding up a pair of shoes on his hands, but he ignored the sideways glances and raised eyebrows. Just like the truth spell he'd used on Azriel, the tracking spell wasn't supposed to be known by anyone outside of law enforcement, so he certainly wasn't about to explain to anyone what he was doing.

"Oh, we're turning again," he said, watching the shoes shift toward the right now.

"I think we may have reached our destination," Olly said.

Dex looked up. The house he stood in front of was tall and skinny with an ivy-covered trellis covering part of the front. "Yeah, it could be." He looked around. "We're not far from the street where we dropped Elle off the first night we met her, so it makes sense."

"She obviously didn't want you knowing where she lives," Olly reminded him quietly. "Probably because—"

"She's a slave, yes," Dex said with a sigh, gripping the two shoes in one hand and lowering them to his side. He'd decided to tell Olly and Xander the truth this morning before he began the tracking spell. Xander had simply shaken his head before heading out to answer a call from a palace guard, leaving Olly to remind Dex that getting involved with a human slave probably wasn't going to end well. "But I'm going to free her," Dex said as he walked toward the stairs that led up to the front door. "And then she won't be a slave anymore."

"Yes, as you've repeatedly told me. But—"

"But she'll still be human, as *you've* repeatedly told me," Dex said.

"And your father will hand the country over to vampires before he lets you marry her."

Dex laughed as he reached the top of the stairs and faced Olly. "Who said anything about marriage?"

"Well she's the only person you've shown more than a vague interest in, and we all know your parents are forcing you in that direction, so what am I supposed to think?"

"I'm just here to make sure she's okay." Dex turned to the door, raised a fist, and knocked. "And then I'm going to confront whoever her slave master is and get him or her to remove that damn charm from her leg."

"And then?"

"And then …" Dex rubbed his free hand along the back of his neck. Everything Olly said made sense, and yet he couldn't get Elle out of his mind. He wanted to know everything about her. He wanted to hang out with her in a normal setting that didn't involve hunting for vampires or running away from them. He wanted to kiss her again. Man, he was so screwed.

"Right," Olly muttered, as if he could hear Dex's thoughts. "Exactly."

"Look, I know everything you're saying is true. I know I'm only making my life harder. And not just because of my father, but because of—"

Because of the Darkness, he'd been about to say. It wasn't fair of him to get involved with *anyone* when he had a death sentence hanging over him. But at that moment, the door swung open. A young fae woman with shiny red hair and vibrant green eyes stood there. She smiled prettily. "Hi. Can I help you?"

Dex blinked. "I—I want to marry you." He slapped a hand over his mouth. Where the hell had that come from?

"You—what?"

"Oh dear," Olly groaned from behind him.

The young woman hesitated, then gasped. "Ohmygoodness. Holy stars. You're *him*! You're Prince Chevalier!"

"Uh, what? No, I didn't say—"

"I made a wish that you'd want to marry me when you saw me, and now you're here, asking me to marry you!" She clasped her hands together and bobbed up and down. "Yes, absolutely, a hundred yeses. I accept your proposal."

"Whoa, hang on." Dex clutched both combat boots to his chest, silently cursing whoever it was that first came up with wish magic. "I didn't propose. I'm looking for—"

"Your royal highness." A woman—probably older than the first, though also fae—swept from the shadows of the house toward the door. "What an honor! My daughter Meredith is *most* willing to accept your proposal."

"I'm sorry, ma'am, I didn't actually propose. I'm—"

"But you said you want to marry me," the daughter, Meredith, interrupted.

Dex *had* said that, and there was an irresistible urge inside him to say the stupid words again. He could picture Meredith in a white dress, standing across from him beneath a canopy of flowers while saying 'I do,' and some completely helpless part of him *wanted* that, even while the logical part of his mind was repulsed.

"I wished for it," she repeated, "and you confirmed it, which means you have to—"

"Which means he now has to wish *not* to marry you," Olly said, moving a little closer. "Not the first time he's had to do that, by the way," he added with an awkward chuckle.

Dex gave Meredith what he hoped was a polite smile. "I'm sorry. I'm sure you're very lovely, and someone will be a lucky man to marry you one day, but I'm afraid that man is not me." *Thank the stars for that*, he added silently. If he remembered correctly from what Elle had told him, Meredith was the stepsister she didn't particularly like. "Ma'am," he said to the other woman, who he guessed was Elle's stepmother. "I'm looking for someone. Her name is Elle. Is she here?"

The woman's expression darkened, and her lips curled into the furthest thing from a genuine smile as she said, "No, she is *not* here. But I do apologize on her behalf for whatever she has done to you, your highness."

"Oh, no, she hasn't done anything to me. Do you perhaps know when she might be home?"

"No. My sincerest apologies, your highness, but I do not."

"Did someone say something about Elle?" Dex's gaze darted further back into the house as a girl poked her head into the entrance hall.

"Sienna, now is *not* the time," Elle's stepmother hissed over her shoulder.

Sienna. That was Elle's other stepsister. The one she cared for and said was more like a real sister. Dex craned his neck, trying to get a better look at her, to see if he could at least read something in her expression. But the two women in the doorway moved closer together, blocking Sienna from view.

"Perhaps I could talk with—"

"I'm so sorry, I wish one of us could help you," the older woman said, "but I'm afraid we're all as much in the dark as you are. Elle disappeared last night while we were out—at your magnificent ball—and we haven't seen her since."

"Okay. Uh, perhaps I could leave a contact number," Dex suggested, "and when you know something about Elle you can get in touch."

"I'll take your number," Meredith said, thrusting her hand forward with a crazed glint in her eyes.

"Oh, well, it wouldn't be *my* number specifically," Dex told her with a strained smile.

"We will, of course, inform your people the *second* we know anything," Elle's stepmother said, her voice dripping fake politeness. "But I feel compelled to tell you that we're also required to contact the police once we know of her whereabouts. They want to know all about her, uh, criminal activities."

"Her criminal activities?" Dex asked, not believing the woman for a second.

"Yes. Elle is our *slave*, you see, but she's become completely out of control. She's attempted to break the slave charm multiple times, she's stolen large amounts of Essence, and now it appears she may have succeeded in running away, despite the slave charm's effects. Your highness, I would *hate* for you to taint yourself by having anything further to do with her."

For several moments, Dex couldn't speak. *This* was Elle's slave master? Or mistress, to be more precise. Someone who was a member of her *family*? Heat rushed through his veins. "You—"

"We should go," Olly said hastily. "Sorry for taking up your time and for, uh, disappointing you." He nodded at Meredith. "Have a good day." He gripped Dex's elbow and forced him to turn away from the door. Behind them, Elle's stepmother was saying something else, but he could barely hear it over the pounding of blood through his ears.

The door shut, snapping him out of his shocked state. "That despicable woman," he hissed.

"You're absolutely right," Olly said, trying—and failing—to pull Dex down the steps. "But what were you going to do? It's perfectly legal for fae to keep human slaves, and there's nothing that says the slave can't be a family member by marriage. I'm guessing it's not *common*, since—"

"Olly! That woman—"

"Let it go!" Olly insisted, gripping Dex's arms tightly and giving him a shake. "Forget about her. She looks like the kind of woman who'll cause trouble if you make her unhappy, and trying to force her to set her slave free is bound to make her unhappy. Your priority is finding Elle, so let's focus on that."

Dex blinked at his friend, surprise cutting through his rage. He might have expected Xander to shake him and speak so sternly, but Olly was usually the quieter, politer of the two. Dex breathed out slowly. "You're right. I'm sorry. Thanks for the reminder."

Olly nodded. "Sure. You're welcome." He stepped back and rolled his shoulders. "Sorry about the manhandling."

"Not a problem." Dex took the stairs two at a time, then turned at the bottom and looked back at the house with a frown. "Do you think she was lying? Maybe Elle's locked up in there somewhere. I mean, the tracking spell did bring us here. Why would it do that if Elle's not inside?"

Olly reached the bottom step and looked back over his shoulder. "Well, either it brought us here because this is her location, or the spell can't find her, and therefore it's brought us to where she's spent the most time. Where she's left the strongest imprint."

"The only way the spell wouldn't be able to find her is if she's magically hidden, right?"

"Yes. If she's hiding—or being held—in a place where magic can't reach her. Somewhere protected. If a slave were to run away, as this woman suggested, that's the kind of place she'd have to go so her master or mistress can't find her."

Dex shook his head. "I don't think Elle ran away. It wasn't her choice to leave last night. Something *took* her. She was completely out of control. Could it have been the slave charm? It happened at midnight, which is the same time the charm burned her leg the last time I saw her."

"Perhaps," Olly said, doubt evident in his tone. "But I don't think the slave charm normally works that way. It—wait." He looked around. "Did you hear that?"

"Uh …" Dex glanced around the empty street as a hiss reached his ears. "Yeah, I did." Movement caught his eyes, and he realized the girl from inside—Sienna—was leaning around the side of the house, beckoning him and Olly closer. They hurried toward her.

"I can't talk for long," she said, sending a furtive glance over her shoulder, "but I just wanted to ask … why are you looking for Elle? Did something happen last night? Did you see her somewhere?"

"She was at the ball," Dex said, "but then something pulled her away. Something magical."

"She was …" Sienna's eyes widened. "She was *at the ball*?"

"Yes. Is she inside the house now? Was your mother lying?"

"No. She was telling the truth. Elle disappeared while we were out. I don't know how because there was a confinement charm on the attic, and there was no sign of her having forced her way out. She was just … gone. My mother should be able to locate her because of the slave charm, but she can't. It's driving her nuts." Dex may have imagined it, but it seemed a hint of amusement crossed Sienna's features at the idea of something driving her mother nuts. But her expression fell an instant later as she asked, "Do you think vampires got her? There was an attack at the palace last night, wasn't there? I was already gone because … well, it was weird. Elle warned me that something bad would happen last night, and that as soon as it did, I must leave and come back home to meet her here. So that's what I did when the protest started, but then afterwards I wondered if she meant the vampires."

Dex frowned. "I don't know. Some kind of magic pulled her away from me. She was literally flying through the air. So I would have said no, it couldn't have been a vampire that took her, but …" He hesitated before adding, "You must have heard by now. The vampires last night were using magic. So maybe it *was* one of them."

Sienna clenched her hands tightly together and pressed them to her chest. "Stars, I hope not. And yes, I did hear about that." She tossed another look over her shoulder, then said, "Could you maybe—I mean not *you*, necessarily. Being a prince and everything, you must be very busy—but could you maybe send a message here if you find out anything about Elle? Nothing that would tell my mother exactly where she is, because that would be bad, but just to let us know she's okay? Um, your highness. Please." She did a weird sort of half curtsy.

"Yes, of course."

"And if she's somehow successfully broken the slave charm, or if she's able to hide permanently from my mother, then tell her not to come back. She doesn't have to worry about me. I'll be fine."

Before Dex could say there was no way he'd ever encourage Elle to come back to the woman who was keeping her enslaved, Olly asked, "Is there a reason Elle would think you're *not* fine?"

"Oh." Sienna's eyes grew even wider. "No, of course not. She's just … you know … my protective older sister."

Dex frowned. "Are you sure—"

"Yes, absolutely." She started backing away. "Thank you again for speaking with me. Your highness, and … sir. And I'm so sorry about Meredith and her stupid wish." After another quick bob that was neither curtsy nor bow, she turned and hurried away.

"Well," Olly said as Sienna vanished around the side of the house. "At least we know Elle's not here. Which is good news because she's nowhere near her horrid stepmother. But bad news because—"

"We have no idea where to look next," Dex finished with a sigh. He turned and began walking away from the house, ignoring the part of himself that desperately wanted to run back up the stairs and into the house, grab Meredith's hand, and ask her to marry him. "Next step," he muttered, "is to wish away the unnerving feeling of wanting to marry that girl. After that, we figure out what kind of magic might possibly be hiding Elle."

"Actually," Olly said, and Dex looked over his shoulder to see Olly frowning at his phone. "We might not need to do much figuring out. Xander's been trying to call. He managed to gain access to the security control room at the palace. Which involved a few favors and a few distractions, since your father's always been very strict about who—"

"Yes, okay, and what did he see?" Dex asked, walking back to Olly.

Olly thumbed at something on his phone. "Elle didn't make it off the property before someone grabbed hold of her last night. Xander thinks he recognizes the guy who took her." Olly looked up, and his grim expression left Dex with a sinking feeling in his stomach. "Our vampire friend Azriel."

THREE

Elle rose from the grogginess of her tangled dreams with the same difficulty as one clawing their way through thick, sticky syrup. It wasn't the first time she'd woken, but it was the first time her mind seemed clear enough to take in her surroundings. Perhaps it was the dull burning pain on the side of her ankle—slowly increasing in intensity—that was helping to cut through the fuzziness of her brain.

She blinked repeatedly as she pushed herself up to a sitting position. Her eyes traveled across the richly embroidered bedspread, the ornately carved wooden posts of the four-poster bed, the plush carpet, thick curtains and abstract art prints. She wasn't sure what she'd expected to wake up to, but this wasn't it. There weren't even any restraints tying her hands or feet together. There was a closed door though. It must surely be locked.

Elle's mind worked slowly back through her most recent memories, hoping to find something that would help her current situation make sense. The Godmother's magic had been pulling her through the air, carrying her back to her attic, and then a vampire had caught hold of her. Azriel. Somehow, he'd been strong enough to hold her in place. She remembered struggling, and then there was a flash of pain, and then—nothing. He must have knocked her out. Hit her head or something.

Since then, she'd woken a few times, but never long enough to make sense of anything. She remembered the burning agony of the slave charm on her ankle—a pain that was oddly subdued at the moment, but definitely growing worse—Azriel's face looming over her, and the sharp prick of something in the crook of her left arm before she fell into oblivion once more. How many times? She had no idea, but it felt like she'd been falling into that dark abyss over and over for an eternity. All while she lay in a luxuriously furnished bedroom. Did vampires treat all their prisoners this way?

She pulled her left sleeve up—holy stars, whose pajamas was she wearing?—and looked for needle marks on her arm. She couldn't see any, but that meant nothing. Perhaps Azriel was good at jabbing needles into people without leaving any trace behind. What he wasn't so good at, apparently, was continuing to administer said jabs at regular intervals. Why else would she be awake now? Unless he *wanted* her to—

Her heart jolted at the sound of the door knob rattling. She instinctively scrambled backward, but there was nowhere to go beyond the wall of pillows behind her head. She pushed the bedcovers back and scooted to the edge of the bed, silently berating herself for not investigating her options the moment she woke up. There must be a window behind those curtains, and perhaps it wasn't barred. If she was close to ground level, she could—

"Why is it *locked*?" someone shouted on the other side of the door.

Elle's feet sank into the carpet, and she pushed away from the bed. A moment later, her vision clouded with white. She lurched toward the window as the floor flew up to meet her hands. "No, no, no …" she gasped, shuffling on hands and knees toward the window. At least, she hoped that's the direction she was heading in, but everything was spinning around her, and the door was clicking open, and a voice that sent chills down her spine growled, "It's *locked* so unwanted visitors can't find their way in."

"Elle?" someone else called. "Elle!"

That voice. It filled her with warmth, but it was all wrong in this setting. She half turned, half fell, her backside meeting the carpeted floor as strong hands gripped her shoulders. "Dex?" she mumbled, blinking at his familiar silver-blue eyes. Maybe she'd never woken up after all. This was another confusing dream filled with the wrong people in the wrong places. Soon Salvia would appear, and then some of Elle's clients, and then—*Yes, there we go*, she thought. As the world tilted yet again, Cress's sleek purple hair and flawless face hovered just beyond Dex's.

Elle's body sank into the soft mattress and pillows as dream-Dex placed her on the bed, and she heard herself say, "I hate … playing … the fainting damsel. Even in … my dreams."

"You're not a fainting damsel," Dex said. "You haven't eaten anything in three days. That's why your legs won't hold you up." He smoothed her hair away from her face, kissed her cheek, and said, "I'm so glad we found you."

She tried to reach for him as he pulled away, but the world hadn't quite stopped turning yet, and she saw her hand grasping at empty air somewhere near Dex's head. "I wish … you were real," she said. It was only about the hundredth time she'd said it. Maybe the thousandth. How many tangled dreams had Dex managed to find his way into since Azriel had taken her? All of them, however many that was.

Dex took her hand, then looked back over his shoulder. "How's it going?" he asked, and Elle realized that dream-Cress was still here too. Bending over something near the bottom end of the bed. The pain from the slave charm abruptly disappeared, so perhaps Azriel was jabbing needles into her again, and her brain was trying to protect her by showing Cress and Dex instead. "And you had something for her to drink?" Dex added, still watching Cress.

Cress was suddenly right beside Elle, bringing a glass of brown liquid toward her face. Elle thought of trying to knock it away—she wasn't going to willingly drink anything Azriel wanted to force down her throat—but then she caught the scent of it, and she almost started drooling. She couldn't tell what it was, or even if it was sweet or savory, but she wanted to consume it immediately. *Wonderful,* she thought as dream-Cress tipped the liquid down Elle's throat. *Azriel's got me hooked on some kind of drug. Maybe that's why he hasn't bothered tying me up. He knows I won't go anywhere while I'm craving more of this stuff.*

She relaxed against the pillows, promising herself she would fight harder next time she woke. She would get to the window before anyone came back into the room. She would escape. She didn't need anymore of that delicious drink.

But as the world slowly righted itself, and Dex and Cress didn't disappear, and a yawning abyss of darkness didn't swallow her whole, Elle began to wonder if she might actually be awake. Dex and Cress peered anxiously at her from either side of the bed. She blinked, staring at one and then the other. Slowly, she pushed herself up a little.

"Are you okay?" Dex asked hesitantly.

"I don't know. Are you real?"

Dex's face broke into a smile. He leaned closer and pulled her into a tight hug. He was so solid, his arms so firm around her, and he smelled just like the real him—though Elle hadn't realized until this moment that she identified any particular scent as his. "You feel real," she mumbled against his shoulder.

"I'm definitely real," he said, laughing into her hair. "And I think you're okay."

"You should start to feel stronger soon," Cress added as Dex gently pulled back. "You haven't consumed much in days, but that tonic will help a lot. We'll get some food into you soon."

"But … how are you here?" Elle asked. "*Where* is here? I'm so confused. Did you catch Azriel?"

Dex sighed. "We didn't have to. He reached out to us."

Elle blinked and shook her head. "I'm still confused."

"He never actually wanted to be one of the Allegiant. But he had a good reason—in his eyes, at least—for doing their bidding. And I'll admit I might have done the same thing in his position. But that reason no longer exists for him. He's turned his back on the Allegiant."

"He—wait. That's what he told you? And you *believe* him? Dex, this is probably some kind of trap."

Dex shook his head. "Olly and Xander caught him that night you and I ran from the other vamp at the bridge. I questioned Azriel under the influence of a truth spell, and it turns out he doesn't agree with the Allegiant at all. I told him he should work *with* us instead of against us, but he said he couldn't because they have the woman he loves. Then he escaped us. And then … I guess something changed. He contacted me after the ball. It took him two days, since a vampire wanting to have a private conversation with a fae prince isn't the easiest thing to arrange. He told me he was hiding you here, at his family's home in one of the Eternal Nights, because of your slave charm and because of that magic that kept pulling you away. Fae spells can't reach through the barrier dividing the normal world from the Eternal Nights, so he figured you'd be safe here."

"So the magic that pulled me away on the night of the ball," Elle said slowly, "can't reach me while I'm here."

"Correct."

"But he's been drugging me, Dex. I've been asleep for however long he's had me here."

"Because the slave charm was causing you so much pain," Cress said, "and he didn't know how to stop it."

"Oh." Elle thought about that for a moment, but she couldn't remember enough from her hazy interactions with Azriel to know if this might be true.

"Azriel explained the situation and told me where to find you," Dex continued. "We're in the Beryl Eternal Night, which is in Verance. That's why it took me another whole day to get here."

"Wait, we're in another *country* right now?" Elle asked. Then she shook her head. "Sorry, I suppose we'd have to be if we're in one of the Eternal Nights. There isn't one in Astranerica."

"Yes, so I had to organize using my father's plane," Dex said, "and I had to see Cress so I could ask her to come with. She said she can't remove the slave charm, which I suspected, but she figured she could do something to contain the pain."

Elle leaned forward and took a closer look at her right ankle. Something like transparent plastic wrap covered her skin. The slave charm was still visible, but she realized—for the first time since discovering this wasn't a dream and Dex and Cress were real—that the pain was gone. "Oh, wow, thank you. That's amazing."

"Elle, that's not all." Dex shifted a little closer. "I mean, that's not all I wanted to see Cress about. I asked her how to remove a slave charm if I'm not your slave master, and she said I could wish for it with a third-tier wish. So I was going to buy one. My family has Essence supplies for emergencies, and I figured I could probably … well, *borrow* some without anyone noticing. But …" His eyes shifted across the bed toward Cress, but not before Elle caught a glimpse of the desperation in his gaze.

"It's gone from the catalog," Cress said quietly. "Freedom from Enslavement Charm. It's been removed. It isn't possible to wish for that any longer."

"But … that … how?" Elle looked back and forth between Cress and Dex.

"My father," Dex said grimly. "Because of what happened at the ball the other night."

"The anti-slavery protest?" Elle asked.

"Yes. He was furious about it. In fact, he seemed just as upset about humans showing up at his party and starting a protest as he did about vampires sneaking in and trying to kill him. I told him to try to keep things in perspective, but that didn't go down well. He was yelling about humans now posing a security threat instead of simply being a useless nuisance." Dex grimaced. "Sorry. His words. Definitely not mine."

"I know," Elle said, though it still angered her to be considered a 'useless nuisance.'

"He still wants to get that law voted in by the National Council—the one that makes the slave charm mandatory for all humans, like it was in the past— but that takes time. However, he suddenly remembered that he's technically Supreme Head of the Mages' Guild—"

"The what?" Elle asked. "I didn't know there was a Supreme Head."

"Yes, it's an old title," Dex said with a dismissive wave of his hand. "It's the same in all fae-ruled countries. He has nothing to do with the day-to-day running of any of Astranerica's guilds, but he technically has ultimate say over all their policies. That was the last thing I heard him muttering about the morning after the ball, before I managed to get away."

"But are you sure it was him who altered the catalog?" Elle asked. "It wasn't … I don't know, the Godmother? Her magic is powerful. She could probably mess with the catalog if she wanted to." *And I wouldn't put it past her to do something like this in retaliation for failing to pay her price*, Elle added silently.

"I placed a query after Dex and I left Vale City," Cress said. "I wanted to know if there might be a glitch in the online catalog that meant I wasn't seeing all the available wishes, but I was told, 'No glitch. King's orders.' And the person I spoke to reminded me that no one would miss that wish, since it's hardly ever used."

"I guess no one expects a slave to be able to purchase a third-tier wish," Elle muttered. "I've been saving for years and I still didn't have enough before—well, it was taken from me."

"Of course, the Essence," Dex said. "I didn't make the connection before. That's why you were collecting it. So you could buy a wish. Though you've still never told me what service you provide. Wait." A deep frown creased his brow. "You said all your Essence was taken from you?"

"My stepmother found it and confiscated it." Elle took a deep breath, looking down at where her hands had begun absently playing with the edge of the bedspread, and added, "She's the one who enslaved me."

"I know," Dex growled. "I … well, I went looking for you the day after the ball. I used a tracking spell on your shoes, which I found on the stairs outside the front of the palace. The spell took me to your home. I know it was an invasion of your privacy, but something carried you away against your will, and I was so worried—"

"It's fine, really," Elle assured him. "I'm just … I'm so sorry you had to meet my stepmother."

"Hold on," Cress said. "Back up. Your *stepmother* is your slave mistress? Your own family? That's despicable."

"Yeah, she turned out to be pretty despicable after my dad died. So that's why I … I eventually …" Elle clenched her teeth together, hating to admit this part out loud. But at some point, Dex would ask her how she'd ended up at the Moonlight Masquerade, and she didn't want to lie. "I made a deal with the Godmother."

"Wait, you *what?*" Dex stared at her in horror. "Elle, don't you know how dangerous that is?"

"Yes, of course I know. That's why it took me this long to summon her. It was never an option before, but then … then it became the only way. And this isn't just about me. It's about Sienna too. My stepsister. My stepmother is just as abusive to her as she is to me, so—"

"Abusive?" Cress repeated sharply.

"So that's why I need to help her escape," Elle finished. Then she sucked in a breath as she realized something for the first time since waking up. She had never returned home, but Sienna had, which meant Sienna was probably being punished for Elle's disappearance. "Ugh, no, it wasn't supposed to work out this way," she muttered, pushing her fingers through her tangled hair. "But wait." She looked at Dex. "You said you went to my house. Did you see Sienna?"

"Yes, and she seemed fine. She told me that if I found you, I must tell you not to worry about her."

"Well of course she'd say that. And just because she *looks* fine doesn't mean she actually is—"

"Calm down," Cress said. "I can take care of this. You can give me your address before I leave, and I'll go and see Sienna. I'll make sure she really is okay."

Elle breathed out slowly. "Okay. Thank you."

"Elle." Dex took her hands and laced his fingers between hers. "You made a deal with the Godmother. What was her price?"

"Whatever it was," Cress said, looking pointedly at the slave charm, "You clearly haven't paid it yet."

"No, I haven't. And I never will." Elle looked into Dex's piercing blue eyes and swallowed before speaking again. "Dex, she asked me to kill you."

FOUR

ELLE WATCHED AS DEX'S MOUTH SLOWLY DROPPED OPEN. "WHAT?" HE ASKED, HIS voice little more than a whisper.

"Well, I didn't see that coming," Cress muttered.

"The Godmother wants me *dead*?" Dex asked.

"Yes." Elle searched his eyes. "Why would she want that?"

Dex let out a long sigh. He looked away, his hands slipping free of Elle's. "She must have found out."

"Found out what?"

"That I plan to kill her."

Elle's eyes widened. "You—wow. Okay. I guess I can see why she might want to take you out first then. Can I ask *why* you plan to kill her?"

Dex looked at Cress and tilted his head ever so slightly toward the door. "Well, this a very interesting conversation," Cress said, "but I think you two need to continue it alone. I'm going to find our host. I see he disappeared very quickly after letting us in here." She rose from the edge of the bed. "I wonder if he can find us some food," she added as she made for the door, "or if I'm naive to think a vampire's pantry might have anything other than blood bags."

"Blood bags," Elle repeated with a shiver. That was a disturbing thought.

"So that's why you were at the ball," Dex said quietly. "I wondered, but I didn't get the chance to ask before that magic took you from me."

"Yes, that's why I was there. The Godmother dressed me up and told me to go and kill the prince. I didn't know *you* were the prince, of course. I never would have agreed to her price if I'd known."

Dex frowned. "But you were happy to agree when he was just a faceless person? You were willing to—"

"No! I was never planning to kill anyone. I told the Godmother I would, but I never actually meant it. I knew I would have to pretend somehow. I sent a message to Cress, and she made me a potion that simulates death, so it would *appear*—for a short time—that I'd killed him. That's what I gave to the guy everyone thought was you. Your body double."

"I see. I heard something about him being unconscious after the ball, and I assumed he'd been hit with something during the vampire attack. But I don't think he ever appeared to be dead."

"Maybe because of the champagne," Elle said. "You mentioned there were protective charms?"

Dex nodded. "Yes, that might have helped him."

In the awkward quiet that followed, Elle looked around and noticed a half-full glass of brown liquid on the nightstand beside the bed. "Is that the tonic Cress gave me?"

"Oh, yes, you should probably drink the rest of it." Dex reached for the glass and handed it to Elle.

She sniffed, took a sip, then said, "Sweet."

"What's that?"

"I couldn't decide before, when I was close to passing out, if it was sweet or savory. All I knew was that it tasted delicious. I still can't figure out what it is, but it's definitely on the sweet side."

"Okay."

She took another few sips, watching him closely. "So ..." she said eventually. "Why do you want to kill the Godmother?"

Dex exhaled slowly. "Because of a wish." He looked away before continuing. "Years ago, my father made a wish. He wished that no one would ever be able to take the throne from him. But the wish went wrong. Or so I've always been told. My parents said it was an illegal wish, and that's why it backfired. They have plenty of Essence with which to buy legitimate wishes, but apparently this was the kind of wish that couldn't be bought. The Mages' Guild said it was impossible. My father might be able to add and remove wishes from the catalog, but only wishes that are actually possible."

"Yeah, I guess ultimate power isn't the kind of thing that should be possible to wish for," Elle murmured.

"Exactly. So my father told me he bought this wish from one of the illegal suppliers—someone who said he'd had partial training at the Mages' Guild before being asked to leave because he was 'too powerful.' I always thought my father was stupid to fall for a story like that. Anyway, he used the wish, but it backfired. Something about the unstable magic of the wish's core being set free and latching onto my brother and me, with horrible side effects."

"Side effects?" Elle asked.

"Yes. Anyway, it turns out that nothing my father told me about that wish was true. He accidentally let part of the truth slip out a few months ago, and after that he had to tell me the full story. He didn't buy that wish from anyone." Dex's brow pulled lower as his expression darkened. "My father bargained with the Godmother. He knew there would be a price, but she wouldn't tell him what. Only that it would reveal itself in time and that it was a terrible price. She asked if he was still willing to pay it without knowing what it was. He said yes, never imagining how truly terrible it would be. But the Godmother knew. *She* decided on the price. She caused unimaginable pain for my family—and for thousands of others who've bargained with her and had to pay a terrible price—and that's why I want her dead. She shouldn't get to play around with people's lives."

Though she had a feeling she may already know the answer, Elle asked, "What was the price, Dex?"

His eyes met hers. "The Darkness," he answered quietly.

"Is that ... is that what killed your brother?"

"Yes."

"So you ..." Her words were barely a whisper now, and she couldn't finish the sentence. But it seemed Dex knew what she was trying to say.

"Yes," he answered again. "One day, probably not too long from now, it will take me too."

Elle was already shaking her head. She leaned to the side and returned the glass of tonic to the nightstand. "That can't be true. There must be a way to stop it. Surely Cress or—or someone even more knowledgeable than her can find something. Some spell or potion."

Dex shook his head. "It's slowly eating away at me. The astaleaf potion Cress makes for me keeps those … *episodes* at bay. You know, where my eyes go dark, and shadows move across my skin. But it's still there inside me, weakening me ever so slowly. My brother grew weaker and weaker until eventually he passed away, and the same will happen to me. My father wished that no one would take the throne from him, and apparently that included his own sons."

"But … can't your father try to undo the bargain?"

"He and my mother have both tried to wish away the Darkness, but the Godmother's price was to take away the power she granted him, and apparently that was too high a price for them to pay."

"*What?*"

"What you saw at the ball the other night—when a vampire tried to directly attack my father, and all that magic mixed in with dark shadows radiated away from him, killing all the vampires in the ballroom—that was a result of the wish he made. If he'd successfully undone that wish, he might have been killed the other night. A fact he was kind enough to remind me of after the ball, as if I should be *grateful* that I'm the one who has to suffer so he can survive any attempt on his life."

"That's horrible," Elle whispered. "How can your own father suggest something like that to you?"

Dex pressed his lips together and shrugged.

"So does the continuation of the Belmont line mean nothing to him?" Elle asked. "If you and your brother are both gone, then your father has no heirs. Is there some distant relative who might inherit the throne? Or will fae from the other noble houses end up fighting over it? Surely your father would rather have one of his sons continue his legacy than to simply be king for as long as possible before dying and then … that's it."

Dex sighed. "That brings us to the ball and the fact that my father is desperate for me to marry. There is no one else in our family to inherit the throne. When he dies of natural causes one day, another house will rule. The Belmont line will be over. He decided long ago not to part with the power he was granted and instead pin his hopes on one or both of his sons marrying and having children. He hopes the next generation will be free of this curse the Godmother placed upon us."

"But he might be wrong."

"He might be. And I don't want to inflict that kind of suffering on my own wife and child. And that's why I shouldn't have kissed you, Elle. That's why I shouldn't be getting close to *anyone*."

Elle blinked. "Oh." That kiss was one of the most marvelous things that had ever happened to her, and now Dex was telling her he regretted it?

"I mean I *wanted* to," he added quickly. "Very much. And that's why I did. But I shouldn't have. And it has nothing to do with the fact that you're human. That really doesn't matter to me. I'd marry you no matter what race you were. I-I mean …" His eyes widened and his cheeks turned visibly pink. "A *long* way down the line, if it turned out we both loved each other, and if I wasn't going to die because of this stupid Darkness, and if you actually *wanted* to marry me." He pushed one hand through his hair and muttered, "Stop rambling, idiot. *Anyway.*" He gave Elle a strained smile. "What I'm trying to say is that I shouldn't have encouraged anything between the two of us because one day— possibly soon—I'll be gone, and that isn't fair to you."

"Oh." Elle nodded slowly, but a frown crept onto her face. "What if I disagree?"

"You … disagree?"

"I'm sorry, you probably don't hear that very often. Being a prince and everything. There's probably a law or something that says people can't disagree with you."

Dex gave her a wry smile. "Fortunately not. Xander and Olly disagree with me all the time, and they make sure I know it. Especially Xander."

"Well, then, I disagree with you. You don't get to decide what's unfair to me, and you don't get to give up on finding a cure for this Darkness thing."

Dex sighed. "Elle …"

"No." She shook her head. "You might not know this about me yet because we only just met, but *I don't give up*. I've always believed I'd find a way out of my own horrible situation, and I believe the same for you. And *don't* tell me I'm naive, because I've had my fair share of major disappointments. I know the world sucks and plenty of people don't get their happy ending, but I refuse to accept that for myself, and now I refuse to accept it for you."

Dex stared at her. His lips twitched, and Elle got the feeling he was trying to hold back a smile. "You're making this really hard," he said.

"This?"

"Yeah." He added no further explanation, but his gaze darted to her lips before moving back up, and Elle realized with a rush of heat that she knew what he was talking about.

"I see. Well, let me make it easier for you." Before she could lose her nerve, she reached out, grabbed a fistful of Dex's sweater, and pulled him closer. She pressed her lips to his, half expecting him not to respond—maybe even to push her away—but a second later, his hands were in her hair, and she felt him shifting closer on the bed. She wasn't thinking about a one-day-in-the-future marriage, or even a fae prince boyfriend. Allowing those thoughts to take hold might have paralyzed her. All she focused on was Dex. The guy she'd bumped into one night outside a club. The guy whose beautiful eyes never left her imagination. The guy who'd traveled into an Eternal Night to find her.

She loosened her grip on Dex's sweater, spreading her hand flat against his chest and feeling the beat of his heart against her palm. His hands slid down her back and pulled her closer, wrapping her in his strong embrace as their kiss deepened. Her blood rushed dizzyingly fast through her veins, undoing the strengthening, steadying effect of the tonic, but Elle let herself fall into it, not caring whether she knew up from down as long as Dex's arms were around her.

As he kissed her chin and neck, she managed to find the breath to say, "You're not very good at the whole I-shouldn't-encourage-anything-between-us idea."

"I know." His lips moved along her jaw to the sensitive skin beneath her ear.

"I usually am, but with you … I don't know." He kissed her earlobe. "Apparently I have zero self-control." It seemed that wasn't entirely true, though, because he managed to pull away for long enough that Elle opened her eyes, blinked, and focused on his conflicted expression. "I'm so sorry," he said. "I shouldn't have let myself—"

"Dex, if you don't care that I'm human—"

"I don't."

"—and you don't care that I'm not only a commoner, but also a slave—"

"*Nobody* is worth anything less simply because someone decided to enslave them."

"—and the possibility that you *might* die at some point in the near future is the only thing holding you back—"

"It's quite a big thing."

"Then I'm sorry, but you can't get rid of me." She kissed him again, wanting to lose herself in a moment where vampires and slave charms and Godmothers didn't matter. But she couldn't keep reality from creeping in at the edge of her mind, and it wasn't long before the heat in her veins began to cool, and their kisses slowed, and then her head was resting against Dex's shoulder as his arms remained securely wrapped around her. She stared unseeingly at the curtains, listening to Dex's steady breathing and trying to decide on which of the many questions running through her mind she should ask first.

"So," she said eventually. "If I leave this Eternal Night, will my stepmother be able to find me?"

"Unfortunately, yes. Whatever magic Cress applied to your leg, it was only to keep the pain at bay. She said she couldn't figure out how to hide a slave from his or her master. The fact that we're technically in a different realm right now is all that's hiding you from your stepmother."

"So I have to stay here."

"Just until we can figure something else out. And you said you don't give up, right? Which means we'll find something. We have to."

Elle nodded, her cheek brushing against Dex's shoulder. "At least there's no pain anymore."

"Yeah, about that …" Dex removed his arms from around Elle and sat back. "Cress said her spell won't work permanently. That transparent stuff she put around your ankle will slowly be absorbed into your skin—probably over the space of a few days—and then the pain will return. She'll have to do the spell again, and she thinks it might get less effective the more she does it."

"Wonderful," Elle muttered. She pushed her hands through her hair. "So what's happening back home in Vale City? What have I missed since the ball? Is the Allegiant threat over now?"

"No," a voice answered from the doorway, and a chill of fear rushed across Elle's skin as her eyes darted toward Azriel. "Savoy is still alive," he said, "and that means the threat is definitely not over."

FIVE

Azriel stepped into the room, and Elle realized he was carrying a plate with some sandwiches on it. Cress walked in behind him. "We didn't have any food when I first brought you here," Azriel said. "The house hasn't been used in a while. But my sister made sure to pick up a few things after I told her you were here."

"Sister?" Elle asked, unable to keep from leaning away as Azriel moved closer. "I'm hoping she was the one who put me in these pajamas and not you."

"Yes. You've met her before. At that celebrity party. She was trying to keep you away from me."

"Oh. Alissa? She's your sister?"

"Yes." Azriel stopped beside the bed and held the plate toward Elle. She hesitated, eyeing the entirely normal-looking sandwiches with suspicion. "I understand if you don't trust me," he said, "after our last few interactions. But I assure you it wasn't personal."

"So I heard," Elle said as she reached slowly for the plate. "Still, you would have done anything to me that the Allegiant asked."

"Yes. For a good reason."

Elle gave him a questioning look. "And now that reason doesn't exist anymore? And we're supposed to believe you?"

Azriel paused, then walked past the bed to the curtains. He pulled one aside a few inches, peered out, then let the thick fabric fall back into place as he turned to face Elle, folding his arms across his chest. He sighed. "Fine. I'll tell you. Hopefully then you'll understand. I was part of an army of vampires. We were experimented on. Enhanced. We're stronger and faster than normal vampires. The man who owned this army had a daughter, and I fell in love with her. She loved me too, and together we plotted to escape. We managed to free the entire army.

"But then she went missing. Word reached me that the vampire heir Vincenzo Savoy had caught her. He refused to free her unless I worked for him. So I decided to do what he asked. I pretended I was loyal to his cause, though I'm sure he saw right through that. I even tried, at one point, to convince myself that maybe the Allegiant were right. That Savoy should be king of Astranerica. After all, his family did rule that country centuries ago. But I couldn't convince myself. In certain parts of the world there are vampire rulers who are good, but Savoy is not one of them. He should never be ruler over anything."

"But you did what he asked anyway," Elle said quietly.

"Yes. Because of Mariel. When you love someone …" He shook his head and sighed. "Love is supposed to be *good*, but it can make you do terrible things. I tracked you down. I tried, as you know, to catch you. After the last time I failed, Savoy told me I'd run out of time to prove myself. He wanted to get rid of me. I tried to run, determined that this time, I would get hold of you. I would hand you over to Savoy and finally free Mariel. But there were others—others from the army I'd helped free—working for him. They caught me. They threw me down in front of Mariel, and I saw that she wasn't in chains. She wasn't confined in any way.

"She told me the truth then. That she'd never loved me. She'd used me to help her get the army away from her father so she could sell us to Savoy and take the full payment for herself. Some of us did manage to escape—myself included—but she handed everyone else over to Savoy. And then, because of my stupidity, I ended up working for him anyway."

"So … you must have got away from him," Elle said quietly, "if you ended up finding me and bringing me here."

"Yes. Something inside me snapped. I realized everything I'd done for Savoy was because of a lie. My fury … well, I suppose it gave me even more strength.

I fought the others off and got away."

"Didn't they have magic?" Dex asked.

"No. Savoy was keeping his magic-empowered vampires aside for the ball. They were all volunteers. He won't give his special enhanced army any magic until he knows he can do it properly."

"So you got away, and then you just happened to find me outside the palace?" Elle asked.

"I couldn't find your home. It seemed to have somehow been hidden from me. I couldn't even find the street. I knew you'd gotten yourself involved with the fae prince somehow, so I figured it made sense to check out the ball."

"Why come looking for me anyway?"

Azriel gave her a puzzled look. "To keep Savoy from catching you. Those vampires he sent to the ball had magic, but it wouldn't have lasted. If they'd survived the ball, they would probably now be suffering in agony as the magic left their bodies. Then they'd have to do the ritual again. Whatever the process is that Savoy keeps putting them through, it isn't complete. He needs you for that. That's why he's been looking for you all this time."

Elle shook her head. "Why? I know absolutely nothing about giving vampires magic."

"I don't know."

"And what does my mother have to do with any of this?"

Azriel frowned again. "Your mother?"

Elle squeezed fistfuls of the bedcovers in her hands, adrenaline racing through her body now that she finally had the chance to ask Azriel the questions she'd wanted to ask since he first abducted her. "She tried to keep me from you. That's what you said when you dragged me from that club and took me to the fairground."

"Oh, yes. Well, she didn't keep you from *me* specifically. I think I must have said 'us.' And by 'us,' I mean Savoy and the rest of his Allegiant. All I know is that there was … an incident of some sort. Many years ago. You and your mother were there, along with Savoy and his father, Nazario Savoy. I wasn't told precisely what happened, but by the time you and your mother fled, Savoy senior was dead."

Elle's heart pounded uncomfortably fast in her chest. "And Savoy—Vincenzo Savoy—didn't say how his father died?"

"No, but I assume your mother did something. You were just a child at the time, so I doubt it was you."

Elle nodded slowly, Azriel's voice fading into the background as the Godmother's words slammed into her, as clear as if she were in the room uttering them out loud: *Your power doesn't simply remove memories. If you take it further—if you remove* all *memories, if you remove the mind itself—the body cannot survive on its own.* And then the most shocking part of all: *You've done it before.* Elle shoved the possibility away. She didn't know if the Godmother had been lying. And even if she'd told the truth, it probably wasn't a *vampire* she'd been talking about. Someone like Nazario Savoy, a man working to take back the throne of Astranerica, would never have let his guard down long enough for Elle to get into his mind.

"Elle?" Azriel said, startling her from her thoughts.

"Yes, sorry? What did you say?"

"Savoy—the current Savoy—told me you took something vitally important that day. I asked you if you know what that might be." Something in his gaze suggested he thought Elle should know what he was talking about.

"I have no idea," she answered.

"Really? Well, he desperately wants it back. He's been searching for you for years, but your mother kept you hidden. When I ended up working for him, he told me everything he could remember about you and your mother, and I was tasked with tracking you down. He told me about the strange, unnatural ability you possess. It was that which eventually led me to you."

"A strange, unnatural ability?" Dex asked.

Mild surprise crossed Azriel's face. "You haven't told him?"

"Told me what?" Dex asked, but Elle's focus remained on Azriel.

"So you don't know anything else?" she asked. "Nothing about how my mother originally got herself involved with vampires?"

"No. That's the only information I was told."

"Elle, what is he—"

"Can we, um, can we talk about that part later?" she asked Dex. She had too much to process right now. She might have *killed a vampire*. At the very least, she'd taken something from him. And that something was probably a memory. If so, Savoy's hunt for her was useless. Once she'd wiped a memory, it was gone.

"Okay," Dex said slowly. "Sure, we can talk later." But his brow remained creased as he watched her.

"Tell me about this ritual that gives magic to vampires," Cress said, perching on the edge of Elle's bed. "I've never heard of such a thing. And you—" she looked at Elle "—should be eating right now."

"Oh. Right." Though she felt far from hungry right now, Elle lifted one of the sandwiches and sniffed it.

"It's safe," Cress assured her. "I made it myself. The ritual?" she prodded, her gaze turning back to Azriel.

Elle took a bite of the sandwich—ham, cheese, tangy mustard, and a few salad items—as Azriel said, "I don't know the details."

"How convenient," Dex muttered, looping one arm around a bedpost at the foot of the bed. "There seem to be a lot of details you aren't aware of."

"Cast another one of your truth spells, if you must," Azriel said. "You'll soon learn I'm not lying. All I know is that humans are required. And there's some ritual or process the humans must first undergo on their own before they can be used to give magic to a vampire. But how any of it works, I have no idea. I'm not exactly on Savoy's list of most trusted confidants."

"So that explains all the recent human abductions," Dex said.

"Yes. And as long as Savoy is still alive, humans will continue to disappear, and he'll keep giving magic to more vampires. And that—" he looked at Elle "—is why the threat is not over."

"This is going to be such a mess," Dex muttered. "My father wants to wipe out any remaining Allegiant—and Savoy—as soon as possible. He doesn't care if he has to start another war. Now that he knows about them, he wants them all dead."

Elle finished chewing her current mouthful of sandwich and looked at Dex.

"Didn't he know about the Allegiant before?"

"No. Not until a few days ago. He was vaguely aware of all the human abductions, but he didn't care about those. And the police were taking too long to find answers, so I decided to start investigating on my own. Well, with Olly and Xander. I warned my father before the ball, but he wouldn't take me seriously. Perhaps he did believe me, but he didn't care enough to cancel the ball. He knows no one can take the throne from him, and I suppose he thought a bit of extra security would keep everyone else safe."

"When you say no one can take the throne from him," Azriel said, tilting his head a little to the side, "do you mean that literally, or is it simply your father's sheer arrogance?"

"I mean it literally." Dex sighed. "He wished for it."

Azriel's eyebrows rose a fraction. "The Godmother?"

"Yes."

"Well, since the Godmother doesn't deal with vampires, I'm fairly certain Savoy has made no such wish."

"Right, so my father should be able to defeat him. I'm just worried about the number of people who'll have to die in the process."

"Your father can only defeat him if he knows where to find him."

"True, but he already has a lead on Savoy's last known whereabouts."

"I doubt it," Azriel said. A beat of silence passed in which Elle looked between him and Dex. She waited for Azriel to elaborate, but he remained silent.

"I assume you know where he is?" Dex pressed.

"I do."

"One of the Eternal Nights, correct?" Dex asked. "Somewhere the fae can't enter without vampire assistance, like this one. I couldn't have entered here if you hadn't met me at the border and allowed me to cross. But my father has a few vampires in his employ. Crossing into an Eternal Night won't be a problem for him."

"And if most people in the world aren't even aware of the existence of this particular Eternal Night where Savoy currently resides?" Azriel asked.

Elle watched Dex's brow furrow. "How is that possible?"

Azriel's laugh was devoid of humor. "Because the fae think they already know everything, and the rest of us are happy to let you continue believing that."

"Okay look," Cress said. "The two of you might have all day to dance around this issue, but I don't. Are you going to tell us where this mysterious uncharted Eternal Night is or not?"

"I am not," Azriel said.

"Come on," Dex groaned. "Seriously? You want to let Savoy go on happily creating a magic-wielding vampire army? So that one night they can all race into Vale City, kill whoever's in their path, and then wind up dead when they try to kill my father?"

Azriel narrowed his eyes. "No, I don't want that. But neither do I want to give up a secret that vampires have kept for centuries. Basically, I'm stepping away from the situation now." He held his hands up in a show of surrender. "I've helped where I can—I brought Elle to a safe location so Savoy can't find her—and now I'm staying out of things." He looked at Elle. "If you need to stay here, that's fine. But beyond providing safe haven, I'm not getting involved any further."

"So you're choosing the coward's way out," Dex muttered.

A growl rumbled in Azriel's throat. The kind of sound Elle would have expected to hear from a wolf shifter rather than a vampire. "Don't you dare—"

"Dex, I think we should go," Cress interrupted, rising from the bed. "We've been cut off from communication with the rest of the world for several hours now. I have responsibilities at the apothecary, and you have no idea if your parents may have been trying to contact you."

Dex exhaled sharply. "Cress, we haven't decided on a course of action yet. And Elle and I ..." He looked at her. "We have things to talk about."

"I know, but we both need to get back now that you've confirmed Elle is okay and it's fine for her to stay here. That is, unless you'd like to piss off her host to the point where he takes back his invitation?"

Elle paused with the last sandwich raised halfway to her mouth. She didn't think her eyebrows could rise any higher. Apparently Cress was just as willing as

Xander and Olly to make it known when she disagreed with Prince Dex.

"It's fine," Azriel grumbled before Dex could answer Cress. "Elle can stay here. When you're done saying your goodbyes, you know where to find me so I can show you out." He stalked past the bed and left the room.

Elle let go of the breath she hadn't realized she'd been holding. "For a moment there, I thought things were about to get ugly."

"I'm sorry," Dex said. "It's just that we need his help."

"Do we?" Cress asked. "Isn't it better if your father *doesn't* know where to find Savoy? We don't exactly want to encourage a war."

"But someone needs to keep Savoy from turning all his enhanced vampires into enhanced vampires with *magic*."

"I don't know what to say, Dex," Cress answered. "I don't know the best way to fix this problem. But remaining in this Eternal Night any longer isn't going to help us. We need to return to Vale City. You took your father's plane without his authorization, which means he's probably trying to contact you right now to find out what's going on."

"I doubt it," Dex muttered. "He probably hasn't even noticed I'm gone. And my forgery skills are excellent. No one questioned any of the authorization papers I handed over."

"Dex!" Elle admonished. "Is that how you got here? You're going to land yourself in serious trouble."

"My point exactly," Cress said. "And I don't want to wind up in trouble along with you, so it's definitely time to go. Whatever you and Elle need to talk about, you can save it for when you next see her."

"Yeah, we can do that," Elle said. She needed to tell Dex the truth at some point about her strange ability, and the service she offered to clients, and all the horrible cons Salvia had forced her to participate in, but she didn't mind putting it off a little longer. "Oh, wait. One of you will come back at some point, right? Or you'll send Olly or Xander if that's less trouble? I know I have to stay here right now because of the slave charm, but I don't want to be here *forever—*"

"Of course I'll come back," Dex said. He took her hand and laced his fingers between hers. "Cress can show me the spell she used on your ankle, so I can get rid of the pain when it returns. And we'll figure out this slave charm thing. Even if I have to negotiate with your stepmother in order to—"

"Oh, nonono!" Elle interrupted hastily. "Don't do that. She's—just stay away from her."

"Um … okay. Then we'll figure something else out. I'm just not sure when exactly I'll be able to come back. And I won't be able to let you know, since communication from the outside world into an Eternal Night isn't possible."

Elle nodded. "That's okay. I understand." At the sight of Dex's guilty expression, she added, "It's fine. It really is." She gestured to the room around her and added, "Things could definitely be worse. At least I'm not a prisoner in an attic."

Cress narrowed her eyes. "I look forward to sharing a few words with your stepmother when I go to check up on Sienna." She rubbed her hands together until, with a spark of gold dust, a small notepad and a pen appeared on one palm. "Please write down your address for me."

"Oh. Actually … that might not be the best way to go about things." Elle reached for the notepad. "I was thinking you should probably go to Sienna's school. At home, she won't tell you if she's really okay. She'll be too afraid of my stepmother overhearing something. But if you find her at school, and you tell her I sent you, hopefully she'll be honest about whether … well, if things are still bad at home."

Cress hesitated, then said, "Okay, perhaps that's a better place to start. One step at a time."

"Thanks." Elle quickly wrote down the address of Sienna's school, then handed the notepad and pen back to Cress.

"Oh, and … I know this is a lot to ask, but … actually, never mind."

"Just ask," Cress said with a sigh. "I can decide if it's too much."

"Okay. If Sienna's happy to meet you a second time, can you ask her to bring some things for me? My father's pocket watch necklace, and the quilt my mother made, and the photo album from inside my wardrobe."

Cress raised an eyebrow. "An entire quilt?"

"I know, I know. If it's too much for her to sneak all of that out of the house, then she doesn't need to worry. It's just that those are the only things I have left from my parents, and—"

"I'll see what I can do," Cress said.

"Thank you."

"I'm so sorry we have to leave you here alone," Dex said. His hand squeezed Elle's, and he moved a little closer. Though there were far more important things to be concerned about at this point, Elle's heart leaped into high gear at the thought that he might be about to kiss her in front of Cress. "But I think we can trust Azriel," he continued. "He wouldn't have—"

"She won't be alone," a female voice said from the direction of the door. Elle turned toward the voice and saw a woman she recognized—dark hair, ivory skin, and a smile curving one side of her lips—leaning casually against the doorframe.

"Alissa," she said.

"You remember me." Alissa looked pleased as she pushed away from the doorframe and entered the room.

"Of course I remember you. I'm still not sure if you were trying to help me or trick me that night at Gizella's party."

"I was trying to *help* you, of course. I knew Azriel was after you, and I didn't want him handing you over to that vampire savage, Savoy."

Dex took a step toward the door and blocked Alissa's path forward. "You attacked me," he said. "Twice."

"Twice?" Elle asked, leaning sideways to see Alissa's reaction.

"The second time was at Xander's home," Dex said, "after we captured Azriel. She knocked me unconscious and helped him escape."

"It was actually my friend who hit you on the head," Alissa clarified. "And if you cast your mind back, *your highness*, you'll remember that right before it happened, I said I didn't want to hurt you. And I meant that. You and I are not on opposite sides. But my family comes first, and that's why I had to help Azriel. Fortunately, he no longer has any ties to the Allegiant. That means he isn't trying to capture Elle, you aren't trying to capture him, and I don't have to try and keep you all apart. We can all be friends now." She stepped sideways, and in a rush of motion almost too fast to follow, she ended up on the bed beside Elle.

Dex spun around to face her. "Was that really necess—"

"Don't worry, Prince Chevalier. Or is it Prince Dex?" She looped an arm around Elle's shoulder and gave Dex a wide, innocent smile. "I'll take good care of Elle. Whatever it is Savoy wants from her, he won't be getting it."

SIX

"YOU KNOW," ELLE SAID TO ALISSA ONCE DEX AND CRESS HAD LEFT, "WHEN YOU said you'd 'take good care' of me, it sounded a little bit like a threat."

Alissa laughed, removed her arm from around Elle's shoulders, and leaned back against the pillows. "I know. But your prince knows I didn't mean it that way. He wouldn't have left you here if he didn't trust me." She cocked her head to one side, her dark hair spilling across a cream-colored pillowcase. "Would you like to take a bath?"

Elle frowned. "Are you saying I smell bad?"

"Not at all. I've been putting you in fresh pajamas every day, and I spritzed your hair with Enduring Rose, that scent that everyone's going nuts about right now. Nobody wants to take care of a smelly patient."

Elle clutched a handful of her tangled blond waves and sniffed, noting that her hair did indeed smell faintly like roses. "That's weird," she muttered. "But thanks, I guess."

"You're welcome. I'm sure Prince Not-so-charming appreciated it too, which, of course, was the main reason I made sure you didn't smell as stinky as you no doubt feel."

Elle's skin flushed. "Thanks again?"

"Don't mention it. Anyway, I thought you might want to have a bath because your body's probably achy and uncomfortable from lying in a bed for so long, and because a hot, soaking bath filled with mounds of bubbles is one of life's greatest pleasures. And I say that as someone who's lived a long time."

"Okaaaaay."

Alissa sat up and pushed herself off the bed. "You clearly haven't experienced enough of them if you disagree with me."

Elle's mind jumped to the tiny shower in the makeshift bathroom section of her attic back home. "Let's just say it's been a while."

"Well, come on then." Alissa headed for the door. "I'll show you where the nearest bathroom is."

"Okay, thanks." Elle climbed off the bed and followed her, bare feet padding silently across the carpeted floor. Out in the hallway, they passed numerous closed doors before reaching the end and turning left. "Is this a large house?" she asked.

Alissa laughed. "Remember that celebrity home we were in when Azriel tried to catch you?"

"This house is *that big*?"

"Not quite, and the artwork isn't as disturbing as that weird thumb sculpture we saw, but this home is unnecessarily large. I think my parents went a little overboard when they designed this place. The library probably could have been a bit smaller."

"There's a *library*?"

"Overkill, right? Anyway, here's the bathroom." She flicked a switch on the wall before sweeping into a room almost the size of Elle's whole attic. Marbled gray and white tiles glossy enough to see one's reflection in covered the floor, and in the center of the room stood an enormous oval-shaped bathtub. The shower took up one entire wall, while on the opposite side of the bathroom, there was no wall at all. A pane of glass stretching from floor to ceiling separated the bathroom from the outside world, a landscape of leafless trees and jagged mountain peaks. The sky held neither moon nor stars, yet the land wasn't shrouded in complete darkness the way Elle had imagined. Dim light of some sort illuminated the landscape, though she couldn't figure out its source.

"This is … wow," was all she could say.

Alissa leaned down into the bath and pressed a plug into place, then opened both taps. "Yes, it's nice to have the view to look at while you're contemplating life. And don't worry, no one can see you from out there." She crossed to the cabinet beneath the pair of oval basins standing atop the vanity and retrieved a bottle. Elle watched as she removed the cap, tipped the bottle upside down over the bath, and poured blue liquid into the stream of gushing water.

"So, you seem to have found yourself in quite an inconvenient situation," Alissa continued, twisting the cap back onto the bottle.

Elle moved closer to the bath and looked down at the mounds of bubbles gathering beneath the heavy stream of water. "Being stuck in a world of everlasting darkness because it's the only way my stepmother can't find me? Yeah. Definitely inconvenient."

Alissa looked up. "I was actually referring to your love life."

"My—what?"

She returned the bottle to the cabinet before leaning against the vanity. "Human slave falls in love with fae prince. You haven't exactly made things easy for yourself."

"Falls in—*love*? No. No, no, no." Elle forced a laugh. "I'm not in love. This is more of a … you know … like a crush."

"I see. Well that's a little embarrassing for Prince Chevalier Adex Norville Belmont."

"It is?"

"I'd say it's *definitely* more than a crush for him. The guy took his father's plane without permission, flew to a different country, and crossed the border into an Eternal Night—not the safest of places for a non-vampire—just to make sure you're okay."

"Well, he … I mean, I guess he … cares?"

Alissa raised an eyebrow and gave her a look that said, *Duh.*

"So, um …" Elle focused on the bubbles again. "That's really horrible for Azriel. The fact that the woman he loves turned out to be using him. He must be heartbroken."

Alissa sighed. "Yeah, he's not exactly in a good place right now. Then again, he hasn't been in a good place for a long time."

Elle cast her mind back to the story Azriel had shared. "He mentioned he was experimented on. Forced to be part of some kind of enhanced army. Is that why he has that tattoo on his neck? The barcode?"

"No, that's—" Alissa paused and looked away. "That's from before. It's … he doesn't like to talk about it."

"Oh. Okay." The level of the bubbles had almost reached the top of the bath, so Elle leaned over and turned the taps off. "Azriel said he won't tell us where this other Eternal Night is," she said to Alissa as she straightened. "The one where Savoy is hiding."

"I know."

Elle took a deep breath and decided to try her luck. "Do you know where it is?"

Alissa hesitated before answering. "I do …"

Elle's heart sank as she recognized the reluctance in Alissa's tone. "But you also don't want to tell us."

Alissa sighed. "The location of the uncharted Eternal Nights is a secret vampires have kept for centuries. It goes against everything in us to reveal this information to another one of the High Races. You're not supposed to know that any uncharted Eternal Nights even exist."

Elle let out a long breath. "I understand."

"But I plan to talk to Azriel about this," Alissa added. "Perhaps we can still help your prince without actually telling him the location."

"You mean like blindfolding him and leading him there?"

Alissa smiled. "Maybe. But you definitely wouldn't be allowed on that trip, I'm afraid. We need to keep you far away from Savoy." She pushed away from the vanity. "Anyway, enjoy the bath. The towels are over there." She pointed to a collection of fluffy white towels hanging over a rail on one side of the shower. "I'll find some clothes for you and leave them outside the door. Come downstairs when you're ready, and I'll show you around." She crossed the bathroom, stopped in the doorway, and reached back for the doorknob.

"Alissa?"

She looked up, her hand pausing in the air. "Yes?"

"Why exactly do you want to keep me from Savoy? I mean, you're a vampire, and he's trying to figure out how to give magic to your kind. Even if you don't want *him* specifically to have that kind of power, surely you want it for yourself and other vampires? This is *magic* we're talking about. The glittery, gold, full-of-potential kind, not just the simple kind that allows shifters to change shape and gives vampires their abilities. Aren't you at all tempted by that?"

Alissa looked away, slowly lowering her hand to her side. She remained silent for several moments before saying, "The thought of being able to do all the amazing things the fae can do … it is tempting, I'll admit. Very tempting. But I don't know enough about the process, and the fact that humans are utilized disturbs me. If they were volunteers, the same way humans can volunteer their blood to vampires or *ask* to be turned, that would be different. But I'm about a thousand percent certain that's not the case here. These humans disappear and never turn up again. This process is probably something that kills them, and I'm one of the many vampires who's *not* okay with that. I believe the four High Races are all equal, and one shouldn't have to die in order to give another more power."

"So … you're not just keeping me here until you and Azriel can get rid of Savoy, and then you can use whatever knowledge I apparently possess—which I don't, by the way—to complete this ritual and give magic to yourselves and anyone else you deem worthy?"

Alissa's mouth fell open. "Is that really what you think?"

Elle spread her hands wide and gave a helpless shrug. "I don't know what to think. I'm trying to understand things from your perspective. You're being so nice to me, so obviously I want to figure out the reason. Unless … is it possible you're just being nice for the sake of being nice?"

Alissa looked genuinely confused. "It's just plain decency, isn't it?" Then her eyes darted down for a moment—somewhere near Elle's leg—and understanding replaced her confusion. "Which I suppose you haven't experienced much of in your life." She smiled and added, "Hopefully that'll change soon." Then she reached again for the doorknob and pulled the door closed.

Despite wanting to take Alissa at her word, Elle remained still for a moment, listening for a key turning in the lock. But no sound reached her ears other than the faint pop of the bubbles sitting in her bath. She let out a long breath as her shoulders relaxed. Perhaps it was naive, but she felt instinctively that Alissa was being truthful.

Elle removed her pajamas and stepped carefully into the bathtub. She lowered herself into the hot water, her eyes sliding shut as she sank down until the bubbles covered her shoulders.

Bliss.

But her busy mind wouldn't leave her alone. And so, with her eyes still closed and a cocoon of bubbles surrounding her, she allowed herself to consider a terrifying possibility: Not only had she wiped away memories—she had wiped away a life.

SEVEN

Three days later, Elle was seriously starting to miss the sun. Even while stuck in her attic back home, she'd been able to enjoy the bright rays filtering in through her dusty little window. Well, 'enjoy' probably wasn't the right word. Hanging out in Azriel and Alissa's beautiful family home was certainly more *enjoyable*, though she felt a little as if she existed in a state of limbo. It was frustrating not knowing what was going on with Dex, or if Sienna was okay, or whether Vale City had been overrun by magical vampires. "It'll be a while before that happens," Azriel assured her multiple times, but she still hated feeling so detached from the real world.

She looked up from the book she'd been trying to focus on as Alissa walked into the lounge and dropped onto the couch beside her. "Finished work?" Elle asked.

"Yes," Alissa answered with a sigh. "It's Friday, and it's wine o'clock. I'm done for the week." Though Alissa's family had plenty of wealth—her parents were currently traveling overseas and hadn't been home for almost a year—and Alissa had amassed her own small fortune from the various occupations her long life had allowed her to try out, she apparently liked to keep herself busy. Currently, she worked as a freelance graphic designer, which meant it had been easy enough for her to leave her fancy Cavalli Avenue apartment for a few days and work from her parents' home so Elle wasn't left alone with a grumpy Azriel.

"I've always wanted to know," Elle said, "if vampires actually enjoy the taste of things other than blood, or whether you consume normal food and drink in public just because it's more socially acceptable."

"Oh, wine is still quite delicious," Alissa said, leaning her elbow on the back of the couch and twirling a strand of hair around her finger. "As are plenty of other foods. They just don't provide any sustenance for us the way they do for other races. Blood is the only thing that's *necessary* for us to consume." She turned her head toward the flickering orange flames lined up in the gas fireplace and asked, "Were you feeling cold?"

"No. I just like the ambience. It makes things feel a little less … gray." Elle glanced out of the bay windows, where the sky was the exact same color it had been day and night since she first woke up here.

"It's hard for humans, I know," Alissa said. "You'll start to get depressed if you spend too much longer here."

Elle turned to face her again. "How did you …" But her words trailed off. She hadn't yet been able to bring herself to ask Alissa anything personal, like exactly how old she was, whether she'd ever been married, and how she ended up a vampire. Vampires weren't born, only made, and since it seemed all her immediate family members were vampires, Elle wondered if they'd all been turned at the same time, either voluntarily or against their will—which was illegal.

"How did I what?" Alissa asked.

"Um …"

"There you are," Azriel said, striding into the lounge. Elle hadn't seen him in over a day, and she wasn't sure if he'd been elsewhere on the property or if he'd left. "That friend of a friend who finally managed to put me in contact with the prince just called. He's at the border. Just helped Prince Dex to cross through."

"Oh. Great." Elle snapped her book shut as anticipation curled inside her and a flush heated her skin. Alissa gave her a knowing look, which turned quickly into a smirk, and Elle frowned at her. "So, uh, communications are possible inside an Eternal Night?" she asked before Alissa could utter whatever embarrassing comment had been about to pass her lips. "Just not between an Eternal Night and the outside world?"

"Correct," Azriel said. "We have networks and all of that set up within our

Eternal Nights, just like in the rest of the world." He frowned. "I thought that was common knowledge. Most of what goes on inside the Eternal Nights—the known ones, anyway—isn't a secret."

"Right, of course," Elle said. If she hadn't been forced to leave school at such a young age, she probably would have learned this at some point. Perhaps Sienna had mentioned it as part of one of her classes, but if so, Elle had forgotten.

"So, should we give you and Prince Just-a-crush some alone time when he gets here?" Alissa asked with an innocent smile.

"Alissa," Azriel grumbled.

"I'm sorry, she's just so easy to tease," Alissa answered with a laugh.

Elle picked up the book and smacked Alissa's leg. "Yes, actually, some alone time would be good. We might want to talk about things that have nothing to do with you."

"Oh, like how he's in looooove with—"

"Wow, when did you turn five years old?" Azriel asked, his tone perfectly deadpan.

"Hey, don't hate me just because I'm not grumpy like you," Alissa replied, reaching for a cushion and tossing it across the room at her brother. Azriel dodged easily, sighed, and left the room.

Elle opened her book again—a history of magical maladies that all had something to do with blood—and pretended to study it intently. After a few minutes, Alissa gave up on teasing her and went in search of a glass of wine. Elle's eyes scanned the pages of the book, searching for any mention of the symptoms Dex had exhibited, but it was hard to remain focused when she knew he might arrive at any moment.

When the sound of the front door opening reached her ears, she lowered the book to her lap and looked up. Her heart thumped unusually fast as she listened. Was that Dex's voice? Were those his footsteps coming toward the lounge?

He appeared in the doorway, and Elle stood abruptly, her lips stretching into a smile. The book fell and hit her bare foot. "Oh, ow." She dropped down quickly, picked up the book, and placed it on the glass coffee table before straightening hastily. "Hey. Hi." Despite the fact that she was making an idiot of herself in front of him yet again, Dex's face lit up with the kind of smile that Alissa—who stood at his side—would no doubt tease her endlessly about later.

"I'll let you guys … *talk*," she said, throwing a smirk in Elle's direction before turning and disappearing.

"I know I said I trust Azriel and his sister," Dex said, walking forward, "but I have to admit I'm relieved to see you're okay. Part of me dreaded the possibility that I may have been wrong about them, and that they wouldn't allow me in a second time."

"Yeah, I'm fine," Elle said. "I've just been reading and … well, mainly reading." Dex stopped in front of her, and an awkward moment passed in which she moved to hug him, he moved to kiss her, and his chin ended up bumping her forehead. She laughed, and he apologized, and then he pulled her against his chest and wrapped his arms securely around her. She melted a little bit.

"It's only been a few days, but I missed you terribly," he murmured against her hair.

"I missed you too," she said. She knew it was silly. Two weeks ago, she hadn't even met Dex yet, and now she couldn't get him out of her head. "What's going on out there?" she asked as they parted. "Has your father done anything drastic yet? Have the vampires made another move?"

"No. Nothing major's happened yet. My father's trying to locate Savoy, and he's tasked my mother with organizing The Ball 2.0, because apparently I still need a wife and the first ball wasn't enough of a disaster to deter him from hosting a second, more intimate, more *exclusive* party. But that's not important right now." As they sat, Dex took her hand in his and rubbed his thumb reassuringly across her skin. "I have some bad news."

"Oh no."

"Well, it might not be bad, depending on your point of view." He took a deep breath, then said, "Cress went to see Sienna."

"Ohnowhathappened?" Elle gasped as the icy fingers of fear squeezed around her chest.

"She's fine," Dex added hastily. "I mean, I'm pretty sure she's fine. But …

Elle, she ran away."

"What?" Elle pulled her hand free of Dex's. "No. Are you sure? She wasn't just … late for school or something?"

"I'm sure. After Cress checked Sienna's school, she went to your house. According to your stepmother, a bag and some of Sienna's things were gone. It's been a few days now, and when I sent a message this morning, Sienna still hadn't shown up."

"No, no, no," Elle moaned, pressing her palms to her cheeks. "She wasn't supposed to do that. It isn't safe out there for her on her own. I was supposed to go with her."

"She's fae, Elle. I'm sure she'll be fine."

"I know, but she's only seventeen."

"And you're a grand total of—what? Twenty-one? Twenty-two?"

"Well, nineteen, actually," Elle admitted.

"Oh. But … you were in that club. The night we met."

"Fake ID. Obviously. I had to pretend I was both fae and old enough to get in there. Anyway, I might be only two years older than Sienna, but I've had more experience out there in the big bad world than she has. I know that doesn't make sense, seeing as I've been a slave for so long, but it's the truth. I've seen more and survived more. I should be with her to protect her. She shouldn't have left on her own."

"I understand what you're saying, but isn't it more important that she got away from her abusive mother?"

"Well, yes, that's definitely a positive, but—"

"And she has magic, Elle. She isn't powerless. And if she's survived her abusive mother this long, then she has more resilience than most her age. She'll be fine."

"Ugh." Elle slid her hands into her hair and tugged. "I suppose I don't have much choice but to believe that you're right."

"Your stepmother reported her missing, and the police have been through the standard tracking procedure, but the spell just takes them to your home, the same way it did when I was looking for you."

"So she's hiding somehow, like me," Elle said, staring past Dex. "Either in an Eternal Night, or by using some form of magical protection."

"Yes. But I asked Olly to make sure we hear about it if the police find her."

"Okay. Thank you." Elle lowered her hands and clasped them together in her lap. "She got away. I have to focus on that part. She got away from Salvia."

"Yes."

"Wait." Elle focused on Dex again as her mind backtracked a few steps. "Is it a problem for you that I'm younger than you thought?"

"Hmm?" Dex frowned at the sudden change of subject. "Oh. No. I was surprised, that's all. But you're still the same person. Age is only a number, right?"

"Well, it could one day be a very big number for you, if we cure you of the Darkness. It'll only ever be a small number for me."

He gave her a sad smile. "I think it's more likely it'll be a small number for me too. Probably much smaller than the age you'll one day reach."

Elle took Dex's hand again and gave it a determined squeeze. "There's a library here—a huge one—and I've been looking through as many books as I can find that mention any sort of magical illness. Unless the Godmother invented something brand new specifically for you and your brother, then we should be able to find it in a book somewhere, right?"

"Maybe," Dex said, his tone suggesting he didn't quite agree. "But remember that my parents have had people searching for a cure for this for years. If they haven't found anything yet maybe it's because the Godmother really did conjure up something no one's ever suffered from before. Then the only way to get rid of it would probably be to make a deal with her, and there's no way I'm doing that."

Elle let out a heavy sigh. "Maybe it's a waste of time looking through these books, but it's not as though I have much else to do. So as long as I'm here, I'll keep looking."

"Thanks."

She hesitated, wondering if bringing up the past might be too painful for him. "When your brother died," she said carefully, slowly, giving him a chance to tell her he didn't want to talk about this. But his expression remained open.

"Yes?" he asked.

"He was younger than you are now."

"Yes, he was."

"Is that why you think you might die soon?"

Dex breathed in, breathed out, and swallowed. "Yes. Though I'm not as weak yet as he was when he passed away. The potion Cress makes definitely helps. My brother didn't have that." He rolled his eyes and added, "My parents never trusted any of Cress's experimental potions. They were always worried she was using unauthorized shifter magic or something, though what that could possibly be, I have no idea, since shifters generally can't do anything with magic except shift. But they were worried about something ancient to do with dragons? I don't know. Cress assured me she wasn't using any non-fae methods." He shook his head. "Anyway, I told my parents I didn't care. If something made a positive difference, I wanted to keep taking it. So I did—without their knowledge."

Elle tipped her head to the side a little and examined Dex. "It sounds like there's a lot you do without your parents' knowledge."

He lifted one shoulder in an easy shrug, a smile curving his lips. "I can't really argue with that observation. I've been breaking their rules for a long time. Ever since ..." He trailed off, his expression becoming thoughtful. "Yeah, probably ever since the day I convinced my nanny to sneak me off the palace grounds and into the forest beyond. You know, not on the side where the main entrance is. The other side. I could see the trees from the windows of the palace, but I could never get to them. I begged for her help until one day she gave in."

"You know," Elle said, "your parents probably set those rules for a reason. You were just a child. What if something had happened to you while you were outside the palace walls with no one to protect you but your nanny?"

"I know. I realize that *now*, but back then, I thought it was the best adventure ever. After I'd been out once, I wanted to go again, so I convinced Liana to help me sneak out more often. We would meet up with her friend and her friend's daughter, race around for a few hours with the forest as our playground, and then return home."

"And nothing ever went wrong?"

"No. Not until …" Dex looked down, his shoulders slumping a little. "I got up one day and she was gone. My mother told me I didn't need a nanny anymore, that I was too old for one. Which was probably true, but I always wondered if there was more to it than that. If maybe my parents found out she was sneaking me out of the palace grounds and fired her—or worse. Years later, when I was older and people actually took my questions seriously, I tried to find out. But no one seemed to know what happened to her."

"So you don't actually know if you have anything to feel guilty about," Elle said.

"Well, there's the fact that I involved her in my rule-breaking. I definitely feel guilty about that. Anyway." He shook himself a little. "That's in the past, and we should be discussing the present. Specifically, your slave charm."

"Oh, yes. Did you find anything useful? I think I'm starting to feel a little bit of pain, but nothing serious yet."

"I think we did find something useful. Cress and I were talking after we left here last time, discussing all the legal aspects of casting a slave charm upon someone. You know, like how it's illegal to enslave a human once he or she has already been freed. And we both suddenly remembered that if a human is *born* free, it's illegal to enslave him or her. That was one of the changes my grandfather made. And you were born free, right? If this woman is your stepmother, she must have married your father, which means he must have been a free human, and therefore you were free too."

"But," Elle interrupted before Dex could go any further, "if a human is underage and her only legal guardian is a faerie, that faerie has the right to enslave her."

Dex remained silent for a moment, his mouth half open. "Seriously? That's legal?"

"Yes. And that law about not being able to enslave a human once he or she has been freed? That doesn't always stand. If a human is convicted of a crime, one of the possible sentences is the slave charm."

Dex's fingers curled into fists. "It makes me sick that my father allows this kind of thing."

"Your father wants far worse than the laws that currently exist," Elle reminded him quietly.

"I know. It's disgusting. He doesn't deserve to be—" Dex pressed his lips together, cutting off the remainder of his words, which sounded suspiciously as though they may have been bordering on treasonous. He let out a long breath, then continued, sounding calmer now. "So. The only way out of this is to negotiate with your stepmother."

"What?"

"It's simple. I'll ask her what her price is. Whatever she wants, she can have it, as long as she removes your slave charm."

For several moments, Elle couldn't speak. "You … you would do that for me? You'd give her anything she wants? To save a person you barely know?"

"Elle, I feel like I know you better than anyone I've met in years. I may not know all the *facts* about you. All the experiences you've had, your history, your likes and dislikes, but I feel like I know what kind of person you are. And that kind of person …" He trailed off, shook his head, then smiled. "Yeah, that kind of person is absolutely worth saving."

Elle raised her hand and gently brushed her knuckles along the faint stubble of Dex's jaw. "I really want to kiss you right now."

He lifted his hand to cover hers, a light sparking in his silver-blue eyes. "I wouldn't stop you."

"But," she said, pulling her hand out from beneath his and leaning away from him, "I don't want to distract myself from telling you that negotiating with my stepmother is a *terrible* idea."

Dex paused. "Why?"

"I know exactly what she'll ask for, Dex, and you can't give it to her."

"Why not?"

"Because she'll ask that you marry Meredith."

Dex blinked. "But … that's … I mean, that's a really high price. Why would she even try that?"

"Because I'm worth that much to her."

Dex's eyes narrowed. "Why?"

Elle allowed herself a deep inhale and one long exhale before speaking again. "This is the thing Azriel said I hadn't told you yet. It's the thing that people pay me Essence for. The thing that makes it easy for my stepmother to con people out of money and jewels so she can continue living a comfortable lifestyle without having to actually work for it."

"Okaaaaay," Dex said slowly.

"You know that I'm human, right? You've seen the color of my blood. But there's something about me that's … different. I can …" She swallowed. "I can remove memories."

Dex's frown deepened. "I'm sorry, you can what?"

"Remove memories. I can slip into a person's mind and remove a chunk of time and all the memories that go along with it. Just a simple nudge, and the memories are gone forever. That's what people pay me for. They come to me when there are things they want to forget."

"How … how is that possible? You're *human*. You don't have magic."

Elle opened her mouth to say she had no idea, but before she could utter a word, a door banged shut somewhere nearby. Footsteps—sharp, confident— grew closer, and into the lounge strode the Godmother.

EIGHT

Dex leaped immediately to his feet and lunged at the elegant, white-haired woman. Bright, golden light flashed, throwing him clear across the room. He slammed into a wall and slumped to the ground.

"Dex!" Elle jumped up and hurried between the couches toward him, but he was on his feet again before she reached his side.

"Silly boy," the Godmother said. "Don't you remember all the wards that have been placed around you to protect you from me? Conveniently, they also protect *me* from *you*. You don't seem to have factored that into your little kill-the-Godmother plot."

Dex began making strange hand motions near his body, muttering things Elle couldn't hear properly. "Are you okay?" she asked, reaching for him.

"And *you*," the Godmother said. Elle lowered her hand and twisted to find the woman's dark brown gaze boring into her. "You failed to pay the price I set. I assume you don't want your freedom as badly as you told me you did."

Anger rushed hotly through Elle's veins. "How did you find us?" she demanded.

"I'm the Godmother," she stated simply, as if that should be answer enough. She stalked past Elle and Dex and took a seat near the fireplace. "Now. We need to talk." Before she could continue, two streaks of color flashed across the room, coming to an abrupt halt in front of her. Alissa's hands were curled into fists, while Azriel leaned forward, gripped both sides of the armchair, and brought his face right in front of the Godmother's.

"How dare you—"

"Everyone, calm down," the Godmother said, pulling her head away from Azriel's. "Why don't you all take a seat, and we can act like the rational beings that we are."

"You have no idea who I am or whether I possess a rational bone in my body," Azriel growled, his hands squeezing tighter on the arm rests.

"Don't lie to me, Azriel. You used your love for Mariel to rationalize everything you did for the Allegiant. You know exactly what it is to be rational. Now sit down."

Azriel straightened, his mouth hanging open and a deep crease forming between his brows. "Fine," he said eventually. "But if you show the slightest hint of hurting anyone beneath my roof—"

"Oh, for goodness sake. I didn't come here to hurt anyone. I could have sent other people to do that. I came here to talk."

"Better talk quickly then," Dex said, still moving his hands and fingers in strange motions around his head and body. "As soon as these wards are gone, I'm coming for you."

"Yes, I see." The Godmother arched an unimpressed eyebrow, sounding bored as she added, "I'm shivering."

"So you're here to *talk*?" Elle asked, moving to the nearest couch and lowering herself to the edge. She remained poised to leap to her feet at the first sign of a threat from the Godmother. On the couch opposite her, Azriel and Alissa sat slowly.

"Yes," the Godmother said. "And if you must know, Elle, it really wasn't that difficult to track you down after you escaped my magic. I got hold of the palace's security footage."

Dex looked up. "How did you—"

"Then I had my people examine it until someone identified the vampire who took you. I found out everything I needed to know about Azriel, including the location of every place he's lived. Within a day of sending my people out to look, I'd narrowed down the options to his family home in the Beryl Eternal Night. One of my vampire contacts brought me across the border from the outside world into this one. And here I am." She spread her hands wide, palms up.

"Well done," Elle said, her voice heavy with sarcasm.

"So my strength is greater than the Godmother's magic," Azriel said. "Good to know."

The Godmother narrowed her eyes at him. "It was a simple spell. If I'd known Elle might encounter anything more than *air* on her way home, I would have cast a stronger one."

"So are you here to talk about how I disappointed you by not killing Dex?" Elle asked. "Or is there something more important on your mind?"

The Godmother folded her hands neatly in her lap. "Savoy is coming after me and my empire. Apparently not all of his magic-enhanced vampires perished at that disaster of a ball the other night. He sent a few of them my way the next day. You know I've never conducted business with vampires, and it seems that this new world Savoy is hoping to establish for himself once he's king does not include me."

"Amazing," Dex muttered, his hands pausing for a moment. "Who would have thought I'd have something in common with Savoy?"

The Godmother let out a dramatic sigh. "I know you think I ruined your life, Chevalier Belmont, but it was your father who made a terrible wish and was never willing to make another one to undo it."

"*You* set the price," Dex hissed. "*You* killed my brother."

"This is all quite enlightening," Alissa murmured.

"And also none of your business," Dex replied.

"*Anyway*," the Godmother continued, "my plan is simple. I find Savoy and kill him."

Azriel let out a humorless grunt of a laugh. "Even if you knew where to find him, you'd never get close enough to actually kill him. You won't even make it through the front door. And if you do, there are his guards to deal with. And if you get past *them*, there's still the additional magic he bought from some faerie or other to protect himself."

"I know. Which is why I'll be taking him the one thing he wants more than anything else right now." She looked at Elle. "You."

"Excuse me?" Elle asked.

"I know he wants you. He's been searching for you for years. If I pretend I want to form an alliance with him and offer him you as a show of good faith, perhaps he'll allow me to get close enough."

Elle swallowed. How did the Godmother know he'd been searching for her for years? How did she know *any* of the things she knew? The memory of what the Godmother had said during their first conversation—that Elle had *killed* someone with her memory-wiping ability—knocked on the inside of her brain. She wanted to ask if it was true—if it was Savoy's father—but at the same time, did she really want to know?

She cleared her throat, pushing her fears aside. "So you need help. That's why you're here."

"Don't pretend that the death of the vampire heir would benefit only me. He's putting the stability of our whole country at risk. Surely *none* of you want that?"

"All I'm hearing," Elle said, "is that when someone needs help from you, they have to pay a terrible price in order to get it. But if you need help? Oh, that's different. We should all jump to help you."

"Not at all." The Godmother crossed one leg over the other and smiled. "Why don't you make another wish, Elle?"

"How dare you make such a suggestion," Dex muttered, his hands moving even faster now. "Elle, I'm nearly free of this damn protective magic."

"Wish again for your freedom," the Godmother continued, disregarding Dex's interruption, "and this time, the only price I ask is that you accompany me on my journey to visit Vincenzo Savoy. Once I've killed him, you'll be free to go. *Properly* free."

Elle folded her arms over her chest. "I thought you didn't deal with people a second time if they refused or failed to pay their price the first time. That's *your* rule."

"Precisely. It's my rule, and therefore I'm allowed to break it."

"So all you want me to do is remain with you until you get close enough to

Savoy to kill him?"

"Yes. Oh, and keep the prince from killing me," she added hastily as Dex rushed toward her. "If he kills me, I'll never be able to give you your freedom."

Dex stopped mere inches from her, his hands raised, faerie dust glittering on his fingers. "That's not the only way for Elle to gain her freedom," he said through gritted teeth.

"Really?" the Godmother asked. She looked at Elle. "Do tell me about this other option that has suddenly materialized."

Elle let out a resigned breath. "Don't kill her, Dex. I'm pretty sure she's still the only chance I have at freedom—other than you marrying my stepsister, which I don't consider a viable option. And, more importantly, she probably has a better chance of killing Savoy than any of us."

"Trust me, Elle, we can make a plan without her."

Elle stood and moved to Dex's side. She placed her hand on his arm. "Please," she said quietly. "Killing her isn't going to fix anything."

"No, but it'll keep her from messing with the lives of all the people who have yet to summon her for a wish."

"But you're not a murderer," Elle said, her voice even quieter now. "You can find another way to bring down her empire." To her side, the Godmother snickered, as if that idea were preposterous.

Dex lowered his hands and scrutinized Elle's face. "You really want to make another bargain with her?"

"I don't *want* to, but if I can get my freedom *and* she can stop Savoy? That sounds worth it to me."

"Excellent," the Godmother said.

"You're forgetting something," Azriel interrupted, and Elle turned to look at him. "I haven't agreed to tell anyone where to find Savoy."

"An uncharted Eternal Night," the Godmother said. "I don't know which one, but I have enough vampire contacts that I'm almost certain I could find out."

"Wonderful," Azriel said, his tone suggesting there was nothing about this situation that he found wonderful in the least. "I'm glad to know I don't need to get involved."

"But it would waste far less time, Azriel," the Godmother said, "if *you* told me."

"The amount of time you waste on this little mission of yours isn't my concern," he replied.

"This *little mission*? Not your concern?" The Godmother shook her head. "I know you don't agree with what Savoy is doing. Will you enjoy living with the guilt when he manages to make a mess of our country because I didn't have enough time to complete my *little mission*?"

"I don't want to be the one to give away a secret vampires have kept for centuries."

The Godmother laughed. "Trust me, there are people other than vampires who know about the uncharted Eternal Nights. They know how many there are, and where to find them. Not all vampires can keep a secret."

"Well I can," Azriel snapped.

"Azriel," Alissa said quietly. "What if you don't *tell* her. What if you don't *show* her either. What if you just take her there and don't let her know where you're going."

"If you're planning to tie a blindfold over my eyes or put a pillowcase over my head, I may have to object," the Godmother said. "Strongly."

Azriel nodded slowly. "I think I like that idea."

The Godmother rolled her eyes. "Of course you do."

Azriel remained silent another few moments, during which Elle returned to her spot on the couch. Dex sat stiffly beside her, his hand gripping her knee. "Okay, I'll take you there," Azriel said eventually, "but only if you do something in return for me."

"Ah, a bargain." The Godmother rubbed her hands together. "You know I like those."

Azriel narrowed his eyes, then continued. "Savoy has something with which he controls the enhanced army he purchased from Mariel. He calls it his scepter. It's a staff with a large red gem sitting atop it. The control charm is within the gem. When you've killed him, I want you to destroy it. Only then will every one of those vampires be free."

The Godmother pursed her lips. "I've heard of this army. Vampires with even more speed and strength. I assume Savoy plans to give them all magic at some point."

"Yes, that was his plan. Get hold of Elle, find out how to complete the ritual properly, and give endless magic to his enhanced army."

"Well, he certainly won't get the chance to do any of that," the Godmother said. "I'll kill him, and then I'll destroy that gem."

"What guarantee do I have that you're telling the truth?"

"I'll make sure it happens," Dex said.

"Oh, and since when are you coming with?" the Godmother asked, though she looked amused rather than surprised.

"Of course I'm coming. Someone needs to make sure you actually do all the things you're promising to do. You can tell Savoy I'm your prisoner, if that'll make it easier for us to get close to him. The fae prince plus the girl with all the answers he's been looking for. He can't say no to that, can he?"

Elle placed her hand over Dex's, letting him know with a gentle squeeze just how grateful she was that she didn't have to do this without him. "Why doesn't this gem thing control you as well?" she asked Azriel. "You were part of that army too."

"I got away after we all escaped the man who experimented on us. I thought everyone else was free as well, but Mariel had told Savoy where we'd be, and he managed to trap almost everyone else. Only once he had the army in his possession did he acquire this gem and place magical control over everyone. I wasn't present for that spell."

"Well, now that we've all agreed on what to do next," the Godmother said, rising to her feet, "let's get moving."

"What, right now?" Elle asked.

"Do you have something more important to do?" the Godmother asked.

"Well, no. But I'm not a prince." She looked at Dex. "I assumed you might need to … I don't know, rearrange your schedule or something?"

He shook his head. "I'll be in trouble anyway when my parents figure out

I've taken the plane again. May as well make it worth it."

"Okay." Elle looked at the Godmother and shrugged. "I guess we can go then. Actually, wait. As soon as I leave this Eternal Night, my stepmother will be able to find me. That could be a problem."

"Shouldn't be," Azriel said. "You'll only be between Eternal Nights for a few hours at the most. That won't be long enough for your stepmother to get from Vale City to where we'll be."

"So, I guess I'll just go back to my normal boring life?" Alissa chimed in, slumping back against the couch cushions.

The Godmother shrugged. "If your normal life is boring, I'm afraid that's your problem, dear, not ours."

"I suppose you're right," Alissa said with a frown.

"So, Azriel." The Godmother clasped her hands together. "Should I be expecting a pillowcase over my head at any moment?"

Azriel sighed as he rose from the couch. "Not just yet. We can drive from here to the edge of the Beryl Eternal Night and cross back into the daylight world. From there, I assume you can get us quickly back into Astranerica?"

The Godmother gave him her most radiant smile. "With a snap of my fingers, darling."

"Good. I'll arrange for a car to meet us. I'll drive from there, and the back windows will be blacked out—magically—so you don't know where we're going. Though pillowcases can certainly be arranged if you'd prefer."

"Hang on," Dex said. "Are you saying there's an Eternal Night *inside my own country*? That's where Savoy is?"

"Yes. And that's all I'll be saying." Azriel turned and strode toward the door. "Let's go."

NINE

Blackness pressed in on Elle, squeezing, squeezing, *squeeeeezing*. When her surroundings finally expanded around her with a pop, she staggered forward and bent over. Sucking in a gulp of air, she tried not to give in to the urge to vomit.

A hand touched her back, rubbing gently. "Are you okay?" Dex asked.

"I'm sorry, dear Elle," the Godmother said from somewhere nearby. "I always forget that humans—"

"Do *not* say you forgot we don't react well to things like being squeezed through space from one spot to another," Elle gasped, straightening and facing the woman. "It's been barely a week since the last time you did that to me. You've forgotten nothing."

The Godmother smiled. "I've told you before that I like you, haven't I."

Elle pressed her lips together to hold back the *Shut up!* that wanted to slip out. The Godmother may infuriate her, but she was still afraid of the woman.

"That spell," Dex said, facing the Godmother.

"Yes, yes, it's ancient and difficult and very, *very* few have perfected it. I'm one of them."

"I was going to say I'm pretty sure it's illegal when used to travel to a different country."

"Oh. Yes, I suppose it is. But we don't have time to waste. I'm sure your pilot won't mind flying your plane back from Verance to Astranerica without you."

Dex sighed and looked around. "I assume I'm not allowed to ask exactly where we are right now?" Elle followed his gaze and took in rolling hills, the occasional tree, and the sun setting in the distance. She smiled at the purple and peach colors lighting up the puffs of cloud as she soaked in the last remaining daylight. It felt indescribably good to see the sun again.

"You can ask," Azriel said to Dex, "but I won't answer."

"You could ask *me*," the Godmother suggested. "Since young Azriel had to tell me where to transport us."

"*Young* Azriel?" the vampire repeated.

"But of course, I wouldn't answer either," the Godmother assured him, "since this is all highly secretive."

"Oh look," Azriel deadpanned. "Here's the car. I'm so excited for this adventure."

The growl of a vehicle reached Elle's ears, and she looked around to see a black limousine driving up the winding gravel road, a smaller car just behind it. Azriel stepped into the road, and both vehicles came to a smooth stop in front of him. From the driver's side of the limo, a vampire stepped out. "Thanks, I owe you one," Azriel said to her.

She shrugged. "Not a problem for an old friend."

"And the windows in the back compartment are enchanted?"

"Yes. Placed by a friend who knows all about these things. But if this woman is who you say she is—" the vampire surveyed the group, her eyes stopping on the Godmother "—she'll probably be able to mess with the enchantment pretty easily."

"But we won't let that happen," Elle said hastily, "because we respect your desire to keep things confidential." She gave the Godmother a stern look. "Right?"

"Absolutely," the Godmother replied with a smile.

"Let's just get this done," Azriel grumbled. He climbed into the driver's seat and slammed the front door shut. His vampire friend headed for the smaller car without another glance at the group. Dex opened the limo's back door, and Elle bent her head as she climbed inside. She slid across the white leather interior while the Godmother took a seat across from her. Dex climbed in last and pulled the door shut, cutting out the last of the natural light. Elle sighed internally as Dex sat beside her. *The sun was nice while it lasted,* she thought.

"I still don't trust you," Dex said to the Godmother as the limo pulled away with a crunch of tires against gravel.

She smiled. "What a surprise."

"Which is why I'm going to perform a truth spell on you."

She let out a full-bodied laugh. "That's not happening."

"So we're supposed to just believe that everything you've told us today is the truth?"

"Dex," she said, "I have the kind of magic you can only dream of. Now that you've so helpfully removed all your wards, I could snuff you out of existence like that." She snapped her fingers, and Elle flinched, expecting something terrible to happen. Nothing did. "But I haven't," the Godmother continued. "That should be enough to suggest I have your best interests at heart."

"My best interests?" Dex snorted. "A few days ago, you wanted me dead."

"Because you wanted *me* dead. Now that Elle has convinced you that's a bad idea, we can all play nicely together."

"You *say* that, but—"

The Godmother slid forward, her hand flashed out, and she grabbed Dex's. She tugged him closer, holding their clasped hands up between them. Elle moved forward, then froze, unsure whether intervening would make things worse. "Here's your truth spell, young man," the Godmother said.

"What—"

"You've cast it before, so you know what it feels like. You know I'll tell you the truth now."

"How did you … you did that in an instant."

"Because I'm the Godmother. Now, do I want Savoy gone as badly as you do? Yes. Do I have every intention of killing him? Yes. Will I follow through on my side of the bargain and grant Elle her wish for freedom once I've killed him? Yes." She let go of Dex's hand and sat back. "Satisfied?"

"Uh …" Dex slid backward on the seat, breathing heavily. "As much as I can be, I suppose."

Elle's gaze bounced back and forth between them, her heart still galloping in her chest. "Is the truth spell still on her?"

Dex shook his head. "She ended it."

"Oh."

The Godmother's dark eyes swung toward her. "Is there something you wanted to ask, my dear Elle?"

"Yes, but now I have no idea if you'll answer with the truth."

"You can ask anyway. If I don't want to tell you the truth, then I'll say nothing."

Elle breathed shallowly, almost too afraid to voice her question. Then she cleared her throat and asked, "Did I kill Savoy's father?"

The Godmother considered her for a moment before answering. "Yes."

Something cracked inside Elle's chest. At least, that was the way it felt as she struggled to take her next breath. Dex gripped her hand and she held on tight, as if he were the only thing anchoring her to this world. She swallowed and asked, "Then did I take the memory from myself?"

"Yes."

"But … how could I do something so terrible? How was I capable of that? Of actually ending someone's life?"

"You were very young. You didn't know what you were doing. The ability was new to you. You were supposed to take Nazario Savoy's memory of the ritual that gives magic to vampires so that he could never use it, but you took everything. Every memory. His whole mind. Though you were young, you understood afterwards what had happened. So your mother encouraged you to take the memory from yourself."

"How do you know this?"

"Because your mother told me about it afterwards."

"My *mother*? She knew you?"

"Yes, but—"

"But you can't say any more because—let me guess—that's someone else's story. *Her* story."

"Correct."

"That makes no sense. I'm her daughter. Why don't I get to know her story? If she were alive, she would tell me."

"Would she?"

"Yes!"

The Godmother sighed, her lips turning down in consideration. "Perhaps she would. Or perhaps she'd tell you to snuggle up beneath that lovely quilt she made and trace your finger over all the stars."

"I'm sorry, *what*? Is that supposed to be some kind of riddle?"

"No. Your quilt is real, is it not?"

"Holy stars, you're the most frustrating person I've ever met."

The Godmother smiled. "Thank you."

"I'm done trying to have a conversation with you," Elle huffed, turning her head to look past Dex. Angry tears burned her eyes, but she blinked them away.

"Hey," Dex said quietly. "It was a mistake. You didn't mean to take his life."

"I'd prefer not to talk about it," Elle murmured.

And so they sat in silence, the minutes ticking slowly by, and of the three of them, the Godmother was the only one who seemed at ease. Elle's shoulders remained stiff and her breathing refused to return to normal, while beside her, she could sense Dex's tension. She longed to fold into him and let herself cry, but there was no way she would let herself do that in front of the Godmother.

Dex reached into his pocket and pulled out his phone. He unlocked the screen and scrolled through the collection of icons.

"I thought communication wasn't possible between an Eternal Night and the outside world," Elle said.

"It isn't." Dex lowered the phone to his lap with a sigh. "It's just habit, I suppose. Checking one's phone when there's nothing else to do."

"What's that picture you've used for the background?" Elle asked.

He picked up the phone again and showed her. "The view from my bedroom balcony. That's the forest I was telling you about—the one beyond the wall, where I used to sneak out and play—and then past those hills, you can see the ocean."

"It's beautiful," Elle said, taking the phone and peering closer at the picture. It was far prettier than any view she'd ever had, even when she lived at Fernvale, Salvia's old home.

"There was this stream running through the forest," Dex added, "and I managed to use my *very* basic knowledge of magic to build a little hut of sticks that floated above the water. With Liana's help, of course. Here, I'll show you." He took the phone and began thumbing through apps.

"You have photos from way back then?" Elle asked. "On your phone?"

"Yes. They were in printed albums originally—Liana, my nanny, gave them to me—but my mother demanded I clear out all the clutter from my rooms last year, so someone digitized everything for me."

Elle watched as Dex's thumb moved quickly across the screen and photos sped by. "Wait, stop," she said, her hand reaching out to grab the phone before she could stop herself. "I—I'm sorry. Can I go back a few photos?"

"Oh. Yes, of course."

Elle's heart pounded faster as her thumb slid across the screen. She thought she'd seen … but it couldn't be. She must have imagined it. And yet, she had to make sure. Her thumb moved again—and her heart almost stopped.

There were two women in the photo, both blond, though one was human and the other was fae. An odd ringing filled Elle's ears as her blood crashed wildly through her veins.

"What's wrong?" Dex asked, his voice piercing through the ringing. He pointed at the fae woman in the photo. "That's Liana. My nanny."

Elle touched the screen, placing her finger delicately on the other woman in the photo. "That's my *mother*."

TEN

RIPPLES OF HOT AND COLD RACED ACROSS ELLE'S BODY AS DEX STARED AT HER. "What? No, that's Liana's friend," he said. "Remember I told you we used to meet her sometimes when we snuck out of the palace grounds? She always came with her …" He trailed off before quietly finishing: "With her daughter."

Elle swallowed, unable to tear her eyes from Dex's face. The confusion she saw there must surely mirror her own. Her mother's best friend was the woman who'd taken care of Dex as a child? Elle and Dex had played together when they were very young? What kind of crazy coincidence was that?

Then, suddenly remembering they weren't alone in the limo, Elle turned the phone to face the Godmother. "Do you know about this?" she demanded.

The Godmother frowned, appearing only vaguely interested. "Why would I know anything about that photo?"

"You said you knew my mother."

"I didn't say I knew her well."

"But you—" Her body rocked sideways as the limo came to a stop.

"Oh good, we're here," the Godmother said, sliding to the edge of her seat.

"Tell me what you know," Elle begged. *"Please."*

"I'm sorry, but I can't help you with that photo, Elle. I don't know anything about it. Right now, we have a vampire to confront."

"This is crazy," Dex said, taking the phone from Elle and shoving it into his pocket. "How strange that we've actually met before. I mean, you were very little—three or four maybe?—so I doubt you remember it."

Elle shook her head. "I don't."

The Godmother exited the limo, and Elle and Dex followed. "I don't see an abode of any sort," the Godmother commented, turning on the spot. Elle looked around at the desolate gray landscape.

"We're not there yet," Azriel said, "but this is as far as I'm going." He pointed to a rock shaped roughly like a bird's head and added, "As you crest that hill, you'll see Savoy's home in the distance. You can't miss it. It's the only one out here."

"You're not driving us to the front door?" the Godmother asked.

"No. You can walk the rest of the way or use your transportation magic, if it works here. But I'm not getting any closer to Savoy than this."

"My magic works here," the Godmother said dismissively. "It can't cross the border into or out of an Eternal Night, that's all."

"How will we get back to the normal world after we're done?" Elle asked.

"I'll wait here for you," Azriel said.

"Okay then." The Godmother raised her hands. "Time for you both to be shackled."

"Shackled?" Dex repeated.

"Yes. Savoy and his people need to think you're my prisoners, remember?"

"I know, but can you restrain us with something a little easier to get out of than metal chains?"

"Oh, these will be easy, don't worry. I won't enchant them. A bit of faerie dust, and they should melt right away." She snapped the fingers of her right hand, and then her left. Dex's shackles appeared first, tugging his hands together in front of him, and a second later Elle was bound in the same way. She watched as Dex tested whether it really was as easy to break free as the Godmother had suggested. After the shackles melted from his wrists and vanished, he held his arms out to be restrained a second time. "Still having trust issues, I see," the Godmother muttered. Then she snapped her fingers again.

The world vanished with a sickening jolt, and when it reappeared moments later, Elle strained to pull air into her squashed lungs. "I wish you'd warn me," she gasped.

"It wouldn't help. Now, please *don't* ruin things before I can get close enough to Savoy."

Elle turned slowly, and right behind her rose a stylish building that appeared to be constructed of numerous white boxes and plenty of glass. Through some of the enormous windows, she could see curving staircases, plants standing in giant pots—how did they grow in a world without sun?—and an art canvas splashed with red and turquoise.

"Wow. You brought us right here. How'd you do that without seeing exactly where the house was?"

"Let's go," the Godmother replied, heading for the glass front doors without bothering to answer Elle's question.

"Why has no one tried to stop us yet?" Dex asked. "With all that glass, we must have been spotted the moment we appeared here. Someone like Savoy would make sure to have plenty of security."

"Perhaps he can see that I've brought him a gift."

As they approached the front door, a vampire appeared on the other side. He held the door open as the Godmother swept inside. Elle and Dex shuffled in after her. "Godmother," the vampire said with a small bow. "I was told to expect you."

"Excellent," the Godmother replied.

Elle exchanged a frown with Dex. That didn't sound right. Or had the Godmother mentioned contacting Savoy? Maybe she had, and Elle had missed that part.

"I'll show you to our lord king's throne room," the vampire said.

"Lovely."

"Lord king?" Dex repeated in a whisper. "His throne room?"

The Godmother shot him an icy glare. "You will not speak unless I ask you to," she snapped loudly, presumably for the benefit of the vampire who was present. Dex rolled his eyes in response.

They crossed the entrance area, skirting a rectangular fish pond, before heading along a glass passageway. Elle looked up through the transparent ceiling at the featureless gray sky. *Utterly depressing*, she thought. Perhaps if she spent too long in a world like this, she would also go a little crazy and want to take over a country where the sun shone at least some of the time.

Leaving the passage behind, they walked into a long room, empty aside from a raised step at the other end, upon which sat a black glass seat that wouldn't have been out of place in a contemporary art museum. Large panes of glass on both sides of the room allowed expansive views of the gray world outside, but Elle's attention was fixed on the man sitting on the black glass throne. Untidy dark hair fell over red eyes and bronzed skin—thanks to his heritage, Elle assumed, since it couldn't possibly be due to the sun. In his right hand, he gripped a polished wooden staff topped by a glowing red gem the size of Elle's fist. His scepter.

"Godmother," he said with a smile. "Welcome to the Jade Eternal Night. It's good to see you again."

Okay, that definitely didn't sound right. Not for someone who'd supposedly sent people to attack the Godmother just days ago.

"Vincenzo," the Godmother replied, warmth filling her voice. "What a lovely home. I apologize for not making time to visit you sooner."

Say what? Elle halted. "Okay, what in all the stars is—"

"Silence!" the Godmother replied, her dark gaze snapping toward Elle.

"Is that her?" Savoy asked, rising from his seat. "The one I've been looking for?"

"Yes."

"And him?" Savoy thrust his chin toward Dex.

"A bonus gift." The Godmother ushered Elle and Dex forward, and the only reason Elle played along was because of the truth spell in the limo. The Godmother said she intended to kill him. So this was all part of the plan, right? It had to be. "This is the fae prince, Chevalier of House Belmont," the Godmother said as she, Elle and Dex stopped a few feet away from Savoy and his throne.

Savoy's brow rose. "You've outdone yourself, Godmother. I wish you'd come to me with your proposal months ago. It would have saved me a great deal of trouble."

"Well, everything happens the way it happens for a reason," the Godmother said smoothly.

"Is the girl going to be difficult?" Savoy asked. "Am I going to have to use special methods to force the information out of her?"

"No, she won't be difficult at all. I know exactly how to get the information you need." The Godmother moved to face Elle. She raised her hands. Instinctively, Elle tried to take a step back, but something held her in place. She tried to move her head, but that didn't work either. "What have you done to me?" she whispered.

"Don't worry, you'll be absolutely fine." The Godmother placed her fingers against Elle's temples.

"Wait," Savoy instructed. In her peripheral vision, Elle noticed streaks of motion. Swiveling her eyes as far to each side as she could, she saw three vampires standing against the right-hand window, and three on the left. "Merely a precaution," Savoy said. "In case you have any unpleasant tricks up your sleeve."

"I understand completely," the Godmother said. "Always better to be careful." Then she pressed her fingers into Elle's skin, and Elle gasped at the pain that shot through her head.

"Elle!" She was vaguely aware of Dex rushing toward her, but she could barely focus on anything but the pain.

"Stay back!" the Godmother shouted. The pain slicing through Elle's mind lessened for a moment. "What did I tell you about *ruining* things?" Dex fell to his knees and didn't move, and Elle suspected the same magic that was paralyzing her now held him in place as well.

The Godmother returned her attention to Elle, and pain rebounded through her head again. Her thoughts became muddled, spinning around inside her mind, until nothing made sense, and she had no idea where she was or what had happened to bring her here.

Then, as abruptly as it had begun, the pain vanished. Her mind cleared instantly. The Godmother lowered her hands, and Elle reared back with another gasp. Then she stilled. Though magic didn't hold her in place, shock did. In front of her, hanging in the air amid a swirling cloud of golden dust, was a semi-transparent image of three people: Elle as a young girl, her mother, and a man who looked very much like the one currently standing in front of a throne holding a scepter.

"Is that it?" Savoy asked in an awed whisper. "The memory?"

"Yes," the Godmother said. "All you need to do is step into it, and it will become yours. You'll know everything your father knew before he died."

"Where did that come from?" Elle whispered. "I thought—I thought all the memories were gone."

The Godmother didn't answer her. Savoy stepped down from his throne. Something rippled and shimmered around him, like the surface of a lake that had just been disturbed—if a lake could be turned on its side. He moved forward, and the rippling layer of magic vanished.

"Finally," the Godmother murmured. Her hand slashed through the air, and black blood spurted from Savoy's chest. He crumpled forward with a cry as she lunged for the scepter. The vampires stationed around the room sped forward, but the Godmother grasped the gem atop the scepter and shouted, "Stop! I am your commander now. You will obey me." The vampires froze, and Elle's wide eyes bounced from them back to Savoy, lying motionless on the floor with black liquid pooling around him. His red eyes, a symbol of the vampire magic coursing through his body, faded to a dark brown.

"Thank you for playing your part, you two," the Godmother said. She stepped over Savoy's body and climbed the single stair to the black glass throne. Turning, she slowly lowered herself to a seated position. She breathed in deeply, then exhaled. "Well, this is the first thing that's going to have to change. Far too uncomfortable. And we may need to add some decor to this room."

"You may need to *what*?" Elle demanded as the meaning of the Godmother's words sank into her.

"You conniving hag," Dex hissed, rising to his feet. Apparently the Godmother wasn't doing anything to keep him or Elle in place anymore. "You're not going to destroy that scepter. Is this what you wanted all along? Control of a vampire army?"

"You, vampires, whatever your names are," the Godmother said, ignoring Dex. "Take this body away. Remove his head and send it to King Belaric. Tell him it's a gift from the Godmother." She smoothed one hand over her white hair, a motion that was entirely unnecessary given that not a single hair was out of place. "And you two." She focused on Elle, then turned her gaze to Dex. "I don't know what you're both so upset about. I did exactly what I said I would come here to do. I killed Savoy. This is the part where you say thank you."

"And *that?*" Dex pointed with shackled hands at the red gem. "You're supposed to destroy it now. And you're supposed to grant Elle her freedom."

"Ah, yes, I may have lied about destroying this lovely little toy." The Godmother caressed the gem. "I'm definitely not parting with something so valuable. At least, not until the time is right. But you're correct about one thing: I do owe Elle a wish. After all, she did pay the price I asked of her." She looked at Elle. "A bargain is a bargain."

For a moment, heat warmed Elle's ankle. Then it vanished. She crouched down and, with hands still shackled together, lifted the bottom of the pants she'd borrowed from Alissa. Her breath caught at the sight of her bare ankle. There was no chain-shaped tattoo marking her skin, nor any sign that one had ever been there. "It's gone," she said. "It's really gone. After all this time."

Dex stepped past the vampires currently wrapping Savoy's body in what appeared to be a large piece of cloth. Faerie dust appeared on his hands, and his shackles melted away before he bent beside Elle and wrapped both arms around her. He kissed the top of her head and whispered, "You're finally free." His hand brushed over her shackles, and they softened, fell away from her wrists, and disappeared. Then he straightened and faced the Godmother. "Destroy the scepter," he said quietly. "That's the only other thing you need to do. Then we can part ways and never have to deal with one another again."

"Until you find a way to bring down my empire, that is," the Godmother said.

"Just. Destroy. It."

"What will you do to me if I don't, young prince?"

"You don't want to find out," he growled.

She chuckled. "Oh, I really think I do."

As the vampire guards lifted Savoy's wrapped body, Dex lunged forward and wrenched a dagger from the scabbard strapped to the nearest vampire's leg. With an expert aim, he threw it straight at the Godmother. She flicked her hand, and the blade spun around and shot back toward Dex. It pierced his chest and sank right up to the hilt.

"No!" Elle gasped. Shock froze her to the spot, and she watched, helpless, as Dex staggered a few steps backward. His shaking hands rose to the hilt, but he dropped to his knees before he could grasp it. Then he fell onto his side, struggling for breath. Blood, as blue as the blood of any other fae, seeped into his shirt as his eyes slowly closed.

ELEVEN

"No, no, no!" Elle rushed forward and dropped to the floor beside Dex. Her hands gripped his arm, touched his face, smoothed his hair back from his brow. What was she supposed to *do*? She turned her desperate gaze toward the Godmother. "*Why would you do that?* You could have ducked, or flicked the weapon away, or frozen Dex in place before he reached the blade."

Unruffled, the Godmother said, "I could have. But then you wouldn't be in the position where you feel it necessary to make another wish."

Elle paused, her breathing heavy, only fully realizing in that moment how calculating the Godmother truly was. She gripped the sleeve of Dex's shirt tightly in her fists. "No," she said. "No more wishes!"

"Really? You'll let your beloved die?" The Godmother's lips turned down. "Hmm. I have to say, that's not what I expected of you, Elle."

Elle forced out a slow breath and reminded herself to be calm, to be rational, to *think*. She looked down at Dex. His eyelids fluttered open and closed, and his chest still rose and fell. "He's not going to die," she said firmly. "He's fae. He can survive a stab wound."

"Normally, yes. But he can't survive a poison-laced stab wound."

Elle's head snapped up. She narrowed her eyes at the Godmother. "You're lying. You have no idea what was on that blade."

"I don't, but I've lived long enough to know that it's tradition for vampires to poison their weapons. Who knows how old these vampires are and if they're still following the traditional practices? Are you willing to take that risk?" Her gaze slid down to Dex. "He's struggling, Elle. I'm willing to bet there's poison seeping into his veins, mingling with the Darkness that's already there. Perhaps it's a mercy to let him die now rather than suffer any longer due to his father's selfish wish."

"No!" Elle squeezed her eyes shut. Tears dripped over her lashes. Why was she hesitating? She couldn't let Dex die! If their positions were reversed, he wouldn't waste another moment before bargaining with the Godmother. She hadn't known him particularly long—though that wasn't actually true, she reminded herself as the photo of her mother and Liana flashed through her mind—and yet she instinctively knew this about him. He would bargain with the woman he hated if it meant saving Elle. "So you're saying I should wish for you to heal him?" she asked, opening her eyes and looking up. "What terrible price are you asking this time?"

"Who said it would be terrible?"

Elle swallowed. It probably would be terrible, but it didn't matter. She was going to ask for a wish anyway. And if it was a terrible price then she'd find a way to trick the Godmother, just as she'd been planning to do the first time. "Okay. I don't care. Just do it."

"Do what?" the Godmother asked. "You need to *tell* me, Elle, so that I know exactly what you're wishing for. Are you wishing for him to be healed from a stab wound? Is that it?"

"Yes, obviously!" Elle shouted, but there was something in the Godmother's expression—a tilt to her lips and a glint in her eye—that made Elle pause. "Wait! Am I supposed to say something different? Do you mean … will he still end up dead even if you heal the stab wound? Damn you and your tricks!" she yelled. "Just heal him of *everything*, okay? Everything that could possibly— Oh!" How could she have forgotten when the Godmother mentioned it mere moments ago? "The Darkness! I wish you to heal him of the Darkness. And the stab wound. And any possible poison in his system. I wish for you to heal him completely of *anything* that's wrong with him. Okay?"

"As you wish," the Godmother said quietly. She raised her hands. Gold light pulsed away from her, blowing Elle's hair back and blinding her for several moments. As she blinked and slowly regained her vision, wisps of a dark substance came into view. They rose from Dex's skin—his arms, his neck, his face—and disappeared into the air like smoke. Elle's gaze trailed further down, and she realized the dagger was gone from Dex's chest. So was the blood that had stained his clothing.

When it seemed all the Darkness had vanished, she waited for him to wake. But the seconds ticked by and he didn't move. "Is … is he okay?"

"He'll be fine. Now, we need to discuss your price."

Elle nodded, her heart settling somewhere near her toes. She straightened to face the Godmother. "Fine. Tell me what you want from me."

The Godmother smiled as if all were right in the world. "I want you to go on a quest, my dear Elle."

"A quest?"

"Yes." She stood and walked toward Elle, never letting go of the scepter. "Come. Let the prince rest. It's time for me to tell you a story."

5
THE STARLIGHT QUEST

ONE

ELLE STARED THROUGH A GIANT WINDOW AT A WORLD OF BARE TREES, RUGGED rock formations, and dark, winged creatures swooping across an eternally gray sky. She was standing in one of the many lounges of a palatial vampire home in the Jade Eternal Night, vaguely aware of the Godmother's presence somewhere behind her. She raised her hand and gently placed her fingers against the glass, her mind still fixed on Dex. She had refused to leave the throne room until several of the Godmother's new guards—vampires with enhanced abilities—had lifted Dex's unconscious form and carried him upstairs to one of the bedrooms. When Elle had made certain he was comfortable—and after lingering a few extra moments in case he was about to wake up—she gave in and followed the Godmother through the house into this lounge, where the wall of glass was larger than in any other room they'd passed, and the view more striking.

Elle let her hand slip away from the window and fall to her side. There were so many emotions she should be feeling. Elation at finally, *finally* being free of the slave charm. Relief that Dex wasn't about to die from a poison-laced stab wound or the Darkness that had been eating away at him for years. Fury at the Godmother for not only taking the enhanced vampire army as her own instead of setting everyone free, but also tricking Elle into making another wish. But all she felt was stunned.

"Come and sit," the Godmother said from behind her.

Elle turned and glared at the woman. She hated everything about her, from her short, perfectly styled white hair all the way down to her elegant black heels.

"No. I will not *sit*."

"Very well then, but I have a lot to tell you, so—"

"*You're* the one we should have been worried about this whole time. Not a vampire heir who wants to be king. *You.*" Okay, so apparently she was feeling something after all. And that something was definitely anger. "Considering all the wishes you're capable of granting, you're probably the most powerful living faerie in the world. It might be impossible for anyone to kill King Belaric, but you're the one who gave him that power, which means you can probably take it away. And if you haven't taken it away until now, it's because you've been waiting until the moment is right for *you*. Did you want to get your hands on the enhanced vampire army before making a move? Is that what you were waiting for? Oh yes, and let's not forget that you were also waiting to get that memory out of my brain—the one about the ritual that gives vampires magic—so you can make your new army even stronger."

"I don't need memories of things I already know," the Godmother told her. "And when I said it was time to tell you a story, Elle, I didn't mean *my* story. I meant yours."

"I gathered as much," Elle snapped. "You'd never reveal anything about yourself." Since it seemed likely she would be in this room for a while, she decided it might be a good idea to sit after all. She moved away from the window and chose the seat furthest from the Godmother. Whoever had done the decorating in this room had gone a little overboard with the color scheme: turquoise curtains, a red couch, cushions covered in splotches of turquoise, red and white, and a turquoise wall opposite the window. But it was tastefully done, and Elle couldn't exactly blame anyone for wanting to fill this drab, gray world with some color.

She sank onto the red couch and folded her arms tightly over her chest. "So, if this story is all about me, are you going to finally tell me about my strange memory-wiping ability? Which apparently doesn't *wipe* memories at all. How did I not know that memory was still there in my head? And why can't I see all the other memories I've taken over the past few years? And how did *you* know that memory was there? How did you pull it out of my head?"

The Godmother let out an impatient sigh. "I know everything there is to know about your gift, Elle. I'm the one who gave it to you."

Once again, Elle found herself in that stunned space in between a multitude of emotions. "You … what? Why?"

"If you'll let me start at the beginning of the story instead of continuously prattling on, you'll find out."

Elle sent another glare the Godmother's way, then pulled her knees up to her chest and wrapped her arms around them. She was far too curious not to want to hear what the Godmother was about to tell her, but she needed to get a few things straight first. "Did you lie about Savoy sending some of his vampires to try and take you down after the masquerade ball?"

Without a pause, the Godmother said, "Yes, I did."

"And you lied to me the first time I made a wish. You told me the prince was just as bad as his father and so I shouldn't have any problem killing him. But you know just about everything, which means you probably know Dex is nothing like his father."

"Correct."

Indignation burned in Elle's veins. She couldn't help raising her voice as she continued, "So why should I believe anything you're about to tell me?"

The smallest frown creased the Godmother's brow. "Because this is a story I have no reason to lie to you about."

"And that, right there, could be another lie!" Elle shouted.

The Godmother switched her scepter—the wooden staff topped by a red gem that controlled the vampire army—from one hand to the other. "Well, I'm going to say what I have to say anyway, and at the end of it, you have no choice but to go on a quest, whether you believe me or not. We made a deal, Estelle. Don't forget that."

Elle pressed her lips together as she pictured Dex lying unconscious in a room not too far away. Yes, she'd made another wish, but only because the Godmother had essentially forced her into it. *But it was worth it*, she reminded herself, thinking of the dark wisps of magic that would occasionally swirl beneath Dex's skin and in his eyes, slowly killing him. She'd wished for the

Godmother to heal him of *everything*, and that included the Darkness.

"Fine," she said. "Tell the story."

The Godmother settled back in her chair and crossed one leg over the other. "Let me begin with the woman who was nanny to the two Belmont princes roughly twenty years ago." Elle almost retorted in a mocking tone that that was surely *someone else's* story and not hers, so why would the Godmother share it? But she kept her lips sealed for fear that the Godmother might change her mind about sharing anything. "Though Liana was fae and in the employ of the royal family," the Godmother continued, "she did not share the Belmonts' view of humans. In fact, her best friend was a human woman. Your mother."

"So you lied about that too!" Elle blurted out before she could stop herself. "I showed you that picture of them on Dex's phone, and you said you didn't know anything about it."

"Correct. I know nothing of that specific photo. Where or when it was taken, or what the occasion was."

"Are you kidding me?" Elle asked in disbelief.

"No, I am certainly not kidding you. Sometimes, Elle, you need to be specific when asking questions."

"As if that would have helped," Elle muttered. "You would have just lied if I'd asked you something more *specific*."

"Perhaps. Anyway, Liana accidentally found her way beneath the palace library one day and into the archives. A vast room of historical documents. Her curiosity got the better of her, and she ended up reading some of them. One particularly ancient document—preserved by magic and probably the oldest document there—was tucked away among the others. Perhaps someone had attempted to hide it, but Liana happened to notice it. She opened it and read it, and she discovered …" The Godmother shook her head slowly, a smile creeping onto her lips. "A shocking secret."

"What secret?" Elle whispered.

The Godmother inclined her head to the side. "You asked before how old I am, Elle. I still won't be answering that question, but you no doubt know that I am old. *Very* old." She paused, then added, "Old enough to remember a time when humans had magic."

Elle opened her mouth, but no sound came out. She replayed the words in her mind, but she couldn't make them fit together in the way the Godmother apparently intended.

"Oh good. I've finally said something so shocking that I've rendered you speechless."

"That … can't be true," Elle whispered.

"Or perhaps not," the Godmother sighed. "But yes, it's true, and that is the secret Liana discovered. Details of the quest that allowed humans to obtain magic."

"Humans … had magic?" Elle shook her head. "No. Someone would know. *People would know.*"

"People do know. Not many, of course. And they all happen to be the sort of people who are happy to keep the information to themselves. The dead vampire heir. Some of the people working with him. A few very old fae. Certain rulers around the world."

"Does King Belaric know about this? The document was inside his palace, so—Wait." Goosebumps drenched Elle's skin. "Does *Dex* know?"

"I'm not sure about King Belaric, but I doubt his son knows. Chevalier Adex Norville Belmont has a strong sense of justice and would want the whole world to be aware of this information. If he knew, you would most likely know by now."

Elle relaxed a little at the reassurance that Dex probably hadn't been keeping this life-altering secret from her. "But I still don't understand how it's possible for so few people to remember something like this. If humans once had magic, that would have been a fundamental part of life at some point."

"Yes. But history is written by the conquerors."

"The fae," Elle said.

"Yes. They wanted slaves, so they imprisoned humans, killed those with magic—because not everyone had it—and destroyed all records mentioning the quest."

"But the Blood War wasn't *that* long ago. Only a few hundred years. How could all record of humans having magic simply vanish in that time?"

"I'm not talking about the Blood War. That was between fae, vampires and shifters. Humans weren't involved in the struggle for power because they were all slaves by then. I'm talking about long before that. Many hundreds of years ago. Back when humans ruled parts of the world, just like the other High Races."

Elle gaped at the ancient fae woman. "No way."

"Yes way. *Everyone* ended up fighting back then as all races sought to claim more territory. The fae won, because they've always been the most powerful. That was when they began wiping out all knowledge of the quest and of humans possessing magic. Humans have been slaves ever since then. Over time, of course, vampires and shifters grew in power. They began taking back certain territories, we ended up with the Blood War, fae still came out on top, blah, blah, blah. That was all far more recent.

"Now, back to Liana. The quest and humans possessing magic wasn't the only thing she discovered in that document. There were also details of how a vampire could obtain magic by taking it from a human who had successfully completed the quest and received magic. Liana was stunned by this revelation that both humans and vampires could possess the kind of power the fae had. She shared it with your mother as soon as she had the chance. Your mother shared it with your father, as well as several friends, and unfortunately someone close to Nazario Savoy got wind of this information. So Savoy captured Liana and learned the full truth from her. Then he killed her. It was at that point that your mother summoned me and made a wish."

Elle's breath caught in her throat. "She—she did?"

"Yes. She knew what Savoy planned to do—capture humans and use them to give vampires magic—and she didn't know how to stop him. So she summoned me, explained everything, and asked me to stop him. I said I wouldn't do that. I had my own reasons at the time for not wanting to get rid of Nazario Savoy. So instead she wished for him to forget everything he'd learned from Liana. I agreed to that, but my price was that you, her daughter, would be the tool that made him forget."

"Why?" Elle demanded. "You probably could have snapped your fingers and made it happen. Do you set all these terrible prices simply because you like toying with people?"

The Godmother stared into the glow of the gem atop her scepter. "Partly. Where's the fun in life if you can't play around with people? But it's also because people need to know that everything in life comes with a price." Her gaze shifted back to Elle. "You must make sacrifices for the things you truly want."

"And my mother actually agreed to your price? She was happy for me to be the tool that would make Savoy forget?"

"No, she wasn't happy at all. At first, she refused. She tried to negotiate, just like you did when I asked you to kill the prince. But I wouldn't budge. I told her to truly think about it. Was she willing to put you at risk in order to save dozens, hundreds, possibly thousands of humans? At first, she said no, but I could tell she was torn. Then she asked for some form of additional protection over you. To that, I agreed. I didn't actually want you to die, Elle. I wanted you to succeed. But I also wanted your mother to know that there is always a risk when playing around with wishes."

"And then I accidentally ended up killing Nazario Savoy, so look how that turned out. You should have done it yourself."

The Godmother shrugged. "These things happen. Plans rarely work out perfectly and one must always be prepared to make a new one. Anyway, you and your mother were both protected and managed to get away from Savoy's people. I'm not sure how she and your father hid you after that. I had no further involvement with your family."

"So you just left me with this strange ability and didn't care how I used it?"

"Correct. And your life has been far more interesting than it would otherwise have been, has it not?"

"My life has *sucked!* Salvia might never have enslaved me if not for my ability. I would have been no use to her. She probably would have kicked me out of her house, which would have been far better."

The Godmother's eyebrows rose a fraction. "Perhaps not better for the stepsister you love so much. And you wouldn't have met and fallen for a prince."

"Oh, well that makes it all better then."

"You're getting sidetracked, Elle. I still need to tell you about the quest. The Starlight Quest. The journey you're going to go on in order to obtain magic for yourself."

Again, Elle's lips parted but no sound came out. The Godmother was right. She *had* been getting sidetracked. Caught up in her anger, she had completely missed what this giant secret might mean for her. Magic was possible for humans. *She* was human. Therefore magic was possible for *her*. "Is this like … *real* magic?" she asked faintly. "Like the fae's Essence? Not just the simple shifter kind of magic or vampire kind of magic?"

"It's very much like the fae's Essence, yes. The quest requires you to journey into one of the Never Woods and make it safely to a lake at the very center, where you'll take the magic from within the light of a star. Sounds simple, but the Never Woods are dangerous—you've no doubt heard the nursery rhyme— and you'll face obstacles along the way. Due to legend and superstition, the Never Woods have remained largely untouched over the centuries, and ancient magic and strange creatures still lurk among the trees. But if you follow the instructions along the way, and if you take a member of each of the other High Races with you, which is one of the quest's requirements, you should make it."

Elle frowned as she processed this information. She knew the nursery rhyme the Godmother had referred to. The line 'Never go into the Never Woods at night' was one most children knew. And it wasn't only night that was dangerous; the poem included lines about every other time of day as well. It also warned that those who *did* venture into the Never Woods would lose their minds. There were several areas around the world where neverwood trees grew, but having never lived near any of them, Elle hadn't been in a situation where she needed to consider whether the nursery rhyme might be true. Until now. "So … that part in the nursery rhyme about people losing their minds …"

"Might happen," the Godmother replied. "Like I said, the magic is ancient. It can have strange effects on people."

"And you want me to take other people with me? What if they end up losing their minds or getting hurt?"

"It isn't what *I* want. That's what the quest requires."

"And you're forcing me to go on this quest as the price I must pay for a wish, so you kind of are forcing other people to get involved."

The Godmother chuckled, though Elle couldn't see anything funny about the situation. "How will I get to one of these Never Woods?"

"I'll send you there. Then you'll receive instructions at the start of the quest. A messenger who knows your intent will appear."

"Uh, okay. So it doesn't matter which Never Woods I go into? Do they all have a lake at the center?"

"Yes."

"And then … you said something about the light from a star?"

"Yes. You know stars have magic, don't you?"

"Um, yes, I think so. I mean, there are spells that incorporate starlight, so … that makes sense, I guess?"

"And we're all made up of stardust. *All* meaning humans as well."

Elle's frown grew deeper. "Um … what?"

"Cosmic dust. It's falling all the time. It forms a small part of all of us, therefore we all have some small trace of magic. It's what allows you to absorb a whole lot more magic into your being at the end of the quest." She waved her hand in a dismissive manner. "But all will be explained to you at the appropriate time."

"Of course," Elle grumbled. "Because it couldn't possibly be as simple as you giving me step-by-step instructions right now." She hugged her knees tighter to her chest, then opened her mouth to ask another question—but the words died on her tongue as something occurred to her. Goosebumps rose across her skin. Her heart thudded a little faster. "The quilt," she said. "The one my mother made. It has stars all over it, and all those different embroidered lines about stars. 'It's written in the stars.' 'Look to the stars.' That wasn't just because she had a thing for stars. It was because she *knew*."

The Godmother smiled. "Indeed. I told you I liked that quilt."

"I wonder why she and my father didn't go on this quest."

"I don't know cither, I'm afraid."

"So is this what Savoy's been doing? Vincenzo Savoy. The vampire you just killed. He's been sending all these humans he's abducted on a quest?"

"Yes. He always had a rough idea of the knowledge you took from his father, so he must have been working ever since then to find out more. Presumably he discovered details of the quest, along with part of the process that then allows vampires to take that magic from humans. But he clearly never found out how to complete the process, given that he was still looking for you. Without that last piece of the puzzle, he would have to keep sending humans on quests and keep taking magic from them. A tiresome process, especially considering not everyone who attempts the quest survives. I'm sure Savoy lost plenty of the humans he abducted."

"That's terrible!"

"It is what it is. Essentially, Elle, you have to prove that you're worthy of receiving magic."

"So all other High Races are born with some form of magic, but humans have to prove themselves worthy? How is that fair?"

"Perhaps you've been living under a rock, Elle—"

"In an attic, actually."

"—but no one in the history of the world has *ever* said that life is fair. This is simply the way things are. If humans want magic, they have to earn it. Then, if vampires want it—over and above the basic magic they already have—they can take it. None of that is fair. It's just life."

Elle let out a heavy sigh. "So you want me to convince a faerie, a shifter and a vampire to go with me into one of the Never Woods and complete this quest."

"Yes."

"Why?" That was the most important question. Gaining magic seemed like a *good* thing. If humans had magic, then they had a right to freedom, just like the other magical High Races. This would change everything. No one could force humans into slavery. Perhaps they could even be rulers again one day. And, of course, there was that not so tiny voice in the back of Elle's mind reminding her that this would make her Dex's equal. He'd said he didn't care that she was human, but other people would. Without magic, no one would ever think her worthy of being with a prince. But *with* magic, no one could ever look down on her. Aside from possibly dying or going crazy in the Never Woods, Elle could see only positives. And that was the part that made her most suspicious.

"Why not?" the Godmother countered. "Don't you want magic?"

"Maybe I do, but that's not the point. I'm asking why *you* want me to have it."

"Perhaps I believe it's time for humans to reclaim their former power."

Elle shook her head. "I don't buy that. You said you've been around many hundreds of years. You've had plenty of opportunities to set the record straight. You're only doing it now because you hope it'll benefit you in some way."

"Well, of course. Everything I do benefits me in *some* way. But that doesn't mean it won't benefit you as well."

"So you're not going to tell me?"

The Godmother laughed. "Of course not. I'm not sure why you expected otherwise."

"I'm not sure either," Elle muttered. Footsteps moved toward the lounge, and Elle's eyes shot toward the door, her heart lurching as she wondered whether she'd find Dex standing there. But it was one of the vampire guards.

"Excuse me, Godmother," she said. "We've spotted someone lurking in the distance among some rocks. It appears to be a male vampire."

"Ah. Must be Azriel. How interesting." The Godmother looked at Elle. "Didn't he refuse to come any closer?"

"Perhaps he decided to make sure you followed through on your promise. You know, to *destroy that thing*?" Elle jerked her chin toward the scepter.

The Godmother stood. "Let me go and see him. I'll make sure he understands he's not needed here anymore."

"Wait!" Elle jumped to her feet. "You're not going to hurt him, are you?"

The Godmother gave her an amused look. "Concerned for the vampire who tried on numerous occasions to abduct you? How sweet. But don't worry, I'll send him on his way without harming him."

"That's because I'll be *harming you*!" a voice bellowed as someone raced past the guard. Magic sparked and arced across the room. The Godmother vanished in the blink of an eye, and Dex crashed into the couch she'd been sitting on just as it went up in flames.

TWO

"Somebody has to stop her." Dex paced the lounge as magic glittered around him, drying off his sopping wet clothes. He'd extinguished the flames with a fountain of water that gushed up from the burning cushions, and ended up a dripping wet mess. Moments later, at least ten more vampire guards had filed into the room. They were now lined up in front of the door and against the turquoise wall. Elle stood between Dex and the guards.

"I know, but it can't be us," she told him. "At least, not yet. I have to pay the price for another wish first. And if you kill her before then, I don't know if that might undo—"

"You made another wish?" Dex stared at her, aghast.

"I had to! You had a knife in your chest, and I didn't know if you were dying. But, Dex, just listen." Elle hurried closer and gripped his hands in hers. "I wished for you to be healed completely. *Completely.* She took the Darkness too. It's gone."

With parted lips and heavy breaths, Dex's eyes traveled Elle's face. He shook his head. "What?"

"I'm serious. I saw it rising away from you. Wisps of shifting shadow leaving your skin and disappearing."

"Really?"

"Yes."

"But ..." He shook his head again. "That can't ... Are you sure that's what you saw?"

Elle's smile stretched wider as she nodded. "I wished for her to heal you of the Darkness, along with anything else that was wrong with you, and I watched it leave your body. It's really gone, Dex."

In one swift motion, he took her face in both his hands and pressed his lips hard against hers. For a long moment, everything else fell away, and all that existed was the two of them. His mouth on hers, and her racing heart, and the flush that warmed her skin. "Thank you," Dex murmured, then slid his arms around Elle and pulled her tight against his chest. "But you shouldn't have done that," he added quietly as she nestled against his neck and he rested his chin on her head. "You put yourself in her debt."

"I would do it again."

"Elle …" He pulled away from her, shaking his head.

"Would you have done it for me?"

His expression hardened, and for a heart-stopping moment Elle thought she'd been wrong about him. Maybe his hatred of the Godmother was so ingrained in him that it was stronger than any feelings he'd developed for her. But then his shoulders drooped and his eyes slid shut. "Yes. I would have. Of course I would have."

"Well there you go then. No one *wants* to deal with her, but when you have no other option …"

"I know. But, Elle, she's the *Godmother*. She's insanely powerful on her own, and now she has a vampire army as well. An army she's probably going to give magic to. She's far more of a threat than Savoy was. She'll probably come for the Astranerican throne, and I have no doubt that she'll succeed where Savoy failed. She *will* defeat my father. She gave him his power, and she can take it away."

"I know. The exact same fears have been running through my mind. But I haven't yet paid the price she asked of me, and I'm afraid that if she dies now, her wish magic will somehow be undone and the Darkness will return to you. So *please* just … just leave her. Let's get this price paid and then worry about getting rid of her.

"I'm almost too afraid to ask, but what is it? What's the price?"

Elle couldn't help the grin that spread across her face. The Godmother's story—the true history of humans, and the promise of magic—was so astounding, Elle was still in awe. "I think you should sit down for this."

Dex frowned. "If it's that bad, why are you smiling?"

"It's not bad. I mean, maybe it is. I don't know what her motive is, so that's scary, but it's … it's the most incredible thing I've ever heard. Just come and sit." She led Dex away from the smoldering couch toward one that was still intact, and as they sat, she began the Godmother's story.

THREE

"Cress says she can't," Dex said with a sigh, lowering his phone and leaning back in the lounger beside Xander's pool. "She can't leave the apothecary again, and she has a daughter to worry about."

"Of course, I completely understand," Elle answered. Part of her was secretly relieved Cress had turned her down. She'd already done so much for Elle, and now Elle was asking her to go on a dangerous quest with no guarantee of emerging safely on the other side. She'd been feeling guilty since the moment Dex suggested they ask her.

The Godmother had given Elle twenty-four hours in which to find a faerie, a vampire and a shifter to accompany her on her Starlight Quest, before they were due to meet at a location approximately two hours from Vale City. "And *don't* attempt to betray me. I will be intensely disappointed in you, Elle." Elle had rolled her eyes at that, but beneath her sweater, a chill had skittered across her skin. She didn't want to find out what the Godmother's disappointment looked like. Besides, this was a price she actually *wanted* to pay. The possibility of receiving magic at the other end? The knowledge that this would change everything for humans? It thrilled her. She suspected there must be some twist or trick along the way—that was how the Godmother worked, right?—or perhaps the whole thing was a lie. But she kept thinking back to her mother's quilt. All those stars. It couldn't be a coincidence, could it?

After the Godmother sent Elle and Dex on their way, they left the Jade Eternal Night and headed for Xander's home. Elle spent the night in one of the guest rooms while Dex returned to the palace to make sure his parents hadn't sent out a search party for him. "He disappears all the time," Xander had told Elle when she expressed concern about whether Dex would be able to get away again. "His father doesn't notice, and his mother should be used to it by now. He won't have any trouble getting out again. If this quest thing takes more than a day or so, they'll probably kick up a fuss. Start blaming vampires for kidnapping him or something. But the Godmother said it shouldn't take long, right?"

Elle had given a noncommittal shrug at that point. The Godmother had said it *shouldn't* take too long, but that was if nothing went wrong. For now, Elle's first step was to find three people from three different races willing to go with her. After she'd explained the whole thing to Dex—and after he'd questioned the Godmother repeatedly in an attempt to figure out if she was lying—he'd said there was no doubt he would be the faerie accompanying her. Then he'd suggested asking Cress and one of his vampire allies. But someone else had shown up at Xander's home this morning before Elle could ask anyone.

"At least you're sorted in the vampire friend department," Alissa said, waving from a lounger on the other side of the pool. The sun had set roughly twenty minutes earlier, allowing her to put away her dark umbrella and throw off the blanket she'd draped across most of her body.

"Thank you," Elle said, for what might have been the hundredth time. Early this morning, Alissa had managed to contact Dex via the same chain of people her brother Azriel had originally used. She'd been worried ever since Azriel returned home alone, furious that the Godmother had tricked him and then sent him spinning through the air away from Savoy's home before depositing him on the bonnet of the limo he'd borrowed. Though he had tried, he physically couldn't get any closer to the house after that.

Azriel had disappeared then, leaving Alissa to get in touch with Dex to find out what was going on and how she could help. Dex wasn't particularly excited about a vampire who'd attacked him twice joining them on their journey through the Never Woods, a fact he had made known numerous times throughout the day. "We were already sorted in the vampire friend department," he reminded Alissa now. "I do actually have other vampire friends."

"I'm sure you do, but Elle doesn't, and this is her quest."

Elle met Dex's gaze and gave him an apologetic smile. "You did mention that your vampire allies haven't been able to help you in any way other than providing information," she reminded him quietly, "since they all have families they're concerned about."

"Yes, but that changed on the night of the Moonlight Masquerade when some of them got involved."

"But they still have families," Elle pointed out. "Just because they've risked their lives once doesn't mean I want to ask any of them to do it again."

"I don't have a family to worry about," Alissa said loudly, sticking her hand up again as if she were a student in a classroom volunteering to answer a question. "Well, I suppose I do, but they can take care of themselves. I don't have children or a partner or anything."

Elle gave Dex another shrug and quietly added, "I don't mind her coming with us. She kind of is like a friend, I guess." She'd spent so many years as a slave with Sienna her only companion that she'd almost forgotten what it was like to have a friend who wasn't also her sister. Alissa had shared her home, her clothes, her food and books, and now she was accompanying Elle on what could very possibly be a life-changing journey. That was the kind of stuff friends did for each other, right?

"See?" Alissa said. "Friend. That's me."

Dex looked at Elle. "I guess if we can't trust her by now, then we never can."

"Exactly," Alissa replied.

"Our bigger problem," Dex continued, "is that we have to leave in an hour to meet the Godmother, and we still need to find a shifter to come with us."

"I'll ask Astrid," Xander said, leaning forward on his lounger. He'd been quiet for so long that Elle assumed he'd fallen asleep. Perhaps he *had* been sleeping, given the way he was now stretching his tall, tanned frame from side to side while yawning. He patted his pockets, pulled out his phone, and stood as he said, "I'll call her now."

"Astrid?" Elle asked Dex as Xander walked away with his phone pressed to his ear.

"Wolf shifter. I think you've met her, actually. Well, not officially, but she was there the night of the Moonlight Masquerade."

Elle cast her mind back and remembered a young woman she'd first thought was human. Tangled, honey-colored hair and pretty eyes. But the pupils of those eyes had changed shape when lamplight shone on them, revealing that she was actually a shifter. "Okay, yeah, I think I remember her." She watched Xander pacing slowly across the lawn, just out of earshot, wishing she could do some pacing of her own. Though she currently reclined in a lounger, she was anything but relaxed. Her hands twisted together in her lap and her left foot kept bouncing. Every now and then she would lean forward and lift the bottom of her jeans to check her right ankle. Then she would look up and meet Dex's eyes. He would quietly ask, "Still gone?" and she would smile and nod as that thrill—she was *free! Finally!*—raced through her body once more. Then she would sit back as nervous anticipation thrummed throughout her body again.

"Okay, Astrid's in," Xander said, walking back toward the pool. "She'll be here in half an hour. She doesn't actually believe this whole quest for magic is real. She's pretty sure the Godmother is sending us on a wild goose chase—"

"Which could very well be the case," Elle muttered.

"—but she said if it *is* real and a human is about to end up with magic, she wants to see it with her own eyes."

"I'm in too!" The voice belonged to Olly, who rushed from the direction of the house toward the pool, pushing his pale hair out of his eyes as he went. He'd been around for lunch earlier, then disappeared again. "A human gaining magic is the most astounding thing I've ever heard of. I'm not missing it for anything."

Elle sat up and crossed her legs. "What if I'm not allowed to take three fae with me on this quest?"

"We're Dex's guards," Xander answered immediately. "He can't go without us."

"You're not my *guards*," Dex replied. "And you don't need to put your lives at risk for—"

"Oh, but *you* can put your life at risk? Prince Chevalier, heir to the throne, no longer dying of mysterious dark magic?"

"Xander—"

"If you're insisting on going, then so are we."

"I assume the Godmother will make it pretty clear what's allowed and what isn't," Elle said, hoping to bring an end to the argument. "We can all go and meet her."

They continued discussing the types of magic and obstacles they might find in the Never Woods, and the ways in which they could protect themselves—as well as the possibility that the Godmother's story was a complete lie—until Astrid arrived. Elle thanked her repeatedly for agreeing to come with, and Astrid shrugged and told her it sounded like an adventure, if nothing else. She perched on a lounger beside Xander as Elle sat forward to survey the group of people who'd volunteered to take this journey with her.

Dex, the person she simultaneously wanted most at her side *and* wanted to keep furthest from harm. Olly and Xander, his best friends and self-appointed protectors. Alissa, someone Elle could hopefully call a friend if they came out the other end of this quest intact. And Astrid, who was little more than a stranger to her.

Dex met her gaze and asked, "Ready?"

Without answering, Elle swung her legs over the side of the lounger and pulled on her black combat boots, which Dex had brought with him when he returned to Xander's home that morning. "Yes. I'm ready."

FOUR

"Wonderful," the Godmother said as Elle climbed from the back seat of Xander's car and looked past the Godmother at the coffee shop she'd requested they meet at. "You're all on time." Elle glanced over her shoulder as Astrid's car—older, bulkier and far less shiny than Xander's—pulled up behind them. Astrid and Olly climbed out. The Godmother rose from the small sidewalk table she'd been sitting at, sweeping one hand through her perfect white hair. "Are you ready for your quest?"

Elle moved to stand beside Dex in the glow of a street lamp. "As ready as we can be, considering we have no idea what we're about to face in the Never Woods." Her gaze wandered past the Godmother and through the coffee shop windows, traveling over the vintage filament light bulbs, copper finishings, and exposed brick walls. Though it was more like dinner time now—Elle and her companions had eaten in their cars on the way here—the coffee shop was still open. "Interesting place. Is there any reason you specifically wanted to meet here?"

"Yes. I love their cinnamon rolls."

"That's it? We're here because of cinnamon rolls?"

"Yes. I've been craving them lately."

Elle crossed her arms. "You mean you can't just snap your fingers and have a cinnamon roll appear in front of you?"

The Godmother laughed. "Was that a hint of sarcasm, Elle? Is it possible you're still bitter about what went down at Savoy's house yesterday?"

"Why would I be bitter? Because you killed our enemy only to take his place? Because you stabbed Dex so you could force me into making another wish?"

The Godmother spread her hands wide, palms up, an innocent expression on her face. "The prince attacked me first. I was merely defending myself. And I don't know why you're so grumpy about the wish. The price is hardly a price. It's a *gift*. By the time you reach the end of your quest, you'll have magic."

"And *you* will have finished plotting how to take down Dex's father," Astrid said, arriving at Elle's side, "so you can claim the Astranerican throne for yourself."

The Godmother tipped her head back and released a gloriously rich laugh. "Oh, you are too funny, young shapeshifter." She dabbed beneath her eyes as if wiping away tears of mirth. "As if I hadn't plotted that long ago."

"So that *is* your plan," Dex said, his tone rough.

"Maybe. Maybe not. Are you going to throw a blade at me again, Prince Dex?"

Dex didn't answer, which Elle figured was probably for the best.

"No, perhaps not," the Godmother continued in a thoughtful tone. "Perhaps you'd secretly be grateful if I removed your father from the throne. You certainly don't agree with all his views. Especially not his views on humans. He's going to make things very unpleasant for you when you tell him you want to *marry* one."

"Okay, what exactly does this have to do with my quest?" Elle interjected, feeling warmth steal its way up her neck and into her cheeks. She and Dex weren't even dating yet, and now the Godmother was making things more awkward by suggesting *marriage*?

The Godmother tapped a painted fingernail against her chin. "Remind me again why it is that your father hates humans so much," she said to Dex. "He wasn't always this way, was he, Dex?"

"That's *Prince* Dex to you," Dex said through gritted teeth.

"I wonder what would happen to his hatred if he *forgot* all about that horrible incident."

Dex took a step forward, his hands balling at his sides, but Xander grabbed his arm and tugged him back. "Are we going on this quest or what?" he demanded. "I feel like we're just wasting time right now."

"Yes, of course." The Godmother rubbed her hands together. "I see we have some extras though. You three are all fae." She pointed at Dex, Olly and Xander. "Elle needs only one of you."

"Will it ruin the quest if we all go?" Xander asked.

"You're aware, I hope, that I've never been on this quest myself? I'm not precisely sure what will *ruin* it. I only know what is required."

"You said you've been around since the time humans used to do this quest as a normal part of life," Elle said. "You must have heard of larger groups going into the Never Woods?"

"Why *must* I have heard of this?"

"You're the Godmother," Alissa pointed out. "You keep making out as if you know everything."

"Not *everything*," the Godmother answered with an impatient sigh.

"Look, does it really matter?" Astrid asked. "This quest is all just some kind of trick, isn't it? It would be really cool if it *wasn't*, but I have trouble believing nobody knows about the fact that once upon a time, humans had magic just like the rest of us. So how about you just let us all go into the Never Woods, and together we can all discover the real reason you're sending us in there."

The Godmother regarded her thoughtfully. "I find it interesting that you're here, considering you're apparently so full of doubt."

Astrid shrugged. "Perhaps I just want to see what's inside the Never Woods."

"Or perhaps you're hoping this quest is real after all."

"Uh, remember the part about wasting time?" Xander reminded her.

The Godmother drew herself up to her full height, which still left her shorter than Xander and yet her presence seemed to tower over him. "I'm not sure why you're so concerned about *time*, young man. Once you enter the Never Woods, it will become fluid. It will speed up and slow down without you even knowing. Some have completed the quest in what they believed to be mere hours, when in fact weeks have passed."

"Weeks?" Dex repeated. "We can't be gone that long."

"You don't have to be. No one said you must be the faerie to accompany Elle."

Elle was aware of Dex bristling at her side. "She's not going into the Never Woods without me."

"Wonderful. Then it doesn't matter how long it takes. And since you all want to go so badly, you can all begin the quest. But don't get upset if you happen to reach a point where only four of you can continue. And if for some reason the two extras never make it out alive, don't come complaining to me."

At that point, the coffee shop door opened and a man hurried out. "Here you go, Godmother," he said, stopping at her side and handing her a bag containing several takeaway boxes.

"Ah, thank you."

"Always a pleasure. I snuck in a few extras. Your favorite with the nuts sprinkled on top."

"Marvelous." The Godmother beamed at him. "Do pass on my regards to Helena and little Drew."

"Yes, of course, thank you. Have a good evening." He ducked back inside as the Godmother set the bag of takeaway boxes—presumably containing cinnamon rolls—on the sidewalk in front of her. With a quick swish of her hand and a sparkle of gold faerie dust, the bag disappeared.

"Excellent," she said, smiling at the group. "Now we can go." She raised her hands and positioned her thumb and third finger together. Elle tensed, knowing what was coming, but as the Godmother snapped her fingers and everything vanished, the jolt that rocketed through Elle was just as nauseating as it had been every other time the Godmother sent her hurtling through space in the blink of an eye.

The world reappeared, expanding away from her in a rush of color and light. She stumbled forward a few steps before someone caught her arm and helped steady her. "You okay?" Dex asked.

"Yes, thanks." She straightened and looked around. It was still twilight here— wherever *here* was—and the grassy hills, rocky outcrops and distant civilization were visible in the dim light. "I'm guessing that's it," Astrid murmured behind her. Elle looked over her shoulder, then turned fully.

A hush fell over the group as they regarded the forest of closely packed trees that began only a few feet away. Tall and spindly with silvery gray leaves that lay utterly motionless in the still air, the trees rose higher than Elle could have imagined. A light mist hung between them, making it impossible to see more than a few feet into the woods.

"Which Never Woods are we at?" Elle asked.

"The nearest one, of course," the Godmother answered. "Though it still would have been a very long drive for you, getting from that coffee shop to the northernmost point of our country. Fortunately, you have me as your travel agent."

"Perhaps not so fortunate once we've completed the quest," Dex pointed out, "since it'll be a very long *walk* back to that coffee shop where our cars are waiting for us."

"Oh, I'll be here to meet you, don't worry," the Godmother said. "I'll need to make sure Elle has paid her price." She met Elle's gaze and smiled, but Elle couldn't help feeling there was a threat behind those perfectly painted lips. Would the Godmother reverse the healing she'd given Dex if she didn't manage to pay her price? She was too scared to ask. Better not to put the idea in the woman's head if it wasn't already there. "Well, what are you waiting for?" the Godmother asked. She waved toward the woods. "Off you go."

"What, just like that?" Elle asked. "No further instruction?"

"I told you, a messenger who knows your intent will appear. I'm not certain on the details, but I know that all necessary instructions will be revealed to you as you go. So all you need to do—" she extended her hand toward the woods once more "—is walk right in. You're welcome to take your time if that's what you'd prefer, but I have places to go and people to see." She looked at her watch—the device on which Elle remembered seeing tiny moving images instead of a clock face or digital numbers—and nodded her head once.

"Wait," Dex said, his gaze focused on the Godmother's wrist. "Is that my *mother's* face?" His hand shot out toward the Godmother's arm, but she sent him spinning away from her with a flick of her fingers.

"I don't remember inviting you to take a look at my watch, Prince Dex," she said as he came to a halt and steadied himself with his arms out.

"Was that. My mother's. Face?" he repeated, his tone low and threatening.

The Godmother sighed and examined her watch once more. "Hmm. Could be. But if so, she needs to do something about her hair. It looks nothing like the elegant updos the queen usually sports on TV."

Xander grabbed Dex's arm before he could rush forward again. "Just chill, man. She's trying to get you worked up."

The Godmother chuckled. "It's so easy."

"Have people told you before what a terrible person you are?" Astrid asked.

"Oh, all the time. And yet, people keep making wishes." The Godmother looked pointedly at Elle. "Which is why we're here. Anyway, I'm off now." She raised her right hand, saluted Elle, and vanished.

"Wow," Astrid said. "So that was the Godmother. I've seen her before, but I've never had any interaction with her. Can't say I'm a fan."

"Me neither," Dex said darkly.

Together, the six of them moved to face the Never Woods. "So I guess we should just go for it," Astrid said, taking a step forward.

"Wait." Elle reached out to stop her. She moved forward and turned to face the group. "In case I haven't thanked you enough already—"

"You've thanked us about a thousand times," Astrid said with an eye-roll. "We get it. You're grateful. Now let's get in there. I want to be able to tell people I survived a trip through the Never Woods."

"Agreed," Alissa said, joining Astrid as she stepped past Elle. "I've always been curious about the Never Woods, despite the nursery rhyme. I finally have a good reason to find out what's in there. And I won't have to complain anymore about having a boring life."

As they walked ahead of her, Elle looked at Dex. His eyes filled with warmth as he returned her gaze and gave her the smallest of nods. She took a deep breath and squared her shoulders. "Okay. Let's do this."

FIVE

Silence pressed in around them as they entered the Never Woods. No sound came from the forest itself, and all Elle heard was her own breathing and the crunch of twigs and dead leaves beneath her boots. She had the strangest feeling that if she spoke now, she would find herself in some sort of vacuum, unable to hear her own voice, separated from everyone else by silence. She looked back, her heart thrumming, and called, "Dex?" Relief flooded her chest as she heard the word loud and clear. Dex moved through the mist and took her hand.

"I'd rather we not end up separated," he said, and she nodded in agreement.

They continued forward, making sure to stay close to the rest of their party. Elle had expected it to be darker in here among the close-set trees, but after another few paces, she noticed a glowing white orb, and then another and another. About the size of a person's head, they hung in the air a few feet up, drifting slowly about despite there being no breeze.

"Do you think the Godmother sent us in here to die?" Astrid whispered.

"Why would she do that?" Elle asked.

"For her own amusement?"

Elle thought about that for a moment. "I wish I could say she's not *that* terrible, but I honestly don't know anymore. Perhaps everything she does is for her own entertainment."

"She mentioned that some people have completed the quest in what they believed was only a few hours," Olly said. "So even though time apparently moves differently in here, it's possible that the quest itself doesn't take that long. Or it shouldn't *feel* as if it takes that long. You know?"

"Yes," Elle said. "I know what you're saying. It's not the kind of expedition where we have to camp overnight for several nights because our final destination is so far away."

"I hope not," Alissa said, "since the Godmother didn't tell us to bring tents or sleeping bags or extra food. Can you guys conjure up that sort of thing?"

"Not from nothing," Olly said. "We would have had to gather those things beforehand and reduce their size. We could shrink them to something so small they might *look* like nothing, if we wanted it to appear as though we could conjure them into being from thin air. But we didn't do that, so no. Though the Godmother probably could," he added, "but her magic is like … on another level."

Dex stopped for a moment and turned fully. Elle followed his gaze as he squinted into the mist. "Everything looks the same in every direction. Trees and mist and these weird floating orbs. How are we supposed to know if we're going the right way?"

"I don't think it matters just yet," Elle said as they continued walking. "A messenger is supposed to appear. Someone who senses my intent."

Astrid snorted. "Well, I hope you're projecting your intent loud and clear. Otherwise we might be wandering around like this for a very long time."

Elle looked around. *My intent is to complete a quest that will give me magic.* She formed the thought into words inside her head and tried to push them outward, feeling a little bit silly. If a being of some sort really could sense her intention, he or she would surely know it already.

Ahead of her, Astrid giggled. It was such an innocent, girlish sound compared to the gruff, sarcastic image she'd portrayed so far. "What is it?" Elle asked.

"Nothing, it's just …" She reached up toward something. "Don't you think the trees look so funny?"

"Hey, stop, what are you trying to touch?" Alissa asked, smacking Astrid's hand back down.

"Just *look*," Astrid said, linking her arm with Alissa's and pointing upward, her voice tinged with wonder.

"You're right," Elle said with a smile. "They do look funny." She started laughing. "Their branches are bending into the strangest shapes. Do you see, Dex?" She looked at him, watching a smile grow on his upturned face.

"Yeah, I see."

It wasn't creepy in here after all, Elle realized. The trees weren't frozen in place like long-dead beings with skeletal arms. They weren't dull gray with patches of bone white. No, their bark was actually a rich brown, with knots and ridges that formed comical facial expressions. They were smiling and laughing, and as their limbs contorted into odd positions, she found herself wanting to dance along with them.

So she did. Soon all six of them were jumping and spinning and twirling clumsily beneath each other's arms. Elle's cheeks began to ache from laughing so hard. She couldn't remember the last time she'd had so much fun. She spun around again—and almost collided with a small winged creature. "Oh, hi, sorry," she said breathlessly as she came to a stop. "Oh, you're a pixie. Like Tash. Though you don't have a hat. But I'm sure we could find you something here." She looked down at the forest debris surrounding her feet. "Maybe a—"

The pixie's frenzied squeaks stopped her before she could crouch down.

"Okay, okay. No hat."

The pixie fluttered closer on delicate pearlescent wings. She held both hands out in front of her, and upon her palms sat four silver jelly beans, giant in comparison to her minuscule size. Something about the number four jolted Elle's memory. "Only four," she murmured. "Because there are only supposed to be four of us here. The Godmother said we don't need the two extras." She looked over her shoulder at her cavorting companions. "Hey, come and look here," she said. "There's a pixie with jelly beans."

"Ooh, I love jellybeans," Astrid said, hurrying over. The others joined her a moment later.

"Do you have any more of those?" Dex asked the pixie. "There are six of us."

The pixie shook her head.

Dex faced his friends. "Didn't the Godmother call you guys extras? I don't think the pixie brought jelly beans for you."

Xander crossed his arms and leaned against Olly. "Whatever, man. I don't even like jelly beans."

"Kids' candy," Olly said, nodding in agreement before bursting out laughing again.

Elle took the four jelly beans and handed one each to Dex, Astrid and Alissa. "Cheers," Astrid said, bumping her jelly bean against Alissa's before popping it into her mouth. Elle placed hers between her teeth and bit down. The effect was instant. Though the woods remained misty, a fog she hadn't been aware of cleared immediately from her mind. The trees stopped moving, and adrenaline pumped through her as she realized just how insane they'd all been acting. She chewed faster, desperate to consume whatever protection this strange silver candy provided.

"Holy stars, that was freaky," Astrid said as she finished swallowing. "The trees were ... I was *dancing* with them and ... and their faces were ... I don't know, I thought they were funny and now they just seem insanely creepy."

"I know," Elle whispered, reaching for Dex's hand. Though his expression hinted he was as disturbed as she was, his grip was sure and solid. With her heart still beating rapidly, Elle looked around. The trees were stiff and gray and spindly. No bending arms, no knots forming noses and eyes. Everything was exactly as it had been when they first entered the woods.

Well, not *everything*. Unfortunately, Xander and Olly were still goofing around, falling over each other as they laughed, aiming good-natured punches at the nearest tree every few moments, the way guys did when they hung out together.

Dex cursed beneath his breath. "We can't continue the quest with them in that kind of state. They should never have come with us."

"Ow, that's gotta hurt," Astrid said as Xander grazed his knuckles against the nearest tree trunk once more.

"We have to get them out of here," Elle said. "This is what we were all warned about as children. The part from the nursery rhyme that talks about losing your mind in the Never Woods. It must be."

"Yes, and we certainly can't trust them to find their own way out," Dex said, walking toward his friends. "We'll have to help them get back to the—"

He stopped, cutting himself off as Xander and Olly turned semi-transparent before drifting away like dust on a breeze, leaving behind no trace of their presence.

"What the hell?" Dex said.

"Stars," Elle whispered. "What just happened?"

"They'll be fine," a high-pitched voice said from behind them.

Elle whirled around and found the pixie still hovering in the air. "Hey, I can understand you," she said.

"Yes, it's the jelly beans," the pixie answered. "They help to keep your minds from being so slow. Your brains are working fast enough now to understand me."

"What happened to my two friends?" Dex demanded.

"They shouldn't have come into the Never Woods," the pixie said, shaking her head gravely. "The human requires only one fae, one vampire, and one shapeshifter as her companions."

"But we weren't sure about that," Dex argued. "We didn't know if we were being lied to about this quest, and they just wanted to help keep the rest of us safe."

"I know," the pixie said. "And for that reason, I sent them back to the edge of the woods before the trees' magic could consume them completely. If they'd been stupid enough to wander in here for no good reason, I wouldn't have bothered. But they came in as part of a quest. Their intention was noble. If they're sensible now and remain outside the Never Woods, they'll be fine."

"Sensible," Dex repeated. He groaned. "Yeah, okay, I'm doubtful about that. Though I think I can probably count on Olly being sensible enough to try to keep Xander from rushing back in here. As to whether he's successful ..."

The pixie shrugged. "It's out of my hands now. And it's out of yours too. You have a quest to complete."

"So it's ... real?" Astrid asked, her voice still full of doubt.

"Of course." The pixie turned to Elle. "You must follow the footprints." She flitted away and stopped beside the base of a tree. As she pointed, the shape of a foot—human, or one of the other High Races—appeared on the tree trunk.

"Freaky," Astrid murmured.

"Where will the footprints lead us to?" Elle asked.

"To the edge," the pixie said as she zoomed back to Elle.

"Uh … okay. And then?"

"Then you will have to cross over."

"To where?"

"To the other side of the edge."

Alissa smacked her palm to her forehead at the same time Astrid groaned. "Why do people insist on being so cryptic?" Astrid asked. "It's really not cool."

"I'm sorry, but I don't know what happens on the other side of the edge," the pixie said. "I've never been there. All I know is that the footprints continue."

"Okay, so after the edge, we look for more footprints," Dex said.

"Is it dangerous?" Elle asked. "This whole journey."

"It's possible you might die," the pixie replied.

"Wonderful," Elle muttered.

"But if you help each other, everything should work out fine. We do *want* you to succeed, human. We just want to ensure you are worthy."

"Right," Elle said. "Because that's totally fair. And don't worry," she added, holding her hand up as the pixie opened her tiny mouth to say something else. "I'm well aware that life isn't fair."

The pixie emitted a high-pitched tinkle of a laugh. "Exactly. Good fortune be with you, human." Then she shot away through the air and disappeared.

SIX

"You're worrying about them, aren't you," Elle said to Dex as they followed the footprint marks on the trees. Astrid and Alissa walked together a few paces ahead, and Elle could hear them discussing a TV show they were both addicted to. "Olly and Xander," Elle clarified. "You guys seem close."

"Yeah, I just know how stubborn they are," Dex said with a sigh. "Well, Xander in particular. He'd probably come barreling straight back into the Never Woods, determined that nothing could make him lose his mind. Then again, he isn't stupid, so hopefully that weird incident with the trees' magic is enough to make him second-guess coming back in here."

"And he's not alone," Elle pointed out. "Olly will remind him that it makes no sense for them to come after us."

"Yeah. I hope so."

"I take it you guys have been friends for a long time?"

Dex nodded. "My mother chose them as my companions from among the children of the noble fae families who have connections to court. They've been living at the palace since they were boys. I suppose we could have all hated each other—nobody wants a parent *choosing* their friends for them—but the three of us formed a fast friendship early on, and we've remained close ever since."

"It must have been hard for them to be away from their families."

"Not too bad, actually," Dex said. "I mean, you saw where Xander's home was. Not too far from the palace. And Olly's family is only a little further away. They got to see their families fairly regularly while growing up."

"Hey, does anyone have any idea how long we've been in here?" Astrid asked, stopping and looking back. "I must have left my phone in my car."

Dex slipped his hand into his jeans pocket and pulled out his phone. "It's … Oh, never mind. Either the battery's dead, or something in these woods is keeping it from working. I can't switch it on."

Astrid sighed. "My vote is for weird Never Woods magic. Wouldn't be surprised if it messes with technology."

"Yeah, probably," Dex grumbled, returning his phone to his pocket.

"Can you guys see the 'edge' of anything yet?" Elle asked.

"Nope," Alissa answered. "Just more trees with weird little footprints."

"Well, we still have the whole of season three and four to discuss," Astrid said to her as they continued forward, "so it really doesn't bother me if we don't reach this 'edge' any time soon."

Elle rolled her eyes at that, but if she was honest with herself, she wasn't in the greatest rush either. She was happy to walk beside Dex with her fingers laced between his and his thumb brushing absently up and down her skin. Sure, her poor heart was getting more of a workout than usual—leaping about from his mere touch—but she figured it was worth it.

"There's so much information my brain should be processing right now," he commented. "So many things that have happened recently. But you know what my mind keeps going back to over and over?"

"The fact that you're no longer dying?"

He paused, then let out a brief laugh. "Well, yes, there is that. I mean, that's *huge*. It's so huge that … I don't know, I don't think my mind has accepted it yet. It's been hanging over me for so long, the knowledge that I've been slowly dying for years and that I probably don't have much time left, that it seems a little impossible to imagine my life without that burden."

"Kinda like me and my freedom," Elle said. "I've wanted it for so long, and it's always been out of reach, and now that I have it, it doesn't quite feel real yet."

"Yes, exactly."

"So if that's *not* what you keep thinking about, then what is?"

He squeezed her hand—skip, skitter, stutter went her heart—and said,

"The fact that you and I knew each other as children. It's so weird, isn't it? Weird in a cool way, of course, but still such a weird coincidence."

Elle smiled and nodded. She'd told Dex everything the Godmother had explained about his nanny and her mother. "I wish I could remember it."

"I think I was about seven, so you were probably only … three?"

"Yeah, probably. *Way* too young for you to have any fun playing with as a mature seven year old," she added in a teasing tone. "You were probably far too cool to pay any attention to me."

"No way." Dex nudged her playfully with his elbow. "I was never too cool for you. I thought you were cute."

She laughed. "You're just saying that now."

"Well, obviously I don't mean it in the same way as I do *now* when I say you're cute." He leaned in and gave her a quick kiss on the cheek.

Her skin warmed, but her smile soon slipped away. "I wonder what you would have thought if you knew the little girl you were hanging out with was going to end up a slave." She peeked up at him and saw his brow furrow into a frown.

"I don't know. I can't remember what I knew of slavery at age seven. I know there was never a time when I thought it was okay. My first reaction when I finally understood exactly what being a slave meant was that it wasn't right. It sounded awful, and I didn't understand how anyone could treat another person that way."

"Did you ever ask your father how he could treat other people that way?" Elle asked carefully.

"I … I don't think I ever did. I think I was too scared. I knew what his views were based on the way he spoke about humans, and he wasn't someone to be argued with, so it wasn't a topic we discussed when I was young. But when I was older, I told him I didn't agree with him. I was still scared—as I've admitted to you already—"

"—because of the blood oath," Elle said. "I'm still really sorry about that. I thought we were joking around, and I did *not* mean to force the truth out of you."

"I know, it's fine." He let out a long sigh. "Anyway, once this is over and you have magic, we'll go to my father and show him. He'll finally see that humans have just as much right as the other High Races to be free."

Elle nodded. "Yes, definitely. Even though …"

"Even though what?"

"I don't know. It's just … why do humans have to have magic in order to prove they shouldn't be slaves? Even without magic, we're just as worthy of freedom. I wish the world could see that."

"I know. Believe me, I agree with you completely. But if this is what it takes for my father to see that humans are equal to other High Races—so we can change things in our *own* country, which would hopefully lead to worldwide change—then does it matter?"

"No. I suppose it doesn't. I guess at this point, all that matters is that humans end up free."

"Right. And they will after this quest." Dex gave her hand another firm squeeze. "Our country's constitution says that all magic-blooded High Races have a right to freedom. If the Godmother's telling the truth about this quest, then that includes humans. You all have the potential to be magic-blooded. And not just the *potential.* What was she saying about stardust? We're all made up of it in some way, so we're all magical."

Elle nodded. "So … you think this will really make a difference? Me ending up with magic?"

"Yes, of course. My father will have to get rid of the slave charm. It will become pointless because anyone using it will be violating one of the basic rights that now also pertains to humans. He can't let his personal feelings get in the way."

"Those personal feelings …" Elle said carefully.

"Yes?"

"Is that what the Godmother was referring to? She hinted there was some kind of incident. Something specific that intensified his hatred of humans. Was that … I mean, you don't have to tell me about it if you don't want to, but … was she making that up? Or did something happen?"

Dex was quiet for a moment before answering. "Something did happen. Before that, my father actually had conflicting views on humans. I remember overhearing him talking to my mother about it. He said he wanted to agree with my grandfather, who started changing the slave laws in this country. He wanted to believe my grandfather was right. But he could never understand why humans didn't have magic like the other High Races. It just seemed they were naturally inferior beings, so why should they have the same rights as the rest of us?"

"And then?" Elle asked, trying her best not to feel personally offended by the things Dex's father had once said. "What pushed him over the edge?"

"My grandmother was killed. And it was humans who did it."

"What?"

"Yeah. I don't know if you remember that she was still alive when my father ascended the throne? She could have continued ruling after my grandfather died, but she stepped down. So she was still around when I was young."

"Oh." Elle frowned. "I'm not sure if I knew that."

"She didn't often make public appearances. Anyway, she was in one of our secure vehicles, and she had several security personnel with her, but the car was hijacked by a group of humans—quite a few of them—and she was killed."

"Oh my goodness. I'm so sorry."

"I think a switch flipped in my father that day. The way he's spoken about humans ever since …" Dex shook his head. "I don't know, it's like he thinks they're all heartless, worthless beings. He believes if he gives them an inch of freedom, they'll swarm the palace and try to kill us all."

"I'm sure that protest at the Moonlight Masquerade didn't help."

"No. Not at all."

"And you really think that showing him humans are magic-blooded beings as well will make a difference?"

"It'll have to. The law is the law. Now that we know what we know, it means humans already have the right to be free. Everyone else will see that, even if my father is still blinded by his personal feelings. Maybe he'll go crazy and try to re-word the Bill of Rights, but the National Council can't possibly side with him on something like this. They won't. This *will work*, Elle. This is going to change the world."

"Change the world," she repeated with a smile. "I like that. I think you're—Oh, sorry." She stopped abruptly before almost walking into Astrid. "Everything okay?" she asked.

"Stars above," Astrid murmured, her gaze focused upward.

"What?" Dex asked.

"I just realized something. There are things—tiny creatures—inside those orbs. Please tell me you see that too and I'm not going crazy again."

Elle turned to the nearest orb as it floated by. It appeared there *was* something inside. She stood on tiptoe to get a closer look. It was a tiny person, one of the High Races—impossible to tell which one, since the being was so small—on his knees inside the orb. He gripped his hair with his tiny hands, his eyes squeezed closed and his face contorted into what looked like an expression of anguish.

"That is the creepiest thing I've ever seen," Alissa whispered. "And I've seen a lot."

Elle looked around, her eyes focusing on another orb. It was eerie to know that they weren't alone after all. That dozens of miniature people were floating above them. She wondered if they'd been listening. Had they heard all the things she and Dex had spoken about? And how did they all get here? A thought occurred to her as another tiny, weeping person floated by. "I wonder if these are all the people who've wandered into the Never Woods, lost their minds, and never left."

"You mean Xander and Olly would have ended up like this if that pixie hadn't sent them out of the woods?" Dex said.

"Maybe, I don't know. But I wonder if we can free these people," Elle added, raising her hand toward the nearest orb.

Dex caught her fingers and pulled her hand back down. "You probably shouldn't touch that."

"You think something bad will happen?"

"I just don't think we should disturb the way things are."

"Yeah, maybe not."

"Let's just keep moving," Alissa said, turning away. "I don't want to look at them anymore."

"Hey, look here," Astrid called to them from a few feet away. "I think it's an actual path."

Elle walked forward, realizing that the mist must have begun to dissipate at some point. The air seemed clearer now, and as she looked ahead, she saw a straight line of space cutting through the trees, ending at a clearing of some sort.

"Do you think that's the 'edge' the pixie was referring to?" Astrid asked.

"I don't know, but the footprint marks continue that way," Elle said. "Let's keep going and find out."

They followed the path, and before even reaching the clearing, Elle could see the 'edge' the pixie had spoken of. At the end of the path, the ground gave way abruptly to a steep cliff. On the other side of a great chasm, the Never Woods continued. "The pixie said we have to cross over," Dex said as the four of them stopped a few feet back from the edge of the cliff.

Elle looked first to the left and then the right, her eyes scanning the moonlit landscape for a way across the chasm. "No bridge," she said when her eyes found nothing.

"Of course not," Astrid muttered. "That would be far too easy."

"Climbing down, walking across, and climbing back up doesn't look like a great option either," Alissa said.

"Definitely not," Elle said, looking down. The bottom of the abyss was so far below, she could barely make out what was down there. "Anyone see any footprints anywhere—Whoa!" She threw a hand out and grabbed hold of Dex as the ground shuddered beneath her feet.

"What the hell?" Astrid gasped as the four of them scrambled a few paces backward.

"Stars," Alissa hissed. "Look there." She pointed toward the left, where boulder-sized pieces of rock were starting to fall away from the edge of the cliff.

"Same on this side," Dex said.

"Oh, are you *kidding* me?" Astrid shouted. "You said we had to cross over, but you forgot to tell us about the *time limit* part!" she yelled into the chasm.

"Okay, let's not panic," Elle said, gripping Dex's arm tighter as another shudder rolled through the ground. "There's a reason you're all here, right? I was told I had to bring a vampire, a shifter and a faerie. So one of you must be able to get us safely across."

"Well don't look at me," Astrid said. "He's the one with all the power." She pointed at Dex.

"Well, yeah," Dex spluttered, "but it's not the kind of power that can build a bridge in five seconds. I mean … anything that might help us get across will take time." His wide-eyed gaze focused on the other side of the chasm. "Okay, the quickest thing is probably rope." In the darkness, gold dust shimmered around his hands. "I can throw it across. Magic can secure it on the other side. I can do one for each of us. But securing it on *this* side is going to be a problem if this part of the woods falls into the canyon. But magic can at least keep us from falling too fast if we—"

"Can you make us fly?" Astrid asked. "Give us wings?"

Dex gaped at her. "No! What kind of world are you living in that you think fae can do that?"

"I don't know, a world of *magic*?" They all stumbled another few steps backward into the woods as the ground began to crumble away in front of them. "A world where the fae like to remind us they're powerful and secretive and never share all the things they can actually do?"

"What?"

"Dex!" Elle shouted. "We're running out of—"

"Hey," Alissa said, looking over her shoulder and then back at the chasm. "I can get across."

"You can?" Elle grabbed onto a tree branch as the ground cracked beneath her feet.

"Yes, I'm pretty sure. You know how fast we vampires are. And that path back there is so straight. I can easily gather enough speed to leap across."

"Well, isn't that wonderful for you," Astrid snapped. "What about the rest of us?"

"I can take you with me. One at a time."

"Like … you would pick us each up and carry us?" Dex asked, eyeing Alissa's slim frame with doubt.

"Hello, I'm a *vampire*," she snapped. "I'm stronger than you are, *your highness*."

"Yes, okay, that sounds great," Elle said hastily. "Let's do it. We'll all be at the bottom of the chasm soon otherwise."

"Take them first," Dex said immediately. "Elle and then Astrid. I'll send rope across in case you don't get back in time for me."

Elle barely heard Dex's last few words as she was abruptly whisked through the air and landed with an *oof* of breath over Alissa's shoulder. A blast of wind blew her hair back, and then they were stationary again, back in the woods. Elle tried to catch her breath as a memory flashed through her mind: the image of being tossed over Alissa's shoulder as she jumped from a window of Gizella Munroe's home. *I'm going to run now*, Alissa had said as they landed at the bottom. *Please don't throw up on me.*

"I'll try not to throw up on you," Elle managed to say with whatever breath remained in her lungs. A snort of laughter escaped the vampire, and then in a rush of speed, the Never Woods blurred around them. The quick, jerky motions morphed into a smooth, soaring motion, and everything slowed just enough for Elle to make out the gaping hole of the chasm for a second before ground flashed into her view again. A sudden landing and several stumbling steps made certain she had absolutely no breath left, and by the time Alissa dumped her on the ground and raced away, she was sucking desperately at the air.

Elle scrambled onto her feet and approached the cliff. A glittering gold line hung across the chasm. She squinted into the night and just managed to make out Dex's shape at the other end of the rope. The ground was still crumbling away on either side of him, leaving him standing on a rapidly narrowing ledge of rock. Alissa sped past him and streaked through the air, but Elle kept her eyes on Dex as the vampire landed somewhere behind her with Astrid. What was Dex planning to do? Tie the other end of the rope around himself and leap into the abyss? Was his magic enough to keep him from slamming against the cliff on this side at a deadly speed?

"I think there's still time," Alissa said breathlessly. "I can get back across."

"Are you—" Elle didn't get a chance to finish her sentence before Alissa raced off again. She squeezed her hands together and pressed them beneath her chin. "Please don't die," she whispered.

"They'll be … fine … I'm sure," Astrid gasped, coming to stand beside her. "Man, that was … a rush."

Elle ignored her, barely blinking as she watched Alissa and Dex disappear into the trees on the other side. "Come on, come on, come on." While the ground on this side was utterly still, she could see rocks, stones and dust tumbling away into the darkness on the far side of the chasm. The ledge Dex had been waiting on was now hardly big enough for a single person, and as a flash of color raced out of the woods, the final piece of rock cracked off and slid down, taking several trees with it. "Oh no," Elle gasped. "Do you think she launched off the edge with enough speed? The ground was already falling when she …"

Her words trailed off as she watched her two companions sailing through the air. Less than halfway across the chasm, they reached the highest point of their arc and began falling, leaving no doubt in Elle's mind: they weren't going to make it.

SEVEN

GOLD LIGHT FLASHED AWAY FROM ALISSA AND DEX, FORMING A LINE THAT HIT THE nearest tree and wrapped itself around the trunk several times. Elle's eyes darted from the conjured rope back to the falling pair. They clung together as Dex's magic looped around them. While Alissa's scream echoed across the cavernous space, Elle held her breath. The rope snapped taut, and instead of falling straight down into the darkness of the chasm, Alissa and Dex swung toward the cliff face at an alarming speed.

Elle dropped to her knees and scrambled toward the edge of the cliff, mumbling, "Don't die, don't die, don't die." She reached the edge and peered over just as a glow surrounded Alissa and Dex and they slowed suddenly. They bumped gently against the cliff face a few times as if it were a mattress instead of a solid rock surface. Alissa yelled out a few obscenities while Elle breathed, "Ohthankgoodness."

Astrid landed on her knees beside Elle and started laughing as she looked down. "I'll bet that was way more of a rush than our ride over the chasm."

Elle didn't answer, her eyes still pinned to Alissa and Dex dangling at the bottom of the rope. "Okay, I'm coming up," Alissa called out in a shaky voice. She began pulling herself up, arm over arm. After a few moments, Dex followed.

"Holy frikkin' stars," Alissa gasped when she reached the top and let Elle and Astrid help her up and over the edge. She crawled a few feet away before lying on her back and staring up at the sky. "There were a few moments when I seriously thought we weren't going to see the rest of this quest. I know a vampire and a faerie can survive a lot, but it is a *looooong* way to the bottom of that gorge."

"Yeah, I'll say," Dex grunted as he made it to the top of the rope. Elle grabbed his arm and tried to assist as he hefted himself over the edge, which was completely unnecessary because, like Alissa, he didn't exactly need the help. Once he was on solid, flat ground, he collapsed against Elle and pulled her into his arms. She clung to him as tightly as if she planned to never let go, blinking away tears of relief.

They sat in silence for a few moments, their breathing the only sound that filled the air, and then Dex looked toward Alissa. "Hey, thanks for getting us halfway across."

She sat up, stuck her tongue out at him, then laughed. "Thanks for getting us the rest of the way, I guess."

"I can't believe you guys are joking about this," Elle said.

Dex pulled away but left one arm around her shoulders. "Hey, it's fine," he said as he rubbed her back. "We're fine."

"I know, but if you weren't, it would be my fault. *I* would be the reason you both died."

"Hey, we volunteered for this, remember?" Alissa said as she pushed herself to her feet. "And since we're all still fine, we should probably carry on."

"Yep, there's the next footprint," Astrid said, pointing behind them. Elle watched the imprint of a foot appear at the base of a nearby tree. "And look," Astrid added. "Those creepy little orb prisoners are on this side too." Elle raised her eyes and gazed further into the woods. Sure enough, a few glowing white orbs floated here and there.

"Marvelous," Alissa grumbled. "I'll keep my eyes pointed down."

Dex helped Elle to her feet—she seemed to be the only one still shaken by the fact that two out of their group of four had almost *died* mere minutes ago—and walked beside her as they headed back into the woods. There was no path this side, but they kept their eyes peeled for each new footprint as it appeared on the trees ahead of them.

"I wish we knew how much longer this quest would take," Astrid said. "I don't know if I should be rationing the energy bars zipped up inside my jacket. I don't want to finish them all and then in two days time I'm eating tree bark and rotting leaves."

"That's disgusting," Alissa replied.

"I haven't even seen anything that resembles a berry," Astrid continued. "There's *nothing* in this place that could be considered—Oh!" She let out a yelp as the ground suddenly tilted at a steep angle.

"Holy staaaaars!" Elle shrieked as she slipped onto her backside and skidded uncontrollably down the steep slope that had appeared out of nowhere. She tried to grab onto roots and tree trunks, but she was sliding too fast to get a good grip on anything. The ground finally leveled out, and she rolled several times before coming to a halt. She sat up, brushing leaves and twigs from her hair. "Everyone okay?" she called as she looked around. They appeared to be at the bottom of a small, circular valley, with an open clearing ahead and the woods surrounding them on all sides.

"Yeah, I think I'm okay," Astrid answered.

"Me too," Alissa added, followed by a similar answer from Dex.

"The footsteps lead across the clearing," Alissa said as she climbed to her feet, pointing to the imprints in the ground..

"Seems simple enough," Dex said, "and yet I'm willing to bet something unpleasant will happen before we reach the other side."

"Yeah, like we'll get halfway and some horrible creature will jump out of the ground and attack us," Astrid replied.

"Or the ground will become sinking sand," Elle muttered. She rose to her feet. "But if that's the way the footprints go, then that's the way we have to go. I must just keep reminding myself that the pixie said she *wants* us to succeed. So even when there are obstacles, we should be able to get past them."

Dex nodded. "True. So … I guess we should start walking then."

Elle took a tentative step forward, expecting the ground to try to gobble her foot right off. But nothing happened. She took another step, and then another, and when nothing bad happened, she started walking normally. If she had to tiptoe the whole way across, it was going to take forever.

"So far, so good," Dex said as the four of them continued forward.

"Why would you say that?" Astrid grumbled. "Now you've probably—Oh, see? Now it's raining. You brought the rain down on us."

"It's just *rain*," Dex replied. "Probably a coincidence."

"You think?" Elle said, looking up. "I hate to point this out, but there are no clouds."

"So freakin' weird," Astrid said, tilting her face toward the sky. "Nobody's going to believe half the things we tell them when we get out of this place."

Elle smiled. "I like the fact that you said 'when.'"

"Well of course. I don't plan to be stuck in these woods for—Ow! Okay, does anyone else feel like this rain is stinging?"

"Oh, ow, yes." Elle brushed the water droplets off the backs of her bare hands. When she felt her left foot stinging she looked down. "Hey! This rain is burning holes into my favorite shoes."

"Dex!" Astrid shouted.

"Yeah, I'm on it!" Sure enough, the gold glow of magic was already surrounding Dex's hands. He raised them above his head, and a rippling, shimmering layer began to form in the air above them. "Keep moving," he told them. "I can do this while we're—"

"Holy *stars*!" Elle yelped, leaping to the side and crashing into Alissa as a ball of flames the size of her fist landed where her right foot had just been.

On Dex's other side, Astrid let out a squeal and ducked closer to the group. "You can't make people fly, but you can deflect magical fireballs, right?"

"Working on it," Dex said through gritted teeth. He was focusing left and then right, both hands raised as the shimmering layer above him became a mesh-like barrier, similar to what Elle had seen in the palace gardens on the night of the Moonlight Masquerade—the barriers she'd assumed were to keep guests from intruding on certain parts of the grounds.

Alissa pressed closer, forcing Elle against Dex's side. "Crap, crap, crap," she hissed. "Can you bend that magic around us? To protect us from the sides as well? Something just hit my ankle."

"Uh, yeah," Dex said, all his attention still focused upward on the barrier.

"It's just … complicated. With us moving. But I've got it."

They rushed forward as quickly as they could while remaining in a huddle, and the fireballs began to increase in size and number. Looking ahead, Elle said, "We just have to make it to the edge of the clearing. As far as I can tell, there's no fire in the trees."

"Great," Dex grunted. "Because—dammit!" He ducked his head, but nothing came through the barrier. "What the hell? They're the size of boulders!"

Elle looked up. It seemed as if the enormous fireballs were melding together as they fell, forming larger and larger masses of fire, until eventually there was no break, no gap through which she could make out the sky. Only a continuous stream of flames, as if a giant dragon had opened its maw over the clearing, taken one enormous breath, and was planning to breath out fire for the rest of time.

They could no longer see where they were going, but they hurried blindly onwards inside their moving bubble of protection. "Come on," Elle panted. "We must be almost there. We must be." Heat burned her face and sweat formed across her brow. When she looked up again, the mesh-like layer was starting to glow red instead of gold, and tiny patches here and there seemed to be disappearing like paper held over a flame.

"Dex!" Alissa shouted. "Argh, jeez!" She shook her hand repeatedly. "Something just got through. Why isn't the barrier holding up?"

"Because there's a damn *inferno* on the other side of it!" Dex yelled back.

Elle gritted her teeth as the heat began to reach an unbearable level. But just as she thought her skin might be about to blister, the flames vanished, and the four of them raced into the cool air between the trees on the other side of the clearing.

"We did it," Dex gasped as they all slowed. He bent over and pressed his palms to his knees, his back rising and falling rapidly.

"You did it," Elle corrected, her chest heaving as she rubbed his arm. "That was quite impressive. We would all have been roasted within seconds if not for you."

"Yeah, um, sorry about yelling at you," Alissa said.

"Where'd you get burned?" Elle asked, turning to her with concern. "You said your ankle, and then … your hand?"

"I'll be fine. I'm not as fragile as a human." She grimaced. "Sorry, I didn't mean that to come out condescending. It's just … it is what it is."

"Yeah, yeah, I know," Elle said, waving away the apology. "So you're okay then?"

"Yes. We should get moving. We've got a steep hill to climb to get out of this valley."

"And, you know, we don't want to be standing here if those flames decide to start burning down the trees," Astrid added, looking back over her shoulder at the crackling mass of flames.

"Definitely not," Elle said.

They gave Dex another few moments to recover, then began the long ascent up this side of the valley, their conversation minimal as they chose breathing over talking. The hill seemed to go on and on, and Elle wondered if this was yet another test of the quest, or if she was simply weak and unfit after spending too much time confined in an attic.

She was just considering giving in to her exhaustion and begging the others for a break when the ground suddenly shifted beneath her feet. She toppled forward and landed on her hands and knees. "Not again," she groaned, bracing herself for the motion of falling down another steep hill. But she remained in the same position, hard earth pressing against her knees and twigs digging into her hands.

"Hey, the ground is flat again," Astrid said. "Like, horizontal flat."

Elle pushed herself carefully onto her feet and looked around.

"It's gone," Dex said, surprise coloring his tone. "The hill. The valley. All of it."

Turning slowly, Elle found that he was right. The Never Woods appeared exactly as they had before the ground first tilted and sent them sliding down toward the clearing: skinny trees growing a little too close together, mist hanging between them, and glowing orbs drifting slowly above their heads.

"That did happen, right?" Dex said. "The clearing, and the fire, and the magic I used to keep it from consuming us? Please tell me that wasn't all in my head."

"It wasn't," Elle assured him.

"Yeah, that definitely happened," Alissa said, gingerly touching a spot on the back of her hand.

"These woods just like to keep confusing us, that's all," Astrid murmured. "So the sooner we get out of here, the better." She looked around. "Anyone see a footprint anywhere?"

Elle's eyes traced over the surrounding trees, but no footprint shape appeared on any of the trunks. "I guess we'd better start hunting." She circled a few of the nearest trees, making sure not to stray too far from her companions. "Footprints, footprints, footprints," she murmured. "Where are you?"

"Do you think this is why the quest takes longer for some people?" Astrid called out. "They lose sight of the footprints and end up going the wrong way?"

"Maybe," Alissa answered. "But I feel like we were following them closely until the point the ground leveled itself out and that hill disappeared."

"Just keep looking," Dex said.

So Elle kept looking, checking some trees more than once, just in case a footprint had formed since the first time she looked. At the sound of footsteps behind her, she glanced over her shoulder, expecting to see one of her companions. "Did you find—"

Her words died on her tongue. She whirled around, a gasp catching in her throat. She wanted to scream but the sight of the person standing there regarding her with a malicious smile was enough to snatch her breath away in an instant. She took a hurried step backward and found herself backed up against a tree.

"Well, well," her stepmother said, advancing slowly toward her. "Of all the places I expected to find you, my dear *Estelle*, this most certainly was not it."

EIGHT

"**W**HAT—WHAT ARE YOU DOING HERE?" ELLE STUTTERED.

"You're my slave," Salvia said. "I came looking for you."

"I'm not a slave. I'm—I'm free." Elle took a deep breath, hoping Salvia wouldn't hear the air quivering as it passed her lips. "You can't do anything to me anymore."

"Free?" Salvia laughed. "What a joke."

"It's true," Elle insisted. She reached with a shaking hand for the bottom of her pants. She pulled them up—and there was the gold chain-shaped tattoo that marked her as a slave. "What?" she gasped.

"Don't you understand, Elle?" Salvia said quietly. "You will *never* be free." Magic lashed away from her like a whip, catching around Elle's arm and tugging her forward onto her knees. She cried out and tried to scramble away, searching over her shoulder for her companions.

"Dex!" she yelled. "DEX!"

"Your friends can't help you now," Salvia said, her face close to Elle's. "I'm taking you back to your attic, and there you will stay forever."

Elle shoved away from her and scrambled around the side of the tree, but Salvia was right. Her friends were gone. She couldn't see a single one of them. She was alone in the Never Woods with her stepmother, and she would never be free.

"You're coming with me," Salvia hissed. Her hand was around Elle's ankle, dragging her away across the dirt.

"No!" Elle shouted, kicking hard. She rolled over to face her stepmother—just as a snarl ripped through the air and Salvia vanished. Elle became aware of other sounds then. Someone screaming, and Dex shouting out for her, and a terrible growling, ripping sound. She scrambled onto her hands and knees before pushing herself up and stumbling around the side of the tree. And there were Dex and Alissa, backed up against another two trees, and a wolf—a *wolf!*

"Astrid?" Elle whispered, too stunned to take another step.

The wolf's jaws were clamped around something white and wispy—a creature appearing to be made of dense mist. As the wolf tossed her head from side to side, silver droplets sprayed from the mist creature across the forest floor. After another few moments and one final shake, she let go of the mist. It hung motionless in the air, dripping silver liquid onto the ground.

The wolf moved back, shuddered, twisted, and began to change shape. Elle hurried to Dex's side and grabbed his hand. She hung on tightly, her other hand over her mouth as she watched the wolf transform into Astrid. In human form, Astrid shuffled on hands and knees to the nearest tree, collapsed against it, and let her eyelids slide shut.

"Um, what just happened?" Elle asked.

Astrid opened her eyes. "What did you see?" she asked. "Before I became a wolf. Before I attacked. Did you see something—or someone—you're afraid of?"

Elle paused before answering. "Yes. My stepmother."

Astrid looked at Dex. He nodded. "I saw … someone." He didn't elaborate, but a quick glance at Elle told her she probably knew who it was. If she had to guess, Dex had just seen his father out here in the Never Woods.

"I saw something terrifying as well," Alissa whispered.

Astrid nodded. "I guessed as much. The person I saw … it was the man who turned me."

"You weren't born a shifter?" Elle asked.

"No. I was born human. But there was this wolf …" She shuddered and shook her head. "Anyway, I was searching for that stupid footprint, and I turned around and found him standing right behind me. I ran and tripped, and for a moment, before you all disappeared, it seemed you were each focused on something invisible. Something … scary. I realized we were all seeing something different. Something we're each afraid of." She pushed herself up a little straighter against the tree and ran a hand through her messy hair. "In animal form, we shifters see things differently. Our fears are different." She let out a short laugh. "Essentially, we fear hardly anything. So I transformed, and immediately, I saw the creature for what it truly was. That strange wispy, misty thing."

"Thank goodness that worked," Elle said. "Well done."

"Yeah, well, I was also expecting that it was my turn to get us past the latest obstacle, so I figured there had to be something I could do in this situation that would work." Without another word, Elle walked closer, crouched down, and hugged her. "Oh, wow, okay," Astrid said. "We're on hugging terms now." She patted Elle's back awkwardly.

"Well you don't seem to like it when I say thank you," Elle said, "so you'll have to accept a hug instead."

"Fine," Astrid grumbled.

"So each of you has done something to help," Elle said as she stood, "which makes me wonder if we might be nearing the end of this ordeal." She let out a quick breath of a laugh. "This is supposed to be my quest, and I haven't actually done anything useful yet."

Astrid climbed to her feet. "Maybe all you're supposed to do is survive. You're the only one who doesn't have any magic yet. That's the point of the whole quest."

Elle nodded. "I guess that's true."

"Hey, is that a footprint?" Dex said.

Elle looked to where he was pointing. "That definitely wasn't there a few moments ago."

"No, it was not," Alissa said. "Which I guess means we've successfully completed this part of the quest. Time to keep moving."

They began following the footprints once more, far more subdued now than they were at the start of their journey. Elle suspected they were all quietly reliving whatever terrible moments the mist-like creature had made them experience. That was certainly where her mind was, and more than once, she stopped walking to quickly lift the bottom of her pants and check that the slave charm was well and truly gone from her skin.

She was about to check again—just once more, she told herself—when the urge to hurry forward overwhelmed her. "There's something there," she murmured, walking faster, leaving her companions a few paces behind. The light mist gave way to another clearing, and at its center sat a still, clear body of water. A shiver of anticipation skittered across Elle's skin. "This is it," she said to the others as they reached her side. "The lake at the center of the Never Woods. It's the right place. I can feel it."

Movement caught her attention at the edge of her vision. Her eyes darted to the side as a unicorn, pure white with an elegant silver horn, walked across the clearing and stopped in front of her. A shiver passed through the creature. Then it shuddered, a more violent motion, and Elle took a startled step backward. Then, just as Astrid's wolf form had done earlier, the unicorn began to change shape. She shifted quickly, and within moments, a woman with silver hair stood before Elle. "Correct, young human," she said. "This is the right place."

NINE

"Wait a minute," Elle said. "Since when do unicorn shifters exist?"

"Outside of the Never Woods," the woman said, "we don't." She looked around as if trying to see past the others. "You're here of your own free will? This vampire is a friend of yours? She isn't forcing you into this?"

Elle frowned. "No one's forcing me. Well, I suppose you might say the Godmother is forcing me into this, but that's a different story. These three are my companions, and none of them are forcing me to be here."

The unicorn woman smiled. "Good. That is the way it should be."

"Hang on," Dex said. "So when all those abducted humans were forced through this quest just so that vampires could take their magic from them afterwards, you knew about it?"

The woman's expression turned downcast. "I saw it, yes."

"And you couldn't do anything to stop them?"

"No. I am bound by the quest to direct any human who comes my way. That is my life's task."

"So you're going to tell me what to do now?" Elle asked.

"Yes. Do you see that boat?" She stepped aside, and Elle watched as a boat faded into view at the edge of the lake. "Take the boat to the center of the lake. Stand up and reach for the brightest star. Close your hand around the light and take it."

"Take it? How? Isn't it millions of miles away?"

"Yes and no," the woman said with an enigmatic smile. "You'll be able to take hold of it. You'll see. It will form a jewel in your hand. Crack it open and let the magic spill over you."

"Like a wish?" Astrid asked.

The woman looked at her. "Where do you think the fae came up with the idea to store wish magic within a gem?"

"So, do I do anything else after that?" Elle asked. "Or is that the end?"

"The quest will be complete when you break the mirror. That action will transport you out of the Never Woods."

"There's a mirror?"

"You'll see it."

Elle took a deep breath. "Okay. Anything else?"

The woman smiled once more. "This was never a quest that was meant to be completed alone."

Elle nodded. "I understand. I never would have made it this far on my own."

"Well then. If you understand that, then it should be easy for you to finish the quest."

"Okay." Elle looked past the woman. She pushed her shoulders back and took one more steadying breath. "Time to finish this."

She took a step forward—and Dex, Alissa and Astrid all slumped to the ground. "Wait, what's happening?" Elle asked, fear coursing instantly through her body. She crouched beside Dex and shook his arm, but all he did was mumble something unintelligible. "What's wrong with them?"

"They're falling asleep," the woman said. "If you don't complete the quest soon, they'll never wake up."

"What? Oh, come on, seriously? Hey, Dex!" Elle shook his arm again, but he barely responded.

"You'd better hurry, young human. This is your moment. You've relied on them to get you this far. Now they have to rely on you to complete the quest and save them."

"Okay, okay." Elle rose quickly and hurried toward the boat. "Get in the boat, row to the middle, take the starlight," she muttered. "I can do this." She climbed in carefully, noting that even though the boat rocked gently in the water, no ripples disturbed the lake's surface. "This place is so weird," she muttered as she sat and reached for the two oars. She'd never rowed a boat before, but she knew what to do, so she clumsily got started. She dipped the oars into the water and pulled. Dip and pull, dip and pull, and soon the boat was sliding through the water away from the lake's edge.

Then it stopped. Elle kept rowing—pulling harder with the oars—but the boat remained perfectly still. "What in all the stars?" she muttered. She paused, looked over the edge of the boat on both sides and behind her. But if there was an obstacle, it was out of sight, beneath the boat. She rowed back a bit, maneuvered past the area where she guessed the obstacle to be, and tried again. But it was like the kind of nightmare where she was trying to run while her feet were stuck in place. No amount of effort moved her forward any further.

"Ugh!" With tears of frustration burning her eyes, she dropped the oars into the boat and turned to look at the unicorn shifter. The woman was still standing near the lake, watching Elle in silence. "What the hell is the point of all this if I get so close to the end, I follow all the instructions, and it doesn't work?" she shouted. "Did the person who came up with this stupid quest just want to have fun watching other people suffer?"

The unicorn shifter smiled her infuriating smile. "Of course not. The quest is simply a reminder of the way the world should work." And with that, she slipped between the trees and disappeared.

"Ugh, that is *not helpful*!" Elle shouted after her. She let out a puff of air, rested her elbows on her knees, and pressed her hands against her cheeks. "Come on, think. Just *think*. There has to be a trick here somewhere. I have to row to the middle, reach for the starlight, crack open the gem, break the mirror, and then we'll all be out of here. The gem comes from the starlight—" she turned her gaze to the night sky "—and then the mirror ..." She looked around, then down near her feet in the bottom of the boat. She turned and looked at the small section of boat behind her, but there was no mirror there either. "No mirror. No mirror, no mirror."

Then her eyes fell on the lake. With no ripples, it formed a perfect glassy surface. "Of course," she murmured. "That should have been obvious from the start. The lake is the mirror. So I have to break it somehow." She lifted an oar again and poked it into the water, but still the surface refused to be disturbed. "*I have to break the mirror*," she said slowly. "Like … my actual body? Do I have to jump in?" She looked around, but the unicorn woman didn't reappear to answer her. "If I jump in and break the surface, then I'll leave the Never Woods. But … I'll be alone? And the others will still be here?" She looked toward them, lying motionless on the ground not too far from the water. "Which means … they should jump into the water with me?"

This was never a quest that was meant to be completed alone.

"So maybe *that's* why the boat isn't moving," Elle said, grabbing the second oar. "I'm not supposed to be alone." She rowed back to the lake's edge as quickly as she could, then climbed out and began the difficult task of dragging each of her companions toward the boat. "This would be so much easier if I had magic already," she grunted. "Oops, really sorry about that," she added as she bumped Dex's head against the wooden seat after finally managing to get his heavy frame over the edge of the boat and into it.

She was breathless and her arms were aching by the time all three of them were lying squashed together in the bottom of the boat. But fear that she was running out of time—that Dex, Alissa and Astrid might remain asleep forever— kept her moving. Trying not to stand on any of them, she positioned herself on the seat and began rowing. "Stars above, you guys are heavy," she groaned. "Okay, come on, Elle. You can do this. You can *do* this, dammit!"

The boat moved achingly slowly through the water, and when she reached the point where she'd first got stuck, she pressed her lips together and held her breath—but the boat kept moving. "Yes!" she shouted out loud. She kept rowing, continually looking toward the far side of the lake and then back toward her starting position, comparing the distance, trying to judge whether she'd reached the middle yet.

"Okay, I think … yes, I think this is it." She lowered the oars into the boat— trying not to hit anyone's face—then patted Dex's arm. He didn't respond. "Just hang in there," she told him. "I'm almost done."

Carefully, she stood up, trying not to think of what a tragedy it would be if she fell and broke the surface of the lake *before* she completed the quest and took magic from a star. "Careful, careful," she whispered as she straightened. She held her arms out to keep herself balanced, then slowly looked up toward the sky. For a moment, she worried that it might be impossible to tell which star was the brightest, but she felt her eyes drawn toward it almost immediately.

"Wow," she whispered. It was brighter than any star she'd ever seen from Vale City. Beautiful, magical, the final piece of a puzzle. It felt completely natural to stretch her hand out toward it and wrap her fingers around the light.

Something hard formed within her grasp, and with a racing heart, she pulled her hand back and slowly opened her fingers. Upon her palm sat a clear gem with silver light glowing at its center. "Crack the gem," she whispered. "But how?" The fae generally used a charm to break open a wish, but Elle had never reached the point where she had to consider how she would do it if she ever got her hands on one. She looked around for a hard surface. "May as well try," she muttered, her eyes landing on the boat itself.

She sat on the seat and positioned the gem over the edge of the boat, the way she might hold an egg over the edge of a pot, ready to crack it open. She brought it down hard, and the outer casing split. With her heart pounding so hard it hurt, she quickly raised the broken gem above her head. She looked up as the glowing silvery liquid cascaded down over her chin, neck and chest. There was something so silly about it, that for a moment she couldn't help laughing.

When all the liquid had fallen, she lowered the empty pieces of the gem to the bottom of the boat near her feet. She wiped her hand over her chin, but it wasn't wet as she'd expected. She peered down at her chest, but there was no silvery liquid there either. "Did it work?" she whispered. Had her body absorbed the star's magic?

She leaned one arm on the edge of the boat and looked toward the trees. "Hello?" she called. "How do I know if ..." Her words trailed off as her gaze caught on something: tiny particles of silver coating her fingers and drifting in the air above her hand. It looked for all the world like ... "Faerie dust," Elle whispered. But it was silver. And it was *hers*. Her skin tingled, and she knew without a doubt that the magic came from within her.

"Elle?" Dex murmured from somewhere near her feet.

"Oh, stars, thank goodness," she said, beaming at him. Then: "Stars! This is why we say 'stars!'" She pointed at the sky, then displayed her hands for him to see. "Because of their magic!"

"Ho-lee stars," Dex whispered, pushing himself up so he was sitting. His eyes traced across her fingers, her hands, her arms. "You did it."

"Ohmygoodness," Astrid mumbled sleepily. "You actually did it." She pushed herself up, and beside her, Alissa began to stir. "It's real. It's actually … You have freaking *magic*. And you're *human*."

"I know," Elle said with a laugh.

"Incredible," Alissa whispered. "Also … why was I asleep? And how did I get into this boat?"

"Oh, stars, what was that?" Elle gasped as something jolted the boat.

"Uh … we're sinking?" Dex asked, looking around.

"No, it's the level of the water," Alissa said, pointing to the bank. "Look, you can see it going down."

"Oh, crap, that's not good." Elle stood while holding onto the side of the boat. "We need to jump into the water before it all disappears. I mean, I think that's what we need to do. We need to break the surface."

"Oh, is the water the mirror?" Astrid asked.

"I don't know. I think so?"

"That makes sense," Dex said. "I don't see an actual mirror anywhere, and the surface of this lake has been perfectly still since we got here."

"Okay, so everyone's agreed," Elle said, reaching for Dex's hand. "We're jumping?"

"We're jumping," Alissa said, grabbing Astrid's hand in one of hers and Dex's in the other.

"Okay," Elle said, her heart thundering wildly once more. "Ready, and … *now*!"

TEN

When Elle woke up beside a forest of spindly trees, her first thought was that she had dreamed everything that took place within it. But as she pushed herself up, she noticed the silver dust glittering on her hands, and adrenaline raced through her body at the realization that it was real.

She had magic.

She had no idea what to do with it, but she wasn't too bothered by that part. She could learn. She was free and she had magic and nobody had died in the Never Woods and *life was good*. And it would be even better once every other human in the world knew that this quest was possible.

"Hey, sleepyhead," Dex said, extending a hand toward her. "You finally woke up."

"Oh, whatever," Astrid said, appearing beside him. "You regained consciousness like ten seconds ago. Don't make out like Elle's been sleeping forever."

"Guys, we actually did it," Elle said as Dex pulled her to her feet. *"We did it!"*

"And survived to tell the tale," Alissa added with a smile.

"Well done," a smooth, familiar voice said. Elle's heart kicked into high gear. She barely had to think of it and shimmering silver dust rushed all the way up her arms. She had no clue how it might protect her, but the Godmother had startled her, and her magic had responded instantly. How could she have forgotten about the woman? Life wasn't good while the Godmother was still a threat.

Elle turned to face the white-haired faerie. The Godmother regarded her, a small smile lifting her lips. "Magic looks good on you, Elle."

"I completed the quest," Elle said. "Just as you asked. But I expect there's some sort of catch now? Some detail I missed that now leaves me forever in your debt somehow?"

"No catch," the Godmother said. "I'm here to officially confirm that your price has been paid."

"Oh. So that's … that's it? I have magic now, and you don't want anything else from me?"

"I don't want anything else from you." She held out her hand. "Shall we shake? To symbolize the end of the deal."

"Oh. Do I have to?"

"Yes."

With a sigh, Elle grasped the Godmother's hand, then flinched at the momentary sting that coursed up her wrist and into her arm. "What was that?"

"Static electricity?" the Godmother suggested. "It's very dry here."

"Yeah, right," Elle muttered with suspicion, tugging her hand free. "You probably just cursed me or something."

The Godmother laughed. "You really are determined to think the worst of me. We're *done*, Elle. This deal is complete."

"Seriously?"

"Seriously." The Godmother shrugged. "But perhaps we'll talk again in the future."

And there it was. A hint—no matter how small—that this wasn't over yet. "I'd prefer *not* to talk again in the future," Elle said. "If my price is paid, and I don't ever summon you for another wish, then we shouldn't have to deal with one another ever again."

"Mm. True." She looked at Dex. "Depends on how close you've grown to the prince."

Elle narrowed her eyes. "Because …"

"Well, if you're around when my army and I make our move on Belmont Palace, then you and I may see each other again."

Dex tensed beside Elle. "So that's happening? That's your plan? You really do want to get rid of my father and take the throne?"

The Godmother shrugged. "He's planning to come for me. To put an end to me and my empire of wishes, once and for all. He just hasn't figured out exactly where to find me yet. So perhaps I'll make things easier on all of us and go to him instead. So." She made a shooing motion with her hands. "You'd better run along so you can help him prepare."

Dex took a step forward, but everything vanished before he could reach the Godmother. That sickening jolt that Elle had come to hate wasn't nearly as bad as she expected, and she wondered, as the world took shape again around her, whether her newly acquired magic had something to do with that.

"Dammit, where is she?" Dex demanded, spinning around on the spot.

"Looks like she didn't come with this time," Astrid said. "I guess she's had enough cinnamon rolls recently."

Elle turned and found herself standing in front of the same coffee shop they'd met the Godmother at before the quest began. Astrid's car was still parked outside, but Xander's was gone. "Well that's a good sign, right?" Elle said, pointing to the taxi that was now parked where Xander's car had been. "Xander and Olly must have managed to get back here somehow."

"Yeah, they must have," Dex said. "I should try to get hold of—"

"Dex!" The coffee shop door swung open, and two familiar figures rushed out. "You made it!" Olly cried.

"Finally," Xander groaned, though he couldn't hide his grin as he slapped Dex on the back. "We've only been waiting five days for you."

Dex laughed, but Olly sobered. "Seriously. It's been five days."

"Really?" Elle asked.

"Five days?" Alissa repeated.

"Five days," Xander said.

"My mother's going to kill me," Dex groaned.

"Yeah …" Olly dragged the word out. "We tried to smooth things over with her."

At that, Dex looked even more concerned. "What did you tell her?"

"We *may* have said that you decided to take off with a girl for a few days."

"What?"

"Which was technically the truth," Xander added, "although your mother didn't take it the way we meant it, and we didn't bother correcting her."

"So you've given my parents even more reason to dislike Elle when they meet her?"

"Nah, they'll be so happy you're okay," Xander said, "that they'll forget all about blaming Elle for luring you away from home for several days."

"Oh, stars," Elle muttered, covering her face with her hands.

"It's fine, it's fine," Olly reassured her. "Nothing to be concerned about. They're super preoccupied with preparing for battles and magic vampires and— Holy frikkin' starballs!" he gasped. "You have magic."

Elle lowered her hands and grinned. "I have magic."

"You have magic," Xander repeated, his face a mask of pure shock.

"I'm not really sure how to turn it on and off," Elle added. "It just appears when it wants to."

"Okay, guys?" Astrid said. "We should go. So how about we save the amazement for the car ride home?"

"Oh, uh, sure." Olly cleared his throat. "Let's get out of here. I've eaten way too many cinnamon rolls over the past few days."

Elle held her glittering silver hand out toward Dex. "Time to get back home and find out what we missed."

He gave her a determined smile and laced his fingers through hers. "Time to change the world."

6

THE EVERAFTER WISH

ONE

Elle stood on the quiet moonlit street outside her stepmother's townhouse, working up the nerve to walk up the front steps and knock on the door. Without a watch or a phone, and after spending hours—which were apparently days—in an enchanted forest, followed by a well-deserved nap in the car during the drive back to Vale City, she'd begun to lose all concept of time. She had no idea how late it was, but lights illuminated the windows of Salvia's home, and the occasional shadow moved behind the curtains, so someone was definitely home and awake.

Elle looked around at the sound of a door banging shut somewhere nearby, but it appeared she was still alone out here. She swallowed and told herself to stop being so jumpy. She'd asked Dex to wait in the next street over, wanting the reassurance of knowing she wasn't completely alone, but *not* wanting the pressure of him watching as she faced her stepmother. "I have to do this on my own," she'd told him.

"They're just possessions," he'd reminded her. "Are you sure you need them?"

"It's not just that. I need this part of my life to be over. I need Salvia to know it's over. Then we can face everything else."

She climbed the stairs and stopped in front of the door. "I can do this," she whispered. "I'm not a slave, and I have *magic*." Adrenaline spiked in her veins at the reminder, and bright silver dust materialized on her fingers in response. Dex had promised that if human magic was anything like fae Essence, he would teach her everything he knew. But exhaustion had knocked Elle out soon after getting into Xander's car to drive back to the city, so Dex hadn't had time to explain a single thing yet.

Elle exhaled slowly, watching the silver glow fade from her skin. Then she lifted her hand to the door. But before she could knock, the image of Salvia looming over her in the Never Woods rose in her mind. She'd been on the ground, so helpless, and the slave charm had somehow reappeared on her leg—

It wasn't real, she reminded herself silently, closing her eyes for a moment. *It was all a trick of the Never Woods.* She opened her eyes, took a deep breath, and rapped three times on the door.

Seconds ticked by.

She considered knocking again.

She considered running.

She didn't *really* need to—

The door swung open, and there stood Salvia, elegant as always with her glossy red hair spilling over her shoulders in perfect waves and her face flawlessly made up. Though the slave charm was gone from Elle's ankle, she almost flinched at the sight of her stepmother. She imagined the burn of magic on her skin. She was late returning home, so very, very late, and surely the pain would eat into her leg any second—

"Salvia," she said before her fear could take over completely. She forced her shoulders back and held her stepmother's gaze. "I'm here for my things."

Salvia's expression, initially one of annoyance—most likely because someone was unexpectedly disturbing her evening—turned instantly to rage. "Where the hell have you—"

"I'm not your slave anymore." Elle bent quickly, lifted the bottom of her pants, and showed Salvia her bare ankle.

Salvia gaped. Then her eyes narrowed to slits. "How did you—"

"I'm here for my things." Elle straightened. "Then I'll be gone, and I don't want to see you ever again."

Salvia pulled herself a little straighter. "As if I give a damn about what you want." She stepped back. "Get inside right now."

"Thank you." Elle marched past her, across the hallway, and into the living room.

"Thank you?" Salvia repeated behind her. *"Thank you?"* The door slammed shut. "You know you're never leaving this house again, don't you? I'll put a confinement charm on these doors so strong you won't even be able to touch the handles without getting burned."

"I told you," Elle said, spinning to face her stepmother, "I'm not your slave anymore."

"Well that—"

"And I have magic," Elle blurted out, raising her hands as silver dust trailed across her skin. "So don't try anything."

For what might possibly have been the first time in Elle's life, she watched genuine shock come over her stepmother's face. For several moments, all Salvia could do was stare. "It isn't possible," she whispered eventually. Her eyes traveled across the silvery glow of Elle's skin. Then she pressed her lips together, appearing to regain some of her composure. "Well, you always were a freak of some sort. I suppose this shouldn't surprise me."

Hatred that had spent years simmering beneath Elle's fear began to bubble. "I'm not a *freak*. There's nothing unusual about me. This is possible for *all* humans. Centuries ago, everyone knew about it. Plenty of humans went on the quest I've just been on, and plenty of them ended up with magic."

"Quest?" Salvia sneered. "Possible for *all* humans? How ridiculous. And of course you're foolish enough to believe whoever told you this."

"It was the Godmother."

"Ha! Exactly. Only the foolish would believe a word out of that woman's—"

"Oh, so just because *you've* never heard of this quest, that means it's nonsense?" Elle took a step closer, her fear all but eclipsed now by the anger that was about to boil over. "Because you're so knowledgable about the world and its history? You don't know *anything*, Salvia. You're narrow-minded and selfish, and you—"

"Don't you *dare* speak to me like that!" Salvia shouted, and Elle flinched, expecting the burn of magic to lash across her skin at any second. Salvia advanced toward her, and Elle, with years of terror ingrained in her very bones, found herself unable to stand her ground. She backed up until she felt the wall behind her. "Do you know how easy it would be for me to burn the slave charm back into your skin?" Salvia hissed, magic crackling around her fingers as she brought her face right in front of Elle's. "You can't fight back. You have no idea how to use that pathetic imitation of faerie dust you're calling *magic*. You're powerless against me, Elle. I could enslave you right now, throw you into a taxi, and by morning, we'd be somewhere new. We could start over again somewhere else, and *no one would know*. Nobody would ever come looking for you because *nobody cares*."

Every single moment that Elle had ever wanted to fight back rose up inside her at once. She raised her hands and shoved Salvia away. Glittering silver light erupted from her in a flash. Salvia shrieked, a heavy thud sounded from the other side of the room, and when the glow diminished, Elle saw Salvia sprawled across an upturned couch against the far wall. Elle walked toward her struggling, cursing stepmother, hands shaking at her sides. "I didn't come here to fight you," she said between heavy breaths, "but if you to try to touch me again—if you so much as *mention* the slave charm or send one speck of faerie dust in my direction—I won't hesitate to defend myself." Then she turned and made for the door. "I'm getting my things and then I'm leaving," she called back. "I suggest you don't move from that spot until I'm gone."

With hands and legs that still shook slightly, Elle headed for the attic stairs. Her rhinestone-studded combat boots clomped all the way up. At the top, the door to the attic was open. She stepped inside and paused as she took in the moonlit space: the worn, striped rug that covered part of the floorboards, the old, creaky bed, the screen that concealed the makeshift bathroom area, the simple table and chair, and the wardrobe. Though she'd lived here for years and had been free for only a few days, it felt as if this space belonged to another lifetime.

She crossed the room, tugged the quilted bedspread off the bed, and folded it several times. Then she slid her hand between the mattress and bed base and pulled out her pocket watch necklace. As she walked toward the wardrobe, she slipped the necklace over her head. She retrieved the photo album that contained pictures of her parents and selected the few clothing items that looked the least bit like faded rags. Meanwhile, questions knocked at the back of her mind— Where would she live now? How would she buy clothes and food and basic necessities? Could she work for Cress, as she'd suggested when she asked Cress to make a potion that could mimic death?—but she did her best not to focus on them. She would confront those questions after she and Dex had spoken to his father and revealed the truth about humans and magic.

Placing her chosen items on the floor, she knelt down and leaned partway into the wardrobe as she opened the hidden compartment at the back. She stuck her hand inside and grabbed hold of the clothes she'd hidden from Salvia. They were mostly of the sparkly, scandalously short, club-appropriate variety, but there might be a few things worth keeping.

She had chosen two tops and was digging around for a third when her hand brushed a piece of paper. With a frown, she leaned further inside the cupboard and fished around until her fingers found the paper again. She pulled it out—a single sheet folded over once—and opened it. At the sight of Sienna's handwriting, her breath caught in her throat. She sat back, cross-legged, and started reading.

Elle,

I don't know if you'll ever return home and see this. I hope you don't, because at least that means you'll never have to be near Mom again. But in case you do end up back in this attic, I just wanted to let you know my plan.

I'm getting as far away from Mom as I can, and I'm coming to look for you. I have no idea what happened or even where to begin looking, but I can't just sit here and let Mom force me into ruining other people's lives with these never-ending cons. So I may as well try to find you. I know she'll go to the police and they'll try to track me, but I asked a friend at school for help, and I'm pretty sure the charm we got hold of will work.

I hope I find you. I hope we see each other again. But even if we never do, please don't worry about me. I'll be fine. I'm stronger than you think.

Love you,
Sienna

P.S. Mom bought a second-tier wish with all the Essence you spent years collecting. She said something about wanting to wish for it to be impossible for the prince to wish against Meredith's first wish. Something complicated that probably doesn't exist in any wish catalog. Anyway, I've stolen it. I'm not going to use it yet. If I hear that you've returned home, I'll come back for you. We can use it together. I know it can't grant your freedom, but we can wish for something else that'll help. For now, don't give up. One day, you'll have your freedom.

Elle squeezed her eyes shut as a single tear traced down her cheek. A quiet laugh escaped her. Dex had been right: Sienna was stronger than Elle gave her credit for. She had taken a wish, and she would be fine. The fact that no one had been able to track her yet meant that whatever magic her school friend found must have worked.

Elle folded the letter until it was small enough to fit into her pocket. Then she stood and picked up the few items of clothing she'd chosen. She had no idea how she would find Sienna—she didn't want her coming near this house ever again—but somehow, she would make it happen. Maybe Cress could help her.

She stuffed her clothes somewhere amid the folds of the quilt, clutched the bundle against her chest, and held the photo album in one hand. Then she marched downstairs, past the living room, and out of her stepmother's life. As the front door shut behind her with a satisfying bang, it seemed a weight lifted from her shoulders. A long and horrible chapter of her life had finally come to a close. She smiled, and if the folded quilt wasn't currently blocking her view of her feet, she would have skipped down the stairs.

With newfound confidence, she walked to the end of the street, turned the corner, and aimed for Xander's car. Reaching it, she opened the back door and dropped her belongings onto the seat. Dex twisted to face her from the front passenger seat. His bright eyes sparkled as he smiled. "I was just wondering if I should come looking for you, but I shouldn't have worried."

"See?" Xander said from the driver's seat. "Told you she's totally capable of handling her stepmother."

As Elle squeezed in beside the quilt and pulled the door shut, Dex added, "Did everything go okay?"

"Not for Salvia," Elle said, "but in general, yes. I'm fine. She'll be fine— when she recovers from her shock and from being thrown across the room by magic that came out of nowhere."

Xander snickered as he lowered the hand brake and pulled away from the curb. "Things are going to be entertaining until you can get a handle on that."

"Entertaining," Elle repeated. "That's one way of putting it."

"You'll be fine," Dex said. He faced forward but reached one arm back and wrapped his hand comfortingly around Elle's lower leg.

"Yeah, I hope so," she answered. "Especially since it's time for me to meet your father."

TWO

Though Elle guessed it was late, a flurry of activity and whispered conversation followed her and Dex as they strode across polished floors, through lavishly furnished rooms, and past artwork, sculptures and flower arrangements that were probably worth a fortune.

"… wasn't kidnapped …"

"… thought he ran away?"

"Has the king been informed?"

Smartly dressed fae with tiny earpieces crossed their path, while another two strode ahead of them. Other fae—employees or guests, Elle wasn't sure—lingered in corners before hurrying away. Elle kept her eyes pointed forward, but she felt the weight of the stares nonetheless. Dex had one hand firmly wrapped around hers, and when she glanced down, she saw her fingers faintly glowing. Had anyone else noticed? Had they realized the glow was silver and not gold? That it was coming from *her* and not from Dex? They were probably far more interested in the fact that their prince was holding a girl's hand—and that he'd returned home safely—than in a few sparkles of faerie dust.

Not faerie dust, she corrected herself. *Human dust?* That sounded so odd. There must be another name for it.

They stopped in an antechamber furnished with a desk and several cushioned chairs. One of the security people—at least, Elle assumed they were part of security—knocked on the ornately carved wooden door on the other side of the room, while the other stood with his hands behind his back, staring resolutely past Elle.

"Do I look okay?" she whispered to Dex, peering down at herself and rubbing at a smudge of dirt on her jeans. She was still wearing some of the clothes Alissa had given her while she'd been hiding out in the vampire's family home in the Beryl Eternal Night. The jeans were newer and more stylish than any Elle had owned before, and the sweater—decorated with gold buttons along the shoulders—fitted her perfectly. But she'd tumbled over the ground in this outfit while traveling through the Never Woods, and there were probably leaves and twigs and bits of dirt in places she couldn't even see.

"You look beautiful," Dex said.

Elle rolled her eyes and rubbed at her jeans again. "I doubt your father will think so." She tucked the pocket watch necklace beneath her sweater while wishing she could change her combat boots for something less chunky.

"You have nothing to worry about," Dex assured her. "Don't be nervous."

He wasn't looking at her as he said that last part, and she wondered for a moment if he was talking more to himself than to her. She remembered his accidental confession about his greatest fear being his father, and now they were about to confront him and tell him something he probably didn't want to hear.

"Hey, are *you* okay?" she asked.

On the other side of the door, a deep voice spoke, and the security guy opened the door. He stepped inside, but Dex remained where he was. He opened his mouth, then spluttered over something. Turning away, he coughed before taking a deep breath. Elle gave him a rueful smile as he turned back to her. "You were going to say yes?" she asked.

"I'm sorry. I didn't even realize it was a lie until I couldn't force the word out of my mouth. I … I guess I'm not?" He turned away from the security guard and muttered, "That was not something I wanted to admit out loud. I'm supposed to be …" He shook his head, pressing his lips together.

"What, all macho and tough and afraid of nothing?" Elle joked quietly.

"Yeah, exactly," he responded with a half smile.

Before Elle could say anything else, the man with the suit and earpiece stepped back out and said, "Excuse me, your highness. His majesty will see you now."

Dex turned back to the door, placed an arm around Elle's lower back, and ushered her forward. Elle took a steadying breath as they stepped into the next room. Her brain registered a vague impression of a richly furnished study—dark wood furniture, thick curtains and loads of books—but most of her attention fell immediately on the man who stood behind the desk. He walked around it, stopped a few paces away, and folded his arms over his chest as he regarded them.

Elle already knew what King Belaric of House Belmont looked like. She'd seen him occasionally on TV. But he seemed taller and far more imposing in person, as if his mere presence took up most of the space in the room. His hair was lighter than Dex's, but the two of them shared the same jawline and eye color—though the king's lacked the warmth and kindness Elle often saw in Dex's gaze.

"Chevalier," the king said. "I hope you have a good explanation for your recent disappearance." His eyes fell on Elle, though it was still his son he spoke to when he added, "And your insistence upon appearing before me in the company of this human instead of alone."

"I do have a very good explanation, sir," Dex said, and for a moment, the only thing Elle could focus on was the fact that Dex called his father 'sir.' An image of her own father—whom she couldn't imagine having ever called 'sir'—crossed her mind before she blinked and refocused on the king. "We've discovered something," Dex continued. "Something huge. Something that will change everything for humans—for all the High Races, in fact, since it will change the way society views humans and interacts with them."

The king's eyes narrowed. "I doubt it."

"It's *magic*, sir," Dex said, his voice alight with passion. "Humans can obtain magic. Hundreds of years ago, it was a normal way of life. Humans can go on a quest, and at the end of it, they walk away with magic. We can't enslave them. They're our *equals*." He looked at Elle and gave her an encouraging nod. "Show him."

Elle raised her hands, afraid that at this moment, when she really needed it to, her newfound magic would refuse to appear. But her heart was pounding so fast, her body so on edge, that glittering silver dust rushed all the way up to her elbows before she'd finished lifting her hands. She inhaled sharply, unable to keep her amazement from spreading a smile across her face. She was certain it would awe her every single time it happened, no matter how long she lived.

She looked up at the king, and her smile faded at the sight of his face. Aside from a slight twist to his lips, his expression had barely changed. No shock. No surprise. No wonder. "You already know," Elle said, the truth of her own words sinking into her bones. The king didn't answer, but his expression was enough to tell her she was right.

"Wait. You *knew* about this?" Dex demanded.

"Of course I knew," his father replied. "I went through all our archives years ago. I discovered the document that refers to the humans' quest for magic. I sent a human with three companions to the Never Woods to find out if it was true. They survived. The human returned with magic, proving that what I'd read was true. I killed all four of them immediately."

"What?" Elle gasped. "How could you do that? Whether you like humans or not, you can't change the fact that we're your equals. How could you ignore the truth once you knew it? How can you continue to—"

"I will do whatever I must to preserve our way of life. To protect the legacy of the fae. Our race has worked hard to be where it is today. I won't let anyone take that from us."

"We don't want to *take* anything from—"

"Silly girl," the king spat. "You're naive if you think that. *Everyone* wants power. Shifters are too weak to take it, vampires are currently *trying* to take it, and humans—if they all obtained the power you now have—would try to take it too."

"But trying to contain this information is pointless," Dex said. A deep frown furrowed his brow. "The secret is already out. There are vampires who know. You saw them all with magic at the ball. They discovered they can take it from humans after humans have been through the quest, and now that there are so many of them who know—*and* there were all those witnesses at the ball who have no doubt been asking questions ever since—"

"The vampires who attacked me at the ball are dead," the king interrupted, "and I will wipe the rest of them from the face of the planet. Of course, a few will remain who know the truth, but that's nothing new. There have always been some who know. It's never been enough to make any difference. Just as it makes no difference that guests of our masquerade ball might be asking questions. Someone will probably come up with the theory that it's possible for vampires to take magic from fae blood after all."

"But everyone knows that's not true," Elle said.

"It's easier to believe than humans with magic," the king countered.

She pushed her shoulders back and tilted her chin up. "Not after I show them what I can do."

The king's expression turned pitying. "You don't honestly think you'll be leaving this palace alive, do you?"

"Dad!" Dex exclaimed.

"Don't pretend to be so shocked," his father said with a sigh. "You know I can't let her live."

Dex moved to shield Elle with his body. "Don't even think about—"

"Restrain him," the king said, his gaze directed behind Elle and Dex. Suddenly there were four men in suits surrounding Dex, magic zapping away from them and tugging Dex's hands behind his back. "I'm sorry, Chevalier, but this is for the best," the king said as Dex was dragged toward the edge of the room. "You'll come to understand in time. If the Darkness doesn't take you soon, that is."

The Darkness … Of course, the king didn't know yet that Dex had been healed. But Elle had no time to contemplate whether blurting this out would make things better or worse because the king was advancing toward her. "Wait," she said, stumbling backward. "You can't just *kill* me."

"I'm the king," he said, raising his hands. "I can do whatever I want." His magic was like the golden sparks of a fire dancing amid black smoke. It rushed toward her with the sound of flapping wings, blocking out Dex's cries and smothering Elle instantly. It enveloped her in darkness. She couldn't breathe, couldn't move, and she knew that this was the end.

The darkness cleared, and Elle blinked at the light. Was this the After? Was death so quick and painless? But when she blinked again and turned her head, she realized she was on the floor of the king's study. Still awake, still alive. And the black smothering magic was gone. She sat up just as the king appeared right in front of her. He snatched hold of her arm and glared at her wrist. "So. You have the Godmother's protection. That's inconvenient." He shoved her arm away and stepped back. "I suppose you'll have to spend the remainder of your days in prison then."

"W-what protection?" Elle stuttered, looking down at her arm. On the inside of her wrist was a symbol, as pale as a scar. An S-shaped curve with three lines and a loop. The symbol Elle had traced into the dust on her window the night she'd summoned the Godmother. "When ... I don't remember ..."

"Take her away," the king commanded. Another two men appeared—were there legions of these dark-suited men simply waiting within earshot to be summoned by the king?—and lifted Elle swiftly to her feet. "And be sure to restrain her with magic."

"Stop!" Dex shouted, struggling against the four who held him in place while the two newcomers attached a pair of glowing gold manacles to Elle's wrists. "Get your hands off her!"

"Don't fight them," his father said calmly, walking back around his desk. "You'll only end up hurt, and it's probably not a good idea to exacerbate your condition."

"What do you think this is going to accomplish?" Dex cried. "*I* know the truth. Others know the truth. Soon *everyone* will know. The National Council won't let you—"

"No one will know a thing," King Belaric said as the two men dragged Elle toward the door. "I have kept the truth from spreading before, and I will do so again. This secret will remain buried forever."

Then Elle was swept away through the antechamber, her mind racing through all the terrible threats the king might currently be making in order to ensure his son's silence. She kicked and struggled until eventually she managed to land an elbow in the ribs of the man on her left. She was rewarded with a heavy grunt in response—before light flashed across her vision and pain struck her head. The world became black for several seconds before color slowly returned. Whether intentionally or by accident, she hadn't been completely knocked out.

Her surroundings became a blur of hallways, staircases, broad metal doors and sliding, mechanical gates. The light around her grew dimmer, and when she was eventually thrown onto a cold, hard floor, it seemed for several long moments that she was in complete darkness. Even the glowing gold manacles around her wrists were gone. But as she blinked and her eyes slowly adjusted to the low light, she made out crisscrossing bars, a simple bed, and shapes that roughly resembled a basin and toilet.

Pushing herself up and squinting further into the dim light produced by a single bulb hanging outside her cell, Elle realized there were no walls separating her from the neighboring cells, only more metal bars, scratched and discolored. The air smelled damp and stale, and she wondered just how long—decades? Centuries?—this part of the palace had existed. It was a world away from the glittering hallways she'd been dragged through just minutes before.

"Hello?" a voice called.

Elle stood hastily, regretting the quick movement a moment later when renewed pain throbbed through her skull. She turned, seeking the source of the voice.

"This side," the voice said, and Elle turned again. The owner of the voice, a woman, materialized from the shadows of the cell on Elle's right. Dressed in ragged, dirty clothes—no prison uniform—she moved slowly toward the bars. "Hello," she said again. "What's your name?"

Without answering, Elle moved a little closer to the bars. There was something about the woman's voice that struck a bell in her memory. She took another step forward.

"Don't touch the bars," the woman said. "They don't look it, but they're enchanted. They'll zap you and shove you backward. The main reason is so you can't throw magic at the guards, but the charm also reacts to your touch. Although ..." She tilted her head a little. "It doesn't look like you're fae, so you probably won't be tossing any magic around."

The bell somewhere deep in Elle's memory jangled louder. Though she couldn't place it, she'd definitely heard that voice before. The woman came to a stop on the other side of the bars, and Elle moved forward yet another step. Through the dim light and dark shadows, she finally saw the woman's face. It was covered in smudges of dirt and framed by blond hair that was straggly and limp, but it was still instantly recognizable. Elle had known this face as a child. She'd seen it countless times in her parents' photo album, and again, only days ago, on Dex's phone.

"Liana?"

THREE

Four security guards shoved Dex into a chair in front of his father's desk and stepped away. He sat awkwardly, his hands still bound by magic behind his back, as his father lowered himself into the chair on the other side of the desk. "I cannot believe you would put our country—the entire *world*, for that matter—at risk for a simple *girl*."

"The entire world?" Dex repeated. "That's a massive overreaction. And don't speak about Elle like—"

"Have you forgotten what happened to your grandmother? Have you forgotten what happened last weekend at the ball? It's far too dangerous for any other race to have the same kind of power we have. If all humans in the world end up with magic, they will destroy us."

"No they won't! Most humans are *not* interested in destroying anyone. They just want to be—"

"YES THEY ARE!" The king brought his fist down on the desk. "You don't know anything. You have stupid ideas about all High Races coexisting peacefully, but that will never be the case. There will always be people who want to take what we've worked so hard for. I was hoping you'd eventually get your head out of the clouds and understand this simple truth, but you'll probably be dead before that happens."

Dex flinched. For a second or two, he couldn't say a word. Then he opened his mouth to tell his father he was no longer sick, but the king spoke again before Dex could utter a word. "I've always hoped we'd find a way to cure the

Darkness running through your blood, but now I wonder if your early death may be a blessing in disguise. You would only fail our people if you ended up ruling them. Our hope lies in the hands of the next generation, not with you. Which is why you *will* produce an heir before you succumb to the Darkness."

Dex sat frozen, his mouth open but not a word able to pass his tongue. An ache formed at the back of his throat and behind his eyes. He blinked once before snapping his mouth shut. He would tell his father nothing. If the king preferred to believe his son would soon die, then that was the way it would stay. "May I be excused?" he asked, his voice tight. Elle was probably locked in one of the ancient prison cells far beneath the palace, and Dex needed to figure out exactly how to get down there—he'd never been allowed access before—and how to free her. He could worry about everything else afterwards.

"Yes, but only after we've discussed one final matter: your desire to spread the truth about the quest and the ability of humans to possess magic."

Dex clenched his jaw, knowing that whatever came next wouldn't be good.

"The human girl. You care for her."

Dex's heart began a slow descent toward his feet. He should never have revealed how much he cared about Elle. Of course his father would use it against him.

"If you breathe a word to anyone, I *will* kill her," his father said slowly, deliberately, his ice-blue eyes unblinking. "I will find a way to get past the Godmother's protection. The girl will die a slow and terrible death, and I will make you watch."

For a moment, Dex wondered when his father had become the cruel man who sat before him now. When he cast his mind back to his childhood, he remembered a different father. One who was mostly serious, but who sometimes smiled and laughed. Someone who occasionally sought out his sons in the palace gardens so he could join in their games for a short while. When had the king begun to change? Was it before or after Dex's grandmother's death? Was it the moment he'd made a wish and been granted great power by the Godmother? Perhaps Dex and his brother weren't the only ones who'd been touched by Darkness that day. Perhaps a different kind of darkness, slow and invisible—a darkness of the soul—had begun to corrupt the king after that wish was made.

"What if someone else spreads the truth?" Dex said. "There are others who know."

"Well, then you'll have to do everything in your power to silence those people. If I begin to hear rumors of this quest, it won't matter exactly who started them. I'll assume they can ultimately be traced back to you, and therefore I'll have to take out my retribution on that poor human girl."

Dex breathed out slowly. There was no point in arguing. "Will that be all?" he asked.

"Yes." The king traced a quick pattern in the air, and with a brief burst of heat, Dex felt the magical bonds vanish from his wrists. Without another word, he stood and walked out of the room. He crossed the antechamber, turned into a hallway—and almost walked straight into his mother.

"Chevalier!" Queen Amra exclaimed. Before he could utter a word, she tugged him closer and embraced him. It was so unexpected—his mother wasn't prone to displays of affection—that all Dex could do was stand there. By the time his arms remembered how to work and started moving to return the embrace, his mother stepped away. "Where have you been?" she demanded. Wisps of dark hair had come loose from the tight knot that sat at the nape of her neck, and a grayish purple hue darkened the delicate skin beneath her eyes.

"I'm so sorry, Mom," Dex said, his insides squirming uncomfortably with guilt. "It's a long story."

"Oliver and Alexander intimated it was because of a girl. Someone who'd tempted you to run away."

Dex sighed. "I did not run away to be with a girl."

"I assumed as much," his mother responded, her tone still sharp. "You've been far too resistant to the whole idea of marriage to elope. But I had to consider there might be some dark magic at play. That perhaps someone bewitched you. Nobody could track you, Chevalier. Not with magic or technology. What was I supposed to think?"

"Nobody bewitched me, Mom. I'm fine. And I'm so sorry for worrying you. I didn't know how much time had passed. I know that doesn't make sense, but—"

"Well, at least you're back now." The queen patted his shoulders. "And you won't be disappearing again. The party is this Saturday, and it is of the utmost importance. With only two days to go, and you still missing, I thought I'd have to cancel it. I'm relieved that's no longer the case."

Dex shook his head, confused by the sudden change of subject. "Party?"

"Yes." His mother gave him the kind of look that suggested he should know exactly what she was talking about. "The smaller, more intimate affair your father asked me to organize, since the masquerade ball was such a disaster. I had hoped you would have found someone by now, but it seems some people don't keep their promises, so this party is still necessary."

Dex's frown deepened. He couldn't remember ever *promising* to find someone to marry. "Mom, the party isn't necessary. I have found someone." He didn't specify whether he'd found someone to *marry*. He had no idea if his relationship with Elle would lead to that. All he knew at this point was that he didn't want to spend time with any other girl.

"You have?" his mother asked. For a moment, something that might have been hope brightened her gaze.

"Yes. You may have seen her leaving Dad's study a few minutes ago."

"That human girl the guards were dragging away?"

"Yes."

"Oh, for goodness sake, Chevalier." His mother sighed. "Please be serious."

"I am being serious."

"You can't marry a *human*. Your father will never allow it. When we invited all the High Races to the Moonlight Masquerade Ball, it was simply to make a show of being inclusive. You know that. You need to find someone fae, and you need to do it fast. You're running out of—"

"Time? I'm not." Dex gripped his mother's arms and gave her a reassuring smile. He knew the truth would find its way back to his father if he spoke it out loud now, but he couldn't keep it from his mother. It had broken her heart to lose her first son, and Dex knew it was breaking her heart all over again knowing she would lose her second son as well. "Mom, the Darkness is gone."

Queen Amra blinked, then shook her head. "What?"

"It's gone. Elle—the human girl you so quickly dismissed—wished for it."

The queen was still shaking her head. "Not possible. The price would have been—"

"The price was specific to Elle, and she paid it. Mom, I stopped taking Cress's potion days ago, before I disappeared, and—"

"*What?* You were still taking that dragon shifter's potion? Chevalier, we spoke about this."

"We did, and I decided to ignore you. The potion helped to keep the symptoms away, so I figured it was better to take it than *not* to take it. But you're missing my point, Mom. I haven't taken it in at least five days, and I've had *no* symptoms whatsoever. The Godmother healed me."

His mother stared at him, a frown pulling her eyebrows low. "I don't believe it," she said softly. "The Godmother is too cruel for that. I thought I may have been wrong about her, but I'm not."

"She is cruel. You're definitely right about that. But Elle wished for her to take the Darkness away, and she did."

"A human's wish saved you?"

"Is that so hard to believe?"

His mother exhaled slowly, her gaze drifting away from Dex's. "Yes." Then she turned and began walking away.

"Mom!" he called after her. She looked back, countless emotions warring in her eyes. "Would it make any difference if I told you Elle has magic?" Dex asked.

Moments passed. Silence settled between Dex and his mother. Eventually, she spoke. "You believe the Darkness is gone, and that a human girl possesses magic?"

"Yes."

Unshed tears glistened in her eyes. "What has the Godmother done to you?"

"Nothing! I mean, nothing *bad*," Dex corrected. "Well, she did throw a blade at me, but she healed me of that as part of the—"

"Stop," the queen said. She set her jaw and pushed her shoulders back. "I need to go. I have a meeting to arrange."

Dex watched her walk away. Then, with a final sigh, he turned in the opposite direction. His father was cruel and his mother was blind, and there was nothing he could do about either of them. But he could find Elle and free her. So that was what he would do.

FOUR

Elle stared into the confused eyes of the woman on the other side of the prison cell bars. "Liana," she repeated. "It is you."

"Who are you?" Liana asked. "How do you know me?"

Elle inched closer, wanting to take hold of the bars so she could pull herself right up against them. But Liana's warning was still clear in her mind. "You and my mom were good friends," she said. "And you were Dex's nanny. You found out the truth about humans and magic, and you told my mom. The wrong people ended up finding out, and the vampire, Nazario Savoy, tracked you down and learned everything from you."

Liana's eyebrows pulled lower. "Elle?"

"Yes." She gave Liana a small smile. "I guess I probably look a little different from the last time you saw me. It's been … I don't know, thirteen or fourteen years?"

Liana let her eyes drift shut. "It feels far longer. It feels as though I've spent many lifetimes down here in the darkness. Sometimes I wonder how I haven't yet gone mad."

"But how did you end up here? When the Godmother told me the story, she said you were killed."

Liana opened her eyes and narrowed them. "Either she lied, or she doesn't know that I survived both the vampires and King Belaric."

"What happened?"

"I made a wish. Not through the Godmother," she added quickly. "It was a third-tier wish for protection against non-accidental death."

"Oh, so you can only die of natural causes? Or an accident of some sort?"

"Yes. Which, if you think about it, you shouldn't have to *wish* for. But evil exists, and sometimes people want to kill you. So I guess someone decided that wish should be possible."

"Yeah, I guess," Elle murmured, wondering why King Belaric hadn't used that wish instead of bargaining with the Godmother. But perhaps it wouldn't have worked for exactly what he wanted. Dex had said his father wished that no one would ever be able to take the throne from him. And someone *could* take it without actually killing him—if they defeated him and overpowered his armies—so protection against non-accidental death wouldn't have helped. The most likely situation was that he'd done both: the third-tier protection wish *and* the wish he'd made through the Godmother.

"So Nazario Savoy couldn't kill me," Liana continued. "I managed to escape him, only to land up in King Belaric's hands. He tried to kill me too, to keep me from spreading the truth I'd discovered. When he realized he couldn't, he locked me up here. And here I've been ever since."

"So … you haven't been moved at all? You haven't seen the outside world in all those years?"

Liana shook her head. "You don't know what I'd give to see the sun again." The longing in her gaze shifted to concern. "But tell me about you, Elle. What did you do to end up down here?"

"I …" Elle moved back a little so she could safely raise her hands without touching the bars. Despite her circumstances, a thrill stirred inside her yet again at the reminder of the power she now possessed. "I did it," she said as silver dust-like particles began to rise from her hands. "The quest. I have magic. The king tried to kill me because of it, but apparently I've somehow ended up with the Godmother's protection. So instead, I'm supposed to spend the rest of my life hidden away down here." She lifted her gaze and found Liana staring wide-eyed at the silver magic glowing in the air around her hands.

"Incredible," Liana whispered. "It's beautiful. Your parents must be so proud of you. I assume they completed the quest years ago?"

The glittering magic dissipated as a dull ache settled in Elle's chest. She lowered her hands to her sides. It seemed strange that Liana didn't know, but of course she wouldn't. When she'd been caught and thrown into this prison, Elle's mother and father were still alive. "My parents …" she said slowly. Even after all this time, it was still difficult to say the words out loud. "They're both dead."

Liana stared, her lips parted but no sound passing them. Slowly, she lowered herself to the floor of her cell. She pressed a fist against her lips, and Elle wondered if she might be crying, but when she lowered her hand and looked up, her gaze burned with anger. "Did the king kill them?"

Elle shook her head. She sat and crossed her legs. "I don't think the king was ever aware they knew his secret."

"Good. I tried to be as vague as possible when I was interrogated with a truth spell. I managed to keep the most important identifying details about your mother to myself, but still, I wasn't sure."

"Well, maybe the king did know, but if so, he never managed to find us. My mom died because she got sick." Elle looked down at her hands twisting together in her lap. "She was so weak and in so much pain, and after she was gone, my dad always tried to explain to me that it was better for her that way. That she was no longer hurting. She was at peace. But I didn't understand or agree. I was only six. I just wanted my mom back."

"Only six," Liana said. "So it wasn't long after I was captured. And what about your father? What happened to him?"

Elle drew her knees up and wrapped her arms around them. "It was just the two of us for a long time. Dad worked hard, and his business did well, and we lived in a nice house. You don't always know or understand the details of a situation when you're a child, but it seemed to me he was pretty well respected for a human."

Liana nodded. "I can see that. He had the kind of personality that drew people in. And his business was already starting to do well when I knew him."

"Then he met this woman when I was twelve," Elle continued. "Salvia." She ground her stepmother's name out between her teeth before taking a deep breath and forging on. "I guess she wasn't too bad in the beginning. She was nice to me, and I could tell she cared for my dad. She had a lot of her own wealth—her first husband had passed away and left her everything—but she liked the fact that Dad was a successful entrepreneur in his field. And I think she also liked ..." Elle pursed her lips, trying to figure out how to put this part into words. "You know when something's new and kind of not that cool *yet*, but you can see it starting to become cool and you want to be one of the trendsetters?"

Liana nodded. "I know what you mean."

"I think that's kind of how Salvia felt about marrying a human. She had to ignore plenty of snide comments from some of her fae friends, but because of the increasing hype around the different High Races accepting one another and seeing each other as equals, there were more and more people who admired her and my dad for being together. They were wealthy and successful and *different*, and people liked that."

"I assume something went wrong?" Liana asked.

"Yes. Very wrong. My dad's business partner cheated him out of pretty much everything. I never knew the details, but I know he stole a whole lot from the business, ran away, and left my dad with a huge amount of debt. I don't know why, but Salvia blamed Dad. She said he took way too many irresponsible risks with no thought for his family. That he gambled his own money and Salvia's inheritance and then lost it all. I remember hearing her yelling at him about how he'd betrayed her and never loved her and only ever wanted to use her for her money. I thought they were going to end up divorced. They probably would have if ..."

"If what?" Liana asked quietly.

"A vampire came to our house one night. It was in that transition period after we'd lost everything but before we were forced to leave Salvia's beautiful home in the Arabesque Hills. I don't know what the vampire wanted, but now I wonder if he may have been looking for me." She lifted her eyes to Liana's and sighed. "That's another whole story. My mom and the Godmother and a wish and me ending up with a weird ability to remove people's memories. That's how I made Nazario Savoy forget everything he learned from you. And then I accidentally took all his memories and ended up killing him."

"Wait, what? *What?*"

"Yeah. That's why vampires haven't tried to go against King Belaric until now. They didn't actually know about taking magic from humans. That's a recent discovery for them. Which I guess you don't know about, seeing as how you've been stuck down here."

Liana slowly shook her head. "No," she said faintly. "I thought maybe they had tried and failed years ago, after stealing the knowledge from me."

"Anyway, back to the vampire who showed up at our house one night. There was a fight, and he bit my dad, and then … I don't know what happened to the vampire. Maybe he ran away, or maybe Dad killed him and I just never saw or knew about that part. It was all a horrible traumatic blur. And then … then Dad started turning." Elle looked away, blinking to keep her tears back. She swallowed and cleared her throat. "He didn't allow the transformation to complete itself. He—he killed himself before that could happen."

"Oh, Elle," Liana whispered. "I'm so sorry."

"It's—I didn't actually see it. See him. Like that, I mean. Some of Salvia's friends were at the house by then, and they kept us—my two stepsisters and me—from seeing anything." Elle exhaled an unsteady breath. "Afterwards, we moved into a little townhouse. The only asset Salvia still owned. I thought she was going to throw me out—she hated me so much by then—but she wanted to use my memory-wiping ability. So she put the slave charm on me instead."

"She *what?*" Liana shouted, startling Elle as she smacked her palm down on the cold stone floor. "She *enslaved* you?"

Something about Liana's burst of anger cleared the remnants of sadness from Elle's mind. A shaky laugh escaped her lips. "I'm free now, don't worry. That's another long story, but I'm free. Well, I guess I'm technically *not* free, since I'm currently locked in a prison cell, but at least I'm not a slave. And hopefully Dex will get me out. And he can get you out too!" she added. "I'm sure he would have tried already if he knew you were down here."

Liana gave her a curious smile. "So you're still friends with Dex? How did that happen? If I wasn't around to help him sneak out of the palace, and your mom wasn't around to bring you to meet him ..."

"Oh, no, we only recently met up," Elle said. "Completely by accident. We had no idea until a few days ago that we actually knew each other when we were children. I walked into him outside a club a few weeks ago. Literally walked into him. And after that ... I don't know. It was like fate threw us together again, and then we ended up teaming up against vampires, and somehow I think I've maybe ... sort of ..." She lifted her shoulders and whispered, "Fallen in love?"

Liana's lips stretched into a grin. Then she started laughing.

"What's so funny?"

"Hey, would you shut up over there?" someone yelled. "Talking, shouting and now *laughing*? I'm trying to sleep!"

Elle clapped a hand over her mouth, then lowered it as she whispered, "There's someone else down here?"

"On the other side of my cell," Liana whispered. "A grouchy shifter woman, plus another faerie woman on the other side of the shifter's cell. Anyway, I was laughing because ... well, it's just that your mom and I used to joke about that very thing. You and Dex. You two were so sweet, playing together as children. I know he would have preferred to play with someone his own age, but he never complained about the fact that you were so young. I think the whole escape-the-palace part was so thrilling that he was happy to do pretty much anything once we got out. Your mom was such a romantic. She saw how patient and caring Dex was, and she used to say that maybe the two of you would grow up and fall in love one day. I guess I was a romantic too, since I kind of hoped her words might come true, even though I thought it was probably unlikely a fae prince and a human girl would end up together."

"Yeah, that part hasn't changed," Elle said grimly. "I mean, Dex doesn't care that I'm human, but it seems his father hates humans more with every passing day. The fact that we can acquire magic and should technically have the same rights as all other magic-blooded High Races means nothing to him."

"I'm sorry. I had hoped that might have changed after all these years. But I'm relieved to hear Dex doesn't share his father's views. I always hoped he would turn out a better man than King Belaric."

Elle smiled, feeling heat rise to her face. "He is. He definitely is. You probably had more of an influence on him than you realize. Not just his feelings about the other High Races, but the fact that he turned out just as daring as you. He started investigating the vampire group that was abducting humans because the police were getting nowhere. And he still sneaks away from the palace without permission whenever he can—even though it seems silly that he has to do the *sneaking* part now that he's an adult."

Liana groaned. "All that sneaking around I helped him do years ago was so foolish. I always knew that. But he begged and begged until I couldn't help but say yes. Not that I hold him responsible, of course. I was the adult. I should have said no."

"Well, Dex is glad you didn't say no." Elle paused as a yawn so wide it felt like it might crack her jaw overcame her. "So there's no point," she continued when she could finally speak again, "in regretting what you did."

"You look like you could probably do with some sleep," Liana said, pushing herself up from the floor. "We can talk in the morning."

Elle nodded. Sometime within the last few minutes, bone-weary exhaustion had settled itself over her. Adrenaline had kept her going until now, but it seemed she'd finally been sapped of all her energy. "I don't know how long it's been since I last had a full night of sleep," she mumbled as she climbed to her feet. "It was before the quest. That's all I remember. Since then, time has become …" She shook her head. "I don't know. Confusing." She frowned at Liana. "Wait, how do you know it's night?"

"Meals," Liana said. "The last one we had was dinner, which must mean it's night time."

"Oh, right." Elle turned slowly to face the skinny bed standing against the back wall of her cell. "Well, good night, I guess."

"Elle, wait," Liana said, and Elle turned back to her. "Do you really think Dex will come for you? Would he go against his father like that?"

"Yes," Elle said without hesitation. "I know he will."

FIVE

Despite the uncomfortable metal ridges of the bed frame digging into her back through the skinny mattress, Elle fell into a deep sleep almost immediately and didn't wake until the door of her cell clanged the next morning. She sat up in fright, her heart racing as she blinked several times at a woman in a palace guard's uniform striding away from her cell. The dim light hadn't changed, but as Liana had said, it was the food sitting on a metal tray on the floor that hinted at what time of day it was.

Elle climbed off the bed and made her way toward the bowl of white mush that smelled like it might be porridge. "Perhaps it's just that I've grown used to it," Liana said from the neighboring cell, "but it's my opinion that the food they give us isn't all that bad."

"You've been here too long!" someone further along the line of cells shouted at her.

"Yeah, well, maybe it helps that I'm not a snob in the food department," Liana shouted back.

Elle bent to pick up the bowl and spoon, then walked toward the bars separating her from Liana, raising the bowl to sniff the contents. She tried a small mouthful, chewing and swallowing as she came to a stop in front of the bars. "Doesn't taste too bad to me either," she said, "but my standards aren't exactly high. I mean, I like to think I cooked pretty good food for my stepmother while I was a slave, but I'm used to shoveling cold leftovers into my mouth while simultaneously cleaning the kitchen. Eating warm food while standing still is something of a novelty for me—even though I've now been doing it for about … I don't know, two weeks?" She paused, thinking back to the few nights she'd spent in a vampire mansion in one of the Eternal Nights, and the week prior to that when she'd been locked in her attic. How long had it actually been since she'd spent a normal day as a normal slave in Salvia's house?

"You could sit," Liana suggested, one eyebrow raised. "You might enjoy the food even more."

Elle smiled. "Right. I guess I could." She sat on the floor in front of the bars and crossed her legs. After rubbing her sleepy eyes, she took another mouthful of porridge.

"One of the guards should bring you a few basic necessities at some point," Liana said, sitting opposite Elle with her own bowl. "Toothbrush, a bar of soap, that kind of thing."

Elle looked around. "Are there showers somewhere?"

"Yes, down one of the passages. They take us to shower every few days. In between, there's the basin and toilet in your cell. You can be grateful we're all women in this section of the dungeon, seeing as how we have practically zero privacy."

"Yeah, I suppose it could be worse," Elle said. She and Liana continued eating, and Liana fired questions at her after almost every mouthful.

"Did your parents complete the quest before they died?"

"No. At least, not that I know of. I never saw either of them with magic."

"Do you still see any of your parents' other friends?"

"No."

"Is that TV show *Three Shifters and a Pizza Place* still really popular?"

"Um, never heard of it."

"Last night, you said something about having the Godmother's protection. What did you mean?"

"Yes, it's—" Elle pushed her sleeve up and looked at her arm, but the symbol was gone from her wrist. "Well, it *was* there. The Godmother's symbol. You know, the one you use if you want to summon her. It was pale, like a scar, and it appeared when the king tried to kill me."

"Interesting. You've obviously had some recent dealings with her? She told you I'd been killed, and I assume she's the one who told you all about the quest and humans having magic?"

"Yes. I, uh, summoned her for a wish—"

"Elle—"

"And before you go telling me what a bad idea that was, I *know*. But I was desperate. And I think—I think?—our deal is complete and I owe her nothing else. That's what she said, but … I don't know. Can you ever really trust the Godmother?"

"Probably not. What were you talking about last night when you said your mother wished for something and you ended up with a strange ability to remove memories?"

"Oh, that was after Savoy caught you and learned that vampires could take magic from humans once they had it. My mom wanted to stop him from doing that, but she had no idea how, so she summoned the Godmother and—Oh!" Elle paused as something occurred to her. "Maybe that's why the Godmother said you'd been killed. Maybe that's what my mom told her. Did you ever see her again after Savoy captured you?"

Liana shook her head. "After I escaped, the king got hold of me before I could speak to anyone else. I suppose it makes sense that your mom might have assumed Savoy killed me."

"Yes. Unless *nothing* happened the way the Godmother told me, which I guess is also possible. Anyway, apparently the Godmother told my mom …" Elle trailed off, her spoon hovering over her half-finished porridge as the sound of footsteps reached her ears. She looked over her shoulder. A woman dressed in ordinary clothing with a scarf covering most of her head walked slowly toward her cell.

"That's not a guard," Liana whispered. Elle placed her bowl on the floor and stood quickly. Behind her, she heard Liana do the same. Further along the row of cells, someone else was whispering now.

The unknown woman came to a stop in front of the gate to Elle's cell. Slowly, she lowered the hood created by her scarf. The dim light illuminated part of her face, and Elle's breath caught at the sight of Queen Amra, Dex's mother. "Are you the new prisoner?" the queen asked.

"Yes. Um, your majesty," Elle added quickly.

The queen's gaze traveled across Elle's face and she nodded. "Yes, I recognize you. You're the one they were dragging away last night." She lifted her right hand and gold light flared into existence, forming a sphere above her palm. Elle blinked and squinted as the queen raised the light until it was level with her face. Then she lowered her hand, and the light vanished. "You're human," the queen said, and Elle realized the purpose of the light must have been to check whether her pupils changed shape or not.

"Yes, I'm human," she confirmed. She realized she was fidgeting with the chain at her neck, causing the pocket watch to twitch beneath her sweater. She hastily lowered her hand to her side.

"Chevalier told me you have magic. Is this true?"

Elle nodded. She cleared her throat and added, "Yes, your majesty."

"Show me," the queen commanded.

"Oh. Okay. I don't really know if it will …" She trailed off as her hands began to glow. Perhaps it was as easy as *wanting* it to happen. Perhaps magic responded to her desire to use it. She lifted her hands as silver particles appeared amid the glow rising from her skin. The queen took a few quick steps backward. "Don't worry," Elle said. "The bars are enchanted. The magic can't get to you."

"I—I know. I was startled, that's all." The queen lifted her chin and made an admirable attempt at smoothing away the shock from her face. "I've never seen … why is it silver?"

"I don't know."

"I recently saw vampires with magic. I tried to convince myself they must be fae somehow masquerading as vampires, but after what Chevalier told me last night, my mind kept going back to them. Do you know how this is possible?"

Elle nodded again. "Vampires get magic by taking it from humans. I don't know *how*, but I've been told that's where they get it from. That's why the rate of human abductions has risen dramatically recently. A group of vampires discovered this is possible."

"And when a vampire takes a human's magic, it ends up gold," the queen mused. "How interesting."

"Y-yes," Elle said. "I suppose it is."

"Well." The queen took another step back. "Thank you." Then she turned and walked away.

Elle stared into the shadows for several long moments after the queen disappeared.

"Hey, Liana," the shifter on the other side of Liana's cell called. "Guess you were telling the truth all these years."

Elle looked back at Liana. "That was weird, right?"

"Definitely. In all my time locked up here, I've never once seen the queen."

Elle walked back toward her. "So the shifter lady knows?" she asked quietly, her gaze moving behind Liana to the woman in the next cell. "About the quest and everything?"

Liana nodded. "Can't exactly spend years in the same space as someone else and not share all your secrets. And even though she's grumpy and we like to yell at each other, she's not that bad. Right, Jax?" she asked in a louder voice, tossing a grin over her shoulder.

"Frenemies for life," Jax called back.

Elle peered further past Liana and raised her hand in a brief wave. "Um, hi."

"Hey, human girl with magic. I'm guessing that's what got you locked down here?"

"There's a human here with magic?" someone called out from further away, and Elle moved to the side until she could see the shadowy figure in the cell beyond Jax's. "I always thought Liana was nuts when she said that was possible."

"Me too," Jax said.

Liana rolled her eyes. "Thanks a lot, guys."

"So she's fae?" Elle asked. "The woman at the far end?"

"Yes. That's Myra. We're all locked down here because King Belaric would like to get rid of us but, for various reasons, he can't."

"He's hoping we'll all end up dying before he does," Jax added, walking back to her bed and dropping onto it. It squeaked loudly in protest.

Elle looked at Liana again. "Don't you think it's interesting that the queen came down here to check if Dex was telling her the truth? Surely she could have asked her husband."

"Perhaps she did, and maybe she didn't believe her husband either and wanted to see it with her own eyes. Or, more likely, King Belaric told her it was nonsense but she wanted to find out for herself anyway."

Elle frowned. "You think he'd want to keep the truth from her along with everyone else?"

Liana shrugged and sighed. "I don't know. Maybe things have changed, but when I used to work for them, he didn't tell her everything. I used to overhear things sometimes, you know? By accident. And then later I'd hear the king and queen talking, and he'd give her a prettier version of whatever the truth was, or he'd outright lie about something. And she never challenged him on anything, even if I knew she had her doubts. I think she's always been a little afraid of him."

"Interesting," Elle mused, her fingers playing with the chain at her neck again. "If the king did lie to her, and now she's seen the truth for herself, I wonder what she—"

"What is that?" Liana interrupted. She moved closer, her hands raised as if to clutch the bars. She stopped just short of touching them. "What's that around your neck?"

"Oh." Elle pulled the pocket watch out from beneath her sweater and held it closer to the bars. "It's just a—"

"Is that your father's pocket watch?" Liana asked, her voice low and earnest.

"Yes. You remember it?"

In a whisper, Liana asked, "Have you used the wish?"

Elle blinked. "What wish?"

"Shh," Liana said, her face almost touching the bars now. Her voice was barely audible as she said, "There's a wish inside it."

"But ... how?" Elle leaned closer and lowered her voice further. "Don't wishes have to be stored inside a gem?"

"Not always. Your father won the pocket watch in a card game or something while traveling overseas. Apparently, in certain parts of the world, they don't use gems. Or at least, they use gems now, but they used to use other objects. I think the process is easier with a gem, which is why wishes are usually stored that way nowadays."

"Okay, so how do I know if there's a wish inside here?"

"You have to look, obviously. Haven't you ever opened it?"

"Well, sure, I've opened the front," Elle said, raising her other hand and demonstrating. "But it's just a glass cover. The watch face still looks the same with the cover open."

"Not that part," Liana said with an impatient sigh. "I assume you'd have to look *inside*. Pull the watch face forward so you can see the mechanism behind it. If there's a wish inside there, that's probably where it's stored."

"I didn't know I could access the mechanism," Elle said thoughtfully, feeling around the edge of the watch face with her nail to see if there might be a small gap somewhere. "I've never needed to try because the watch has never stopped working before. Dad said it was one of those magic-powered ones that doesn't need to be wound up or have a new battery put in or anything like—Oh."

She paused as her fingernail caught on a tiny gap in line with the watch face's number nine. She pressed, inserting her nail between the gold layer encircling the face and the gold layer behind it. With a small click, the watch face popped forward. Heart pounding faster, Elle pushed the face sideways on its hinge until it sat flush against the glass cover. The back of the watch face layer was where all the cogs and wheels and other minuscule parts were located, but Elle's attention was captured by the very back layer of the pocket watch: Swirling between the rear casing of gold and a circular glass layer in front of it was the glowing magic of a wish.

SIX

"STARS ABOVE," ELLE WHISPERED. "YOU'RE RIGHT." ALL THESE YEARS, SHE'D BEEN wearing a wish around her neck. *A wish.* "Do you know what tier it is?" she asked, looking up at Liana. It couldn't be third, could it? She couldn't possibly have had a *third-tier wish*—the price of her freedom—in her possession all this time.

"I don't know. It was a long time ago, but I seem to remember your dad saying something about the amount of magic not being exactly in line with what would be considered first-, second- or third-tier these days."

"So … something in between? Or something even smaller than a first-tier wish?"

"Smaller, perhaps. I mean, it doesn't look like a very large amount of magic. My guess is that it wouldn't grant you anything too amazing."

"I wonder if …" Elle looked over her shoulder at the gate of crisscrossing bars. "I wonder if it would unlock my gate."

"Hmm. Do you think that would work if the bars are enchanted to repel magic?"

"I don't know. I suppose it depends which magic is stronger."

"What's that about a wish?" Jax called out.

"Nothing," Liana shouted back. "Mind your own business."

Footsteps echoed through the cold, dark space, and Elle looked around as a man in a uniform approached the cells. She snapped the pocket watch shut and quickly slipped it beneath her sweater again. "Now that's a guard," Liana muttered. "Probably here to take our breakfast trays. Though they usually wait until later in the day to take them."

The guard stopped in front of Elle's cell, but instead of telling her to slide her tray across the floor or insert it between the bars, he folded his arms across his chest.

"You're new," Liana said before the guard could utter a word. "Haven't seen you down here before."

The guard frowned at her, then motioned with his head for Elle to move to the other end of her cell. He took a few steps to the side and waited until she'd moved closer. "I'm not supposed to be here," he said quietly, though Elle suspected Liana could still hear him, "but it's easier for me than for the prince. The usual guards are under strict orders not to allow him down here, but he wanted you to know he's working on it and he'll figure something out. Basically, if days end up passing and you don't see him, he doesn't want you to think he's given up on you. He will find a way to free you."

"Why don't *you* find a way to free her," Liana called out, "since it's apparently so much easier for you to sneak down here than for the prince."

The guard sighed. His wary gaze flicked toward Liana before returning to Elle. "Look, Prince Chevalier has done a lot for me, and I'll help him in whatever way I can, but I value my life. If I free you and the king finds out it was me, I'll be dead. Not only that, but he'll make sure my family suffers for my crime. I'm sorry. All I can do is deliver the prince's message." With that, he turned and strode quickly away.

"Days," Elle murmured, wandering back toward Liana.

"Sorry," Liana said. "I'm sure you didn't expect to be stuck in this grimy hole that long, but look on the bright side: at least it's not years."

Elle shook her head. "It's not that I mind being stuck in here for days. It's a lot worse than my attic, but I'm sure I could survive just fine. What I'm worried about is what might happen up there—" she nodded toward the ceiling "—during the next few days."

"Why?" Liana's brow crinkled. "What's going on up there?"

In low tones, Elle explained to Liana that the Godmother had killed

Vincenzo Savoy, the man most vampires wanted to see on the Astranerican throne, and taken control of his army of enhanced vampires. "She knows how vampires can get magic from humans, so she's probably putting them all through the process or ritual or whatever it is right now. Then she's going to make her move against the king."

"Are you sure?"

"That's what she said. She said the king is planning to come for her—once he can figure out which Eternal Night she's been hiding in—and that she may as well make things easier by coming to him instead. I don't know when that's going to happen, but she doesn't seem like a woman who wastes time."

"You think it could happen within the next few days?" Liana asked.

"I don't know. She's the Godmother. Anything's possible."

"And if it *does* happen within the next few days, she'll probably defeat the king, seize control of the throne, and Dex will never get the chance to come down here and free us."

"Probably not. And while that would be truly terrible," Elle added, "I'm not just worried about our freedom. I'm worried about the whole country. I'm not a fan of our existing king, but do we really want the *Godmother* ruling? She's insanely powerful, and she likes playing games with people. She'd probably start plotting to take over neighboring countries as well."

"So what are you suggesting?" Liana asked. "You want to try use the wish instead of waiting for Dex?"

"Maybe." Elle pushed one hand through her tangled, dirty hair—how long had it been since she'd washed it?—before letting her arm fall to her side. "I don't want to waste it, and that's exactly what will happen if it doesn't unlock our cells. But I don't want to wait too long and then by the time we try it, the Godmother's taken over everything, and the royal family's dead, and Vale City's in flames, and ..." She shook her head, her mind snagging on the words *royal family's dead.* Now that she'd voiced her fear out loud, she couldn't shake the mental image: The king and queen and Dex, lying motionless amid the smoking ruins of a destroyed Belmont Palace.

"So do it then," Liana said. "Use the wish. You don't have much to lose at this point."

"Hey, what are you two whispering about over there?" Jax shouted.

Ignoring her, Elle reached for the pocket watch again. Pulling it free once more, she said, "Yeah, you're probably right. Besides, how much magic can it really take to unlock a few gates?" She looked up and met Liana's gaze.

Liana grimaced. "You probably shouldn't have said that."

"You think I jinxed it?"

She shrugged. Elle rolled her eyes. "Whatever. I'm doing it." She stepped back and turned away from Liana's cell as she opened the pocket watch again. The glow of wish magic illuminated her palms as she stared at it in wonder. She would have to break the glass to free the magic, a thought that caused a stab of anxiety to pierce her chest. It went against everything inside her to break something that served as such a special reminder of her father. But she wouldn't be breaking it completely, she reminded herself. She would just be freeing the wish. She could close all the layers afterwards, and the watch itself would still work.

She ran her left thumb over the glass layer, wondering what to break it with. Any faerie would have used a charm, and Elle *did* possess magic now, but she had no idea how to use it. Even if it was simply a matter of Liana telling her exactly what words to use, she didn't want to risk getting them wrong and breaking the entire watch. Besides, who knew if the same words and spells that applied to fae Essence also worked with human magic?

Elle cast her gaze about, looking for something sharp and hard enough to break glass. She turned slowly, her eyes traveling across her almost empty cell, until she spotted the spoon sitting in her half-eaten bowl of porridge. That should do it. She bent and picked up the spoon, tapping it against the bowl to remove any remaining bits of porridge before she rose. Then, gripping it with the handle pointing down, she held it over the pocket watch.

"What are you doing, girl?" Jax called.

"Hush," Liana told her.

Elle turned her back to the women again, but she couldn't help considering the two she didn't know. Jax and Myra. They probably didn't deserve to be down here any more than she and Liana did. Should she try to free them too? If she didn't, she'd probably never forgive herself for leaving them locked down here in this dark, musty dungeon. But what if there wasn't enough magic to unlock all the cells? Would it only open one or two? Or would it open none of them?

Just get on with it, she told herself. *You'll never know until you try.*

She arranged the words in her head, going over them several times to make sure she would be wishing for exactly what she wanted. Then she lifted the pocket watch until it was level with her face, and raised the spoon a little higher. This moment—the act of breaking open a wish and letting the contents spill over her as she whispered her heart's desire—was one she'd dreamed of for years. It didn't escape her notice that while she no longer had to wish away the slave charm, she was essentially wishing for the same thing she'd always planned to wish for: her freedom.

Elle squeezed her eyes shut for a moment, then opened them as she brought the spoon down swiftly. The glass shattered. A glowing gold substance, almost liquid like water, but somehow lighter, spilled from the pocket watch, ran down her hands and arms, and dripped onto her chest. As her entire body glowed, she whispered, "I wish for the gate of my cell, Liana's cell, Jax's cell, and Myra's cell to be unlocked and opened."

The glow diminished. Darkness settled over her cell again. Elle looked at her gate, holding her breath, waiting and hoping desperately. Then, with a grinding, rusty screech, the lock turned and the gate swung open.

SEVEN

Elle twisted around in time to see Liana's gate swing wide, then Jax's, and then Myra's. Silence followed. No one moved an inch. Finally, Jax spoke: "Ho-lee heck. What the hell just happened?"

A grin stretched Elle's lips. "It worked. It actually worked!" She hurried forward through the open space, half expecting some unseen form of magic to toss her back into her cell. But nothing happened.

"We're actually … free," Liana said in a stunned tone, walking slowly out of her cell. Jax and Myra joined her a moment later, and Elle finally got a proper look at them. Their clothing was just as ragged and dirty as Liana's, and Myra, being fae, had the same youthful look. But Jax's lined face and gray strands mixed in with her dark hair suggested she was in her forties or fifties.

"Normal magic could never have done this," Myra said. "Liana and I have tried so many times. Was that wish magic I saw glowing in your cell?" Elle nodded, and Myra asked, "How on earth did you manage to smuggle a wish in here? Didn't the guards search you?"

"I don't know," Elle said as she carefully closed the pocket watch and slipped it beneath her clothing once more. "I was a little bit out of it when they brought me here. Maybe they did pat me down or something, but they wouldn't have known I had a wish with me. It wasn't inside a gem." She met Liana's eyes. "*I* didn't even know I had a wish with me."

"So you wished for our gates to unlock," Jax said. "That's great and everything, but how are we supposed to get out of this dungeon and away from the palace?"

"Yeah, that may not have been the best wish," Myra added. "Wishing for us to be instantly transported outside of the palace grounds would have made things a lot easier."

"Hey, look, I didn't know if there was enough magic in that wish to unlock even a single gate. I didn't want to wish for too much and end up with nothing."

"We're grateful," Liana said hastily. "We really are." She shot a glare in Jax's direction. "Let's not ruin this opportunity by arguing for so long that the guards end up—" Her words cut off at the sound of someone approaching. "Dammit," she whispered, throwing a glance back over her shoulder at her cell. Elle began to backtrack toward hers, though the logical side of her brain told her there was no way all four of them could get back into their cells and pretend the gates were closed before—

A growl shredded the quiet, and with a shudder, Jax fell forward onto her hands and knees. Her body twitched and began to change shape, and as a female guard rounded the corner and froze, Jax launched, now a fully formed wolf. She tore at the woman's throat, and Elle gasped and instinctively squeezed her eyes shut as she turned her head away.

Within seconds, the snarling, ripping sounds came to an end. Slowly, Elle looked toward Jax. She shuddered and arched her back before returning to non-animal form, breathing heavily. Blood stained her mouth, and she used her dirty sleeve to wipe it away as she pushed herself to her feet. Elle's horrified gaze moved to the blood-drenched guard lying motionless against the wall. "Is … is she dead?"

"I hope so," Jax said. "She was one of the guards who threw me into a cell years ago. You don't expect me to go lightly on her, do you?"

"I …" Elle swallowed. "No, I suppose not, but I don't expect you to *kill* everyone on our path between here and the main gate."

"Why not? They're all our enemies."

"Actually, they're not. The prince and his friends are on our side."

"Well, good for them. Hopefully they're the only ones we come across on our way out of here."

"Let's get moving," Liana muttered. "And try to keep the killing to a minimum," she added, looking at Jax.

As quietly as possible—easy for the other three women, who were all barefoot; not so easy for Elle—they headed around the corner and along a shadowed corridor. At the top of a staircase, they came to a gate. "Not locked?" Liana whispered as she carefully slid the gate sideways.

"Probably left open by the guard who came to fetch our trays," Myra said. "It's not as though they've experienced a security breach in all the years we've been down here. At least, not from our section."

They continued along another cold, dimly lit passageway, the windowless stone walls feeling as though they were pressing in around Elle. *Not too much further*, she assured herself, though her memory of exactly how long it had taken those men to drag her to the dungeon last night was fuzzy.

When they came to a solid metal door, their luck finally ran out. "Locked," Liana grumbled. There was no handle, only a keypad on the wall, but when she pressed her hands against the door and tried to slide it sideways, it wouldn't budge.

"So we wait," Jax said. "And when it opens, I'll take down whoever's on the other side."

"No," Liana said. "We wait, and when it opens, Myra and I will use magic to knock out whoever's on the other side. Knock *unconscious*," she added. "Not dead."

"You guys are so boring," Jax grumbled.

They waited, and Elle began to question the wisdom of setting free two prisoners she knew nothing about. Though they'd most likely been unjustly imprisoned—the king's secret dungeon wasn't exactly a place people ended up in after going through a fair trial—that didn't mean they were good people.

"I think someone's coming," Myra whispered, pushing away from the wall and raising her hands. "They've probably noticed the missing guard." Magic sparkled at her fingertips. Beside her, Liana's hands took on the same appearance.

"Ready?" Liana asked. Myra nodded.

Though Elle hadn't intended it, she found her hands glowing silver as magic rose away from the surface of her skin. She hastily tucked her hands behind her back, not wanting her magic to leap away from her without her permission. She would gladly have offered to help Liana and Myra, but only if she knew what she was doing.

A click sounded somewhere within the metal door, and then it slid swiftly open. Liana and Myra lunged forward, magic flashing away from them. Elle squinted against the bright light. It subsided a moment later, accompanied by the heavy thump of a body hitting the floor.

"Is there anyone else there?" Jax whispered.

"Doesn't look like it," Liana replied. "Quickly, let's go."

They moved forward, stepping hurriedly over the body on the other side of the doorway. A wider, brighter corridor greeted them on the other side, with polished tiles instead of a dull stone floor, and ornamental light fittings instead of plain, dim lighting. But there were voices nearby. At least two or three. Footsteps, unhurried but moving closer.

"Crap," Elle whispered. The moment the owners of those voices rounded the corner up ahead and saw four disheveled women and an unconscious guard, they would attack.

Liana and Myra stepped forward, hands raised once more. "We've got this," Liana said.

Jax shoved her way between them. "Let me—"

"No," Liana said. "These people are just following orders. You can't go around killing them all. Let us—"

"Hey!" a voice hissed from somewhere on Elle's right. "This way!" Her head snapped toward the sound, and somehow, where there had been only a flat, plain wall before, then was now an opening. A figure stood in the dark space beyond, and the only detail Elle could make out was a beckoning hand. Could it be Dex? No, the voice hadn't been deep enough. Still, there were people inside this palace willing to do whatever he asked. Hopefully this was one of them.

"Come on!" Elle whispered to the others, tugging Liana and Myra. "Someone's helping us."

Liana didn't hesitate to follow Elle—perhaps because she assumed Elle knew whoever it was that beckoned from the darkness behind the wall—and Myra and Jax followed her after only a moment's pause. They slid into the shadows, and the section of wall swung closed behind them with a quiet click, sealing them in complete darkness.

A few stray gold particles danced in the air in front of Elle, and a moment later, a gold light materialized. It soared upward, illuminating the narrow passageway and the woman who stood before Elle: Queen Amra.

Jax rushed forward, her body already twitching, but Liana reached out and tugged her back. "Don't."

"She's not just another guard," Jax growled, shaking Liana off. "She's the damn—"

"I swear I'll knock you out with magic if you dare shift right now," Liana hissed.

The queen narrowed her eyes at the two of them. "Liana?" she asked. "How … You disappeared years ago. I thought …" She shook her head and returned her gaze to Elle. "No time for that," she muttered, reaching for Elle's arm and tugging her forward. "Have you had dealings with the Godmother recently?"

"Y-yes," Elle answered, too startled to let anything other than the truth slip free.

"Did you come to the masquerade ball?"

"Um, yes, I did."

"Why?"

Elle paused, her mouth open. It couldn't possibly be a good idea to admit that she'd gone to the ball to kill the queen's son. "Just to … um …"

"I need the truth," the queen insisted.

Though the truth was likely to get her thrown back out beyond the wall and into the midst of whatever activity now surrounded the unconscious guard, Elle couldn't force a lie past her lips. "The Godmother asked me to kill the prince," she admitted. "I said yes, but I was never planning to go through with it. I got hold of a potion to mimic death. When I realized the prince was Dex … well, I'd already given the potion to his body double, but even if I hadn't, I would never have given it to Dex. I already knew him. I … I couldn't have done that to him. Neither fake death nor real death. I swear."

"And did you wish for the Godmother to remove the Darkness from him?"

This, at least, was something Elle was happy to admit to. "Yes. I didn't want him to die."

The queen's gaze darted to the three women behind Elle. Her breathing was heavy, and a war waged in her eyes. Then she clutched Elle's hand, tugged her even closer, and said, "Thank you. Now follow me. Quickly."

Elle hurried after the queen as the light bobbed ahead of them. She tossed a glance over her shoulder to make sure the others were still right behind her, then looked forward again. The queen brought a phone to ear and spoke quietly to whoever was on the other end. "Meet me in the Rose Suite. Bring three sets of clothing. Oh, and four wigs from that collection Marcio sent over before the masquerade ball. And organize a car to pick me up at the east entrance in ten minutes. I'll be leaving for tea with four of my friends."

She lowered the phone and followed the passage as it bent sharply to the right. When it split into a T a little further on, she turned left without hesitation. Finally, after turning right again, she came to a halt. Elle stopped just short of bumping into her. Thank goodness. Bumping into Queen Amra of Astranerica was probably considered a crime of some sort.

"Remain silent," the queen instructed. Then she pushed a section of the passage wall. It gave way, slowly swinging open and allowing daylight to stream in through the gap. She peered out. "Quickly," she said to Elle. "Follow me."

They filed out of the passageway and into a wide and lavishly decorated corridor. The queen pushed the section of wall closed, and once it was flush with the rest of the wall, Elle could barely make out the panel's edge. "In here," the queen added, hurrying past them and opening a door. She ushered them into the next room, which turned out to be a beautifully furnished bedroom, and slipped in behind them.

"Is this your room?" Elle asked before stopping to consider whether it might be rude to ask.

"No, just a random guest room. Now, we just need to wait for—Ah, Katrina, there you are." A woman in a pantsuit slipped inside the room mere seconds after the queen had shut the door. She flicked her hand behind her, and a suitcase floated into the room before the door quietly shut itself. "Was there anyone else out there?" the queen asked. "Anyone who might have seen you?"

"No, your majesty." She sent the suitcase soaring toward the bed and hastened toward it as it popped open. "I grabbed several of your outfits, and you didn't say anything about shoes, so I brought—"

"Perfect, thank you." The queen turned to Elle. "You still look mostly presentable. Just cover up your hair with one of the dark wigs, and make sure it conceals your ears. You three …" She turned to Liana, Jax and Myra. "Change as quickly as you can. You'll attract far too much attention in those rags. Katrina, did you organize a car?"

"Yes, ma'am. It's probably waiting for you already."

"Good."

As Liana, Jax and Myra changed their clothes, Elle grabbed one of the wigs Katrina had hastily laid out on the bed. She moved to the dressing table on one side of the room and peered into the mirror as she piled her blond hair on top of her head. With some difficulty, she pulled the wig on, then pushed any free strands of blond hair beneath the wig's edge. When everything was positioned properly, she appeared to be the owner of a sleek black bob with a dead straight fringe. Nothing like her natural hair, which, of course, was the point.

"Hurry up," the queen said. Elle turned away from the mirror and smoothed her hands over her sweater. Jax hopped on one foot as she pulled a shoe onto the other, and Liana and Myra finished fixing their fake hair.

"You heard the queen," Liana said, grabbing a wig from the bed and tossing it at Jax.

The queen sighed and muttered something inaudible. She tapped her foot against the carpet, and the second Jax had pulled the wig on, she said, "Right, let's go. And don't *rush*; that'll look suspicious. We are simply five ladies going to tea." She reached for the door handle, but Elle grabbed her arm. The queen swung her hard gaze instantly toward Elle, and Elle snatched her hand back, feeling as though she might shrivel up and disappear into the carpet. But she needed to ask what she'd been about to ask.

"Why are you helping us?"

The queen's gaze softened somewhat as it traveled Elle's face. Quietly, she said, "You care for him."

Though it wasn't a question, Elle answered, "Yes. Very much."

"You saved his life with a wish."

"Of course I did. He would have done the same for me."

"Well, that's why I'm helping you. The others ... I hadn't planned to help them, but you'd already freed them so ..." She exhaled sharply through her nose. "Well, this seems the least complicated way forward."

Without another word, she pasted a serene smile onto her face, opened the door, and walked out. Elle followed, trying her best to smile naturally and walk casually. Liana whispered something about laughing, so Elle forced out a polite chuckle. The queen made a comment about never understanding why Liana had simply vanished years ago, and Liana laughed loudly and told her she should ask her husband about the time he tried—and failed—to murder the nanny. Jax snickered, Elle tried not to cringe, and somehow, the five of them arrived at an open doorway on the ground floor without anyone stopping to ask if they were escaped prisoners.

A man standing at the doorway nodded politely as they passed, and outside, a limousine was already waiting for them. The driver asked no questions as he opened the door to the back compartment, and no one yelled out for them to stop as all five of them climbed inside. Nevertheless, Elle found herself holding her breath as the vehicle pulled smoothly away from the door, drove around the side of the palace, and headed for the gate. Only once they were beyond it did she finally relax against the leather seat and draw a breath.

"The car will stop at the edge of the city and let you out," the queen said, remaining rigid and staring straight ahead. "From there, you're on your own."

EIGHT

"**Why haven't you *found* her yet?**" King Belaric demanded of his Captain of the Guard, bringing his fist down on the desk. Dex flinched, along with the other six or seven people standing in the king's study.

"We've followed every rumor, sire," said the captain. "Every whisper, every hint. But this is the Godmother we're talking about. If she doesn't want to be found, I don't think there's anything more we can do."

Dex pressed his lips together as he stared at the floor. He knew which Eternal Night the Godmother was hiding out in, but he couldn't decide what to do with that knowledge. He should probably tell his father. After all, he didn't want the Godmother descending on Belmont Palace out of the blue and killing everyone in their sleep. But he didn't want his father racing off to the Jade Eternal Night and taking with him an army of fae who would probably all end up dead when they found themselves facing a force of enhanced, magical vampires.

So what was he supposed to do? Which course of action would lead to fewer deaths?

He needed more *time*. He needed to get through tomorrow night. He had a plan for this party his mother was forcing on him, and once that was done, he could focus on everything else.

"Of course there's more you can do," his father snapped at the Captain of the Guard. "Do your damn job, for a start. I want the Godmother dead, and I want to wipe her vampire army into oblivion. That means you need to *find*—"

A knock at the door interrupted him. "What?" he shouted.

The door swung open, and Dex recognized one of the prison guards who'd stopped him from going down to the hidden dungeon this morning. "I apologize for interrupting, your majesty. The, uh, the human girl who was brought in last night. The one with—"

"Yes, I know who you're talking about," the king said.

"She, uh … she escaped."

Dex's heart leaped, but he managed to keep his expression neutral as his eyes darted back to his father. The king appeared frozen, though his face was slowly turning purplish red. He bit out a single word: "How?"

"I—I don't know, your majesty. She had magic. Perhaps human magic is different from ours. More power—"

"Nonsense," the king snapped. "Of course she didn't have *magic*. Now get out. All of you, out!" Everyone shuffled toward the door, but when Dex made to move, his father said, "Not you."

As the last person filed out and the door clicked shut, the king turned his thunderous expression on Dex. "What have you done?"

"I haven't done a thing," Dex said, pushing away from the wall and moving closer to the desk. "I've been stuck in this room all morning with you, and—as I'm sure you're aware—your guards wouldn't let me anywhere near the dungeon when I tried to get down there early this morning to see Elle."

"I know you've done—"

"I've done *nothing*," Dex shouted. "Question every one of your guards. They'll tell you they didn't allow me down there. Though I wish I'd fought past them. I wish I *had* freed her. If she's gone, I'll probably never find her again." Not true, but it was what he needed his father to hear. Let the king think Elle was long gone. Let him think Dex was unlikely to ever see her again. That way, he'd be completely blindsided when together, Elle and Dex revealed the truth about humans to the whole world.

NINE

"You owe me big time," Cress said as she let Elle and her companions in through the back door of Apollo's Apothecary.

"I know," Elle answered immediately. "I am a *thousand* percent aware of that. If there was anyone else I felt safe going to, I'd be bothering them instead of you."

"It's fine, it's fine," Cress drawled, closing the door and stepping past Elle and the others. She walked ahead of them toward one of the apothecary's back lounges. "I'm not exactly surprised that you're here. Dex already sent a message to tell me to keep an eye out for you."

"He did?"

"He didn't mention you'd have three escaped convicts with you, though." Cress gestured to two couches covered in colorful throws.

"I'd like to object to the term 'convict,'" Jax interjected before taking a seat.

"But like I said," Cress continued, ignoring Jax, "it's fine. Mostly, I'm just insanely curious to see your magic, Elle."

Elle pulled the wig of dark hair off her head and tossed it onto one of the couches as a grin spread across her face. "It's amazing, Cress. I have *actual magic*. I have no clue what to do with it, but I *have* it."

"One step at a time, honey," Cress said, her smile mirroring Elle's. "You'll learn. I'm still amazed it's even possible." With a wave of her hand, she moved a few beaded cushions—and the wig—out of the way before taking a seat on the couch. "So," she said as Elle sat beside her, "are you going to show me, or what?"

Elle tipped her head to the side. "Don't you have a store to manage right now?"

"My daughter's in there. She's old enough to take care of things. Now stop being such a tease."

"Excuse me," Liana interrupted as she slowly lowered herself between Jax and Myra on the other couch. "Could I perhaps … use a laptop? Or a phone? After so many years of being locked away without my family and friends knowing I'm alive, I don't even know where to start. I don't know where anyone is, or who to contact first or … anything."

"Same here," Jax said, and Myra nodded along with them.

"Yes, of course," Cress said. "Let me fetch a laptop. Then Elle and I can talk."

She disappeared from the room, and Elle looked at the other three women. "This must be really weird for you guys. Finally free after so many years of being locked away in the dark."

Liana looked toward the window, where sunlight filtered through a peach-colored scarf partly draped across the glass. "The sun is the best thing ever. Seriously. I don't know how vampires survive a lifetime without it."

"It is weird," Jax murmured. "I don't know who's still alive. I don't know what's changed in my pack. If my pack even exists still. I'm both excited and scared to find out."

"It's all the little things, you know?" Myra said quietly. "All the advertisements out there look different. I don't recognize most of the products. We passed people using phones and other devices, and they all look different from what I remember. It's like coming out and finding a slightly different world from the one I left behind."

Elle nodded. "That does sound quite … unsettling."

"Here you go," Cress said, bustling back into the room with a laptop. She handed it to Liana. "And Elle, I sent Dex a quick message to let him know you're here."

"Oh, thanks."

"Now." Cress settled herself on the couch and ran one hand through her sleek purple hair. "Show me this magic of yours."

* * *

Elle demonstrated as much as she could—which wasn't much—and then Cress asked if she wanted to try out a few things to see if human magic was anything like fae magic. Elle's answer to that was yes, of course. So Cress started with the basics. It turned out that a lot of it was simply about intent. She had to push her magic out and *intend* to move the coffee table, or the pot with the giant fern in it, or the stack of books.

By the time Cress's phone pinged with a message from Dex, Elle could lift a cushion, make it move in a shaky circle above her head, and lower it back down to the couch. It took a great deal of effort though. Far more than the kind of magic that happened without really thinking about it—like the force that had thrown Salvia across a room.

"Dex says he'll reach the apothecary in less than a minute," Cress said, looking at her phone. "He's heading for the back entrance. Do you want to let him in?"

"Yes," Elle answered immediately in a voice that was probably a little too loud.

Cress arched an eyebrow. "Excited to see him? It's been, what? Five minutes since you parted?"

"It was last night," Elle said defensively. "And it feels like a lot has happened since then."

Cress shooed her toward the door. "Go and have your happy reunion."

Elle rolled her eyes and stood, leaving Cress with a smirk on her face and Liana, Jax and Myra crowding the single laptop. She hurried to the back door and opened it, but Dex wasn't there yet. So she closed the door a little—who knew if there might be someone dangerous nearby, like a palace guard who'd managed to track her this far and was now looking out for any sign of her—and watched through the narrow gap.

Something small darted across her line of vision and came to a halt somewhere on the ground. She looked down at the doormat and saw a pixie standing there. "Tash?" she asked, bending slightly to get a better look. But before she could figure out if the pixie was familiar—and if the shape on top of her tiny head was half a pistachio shell—the pixie launched forward, zoomed beneath Elle's arm, and disappeared inside the apothecary.

"Elle?" She looked up at the sound of Dex's voice, a smile already on her lips. She pulled the door open fully, and a moment later, Dex's arms were around her. He hugged her tightly, and then his hands slid into her hair, and his lips were against hers, and he was kicking the door shut as they stumbled further inside.

"I'm sorry," Elle mumbled against his lips. "I'm probably gross and smelly—"

"I don't care." Dex kissed her again. "I'm just so happy you got yourself out of that dungeon." He pressed his lips against hers once more. "And I'm so sorry about my father. I honestly had no idea that he already knew—"

"It's okay." Elle pressed one more kiss to his lips before stepping back and taking his hand in hers. "You don't have to apologize for him."

"He's a monster."

"He—" She blinked. "He's your father."

Dex shook his head. "He's not a father. He hasn't been for a long time. He's become something else." He leaned forward and rested his forehead against hers. "I could kiss you all day, but there are things we need to talk about."

"Yes," Elle murmured. "I know." She led him to a smaller lounge—the one where he'd slept on the futon as he recovered after Elle first saw the Darkness come over him—so they could talk in private. "What are we doing about the Godmother?" she asked as they sat. "Have you told your father where to find her?"

Dex sighed. "No. But let's deal with one problem at a time. The world needs to know about the Starlight Quest and what's possible for humans. That has to happen, regardless of who ends up ruling this country—my father or the Godmother. So first, we need to make sure the truth gets out. After that's done, we can face everything else. So my plan for that is—"

"Wait." Elle paused, trying to formulate her tangled thoughts into words that made sense. "Why do you think the Godmother made me go through the quest? Why did she want me to end up with magic? Maybe she *wants* me to spread the word. Maybe she wants the world to know. Maybe, if she defeats your father, it'll actually be easier to get the truth out there."

Dex shook his head. "If that were the case, then why hasn't she told anyone before now? She's the Godmother. She could make sure the whole world knew if she wanted to."

Elle sighed and placed her head in her hands. "You're right. In fact, I'm pretty sure I asked her the same thing. It's just … *I don't understand her.*" She lowered her hands and focused on Dex. "What does she actually want?"

Dex shrugged. "To play around with people's lives?"

"Yeah. Maybe. Okay, so one problem at a time. You said we should get the truth out there first. How are we going to do that?"

"So, tomorrow night, at the party—"

"Party?"

"Remember I told you my mother is organizing another event, since the masquerade ball was a disaster? Something smaller and more exclusive, which I'm pretty sure only fae have been invited to. Another chance for me to apparently find someone to marry."

"Oh, yes," Elle said, trying not to dwell on the idea of Dex marrying someone else. "You called it The Ball 2.0."

"Right. That party. It's tomorrow night, and I'm hoping you'll come with me. It's smaller than the Moonlight Masquerade Ball, but there'll still be plenty of people there. All it'll take is one demonstration for everyone to see the truth. Word will begin to spread immediately. You know everyone will have their phones there. They'll be taking selfies and posting them on social media, letting the whole world know they were lucky enough to be invited to an exclusive royal event. There'll probably be a video online of you demonstrating your magic within minutes of you showing everyone."

Elle shook her head. "No, there won't be, because your father would never let things get that far. He'll throw me back into a dungeon before a sparkle of magic has left my fingertips. And if the guests at the party *do* happen to see something, your father will probably kill them all to stop the truth from spreading."

"He won't get a chance to do that. There's … there's something else I've been thinking about." Dex took a deep breath and stood. "I can't believe I'm about to suggest this," he muttered as he began pacing.

"What?" Elle asked, apprehension creeping in at the edges of her mind.

Dex stopped. He stared at the floor. "Sometimes I wonder if the Godmother knew exactly what she was doing when she decided on the price of my father's wish all those years ago."

"What do you mean?"

"I mean … maybe my soul is just as black as the Darkness the Godmother placed upon me."

"Dex—"

"I've thought about killing him, Elle. That thought has actually entered my mind. If it wouldn't guarantee a swift death for me, I might have seriously considered *killing my own father*. I would never *want* to, but he's so terrible, and I'm so desperate for him *not* to end up ruining our country and the lives of all humans, and I just … there's nothing I've been able to do. Until now."

"What are you talking about?"

He raised his eyes and met hers. "There's something we haven't had a chance to speak of since you first told me about it. Your ability to remove memories."

Elle stared at him, her lips parted. He couldn't possibly be asking her this, could he? "You want me to … take away all your father's memories? Remove his mind to the point of death?"

"What? No! I didn't even know that was—*NO*. I would never ask that of you. It would probably end up killing *you* instead of him—because of that blasted wish he made—but even if that wasn't the case, I would never ask you to murder someone. No, I'm just asking you to take enough of his memories that he forgets his hatred of humans. That's what's poisoned him. That's what has influenced all the terrible decisions he's made in recent years. If he could go back to a point where he's still questioning the way he feels about humans, and *then* we show him that humans can also have magic and are equal to all other High Raes, I think he'll accept that."

Elle stood. She needed to pace. She couldn't seem to think clearly while sitting still. "So … I would need to go as far back as …"

"As far back as my grandmother's death. That was the event that sent him over the edge."

"But that means I'll have to remove *everything* from that time until the present," Elle pointed out. "Surely there would be far too many other important things that I'd be erasing from his memory?"

"Nothing that his advisers can't tell him about. And, fortunately, none of his advisers are as terrible as he is. They would present all the facts in a … well, *mostly* unbiased fashion. And I would be there too, to help influence him in a positive direction."

Elle drew in a deep breath and let it out slowly. She continued pacing, chewing her lip, considering doing the very thing she'd hated most about all the years she'd spent as Salvia's slave.

"Elle, I think this might be the only way for my father to be a better ruler," Dex said. "No one can kill him—well, the Godmother probably can, but then we'd all be in an even worse position with her as a queen. So if we can get my father to be the kind of ruler he was meant to be before fear and hatred twisted him into such a monster—and then if we can figure out how to stop the Godmother from wanting to defeat him—then maybe, somehow, we'll end up with some form of happily ever after."

Elle gave him a small smile. "You're a whole lot more optimistic than the guy I met a few weeks ago who was convinced he was going to die soon and that there was no other way his life would play out."

"Well, that guy was fortunate enough to meet a girl who told him that despite the fact that life sucks, she's always refused to give up." Dex stepped closer and took Elle's hands. "It seems like her outlook on things may have ended up rubbing off on him."

Elle's smile stretched a little wider. "I'm glad." But then her smile faded, and she slowly lowered herself to the futon again. "But this isn't going to be easy. Your father will have to be relaxed for it to work. Super relaxed. Like, almost asleep."

"So we'll give him a potion then. A sleeping potion. I can slip it into his drink at the party tomorrow night. Not too much, but just enough so he ends up drowsy. Then you can come in—not before, because he'll recognize you and have the guards drag you away—and you can do your memory thing. If he's so drowsy he's close to falling asleep, he won't notice."

Elle nodded, thinking of all Salvia's cons that had gone down in a similar way. "And what about the dark magic that protects him?" she asked. "Won't it throw you clear across the room and kill you for doing something like adding a potion to his drink?"

"I don't think so. My intent isn't to kill him or to take the throne from him. I just want to relax him. It should be fine."

Again, Elle nodded. "I assume that doing it while he's sleeping, like tonight while he's in bed, is out of the question?"

"Correct. You'd never get close enough. There are too many guards stationed around his quarters."

"Okay."

"So … you'll do this?"

Elle gave Dex a resigned nod. "I will. If you think it's the only thing that'll make a difference—a positive difference—then I'll do it."

He sank onto the futon beside her and pulled her into a hug. She rested her head against his chest. "Thank you. I was worried you might hate me for even suggesting it."

She shook her head. "I understand that you only want to make things better. You don't want to kill your father. You don't want the Godmother to kill him. You just want him to be a better person so he can rule the way he was meant to rule. If I have to steal some memories to make that happen, I think I can probably live with myself." She let out a long breath. "And then—after tomorrow—we'll figure out how to deal with the Godmother."

"Yes." Dex pulled away and stood again. "I should probably go now. If my mother thinks I've vanished again, she'll cancel the party. I'll get Olly and Xander to smuggle you inside the palace grounds tomorrow night. Shouldn't be too hard for them."

"Oh, wait," Elle said as she stood. "Before you go, there's someone you should see. Someone I found locked in the dungeon. She's been there for a very long time, and … well, I think she'd probably like to see you too."

Elle led the way to the other lounge, then stood aside as Dex walked in. She watched as his eyes fell on the three women bent over the laptop. She watched as recognition flooded his features and his mouth fell open. She watched as Liana finally looked up and shrieked in surprise, throwing her hands up and almost knocking the laptop onto the floor. And as she jumped up and ran to wrap her arms around Dex, all Elle could do was smile and laugh. And cry. Just a little bit.

TEN

Music and laughter mingled, perfume filled the air, and Elle tried not to bite her nails as she waited in a small antechamber off the dining room where The Ball 2.0 was currently underway. Xander had left her here earlier with instructions not to enter the dining room until Dex came to fetch her. She wasn't sure how much time had passed, but it felt like a lot. How much longer could people possibly spend chatting and dancing and sipping champagne? Surely dinner would be served soon, and then everyone would notice that something wasn't quite right with the king?

Elle paced the antechamber, her hands repeatedly smoothing the folds of her skirt. Her dress was something Cress had lent her—far simpler than the beautiful gown the Godmother had brought into existence with a snap of her fingers, but pretty enough that she wouldn't stand out as being vastly underdressed. And, coincidentally, a similar color. She'd indulged in a long shower at Cress's place, and then Liana had used magic to curl her hair into simple, shiny waves. Elle had tried out the spell herself and almost singed part of her hair off, so she'd left the remainder of the hair styling to Liana after that. The makeup painted onto her face was also Cress's, and again, it was simple. Just enough so she would fit in tonight.

Elle had just decided that chewing her nails was worth it after all—it gave her something to do—when Dex suddenly appeared in the small room. "Oh. Hi. Has everything gone okay so far?"

"Better than okay," Dex said. "I kept waiting for him to notice something was off with his drink, but he just kept tossing it back. I think the whole Godmother threat—and you running away—has got him drinking more than usual."

"So … it's time for me to come in?"

"Yes. I've made sure my mother is at the far end of the room chatting with two of her friends, so she won't see you. Though I'm starting to wonder if it would even matter if she did, seeing as she's the one who helped you escape."

"Crazy, right?" Elle said. Before Dex had left the apothecary earlier, she'd told him exactly who had assisted in her escape.

"More than crazy. Anyway, are you ready?"

"I—I guess so." It couldn't be this easy, could it? How could nothing have gone wrong so far? But perhaps, sometimes, things just worked out.

So Elle took Dex's hand and allowed him to lead her into the crowded dining room. "I would love to dance my way across the room with you," Dex said, "but I'm afraid that would draw too much attention. Better just to get you close to my father without too many people noticing."

"Save me a dance for later," Elle said, trying to ignore the nervous shudder in her voice. "When this is over. When everyone's laughing into their champagne because the king drank a little too much and fell asleep. Before he wakes up and everyone realizes he's confused and lost his memory."

"Definitely," Dex said.

"Remember you need to keep him distracted," Elle reminded him as they rounded the impressively long dining room table and drew nearer to where the king was sitting. "Talk about … I don't know. Something that'll keep him calm. Just keep him distracted enough from the fact that I'm touching him."

"I will," Dex assured her. "You've got this. Everything's going to be okay."

Yes, Elle told herself silently. *Everything is going to be okay.* In a weird sort of way, she'd been training for this for years. Every con that Salvia had forced her to participate in had prepared her for this moment. Though she'd hated it every single time, she found herself feeling oddly grateful in this moment.

Then, suddenly, she was standing right behind the king. Dex moved forward a little, into his father's line of vision, and laughed as he said, "So I asked around and got the real story. Derren *did* fall off that horse because he was staring at Angel."

"That's … hilarious," his father slurred, tipping his head back just enough for Elle to see that his eyes were half-closed.

Now or never, she told herself. As Dex continued some nonsense story about a man who couldn't seem to stay on his horse, she gingerly pressed one finger to the back of the king's neck. She froze, waiting for him to whip around and slap her hand away, but of course, he was in no state to notice her featherlight touch.

She closed her eyes, breathed out, and slipped almost instantly into the king's mind. Unfamiliar memories flashed across the surface of her thoughts, but she didn't pause to examine any of them. She had to go back a long way, further back than she remembered ever going into someone's mind. She began flicking through his memories, faster and faster and faster. Dex had told her what date to aim for and what other memories she would see around about that time, but it was a while before she slowed down to check if she was anywhere near the right date. It was odd the way she got a sense of the time and place without actually *knowing* for sure exactly what the date of any specific memory was. She simply knew without knowing—though that made no sense.

She was still far off, so she hurried further backward, more memories flashing across her mind's eye. Until she felt herself nearing it. She felt the pain, the confusion, the way it hardened into hatred. She slowed down and flicked a little further back—and there it was. The moment the king had received the news of what happened to his mother. The way in which she'd been killed. The fact that humans were involved.

Elle went a little bit further back—Dex had asked her to do this, just in case—and then, after a few seconds of hesitation, she squeezed her eyelids tighter and clenched her hand around Dex's. In a single moment, she wiped away everything from that day up until the present.

Elle opened her eyes and blinked. She looked up and met Dex's gaze. "He's asleep," Dex said quietly.

"It's done," Elle told him.

And right then, as if perfectly on cue, a guard came running into the dining room. With her heart sinking beneath a foreboding weight, Elle watched as he pushed his way between the guests. Finally, he stumbled to a halt a few feet away, his nervous gaze darting from Dex to the king and back again. "Is—is his majesty asleep?"

"Looks like it," Dex said with an exaggerated smile. "Too much champagne, I guess."

"But … it's … this is very important."

Dex frowned. "What is it?"

"The Godmother. She's here."

ELEVEN

"The Godmother is *here*?" Dex repeated loudly, and Elle felt his hand clench around hers. He lowered his voice and asked, "Inside the palace?"

"Well, no, not quite," the guard said. "But almost. She just … appeared. With an entire army of magical vampires. At the bottom of Sovereign Hill. They're marching toward Belmont Palace as we speak. The Captain of the Guard is gathering all forces currently present, and he sent me to fetch the king."

"Well, the king is currently indisposed," Dex said. "You have me instead."

"Er, of course, your highness."

Dex nodded for Elle to follow him, then strode away with the guard. "Don't say anything else while you're in this room," he told the guard. "I don't want anyone to panic."

"Of course not, your highness. My thoughts exactly."

Once they were out of the dining room, Dex fell back a step or two and spoke quietly to Elle. "You need to get away from here."

"I know. I'll see if I can get to the Godmother before she reaches the palace."

"What? No, that's not what I meant."

"But maybe I can convince her not to attack."

"How?" Dex stopped walking and took hold of her arms. "Elle, you can't—"

"I have to try something! She won't hurt me. She put her protection on me, remember?" Elle looked at the guard, hovering awkwardly nearby and pretending to pay no attention to the two of them. "You have to go with him," she said to Dex. "You do what you need to do, and I'll do what I need to do. I'll be fine, I promise." She stepped away from him and added, "I've survived every other encounter with the Godmother, haven't I?"

Dex groaned, stepped forward, and grabbed her hand. He brought his face down near hers, and his lips brushed her cheek as he said, "I think I love you, so please don't die, okay?"

"Uh …"

He kissed her cheek, then straightened and let go of her hand. "I'm serious." Then he turned and hurried away with the guard.

I think I love you … I think I love you? Okay, they were going to have to have a serious chat about Dex's timing once this was all over because, as far as Elle was concerned, his was terrible. Who declared their love at a moment like this? How was she supposed to focus on anything now?

Speaking of … She blinked and looked around, trying to figure out where she was. *Focus. Get out of the palace. Find the Godmother.* She should have asked Dex for directions before he hurried away. *See?* she wanted to say to him. *You distracted me, and now I don't know where I am!*

She turned on the spot, taking note of the portraits that lined the walls of the wide corridor. There! The one of the queen sitting in the garden. Elle had definitely passed that one when Xander led her through the palace earlier. She must have come from that side. She hurried past the portrait, her feet—clad in her favorite combat boots, despite Liana and Cress's protests—making no sound on the thick carpet.

She turned into another corridor, this one with a balcony railing on one side. She hurried toward it and looked down, her heart leaping as she recognized the enormous domed area just inside the main entrance to the palace. She ran further along the corridor, toward the grand staircase that led downstairs. She grabbed hold of a pillar and swung herself around it as she reached the top step—

And a blur of motion rushed toward her, slamming into her a second later and knocking her backward. She tripped over the lower edge of her dress and went down, pain shooting through her left wrist as she hit the floor, despite the soft carpet that cushioned her landing. Someone grabbed hold of her other wrist and began dragging her away from the staircase. She shouted and struggled, but the grip on her arm was too strong. She slid jerkily across the carpeted floor and into another room, this one with softer lighting. As she twisted and fought, she made out armchairs and large windows and a grand piano. Then she was dragged into a smaller adjoining sitting room, and her captor kicked the door shut.

Finally, he let go of her arm and stood in front of her. Blond. Piercing red eyes. A familiar face. "Nik?" she gasped, remembering the vampire from the bridge that night in Belgravia. Her very first encounter with a magical vampire. But no, this couldn't be Nik. She'd been almost certain she'd seen him in the ballroom on the night of the Moonlight Masquerade Ball. She was pretty sure the king's magic had killed him.

"No," the vampire said, leaning over her. "Nik was my son, and he's *dead*. But I'm still around, and I need more magic."

Elle scrambled away until her back met the edge of a hard piece of furniture. "Are—are you part of the enhanced army? The vampires who are faster and stronger and—"

"No. But I came along for the ride anyway. Without the Godmother's knowledge. Figured I could get back at the king for killing my son. But I saw you and your magic, and …" He chuckled. "I just can't resist."

Her magic? Elle didn't realize it had been visible as she'd been running through the palace. "But … I don't understand why you haven't completed the ritual already," she said, grasping at the first thing that came to mind. *Keep him talking. Come up with a way to get out of this mess.* "Didn't the Godmother tell you how to do it? Properly, I mean, so that you don't ever run out of magic."

The vampire's expression twisted. "She hasn't told us a damn thing. She hasn't given magic to anyone. Not even the enhanced vampires."

"But … the army that's marching toward the palace right now. Someone said they're vampires with magic."

He crouched beside her and wrapped one hand around her neck. "Tricks. Illusions. More Godmother games. She's full of them." He began to squeeze.

"No!" Elle gasped, her fingers tearing uselessly at his arm. Magic glowed brightly around her hands. *Push out. Push him away.* She tried with all her might, and it seemed like it might be working because he began sliding slowly away from her. But he clenched his teeth and fought back, struggling to remain at her side.

"You don't know what you're doing," he grunted, his hand squeezing tighter. "You humans are *useless* with—"

Elle's arm burned, and the Godmother's symbol flared bright gold against her skin. Magic burst away from her in a flash. The vampire soared across the room and slammed into the wall. Gasping for air, Elle scrambled to her feet and ran for the door. She tugged it open, ran out, then slammed it shut. She backed away hastily, then raised her hands and threw everything she had at the first heavy object her eyes landed on: the grand piano. It screeched across the floor and came to a halt against the door. "Try pushing your way past that," she muttered as she turned away. She hurried from the room, ran across the corridor toward the staircase, and skidded to a stop.

She was too late.

The entrance below was filled with vampires, fae in uniforms, and flashes of gold light. Shouts and crashes and the sizzle of magic filled the air. There was too much commotion for her to tell whether the magic came from both sides, or only from the fae. All she could make out from the vampires' side was a faint red glow that appeared to wrap around the wrists of each vampire.

Elle pressed her hands to either side of her face as her eyes searched the battle for Dex. She spotted him a moment later, dodging aside as a vampire hurtled toward him, then spinning around and sending two glowing balls of magic flying through the air.

I think I love you, so please don't die.

Stars! Why hadn't she said the same thing back to him? What if she never got the chance now? Dammit, she had to find the Godmother and beg, bargain, wish, whatever it took. She had to put a stop to this. But where, in the midst of all this chaos, would she find the woman?

Her eyes landed on a familiar figure running up the stairs toward her. "Elle!" Xander shouted. "You need to get out of here!" He was about halfway up the staircase when a furry shape—a wolf—leaped from the base of the stairs and raked its claws down his back. Xander went down beneath the weight of the creature. He threw magic blindly behind him, but not before the wolf tore its teeth along his arm.

"No!" Elle shrieked. She ran down the stairs, silver magic flashing away from her before her hands were even half raised. Her magic struck the wolf and sent it tumbling down the stairs. It shifted form, and by the time it reached the bottom step, it was Jax who stood to face Elle.

"What the hell?" she roared, blood smearing her face and hands.

"What are you *doing*?" Elle shouted, positioning herself between Jax and Xander. "Why are you here? I thought you—"

"My pack is gone!" Jax yelled. "These people *ruined my life*. I will tear through every single one of the king's men if I want to, and you will *not* get in the way of my revenge. They've had this coming for—"

"That's Dex's best friend!" Elle shouted. "He's not your enemy! He had absolutely nothing to do with your imprisonment!"

"But … he …"

"What have you *done*?" Turning her back to Jax, Elle dropped onto her knees beside Xander. Her hands hovered above him, but she had no idea how to help. "Xander," she said in a shaky voice. "Xander, can you hear me?"

His chest still rose and fell, which was a good sign. His eyelids fluttered, and his expression twisted in pain. "I … I think I'm okay." He attempted to sit but couldn't raise himself more than a few inches before falling back against the stairs. "Holy stars," he whispered, his eyes growing wider. "Is that … is that a bite?"

Elle followed his gaze to the gashes running down his arm. She couldn't lie—the truth was plain for both of them to see—nor could she bear to force the truth past her lips. "You'll be okay," she said. "You'll be fine." She didn't say what both of them already knew. That shifter magic was probably working its way through his system already, mingling with his Essence. That at some point, he would be forced to change form. That he would never be the same again.

But he was alive. That was the important part.

Something buzzed near Elle's face, and she automatically lifted her hand to swat it away. But it grabbed hold of her finger, and before she could shake the tiny creature loose, she realized it was a pixie clinging to her hand. "Tash?"

Tash let out a series of frenzied squeaks, and Elle was already shaking her head before the tiny woman was finished. "I can't understand you. You have to slow down." Tash tried again, pointing frantically upward. "I'm sorry … I still don't …"

Tash shoved Elle's finger away and began darting through the air in random, jerky patterns. Gold dust fell away from her body, leaving streaks in the air, and before long, Elle realized the patterns weren't random at all. Tash was spelling out letters.

Elle rose to her feet, barely breathing as words slowly took form in the air in front of her.

Godmother
North
Tower

TWELVE

Elle had no idea where Belmont Palace's north tower was, but apparently Tash did. She zipped through the air while Elle ran as fast as she could to keep up. She raced along passages and up staircases, the folds of her blue skirt clutched in her hands, and her hair streaming behind her. When she finally reached a spiral staircase within a cylindrical structure, she was pretty confident she was ascending a tower.

The room at the very top was empty save for a simple wooden staircase leading up to a trapdoor in the ceiling. Tash hovered near the top of the steps, pointing up. "Okay," Elle gasped, bending over as her chest heaved and she struggled to catch her breath after all those stairs. "Through the trapdoor. I get it. I just need … a moment."

But people were fighting downstairs, and every moment was a moment too long, so she straightened and began climbing the rickety wooden steps. As her head neared the ceiling, she bent over, climbed another step or two, then reached up with both hands. She pressed against the trapdoor. It opened easily. She pushed further, climbed another step, and let the trapdoor fall open completely. A cool breeze drifted past her face as she climbed the last remaining stairs, stepped onto the top of the tower, and looked around.

And there she was. The Godmother. Sitting on the stone bench that ran all the way around the inner edge of the tower. Tailored pantsuit; short, white, perfectly styled hair; flawless, wrinkle-free skin; and of course, the scepter clasped in her hand, its red gem glowing brightly. "Thank you, Tash," the Godmother said, and the pixie fluttered away.

Elle barely had time to register that Tash was somehow helping the Godmother, not *her*, before the sounds of fighting reached her ears. She stepped toward the edge of the tower and looked down. Far below, figures darted back and forth, and flashes of magic brightened the night. Elle looked at the Godmother and opened her mouth to begin pleading.

The Godmother snapped her fingers. The noise stopped. Elle looked down again, and though her brain told her it wasn't possible, her eyes told her that everyone down below was frozen in place. "What just happened?" she whispered.

"Right now," the Godmother said, "Belmont Palace exists within a bubble of magic. Outside, time marches on. Inside, everyone is frozen. Except for the two of us."

Elle stared at the woman, her pulse throbbing in her ears. "How the hell are you so powerful?"

She smiled. "That's a story for another day."

"How can you *smile* right now? You have the power to put an end to all this fighting—you can stop *time*, apparently—but instead you're sitting up here watching people kill each other? And *smiling* while it happens?"

"I was waiting for you, Elle. You should have got here sooner."

"Oh, so this is *my* fault?"

"Let's stop with all this animosity." She changed her scepter from her left hand to her right and crossed one leg over the other. She patted the stone bench beside her. "Come and sit."

"No."

The Godmother arched an eyebrow.

"Fine." Elle had, after all, come up here with the intention of doing whatever the Godmother asked if she agreed to put a stop to the fighting. May as well start with sitting when the Godmother commanded her to do so. She lowered herself to the stone slab and folded her arms across her chest.

The Godmother smiled once more. "I have a wedding present for you." She held the scepter—the staff with which she controlled the enhanced vampire army—toward Elle.

Elle eyed it with suspicion and made no move to take it. "I'm not getting married."

"An *early* wedding present then. We all know it's going to happen. Hopefully sooner rather than later."

Still, Elle didn't reach for the scepter. "What trick is this?"

"No trick, I assure you."

"We asked you to destroy the scepter before. To free the vampires. You refused. Why should I believe you've suddenly had a change of heart?"

"Oh, there's been no change of heart. I never intended to keep the scepter."

"But … you've had it in your possession since the moment you killed Savoy."

"Yes." The Godmother nodded. "Somebody needed to take care of it while you went off on your quest. And, well, it was backup in case you and Dex didn't return from the Never Woods and the king came after me. I might have needed a vampire army then. But aside from that small potential hiccup, I always intended to give this scepter to the future young rulers of this land, provided things worked out the way I hoped they would." She paused, motioning again for Elle to take the scepter. "That means you and Dex, by the way, in case you hadn't figured that out."

Finally, Elle reached forward and took the scepter. Its smooth, wooden surface was cool beneath her palm. "I can tell you now that Dex doesn't want a vampire army."

"No, I didn't think so. Which means he'll destroy the gem and set those vampires free." The Godmother smiled. "It'll do wonders for fae-vampire relations. Which, again, is what I hoped for."

Elle frowned at the gem. "How is *any* of this part of what you hoped for? You asked me to *kill* Dex. Remember? Now you're telling me you actually hoped he'd one day be king?"

"Yes."

"So … you don't actually want to defeat King Belaric? You don't want the throne for yourself?"

"Oh, goodness, no. I've never wanted to rule anything except the wish trade."

"But … no! None of that makes sense! *You* don't make sense!"

The Godmother leaned back against the tower's edge and sighed. "Elle. Do you have any idea of the extent of the wish granting going on around you at all times? It's happening everywhere in the world, every minute, but even more so in Vale City."

"Because of you and your *empire*."

"Yes. Though I'll happily answer a summons from anywhere in the world, if someone calls for me. I have agents everywhere, in case I can't make it. But what I'm trying to explain, Elle, is that wishes are connected. A single wish rarely affects only one person. A person's wish may have a direct effect on another person who then, in response, wishes for something else. Or wishes for the opposite. Or someone wishes for something and it becomes the answer to someone else's wish. Wishes end up wrapping around each other and becoming entwined. It gets complicated."

Elle laid the scepter across her lap. "What's your point?"

"King Belaric isn't the only member of the royal family I've dealt with."

Elle narrowed her eyes. "Dex would never, and he said his mother tried to wish away the Darkness years ago, but the price—"

"Will you let me speak?" the Godmother asked.

Elle pressed her lips together.

"Thank you. Now, the person I'm speaking of is Queen Amra, and you're correct. She did summon me years ago for a wish that she ended up deciding not to go through with. She tried to wish away the Darkness from Dex, and I told her the price would be to take away the power I granted her husband. I always regretted granting that wish. King Belaric turned out to be far worse than I could have hoped, while both his sons turned out to be fairly decent."

"Why didn't you just undo the wish then?" Elle demanded. "You have that kind of power."

The Godmother fixed a puzzled expression on Elle. "That's not the way magical contracts work. And what kind of reputation would I have if I went back and altered wishes I'd already granted? Honestly, what kind of business do you think I'm running?"

"A business where you make up all the rules?" Elle asked.

For a moment, a genuine smile brightened the Godmother's face as she looked at Elle with newfound appreciation. But she returned quickly to her neutral expression. "Anyway, the queen decided for some reason—most likely fear of her husband's retribution—that she couldn't pay the price I asked. As the years passed, however, she grew desperate once more. She knew that Dex would die. She knew he needed an heir, and she knew he was running out of time. So after her husband planned the Moonlight Masquerade Ball, she summoned me again. As I told you before, I don't generally deal a second time with someone who refuses to pay a price, but … well … I break my own rules sometimes when I'm curious enough. And a queen's wish is always bound to be an interesting one."

"So that must have been quite recent," Elle said. "What did she wish for?"

"She wished for me to find her son the perfect wife, and that the two of them would have a happily ever after, no matter how short it might be."

Elle's heart thudded a little faster. "Did you agree to grant her this wish?"

"I did. And she agreed to pay the price, the specifics of which are not relevant to this conversation. I told her I would find someone, but I couldn't guarantee how long it would take. She said that wasn't acceptable; she didn't know how close her son might be to death. She said he appeared much healthier than his brother, but still, she didn't want to take any chances.

"She gave me the masquerade ball as a deadline. I told her that was too soon. A month after the ball, I said. And I made sure she understood that even if I found the perfect person, Dex would have to decide for himself if he wanted to marry her. I'm not interested in forcing something like that."

"I didn't realize negotiating with you was an option."

"Sometimes it is, sometimes it isn't."

"You make the rules," Elle muttered.

"Exactly. Anyway, I placed a few options in the prince's path to test them out. They all failed."

"Failed? What did these people have to do in order to—"

"It was different for all of them, and none of them knew they were being tested. Some of them didn't even know it was a prince they were dealing with."

"So then—"

"You were the only one, Elle." The Godmother's dark gaze warmed somewhat. "You were the only one who passed."

Elle's mouth dropped open. "But—what? When did you test me?"

"It was perfect." The Godmother stared past her, a smile on her lips. "You summoned me. I took your hand and saw that you'd already met him. You'd spent time with him, and he liked you. But you still needed to prove yourself. So I gave you a test." Her eyes refocused on Elle's. "The price of your wish. That was the test."

"I—are you—are you *kidding*?" Fury ignited a fire instantly in Elle's veins. "Are you freaking *KIDDING*? You asked me to kill him as a *TEST*? What the hell is wrong with you?"

"Well, I needed to see if you were truly selfless. You said your freedom was about saving your stepsister as much as yourself, which *seems* selfless, but could I really believe you? I would have known for sure if you'd only been asking for your stepsister's freedom, but you weren't. So I had to test you."

"But what if I *had* killed him? That would have completely ruined your plan!"

"Not really. It would have ruined the queen's plan, but it wouldn't have bothered me a great deal. In fact, it might have been more convenient to remove Dex from the picture, given how badly he wanted to kill me. If that had happened, then King Belaric and Queen Amra would have had no heir, and someone from one of the old Houses probably would have ended up wishing for the throne. Or multiple people, more likely. That would have been fun for me." She paused for a moment, frowning. "Or perhaps the vampires would have been in power by now. Who knows? I've been around long enough to know that I can survive anything. I've learned to be ... *flexible*. To turn any situation to my advantage. My point, Elle, is that there was no plan for you to ruin. You would either pass or fail your test, and the game board would change accordingly."

"The—the *game board*? Do you even hear yourself?"

"I do."

"Did you know that I tried to *trick* you? That I wanted to give the prince a potion that would simulate death for long enough to get away from the palace and get my freedom from you? If I'd succeeded with that plan, then I would have failed your test."

"But you didn't succeed with that plan. The point is that you discovered Dex was the prince and were unable to either kill or pretend to kill him, even if that meant sacrificing your freedom." The Godmother tapped one finger against her chin as she frowned. "You tried to *trick* me?" she repeated, as if only fully grasping this part now. "Interesting. I'm impressed."

"And then you *stabbed* Dex when we were in that Eternal Night," Elle reminded her. "You were going to leave him for dead."

The Godmother rolled her eyes. "Oh, Elle. You really are quite slow. I needed somebody to wish for him to be healed. *Completely* healed. So I could remove the Darkness from him. Nobody else was going to do it, and apparently it didn't occur to you that you could wish for it—or, more likely, you planned never to bargain with me again—so I had to force your hand."

"You're ... just ... wow. Your level of manipulation is unbelievable."

"Thank you."

"And what if, after all of this, *I* never wanted to be with Dex?" Elle asked. "What if *he's* not the perfect person for *me*? Or does it only matter than I'm the perfect person for him?"

The Godmother gave Elle a knowing look. "This part of your argument is pointless, since you know full well he's perfect for you, and you've been dreaming of white dresses and saying 'I do' and having all his babies."

Elle gaped, her cheeks burning. "I ... I haven't ..."

"But aside from all that, if you can't see that I've been testing him as much as you this entire time, then you're blind. Would he insist on accompanying us into an Eternal Night to make sure you were safe? Check. Would he insist on being one of your companions for the Starlight Quest? Check. Would he stand beside you to confront his father about the slavery of humans? Check. He passed with flying colors, wouldn't you say?"

"I … yes. He did." Elle looked down at the scepter, then over the edge of the tower where the people below were still frozen in place. "So … what now?"

"Well, that's up to you, of course. But if it were me, I'd go downstairs, show everyone the scepter and tell them you got rid of me, free the enhanced vampires linked to the control charm in that gem—which is easy, by the way; doesn't even take magic to smash that gem—and then tell everyone that it's possible for humans to have magic. King Belaric won't even lock you up for it, considering he'll be more concerned about the last decade or so of memories he's now missing."

Elle's gaze jumped back to the Godmother. "How do you know I took his memories? You were already on your way here when I did that."

"Elle, dear, I have ears everywhere. Currently, those ears include Tash's. She was listening in on your plan yesterday at the apothecary. The plan I not-so-subtly planted the seed for, by the way. Dex probably thinks it was all his idea. He's probably forgotten I suggested it first." She placed her hands on her knees and stood. "Now, I think I've been here long enough. Who knows how many wishes I'll have to deal with by the time I get back to the office." She inhaled deeply and smiled at Elle. "Get ready to run. The moment I'm gone, everything will unfreeze."

"Wait." Elle stood hastily, gripping the scepter in one hand. "I just want to check … so you were actually … you were doing something *good* this whole time?"

"Is that so hard to believe?"

"Honestly, yes."

The Godmother laughed. "I told you I like to play around with people, Elle. It was you who assumed that always meant something negative."

"Can you blame me?"

"I suppose not. I do like to make people squirm. But every now and then …" She shrugged. "I appreciate a good old-fashioned happily ever after." With that, she raised her hand, snapped her fingers, and vanished.

THIRTEEN

With one hand gripping her skirt to keep from tripping and the other hand wrapped tightly around the scepter, Elle raced back through the palace to the grand entrance area where everyone was fighting again. She ran alongside the balcony railing toward the stairs, passed a very confused-looking king surrounded by several security guys, and almost crashed into the queen and her security detail.

"Oh, stars, I'm so sorry. So, so sorry." The queen opened her mouth, but before she could say a word, Elle hastily sidestepped her and hurried toward the stairs. Without pausing to wonder whether this would work or if she was about to get herself killed, she ran about halfway down the staircase before stopping. No one appeared to notice her standing there, but she would never get anyone's attention if she didn't at least try.

"Stop!" she yelled, then raised the scepter above her head for everyone to see. "STOP!" Then, for added measure, she pointed her empty hand toward the domed ceiling, summoned up the feeling of throwing her stepmother across a room, and watched as silver sparks flew free from her fingertips.

Slowly, people began to look her way. Vampires first, perhaps because she held the scepter, which meant she was technically now the one who controlled them. Not that she had any idea how that worked; if she did, she would have made them all look this way. Then the fae, when they realized something had caught the vampires' attention. After another minute or so, the area was finally quiet enough for Elle to think about speaking. Which, of course, was around about the time when her nerves started to take over.

She found Dex in the crowd, amazement written all over his face at the sight of the scepter in her hand. The knot of anxiety that had been tightly coiled inside her released itself when she saw he was still okay. He met her eyes and gave her the smallest of nods. With that tiny bit of encouragement, she opened her mouth and spoke.

"This is the Godmother's scepter," she called out. "The one she took from the vampire heir, Vincenzo Savoy, when she killed him. The gem on top of it controls the vampire army. The only reason that army is here—the only reason you're all fighting each other—is because of the Godmother. But she's *gone*. And with her gone, we have no more reason to fight." Several of the vampires exchanged glances. Murmurs passed between some of them, while others looked down at the glowing red magic encircling their wrists. Magic, Elle realized, that probably connected them to the scepter. Magic just like the slave charm.

Anger burned through her. Without waiting a moment longer, she swung the scepter down, smashing the end of it against the hard, polished tiles covering the stairs. The red gem shattered instantly, and a cry went up from the crowd. Elle looked up, and everywhere her eyes landed, the red glow of magic brightened and then vanished. The vampires were free.

"Wait!" she shouted before the murmurs could become loud enough to drown her out. She threw what remained of the scepter down at her feet, and the sound of it rolling down the steps was enough to gain everyone's attention again. When the scepter came to a stop at the bottom of the staircase, she said, "I have one more important thing to tell you." She scooped her hair behind both ears so that everyone would see they weren't pointed. Then she kept her hands raised in front of her. Hands that were already sparkling silver. "I'm human," she shouted out, "and I have magic."

EPILOGUE

Four months later

ELLE LOOKED AROUND AS DEX WALKED ONTO THE BALCONY THAT LED OFF HIS bedroom. She turned her back to the view of the palace gardens—she never got tired of admiring them—and leaned against the railing. "Who was at the door?"

"Someone delivering this," Dex said, holding out a silver box wrapped in a pink ribbon. Elle raised an eyebrow in question, and he added, "Another engagement gift."

She groaned. "This is getting embarrassing. You're *royalty*. You don't need to be showered in gifts."

"But you do," he said, his lips pulling up on one side. "Everyone loves you. As they should." He set the gift down on the glass-topped table. "How many humans have magic now?"

"No idea. I've lost count of all the letters I've received. And I'm sure there are far more people who've completed the quest and *haven't* written to let me know. There was that news story about the long queues of people lining up outside all the Never Woods around the world. All the groups of people about to embark on their quest."

Dex smiled and looped his arms around Elle's waist. "How does it feel to know you've changed the world?"

She rolled her eyes and tried, unsuccessfully, to push him away. "Stop asking me that. It took more than just me to change the world. There was you, and Astrid, and Alyssa, and Olly, and—"

Dex pulled her closer and silenced her with a kiss. "We don't need to go through the whole list again," he murmured against her lips. "I can think of better things to do with our time."

"Oh yeah?" She smiled as his mouth trailed kisses along her jaw. "What things are those?"

"How about I show you?" he suggested, his hands sliding down to her hips before hoisting her up. She wrapped her legs around his waist and tilted her head down to kiss him again. Her hair fell in a curtain around their faces as Dex turned, bumped into a chair, bumped into one of the balcony doors, and finally made it safely inside. By the time they fell onto the bed together, they were both laughing.

"Your mother's going to freak out about propriety if she walks in on us again," Elle said as Dex dragged his lips along her collarbone and slid his hand beneath the edge of her T-shirt.

"No she won't." He raised his head and kissed her chin. "She's having tea with Olly's mom." Another kiss on her lips. "Besides, we're adults. We can do whatever we want in my—"

A knock at the door cut him off. "Stars!" Elle gasped. Dex rolled away, disappeared off the edge of the bed, and hit the floor with a thump. Elle buried her face among the pillows for a moment to smother her laughter. Then she scooted to the other end of the bed and stood, patting her hair and straightening her T-shirt. "We can do whatever we want, huh?" she whispered with a giggle as Dex jumped to his feet and ran a hand through his hair.

"Uh, come in," he called as he walked toward the door.

It opened, and Jarryd, one of the men Elle had grown to recognize in recent months—though she couldn't remember precisely what position he held— stood on the other side. "Sorry, sir, I should have brought this one with the other gift." He handed Dex another small box, this one wrapped in white paper and a red ribbon.

"*Another* gift?" Elle asked as Jarryd shut the door.

"This one's just for you," Dex said, examining the small envelope that accompanied the box. "Like I said: everyone loves you."

Elle took the gift from him and sat on the edge of the bed as she slipped the card out of the envelope. She opened it—and her heart did a somersault at the sight of the handwriting inside. "It's from Sienna!" She had tried numerous times over the past months to find her younger stepsister, but so far, she'd had no success.

Dear Elle,

You have MAGIC! And you're about to become a PRINCESS! And you're FREEEEEE! Congratulations!!!

Hopefully all the amazing things coming your way can make up for the horrible life you had up until a few months ago. (And if you ever need to laugh, just think of what Mom's face must have looked like the day the palace announced your engagement and she realized the girl she'd enslaved for so many years would probably one day be her queen.)

So happy for you!

Love you lots and lots and lots,
S

P.S. I'm fine. No need to worry about me. We're both free now :-)

Elle sniffed and wiped at the tear that had traced its way down her cheek. After lowering the card to the bed, she undid the red ribbon around the box and removed the pearl-white wrapping paper. A tiny note stuck to the lid of the box read, *I finally understand the significance of all the stars on that quilt your mom made. Whenever I see a star now, I can't help but think of you.*

Tears welled again in her eyes as she opened the box and found a silver chain with a silver star pendant hanging from it. "Isn't it perfect?" she whispered.

Dex reached for the box and carefully removed the necklace. Then he placed it around Elle's neck and fastened the clasp. "Perfect."

She sniffed again and asked, "Have you heard anything recently from Xander?" Thinking of Sienna—the closest thing she'd had to a best friend during all the years she'd been Salvia's slave—reminded her that one of Dex's best friends was no longer around. A full moon had forced him to shift only days after the vampire attack on the palace, and he'd left Vale City the very next morning.

"Not since he sent that congratulatory message," Dex said. "And he didn't reveal much about where he is or what's going on. I have no idea how he's actually doing."

"I hope he comes back," Elle said. "He knows we accept him exactly the way he is, right?"

"He does, but it's his family. They refuse to have anything to do with him. There's animosity between them and the shifters that goes back generations."

Elle nodded. She and Dex had spoken about this before, but she always hoped that perhaps something would change. Perhaps someone in Xander's family would realize that old grudges weren't worth hanging onto.

She stood, took Dex's hand, and walked back onto the balcony with him. Leaning on the railing, she said, "Sometimes I still catch myself thinking about the Godmother, wondering if there's something I still owe her and she's going to show up one day and tell me it's time to pay my price."

"I know what you mean. I never even made a wish, and I find myself wondering if things are really over with her, or if there's another twist just out of sight around the next corner."

"Right. Even though I *know* we don't owe her anything else."

"Yeah." Dex moved to stand behind Elle and wrapped both arms around her. She leaned back against him. "But you haven't heard a thing from her since that night. I think it really is over."

"I never got the chance to ask her how to access all the memories I've taken over the years," Elle said. "Maybe it's not even possible. Maybe only *she* can pull a memory from wherever it's stored deep inside my head. I just wish I knew one way or the other."

"You know you just said 'wish,' right?"

"Oh, stars," Elle groaned. "That just slipped out. I definitely will *not* be wishing for that."

"Something tells me she *would* make you wish for it if you really wanted to know."

"Probably." Elle's eyes traveled across the gardens and the sparkling blue strip of ocean in the distance. "What's the time?" she asked, though the last thing she wanted to do was move from Dex's arms. "I think I need to go soon. I have a class at three." She had one private tutor catching her up on the schooling she'd missed over the past few years, and another private tutor teaching her how to use her magic. Turned out it wasn't all that different from fae Essence.

Dex leaned away, probably looking back at the clock inside his bedroom. "All good," he said, wrapping his arms around her again and kissing the top of her head. "You have at least forty minutes before you need to leave. Oh, and you should say hi to my parents on your way out. They were sad you had to miss the brunch this morning."

"They were *sad*? Really? Even your dad?"

"Even my dad. I know he's scary, but he does secretly like you."

Elle turned to face Dex as she raised an eyebrow. "So secret that even he doesn't know?"

"Come on, it's not that bad."

"You're right. I'll take being 'secretly liked' over being thrown into a dungeon any day."

"Exactly. See? He's not that bad compared to the way he used to be."

She tried to turn back to face the garden, but Dex only pulled her closer. "I have another question." He grinned. "How are the dance classes going? Ready to share your moves with me?"

Elle groaned, but she couldn't help smiling. "Are you going to ask me that *every* time you see me?"

"Yes. I'm still disappointed that I missed out on dancing with you at both the Moonlight Masquerade Ball *and* the Vampire Attack Ball."

"I wish you wouldn't call it that."

"The Godmother Surprise Ball?"

"No."

"The Magic Reveal Ball."

"Dex."

"Show me your moves, soon-to-be-Princess Elle, and I'll stop with the terrible party names."

"You want me to dance here? On your tiny balcony?"

"It's not that tiny," he pointed out. "That was a terrible excuse."

"I'm not wearing the right shoes."

"Those are your wedding shoes, aren't they?" Dex asked, looking down at her rhinestone-studded combat boots. They'd already had a serious conversation about whether she could realistically get away with wearing them beneath her wedding dress.

"Fine." Elle rolled her eyes, then placed her arms around his neck. As his hands moved to her lower back, she began swaying slowly from side to side, attempting to keep a straight face as she did so.

"Great moves," Dex said with a nod, his face as serious as hers. "Is this what we're going to be doing at our wedding?"

"Yes. We'll be swaying. I'm attending two lessons a week to learn how to sway."

"Perfect. I could sway all night with you."

Laughter burst free of her lips, and then a yelp of surprise as Dex spun her away and then tugged her back in. She crashed against his chest, still laughing. "I'm terrible at this."

"You're not. I happen to think spinning and crashing and doing lots and *lots* of swaying is the perfect way to dance."

"They'll never allow it."

"It's our wedding," he said, lifting her hands and pressing a quick kiss to one and then the other. "Our happily ever after. We're free to dance however we want."

Elle placed her arms around his neck again, and as they resumed their slow swaying, she laid her head against his chest. "Yes," she whispered. "We're free."

Thank you for reading Elle's story!

For more from Rachel, visit rachel-morgan.com

Rachel Morgan spent a good deal of her childhood
living in a fantasy land of her own making, crafting endless
stories of make-believe and occasionally writing some of them down.
After completing a degree in genetics and discovering she still
wasn't grown-up enough for a 'real' job, she decided to return to
those story worlds still spinning around her imagination.
These days days she spends much of her time immersed
in fantasy land once more, writing fiction for
young adults and those young at heart.

www.rachel-morgan.com